HELPLESS TO LOVE

Without warning, he grabbed her and kissed her hard on the mouth. He shocked Valeria so badly she couldn't breathe. No coherent thought emerged from the jumble whirling about in her head. Everything about her simply came to a dead stop.

Just as abruptly Luke broke the kiss and held her at arm's length from him. "Did you like that? Did you want me to do it? Could you stop me from doing it again?"

Exclamations of surprise, nods of protest, pleas for an explanation stumbled over each other in her mind.

He wrapped his arms about her, pulled her tight against his chest. "You're helpless, aren't you? You can't run away and you can't fight me."

She could if she could get over the shock. She had never been held in such an intimate embrace. Not even when dancing in public would a man have dared let his body touch hers. The shock was enormous, disabling.

He kissed her again.

No other man had kissed her on the lips. She had no way to differentiate ruthless from enthusiastic . . . or impassioned . . . or heedless. Her mind told her she ought to be furious, insulted, violated, even frightened. Her body pleaded with her to give in to Luke's embrace.

The Cowboys series by Leigh Greenwood:
JAKE
WARD
BUCK
CHET
SEAN
PETE
DREW

The *Seven Brides* series:
ROSE
FERN
IRIS
LAUREL
DAISY
VIOLET
LILY

LUKE

The Cowboys

LUKE

LEIGH GREENWOOD

LEISURE BOOKS  NEW YORK CITY

For Cameron

A LEISURE BOOK®

December 2000

Published by

Dorchester Publishing Co., Inc.
276 Fifth Avenue
New York, NY 10001

Cover Art by John Ennis.
www.ennisart.com

ISBN 0-8439-4804-3

The name "Leisure Books" and the stylized "L" with design are trademarks of Dorchester Publishing Co., Inc.

Printed in the United States of America.

Visit us on the web at www.dorchesterpub.com.

Chapter One

Arizona Territory, 1887

Luke Attmore had taken on more than a hundred jobs as a hired gun, but none had been as troublesome as this one promised to be. He'd closed the curtains in his hotel room against the heat of the day, but he could see Hans Demel clearly enough. Luke leaned back in his chair, a bottle of expensive brandy on the table before him, the remains of a cigarette in the ashtray. His visitor sat forward, tense, as though he expected to have to spring to his feet any moment.

"Are you sure you understand what I want?"

Hans kept saying things again and again, as if he didn't believe anyone like Luke could understand him. Maybe the heat was getting to him. His clothes were more suitable for a European court than the Arizona Territory. He wore a white shirt with a turned-down collar, a necktie with a large knot, a swallow-tailed coat with three buttons, a waistcoat, and narrow trousers pulled tight over a protruding stomach. Perspiration stood out on his forehead and upper lip in sharp contrast with his polished shoes and slicked-back hair.

"Yes," Luke replied, bored and irritated by this agitated little man. "You want me to escort your client's wife to his ranch. That seems straightforward enough."

"She's not his wife yet," Hans corrected. "The marriage contracts have been signed, but she must reach his ranch before . . ."

Luke ignored the drone of Hans's voice. He had never gotten used to the way obscure European countries tied their royal families up in marriages arranged for every possible reason except love. Luke figured love and marriage went together, which made it easier for him to avoid both. He didn't believe in love, didn't understand it. He did understand contracts based on wealth. He worked for the man willing to pay the most money. And Prince Matthais had paid him a great deal.

"I'm not interested in the details," Luke said. "I'll get her to the ranch safely."

"It's not that simple. There's a great deal of money involved."

He'd expected that. The fee wouldn't have been so high otherwise. It was more than he'd made in the previous year, and he was the highest-paid gunman in the country.

"Prince Matthais needs the alliance with Duke Rudolf, but it will only come into effect once the princess reaches the ranch."

Luke had no patience with this kind of intrigue. He'd spent two years in Europe as a soldier of fortune. He'd returned to the West because he never knew when a sworn ally would shoot him in the back. Black-hearted criminals had more honor than blue-blooded aristocrats.

"You must understand that Prince Matthais has many

enemies," Hans said, "people who want to see bad things happen to him."

Nobody in the Arizona Territory went around referring to people by royal titles. Heat, dust, and horse manure didn't make a very classy backdrop for royalty.

"The prince isn't my concern," Luke said. "I don't see any problem delivering the princess to her future husband."

"The princess is in danger," Hans said, more agitated than ever. "There are people who will do anything to keep Prince Matthais and Duke Rudolf from joining their houses."

Luke didn't care who married whom, who ascended what throne, who had his throat slit in some dark alley—or some sumptuous bedchamber. He was being hired to deliver his client safe and sound. What happened after that was none of his concern.

"I'll get the princess to the ranch," Luke said.

"Have you hired extra people as I instructed?" Hans asked, nervously wringing his hands.

Luke wasn't used to being *instructed* to do anything. "I've hired two extra men."

"I asked for a dozen."

"These two are as good as a dozen."

"Can you trust them?"

"They're my family," Luke said. Or as close as he'd ever come to having one.

Hans shook his head. "If anything were to happen to the princess, it would be catastrophic. Heads would roll, thrones would topple, empires would—"

"Nothing will happen to the princess!" Luke stood, tired of this little man and his groundless fears. No one bothered Luke Attmore. Those who had been foolish enough to try resided in boot hills around the West. Once it was known Zeke and Hawk were with him, not even the most foolhardy would attempt to harm this princess. He hoped she was pretty enough to warrant all this trouble. The princesses he had seen caused him to doubt it.

"Two isn't enough," Hans said. "We are paying you enough to hire at least a dozen of the best men."

"I don't need anybody else," Luke said. "But if I did, I've got more family, the dozen good men you're looking for."

"Your family is so big?"

"Yes." Hans didn't have to know it was an adopted family, that half of his brothers were married and nearly a thousand miles away, that he wouldn't call on them even if they'd been in town. They had wives, children, ranches to take care of, lives to live safely and happily. Luke wasn't about to involve any of them in his risky enterprises, especially his real brother, Chet. Chet had spent nine years watching Luke's back. If he thought for a minute his younger brother was in trouble, he'd be on the first train to Arizona. Zeke and Hawk were enough. They weren't married, or likely to be.

"When do I meet the princess?" Luke asked.

Hans started to fret again. "She should have reached Bonner before now."

It didn't surprise Luke that she was late. Once Hans had described the retinue that accompanied the princess on the train—tents, trunks of clothes, carloads of furniture, dishes, mirrors, servants, food and the stoves on which to prepare it—Luke had marveled that she'd ever left New Orleans. He considered it the height of stupidity to set out over the hot, often barren lands of the West with a retinue more suitable for Napoleon's Europe. At least Napoleon had roads. The Territory didn't even have trails in some places.

He questioned whether he should have accepted this job. He might not have if he hadn't found himself becoming unaccountably weary of his work. Maybe weary wasn't the right word. Irritable. Nothing pleased him these days. Maybe he ought to head back East to one of those fancy resorts like Saratoga Springs, and sit on the front porch until he could figure out what he wanted.

No, he didn't need to go anywhere. He knew exactly what he wanted. He just couldn't have it. He cursed violently.

"What's wrong?" the little man asked.

"Nothing you can fix," Luke replied.

"Can *you* fix it?"

"No."

Princess Valeria Elizabeth Rose Maria Beatrice Christina of Badenberg didn't like anything she saw as she approached the town of Bonner, but then she hadn't liked anything since she'd been forced to leave her home. This country was impossibly huge, impossibly hot, and impossibly alien. Nothing about it was anything like what she was used to, yet Rudolf expected her to become accustomed to it, to live here and pretend to be happy.

She would never have admitted it, but this country frightened her. She was alone except for her servants. Her parents were dead, her uncle exiled from his throne, her fiancé waiting for her at a ranch above the Mogollon Rim, and her friends scattered across Europe. Everything she'd ever known had disappeared. She didn't understand these Americans or their customs, and she had no one to help her learn. Hans and Otto didn't know any more than she did.

But she wasn't allowed to show fear. She had to remain calm and regal. She was a princess.

At least she used to be. She didn't know what she was now.

Her childhood friend, Lillie, had married a wealthy

New York banker. She had told Valeria wonderful things about New York, but Hans, responsible for her personal safety, and Otto Sacher, responsible for organizing the journey, hadn't allowed her to go there. She'd had great hopes for New Orleans, but they had smuggled her into the city at night and put her on a train out of town before dawn. They hadn't even let her get off in San Antonio.

Otto's explanation had been that he didn't want to attract attention. She'd tried to convince him a princess would attract less attention in a grand hotel than rambling about the desert in a railway car suitable for the Czar of Russia. Hans said only that Otto made all the decisions, that their only consideration was for her safety, that no one could be safe in a city. Hadn't she been attacked in Rome, Paris, even London?

Valeria wasn't certain she could consider such ineffectual attempts to harm her attacks, but they had sent Hans and Otto into a frenzy. Plans for a sensible passage through the United States had been scrapped, and Otto had hatched this scheme to sneak her in by the back door. She was certain it wouldn't succeed, but no one would listen to her. No one ever had.

She was a princess. She could trace her ancestry back five hundred years. She was rich. Her hand had been sought by men of noble lineage. She had been one of the most important persons in central Europe.

But she was a woman.

"Do they call that collection of mud huts a city?" she asked Otto.

"I'm informed it's adobe, your highness. I believe it's a kind of brick made of local material."

"Mud," Valeria said decisively. The place was surrounded by mountains of stone, yet these crazy Americans built their houses out of mud. They were even more eccentric than she'd been told. "I hope my hotel isn't built out of mud."

"I requested Bonner's finest accommodations," Otto said.

Valeria was under no illusion as to why the haughty ex-Duke Rudolf of Ergonia had sought to marry her even though she was now an ex-princess. She had a fortune; he didn't. He had wanted to use her money to restore himself to the throne his foolish, cruel, and extravagant father had lost a decade earlier. She had only agreed to marry him on the condition that he use her fortune to establish a new life for them in America.

"I hope the hotel is cool," she said, fanning her bosom. "I've never been so hot in my life."

"It is warm here," Otto agreed. "I had been informed America experienced cool weather in the spring."

"If you'd taken the trouble to consult a map, you'd have noticed that America is a big country. I imagine the northern part is cool. You brought me across the south. That's why we used to go to Monte Carlo in the winter, Otto, because it's warm in the south."

"I'm only following your uncle's instructions, your highness."

He always said that because he knew it left her nothing to say. He had to follow her uncle's instructions—or Rudolf's. It didn't matter that neither of them knew what they were doing. Surely New York would have been sufficiently far from the tiny principality of Ergonia for Rudolf to escape his enemies. But he had wanted to be assured of his safety, and having seen the American West, she had to agree it was the best place for Rudolf. No sane European would attempt to penetrate this endless wasteland.

A vehicle pulled to a halt next to the train. "Your carriage is ready, your highness," Otto said.

"It looks dirty," Valeria's maid, Elvira, said. "I'm sure the seats are hard."

"It's the only carriage in this town," Otto said. "If your highness would prefer to walk . . ."

He knew she wouldn't walk. She'd be soaked through with perspiration in minutes and stared at by everyone she passed. "I'll ride."

Valeria wondered for a moment what was being done with her horses, the carloads of furniture and household furnishings, and her personal belongings, but the heat drove all thoughts of her possessions out of her mind. "Where is Hans?" she asked Otto.

"Waiting for you at the hotel."

It was almost too hot to breathe inside the carriage, but the trip was mercifully short. Bonner was incredibly small. She couldn't imagine why anyone would want to live here. What good was it to have a fortune if you had to live in a mud house?

Leaving Elvira to see to her personal luggage, Valeria entered the hotel. She was pleasantly surprised by the interior. Though it didn't approach the luxury and style of even an ordinary European hotel, it was more than she'd expected when her train stopped in this small, remote town. The lobby rose two floors in height, the ceiling supported by wood columns that had been carved at the top like the stone columns of ancient Greece. The wooden beams that supported the ceiling had carvings she didn't recognize. The walls were made of a plain brown material. Stone floors helped keep the interior cool. A wide, divided staircase rose against the far wall. Gas-lighted globes suspended from the ceiling illuminated the room. A group of leather-covered sofas and chairs were arranged around a low, slate-topped table covered with magazines and newspapers.

Rather than bow or avert their eyes, the people in the

hotel lobby gaped at her as though she were some sort of exhibit. Their unblinking stares made her uncomfortable, and that angered her. *She* was the one whose presence was supposed to make *them* uncomfortable, make them aware of their lowly position in life. She didn't know how they managed to look so happy and healthy in this desert.

"Take me to my suite immediately," she said to Otto.

"They don't have suites, just rooms."

She always had a suite, but a few weeks in the American West had taught her that not even European royalty could have what they wanted when it didn't exist.

"I hope it's on the ground floor."

"I've asked for the best room on the second floor," Otto said. "We can't take the chance that someone might break in through the windows."

She didn't bother pointing out that a ladder would make the second floor as accessible as the first. She'd tried to reason with Otto before, to no avail. She just wanted to get off her feet, to relax before she had to dress for dinner.

The hallway, with its wood floors, stucco walls, and exposed beams, was nothing like the marble halls of her home, its walls covered with silk, tapestries, or hand-painted wallpaper from France or China; its ceilings painted with pastoral scenes and highlighted with plaster or gold leaf. The beams here were so low she felt they might crash down on her head. She was certain she saw a cobweb dangling from one.

The stairs were so narrow her dress caught on a splinter. She paused while her maid pulled it loose. The floor didn't appear to have been swept recently. She'd been told towns like Leadville, Colorado, or Virginia City, Nevada, had grown up around rich gold mines. She'd been assured the wealthy mine owners lived in great houses with electric lights, steam heat, hot water, and many other conveniences. She wondered where the rich people in Bonner stayed. Obviously not at this hotel.

"This is the room, your highness." Otto pointed to a door with the number 8 on it. The quality of the rough-hewn wood didn't encourage Valeria to expect much. Dark brown paint served merely as a relief to the red-brown walls. It was almost dark as night inside the room, where a single oil lamp provided the only light.

Her maid held the door as Valeria swept into the room, only to be brought up short by the sight of a rough-looking man sitting in a deep, leather-covered chair by the window. Valeria stifled a frisson of fear, a gasp of surprise, then replaced them with a hiss of anger. Except for being absurdly handsome in a rough, unkempt sort of American way, he was exactly the kind of person Valeria was sure would kill her for anyone willing to pay his price.

Valeria had met half the rulers of Europe, danced and dined with villains who stole countries, emptied treasuries, caused whole populations to be destroyed. From the coldness of his ice-blue eyes, the frigid feel of his gaze, Valeria knew this man could be just as ruthless. She turned to Otto. "Who is he?"

"I don't know," Otto replied, looking nearly as uneasy as she felt.

"Who are you, and how did you get into this room?" His gaze might be icy enough to chill her blood, but she was a princess. A hundred generations of warriors stood behind her. She would not cower before this American intruder.

"I'm Luke Attmore."

Just that. No explanation of what he was doing there, no apology for unnerving her, no excuse for invading her privacy.

"I've never heard of you."

He didn't reply, just continued to sit, looking as if he'd come straight in off the desert. His boots might once have been black, but time and use had rendered them a creased brown even a peasant in her country would have been ashamed to wear. His pants hugged his body like a second skin. She didn't know how he managed to sit down without ripping a seam.

His shirt was of the same brown as the adobe, unadorned, and open at the throat. He wore his hat low over his eyes—wearing a hat inside was a breech of etiquette no European would have ever committed!—but not so low she couldn't see his eyes. He had a square jaw and wide, full, sensual lips. Bits of moonlight-blond hair hung down the back of his neck.

Cleaned up and wearing decent clothes, he would be devastatingly handsome. But even in his deplorable condition he projected a sensual aura that reached out and enveloped her like a cloud of warm air in a cold room. Valeria had known many handsome men, but none had ever affected her so strongly by merely being in her presence. She couldn't understand it. She disliked it, and it made her angry.

"Make him leave," she said, turning back to Otto. "And if the hotel can't keep strangers from wandering into my room, we'll have to go to another hotel."

"This is the only hotel in Bonner," Mr. Attmore said. "At least, it's the only one suitable for you."

"You call this suitable?" Valeria said, rounding on him, angry he hadn't left, angry he still appeared to feel more comfortable in her presence than she in his, angry her attraction to the man continued to grow. She couldn't figure out what could possibly be wrong with her, unless the heat had caused her to go mad. There was absolutely nothing about this man that should inspire her interest or admiration. He was a commoner, an uncivilized man . . . an American!

"It's what passes for luxury in Bonner," he said.

Valeria realized she was still standing in the doorway, flanked by Otto and her maid, her entire entourage backed up behind her—all because of this man. "Otto, have someone remove him from my room at once. And tell the owner of this hotel that I wish to speak to him immediately. These accommodations are not satisfactory."

"They're the best you'll find unless you go to Tucson," Mr. Attmore said. He still didn't move. "You probably ought to keep going until you reach San Francisco. I doubt you'll find anything between here and there that'll satisfy your exacting demands."

He said it as if he thought she was a spoiled brat, whining because she hadn't gotten what she wanted. Well, she *hadn't* gotten what she wanted. This room was a disgrace. The floors were plain wood, worn from use, and covered in places by rugs that appeared to be made from randomly chosen rags. A Spanish armor plate, a couple of religious paintings, and a drawing that showed a bear being lassoed and killed by some men dressed very much like Mr. Attmore hung on the walls. Someone had painted designs in bright, primary colors on the ceiling. She had never seen anything like them and had no idea what they represented.

The furniture seemed substantial—the wardrobe commodious, the bed covered in a brightly colored blanket made up of unfamiliar geometric designs, the chairs and tables numerous—but everything had been constructed of nearly black wood and covered in dark brown leather. She was used to spacious rooms decorated in white and gold, elegant chairs covered in embroidered silk or woven tapestry, furniture designed to delight the eye as well as offer comfort.

"Why are you here?" she demanded.

"Because Hans Demel hired me to escort you to your new home. I thought it would be polite to introduce myself."

Valeria could tell from the look in his eyes that whatever he might have thought before she entered the room, he didn't think it any longer. He was looking at her with disdain. The idea that he was her escort was so shocking, so unbelievable, she couldn't speak for a moment.

"I don't want you to escort me anywhere," she said. "Otto will find someone else. You are free to go back to . . . where do you come from?" she demanded, startled to realize that, though she knew nothing about him, she was certain he didn't come from around here.

"All over," he replied.

"Why do you stay here?"

"Some of us like it."

He smiled at her in a self-satisfied, superior sort of way as though he knew something she didn't and he wasn't going to tell her what it was. Well, that was just fine. She didn't want to know anything he knew. It couldn't possibly be of interest to her. She had every intention of convincing Rudolf to move to a more civilized part of the country the moment she reached him.

"Why are you still here?" she demanded when he didn't move.

"I'm studying you."

Nobody studied her. At least, not anybody like this scruffy *cowboy*. She thought that was the correct term. She'd heard somebody use it in connection with a man dressed like Mr. Attmore.

"What do you see for all your studying?" she asked, her chin tilted upward. Her maid had stopped standing like a statue and begun to unpack some of the cases that contained her lotions, ointments, and other beauty aids.

"I see a woman who appears to be far too young to consider herself of such consequence, pretty enough, though not a great beauty."

Valeria heard gasps from her maid and Otto. No one spoke to a member of the royal house like this. She knew she wasn't a great beauty, but everyone said she was, because to say anything else to a princess would have been an insult.

"And you appear to be remarkably foolish," he continued, "willing to judge by outward appearances. But I guess I can't blame you for that. You've been judged the same way your whole life. You've probably been so busy getting your hair fixed or going for a dress fitting you never had time to develop your mind or character. I doubt there's anything of substance behind all that powder and those ridiculous clothes."

Ordinarily Valeria would have been angry at such a brutal appraisal of her character, but how could an ill-bred American be expected to understand royalty? However, she took exception to his remark about her clothes.

"This dress is from Paris," she said, unable to believe even an American would call clothes designed by Worth of Paris *ridiculous.*

"Then you should have saved it for Paris. You'll ruin it in a single day out here. You should also have left your carloads of belongings behind."

"It's impossible to leave everything behind. How could I live?" She knew she'd brought too much, but as long as she was surrounded by reminders of home, she felt a little less frightened, a little less lost.

"You'll soon find that living well has to do with a person's character, not a trainload of belongings."

"Leave my room this instant," Valeria said with all the

regal outrage she could summon. When he didn't move, she practically shouted, "I'd walk through the desert by myself before I'd go so much as one foot with you. Did you hear me?"

"I imagine half of Bonner heard you," he said, finally rising to his feet. "The rest of them will know by dinnertime."

Then he turned and walked out. He didn't bow, nod his head, doff his hat, or take verbal leave of her. He just walked out as if she, Otto, and her maid didn't exist.

She whirled on Otto. "Who hired that man?"

"Hans."

"He couldn't have met him, or he wouldn't have hired him."

"I imagine it was done through an agent."

"Make certain we never use their services again. Now I'd better change for dinner. I hope you've informed the hotel that I have my own chef and my own food. The kitchen must be put at his disposal."

"I instructed Hans to attend to that."

"Good. I'll dine at half past eight."

"Very good."

Otto didn't move.

"Is there something else?" she asked.

"Did you really mean that man wasn't to serve as our guide?"

"I most certainly did."

"We can't possibly find Duke Rudolf's ranch without him."

"Find another guide. There must be dozens like him."

Chapter Two

Luke leaned back in his chair and allowed his eyelids to droop, but he watched Hans closely to gauge the extent of his sincerity.

"You can't quit," Hans was saying. "The princess is in great danger."

"You keep telling me that, but you can't give me any proof," Luke said.

Otto had followed Luke from Valeria's room, confirmed that he really had been fired, but said he could keep the money he'd already been paid. Less than twenty minutes later Hans tracked Luke down and begged him to stay.

"I'm certain they're only waiting until we leave Bonner. Once we're in your wilderness, there won't be anyone to stop them," Hans said.

"Who are you afraid of?" Luke asked.

Hans looked around with the nervous glance of a man fearful he would be attacked from behind at any moment. Luke could have told him the Crystal Palace was the safest and most orderly saloon in town. It was patronized primarily by the solid citizens of the town, along with some mine- and land-owners; the conversation was muted, the alcohol of good quality. Several years earlier the town fathers had hired Luke to clean out a gang of rustlers and gold thieves. People still remembered burying the gang one by one in the local boot hill. Luke's liking for a quiet place to drink his brandy ensured that the boisterous miners would seek their beer and whiskey elsewhere while he was in town.

"I can't be entirely sure who's behind it," Hans admitted. "Otherwise Prince Matthais would have caught the unprincipled cowards. He was not easily persuaded to let the princess travel to this country. For more than a year he insisted Duke Rudolf return to Europe. But such a trip would endanger the duke's life."

"Why?"

"A revolution in Ergonia deposed his father ten years ago. Those in power now would try to kill the duke if he should attempt to return. He's depending on the princess's inheritance. So you see, he, too, is most anxious to see she reaches him safely."

"Still, I don't see who can be behind this danger you are certain hangs over the princess."

Luke told himself he shouldn't be wasting his time. Hans had spent his entire life in the confines of a dull, orderly, protocol-driven European court where being fifteen minutes late for lunch could put a person before the firing squad. Just being in the Arizona Territory was probably enough to start him seeing bandits behind every bush.

"I have lived at court my whole life," Hans said. "I can sense these things."

Luke refrained from pointing out that in the West people liked facts, that all this *sensing things* could get you killed. Being right wasn't always enough. You had to be smart and fast with a gun. Most people weren't smart enough or fast enough. That's where Luke came in. "It doesn't matter," Luke said. "The princess has fired me."

"She has no authority to do that," Hans said. "I hired you at the behest of her uncle. You are still our guide."

Luke sank deeper into his chair. "She doesn't want me. Otto told me I could keep the money, to just go away."

Hans didn't appear surprised, but he did appear disapproving. Or was it disappointed?

"That's how we do it in my country, pay people to ignore injustice and fade away quietly. I was told men in your country were willing to die for their principles."

"Meaning?" Luke didn't have any principles. Yet, once he accepted a job, he didn't consider his obligation fulfilled until he had completed the job. But he'd been fired. So why did Hans's disappointment prick a sensitivity he hadn't known he had?

"You can't desert the princess."

"I've been paid to go away."

"I'll pay you more to stay."

"Why?"

"My family has served the princess's family for more than a hundred and fifty years. During that time we've managed to prevent any of them from being killed. I don't intend to be the first one to fail."

"What's in it for you?"

"Honor."

"I'm talking about money," Luke said. "Nobody does something like this for nothing."

"You consider honor nothing?"

"It can be bought."

"Service can be bought. Honor never."

Hans's words stung. What right did he have to criticize Luke? He was short and unattractive, balding, on the shady side of fifty, his stomach threatening to burst the buttons on his waistcoat. He couldn't see without his thick glasses, and he was too slow and weak to defend himself. "You're mighty free with your criticism," Luke said.

"I don't know your character well enough to criticize you," Hans said, looking more nervous and ill at ease than ever. "But people say once you take on a job, you don't back down, regardless of the danger. That's why I chose you."

"This isn't a matter of backing down," Luke said. "I've been fired."

"Not by me, and I'm the one who made the contract with you."

Luke sat forward so quickly, Hans jumped back startled. "I'll honor our bargain on one condition."

"I understood you never had conditions."

"I do this time."

"What is it?"

How could a silly, defenseless man look so proud and regal? "The princess must ask me to go with her," Luke said.

Hans collapsed like a punctured balloon. "She'll never do that."

Luke settled back into his chair. "Then you'll have to find someone else. I won't take a commission against the wishes of the person I'm supposed to protect. I did that once"—to protect his brother, but Hans didn't have to know that—"and I swore I'd never do it again."

"But how do I get her to change her mind?"

"Let her spend several days in this town."

"She'll insist I hire someone else."

"Then hire someone else."

"They told me Americans were stiff-necked and proud, especially you."

"Who told you?"

"Jefferson Randolph. He's a very successful banker."

"I know Mr. Randolph." Luke would have a few things to say to Jeff when they met again. Not that Jeff would care. He could be extremely foul-tempered when he wanted to. Luke rose. "My honor can't be bought, either. I'll escort the princess to the duke's ranch, but she must ask me herself."

"She's much too proud," Hans said, perspiration the size of raindrops popping out on his forehead.

"So am I," Luke replied.

As he watched Hans walk away, Luke wondered why he'd agreed to reconsider. He'd never done that before. He didn't understand why the princess intrigued him. He despised royalty in principle and in practice. The aristocrats he'd encountered deserved to be dethroned, cast out, and forced to earn their living. They were little more than glorified leeches living off the labors of others.

So what made him believe Valeria might be different? Had her dusky beauty hypnotized him? She had hair black as a raven's wing, thick and glistening, ebony brows, ruby lips. He'd never seen more perfect skin, not the pure white favored by most but almost an almond color. Could it be that the princess had a few drops of gypsy blood? The thought made him smile.

Maybe she had cast a spell over him.

He got to this feet, disgusted with his foolish thoughts. She was a beautiful woman with a tall, slim body endowed with almost enough curves to be voluptuous. He reacted like other men when it came to beautiful women. But he differed from most men in that he never let his physical response influence his actions.

Valeria couldn't sleep. The heat was nearly unbearable, but it was the noise outside that kept her awake. It seemed people in this town didn't go to sleep. For the last two hours they'd gone up and down the street, shouting to each other, shouting *at* each other, fighting, even singing drunken songs. She'd sent Otto to complain, but the miners were a rough lot who didn't appreciate restrictions. In her country, the army would have taken care of them immediately. She wondered why the American army didn't do something.

Then she realized she hadn't seen any army. What kind of country was this that didn't have soldiers everywhere? How were people controlled, revolutions prevented?

The army hadn't prevented a revolution in her country. Nor in Rudolf's. That was why she was in America trying to find her way across its trackless wastes. She wondered what Rudolf was doing on a ranch. He didn't know anything about working for a living.

The noise level on the street below had been dropping over the last few minutes until near-silence reigned. She could still hear footsteps, so she knew not everyone had gone home. Why had the men stopped making so much noise? Curious, she got out of bed and went over to the window. The number of men about didn't seem to have decreased, but they weren't loud and raucous as they had been for the last few hours. They walked quickly, talking softly among themselves, glancing into the shadows as though wary of something they couldn't see.

Valeria didn't see him at first. Then she gradually made out the shape of a man in the shadow of a building, leaning against the wall, his outline barely visible. Who was he? What was he doing on the street at this hour, and why was he hiding in the shadows? A tiny shiver raced down and back up her spine. Could this be the assassin Hans and Otto seemed convinced had been sent to kill her? She told herself not to be foolish. She was thousands of miles away from Belgravia. No one knew where to find her.

Yet she couldn't drive out the fear that this was a killer who had followed her to America. What other kind of man could cause drunken miners to fall silent?

A movement in the shadows caused her focus to become intent. She saw a faint red glow brighten, then fade. He was smoking a cigarette. Nearly every man she knew smoked. She considered it a disgusting habit, but no one cared what she thought.

The man dropped the cigarette, and ground it out beneath his boot. Then he stepped out into the moonlight.

Luke Attmore!

What was he doing? Watching her window? If so, why? Instinctively she drew back, her hand at her throat. She told herself not to be foolish. The man was outside. She was inside. She had no reason to believe he wanted to harm her, but he'd found his way into her room without anyone knowing how. He'd caused the drunken miners to fall silent.

What kind of man could do that?

He looked up at her window. There was no doubt about it. He was watching her room. Otto had paid him to go away. Why was he still here? Then he did something very surprising. He took off his hat and made a sweeping bow, flashed a brilliant smile, returned his hat to his head, and retreated to the shadows once more.

Valeria felt exposed, defenseless. She wanted to jump back into the shadows, to crawl back into the safety of her bed. Luke Attmore had seen her at the window. He knew she'd watched him, and it pleased him.

As much as it unsettled her, she admired his boldness. She had dispensed with his services, so he had apparently decided to show her exactly what she'd thrown away. He intrigued her, she admitted that, but she wouldn't change her mind. She didn't like Mr. Attmore, and she didn't want him anywhere near her.

A light flared. Another cigarette. He obviously didn't intend to leave his position for a while yet. She didn't know whether to feel safe or pursued. She knew nothing about him. He could be the man Hans feared wanted to kill her. What better plan than to hire on as her guide and kill her in the desert where no one would ever find her body.

The pinpoint of light at the end of his cigarette glowed brightly, then faded.

Why was he watching her? Did he know the noise in the street had kept her awake? Why should he care? He had called her shallow, spoiled, and overdressed. Anger at his remarks swept through her. No one had ever dared to say such things to her. No one! But he hadn't hesitated.

The cigarette glowed again.

Valeria turned away from the window and back toward her bed. She prided herself on knowing men, understanding them. It was the only way a woman could achieve any degree of happiness. But she didn't understand Luke Attmore. He didn't behave like any man she'd ever known.

That probably came from living in this strange country. He intrigued her. She almost wished he were going with her. She even considered sending Otto to ask him to be her guide after all.

She lay back down on the bed. She refused to do anything so foolish just to satisfy her curiosity. She closed her eyes. But rather than her fiancé, the image of Luke Attmore, standing in the middle of the street, smiling up at her, filled her thoughts.

"What do you mean, no one will take the job?" Valeria asked. Both Hans and Otto stood before her, Otto looking irritated, Hans nervous and fidgety.

"It seems he's a famous gunfighter," Otto said. "Everybody is afraid of him."

They had interrupted her breakfast. She was already irritated because her chef had not been given free rein to use the kitchen. A reprimand sent through her maid had resulted in a sharply worded reply stating that the princess wasn't the only person in Bonner in need of breakfast. It wasn't so much the lack of respect or the late breakfast. It was more that everything familiar, safe, and comforting had been taken from her, leaving her feeling very much alone, vulnerable, and adrift. But she couldn't confess that to anyone. A princess never admitted weakness. She was hemmed in, held defenseless by the very status which should have protected her.

"They also say he's the best," Hans said, wringing his hands in a fashion that made Valeria want to slap him. He was a good man—honest, dependable, hardworking—but she wished he would act like a man instead of a mouse.

"Thank you for trying to make sure I'm safe," she said, smiling at Hans. "I'm sure dealing with such a man must have been hard for you, but I can't have him in my service."

Both Hans and Otto put forth several reasons why she should retain Mr. Attmore's services—Hans more convincingly than Otto—but she wouldn't listen. She would have nothing to do with Luke Attmore.

Still, something about him tugged at something deep inside her, something that had never come to life before. She knew it was a purely physical response, and that frightened her. Her entire life had been fabricated of arrangements made for reasons of state. Personal likes and dislikes weren't allowed to enter into her decisions. As for physical reactions, well, that was unthinkable. She was a princess.

But telling herself that didn't change the fact that she couldn't stop thinking about Luke Attmore, couldn't stop picturing him sitting in that chair, his deep blue eyes watching her every move, his near-perfect features immobile, his sensual lips parted in speech. Nor was she unaware of his broad shoulders and powerful thighs. He was a man who'd reached full, magnificent maturity, and it was impossible for her—for any woman, she was sure—to be unaware of or unmoved by him.

Then there was his standing on the street outside her window the last two nights. Was he trying to scare her into hiring him back? She didn't think he was protecting her. Men who could be bought didn't have the kind of honor and loyalty Hans and Otto had. But if he wasn't protecting her, what was he doing?

In the middle of a thought that said she was helpless to find out, she remembered she wasn't in Europe any longer. Neither her uncle nor Rudolf could forbid her to do what she wanted.

"Bring him to me," she said.

"Why do you want to see him?" Otto asked.

"He won't come," Hans said.

"Why not?" she asked.

"He said he wouldn't be your guide unless you asked him."

Valeria jumped to her feet. "Me! Beg him!"

"He said *ask*," Hans said. "He was not happy that you dismissed him without a reason."

"He was rude."

"I don't think he meant to be," Hans said. "It's just the way of these Americans."

"Then he should change his ways. I don't like them."

"I don't think he cares what we like," Hans said.

"He made that abundantly clear," Valeria shot back.

Well, he would find himself at a loss this time, this brash American. A princess did not beg.

"Take me to him," she said.

"It would be improper for you to be seen on the streets," Otto said.

That would have been true in Belgravia, but her life had changed forever the moment she entered the United States. If she couldn't go out, she would be bored to the edge of insanity. She'd had parties, balls, visitors, trips, concerts, the library, a thousand and one things to entertain her in Belgravia, and still she'd frequently been bored. She would have none of that at Paul's ranch. She should begin right now to adapt to her new circumstances.

"It won't matter here," Valeria said. "Elvira will accompany me. With you and Hans along, what could be so improper?"

"I don't know where he is," Otto said.

"I do," Hans said.

"Then take me to him," Valeria said.

"I ought to make sure he's still at the hotel," Hans said. "And hire a proper room as a meeting place."

Valeria wouldn't be put off. Hans was fanatically loyal, but he was also a stickler for maintaining her royal consequence. "I'm not willing to wait. Elvira, bring me my cloak. If I pull the hood over my head, no one will notice me."

The moment she reached the street, she knew she'd made at least two mistakes. First, the cloak was too hot. She didn't think she could walk a hundred feet without fainting. And second, she could tell from their stares that the people of Bonner knew her at a glance. They all watched her progress down the street in fascination.

"I advised your highness not to venture out," Otto said.

"They're only looking at me, Otto. That causes no

harm." But people usually looked at her in admiration, not in gape-mouthed wonder.

"Where is this hotel?" she asked Hans.

"It's right here."

"That's a saloon," Otto said.

"Americans stay at saloons, too," Hans said. "Some of them have rooms just like hotels."

Valeria doubted she would ever accustom herself to the strange and unaccountable things Americans did.

"They're not very different from inns in our country," Hans added.

Valeria had never stayed at an inn. But the moment she entered the Crystal Palace, she decided there couldn't possibly be anything like it in her country. Except for a bar of about a dozen feet, tables and chairs filled every inch of space in the long, narrow room. The walls were bare except for a mirror and two racks of glasses behind the bar. The tables looked clean and the floor had obviously been swept recently, but the odor of whiskey and tobacco vied for prominence with the aroma of coffee and the smell of bacon grease.

Valeria expected to be disgusted. She was only surprised.

But not as surprised as the men seated at the tables. Their stares when she entered made it plain women weren't frequent visitors. Even though she'd come to put him in his place, she felt greatly relieved when Mr. Attmore stood up at one of the tables in the back of the room.

"I didn't expect her to change her mind so quickly," he said to Hans when they reached the table.

"Change my mind about what?" she asked Hans.

"My being your guide."

"I didn't." It disturbed Valeria that she was more aware

of the attraction between them than the feeling of outrage that had brought her here.

"Whatever you came to do, it'll attract less attention if you sit down," Mr. Attmore said.

Valeria wanted to refuse to be seated in such a place, but she knew she would probably have to do many things she would never have considered only a few months ago. When Hans held a chair for her, she sat down. The infuriating Mr. Attmore held a chair for her maid.

But taking a seat didn't remove her from the glare of attention. It seemed no one in the room had anything to do but stare at her.

"Could I offer you some coffee?" Mr. Attmore asked.

"No, but I would accept a cup of cocoa."

The look he gave her reminded her forcibly of the one he had given her when she had been foolish enough to ask what he thought of her.

"I'm afraid Sandoval doesn't get many requests for cocoa," Mr. Attmore said. "All he has is coffee. Unless you'd prefer a beer."

She supposed he'd said that intentionally, just to rile her. Well, she could play this game just as well as he.

"I'd love a Blauenstaff," she replied, then tried not to laugh at the shocked looks on the faces around her. "It's the favorite beer in my country."

The faint crinkling of the skin at the corners of his eyes told her Luke knew exactly what she was doing.

"I'm afraid Sandoval's shipment of Blauenstaff was stolen last week. It's a favorite of so many of the miners, they can't wait for it to reach the saloon."

He wanted to joke. She didn't care as long as he realized she wasn't a silly little fool he could insult at will.

"In that case I'll have to decline your offer."

"We have other beers."

"I couldn't think of drinking anything but Blauenstaff. I came here to tell you, Mr. Attmore—"

"Call me Luke."

"—that I have no intention of asking you to escort me to Rudolf's ranch. I wouldn't accept your services if you volunteered them."

Chapter Three

"I never volunteer my services," Luke said, without the slightest change of expression. "I charge an exorbitant price. That makes me even more valuable to my clientele."

"Not to me."

"So you've made clear."

"You're free to leave Bonner."

"So I am."

"I'm sure someone else is anxious to retain your services."

"I've had several requests."

"Then by all means take one of them."

"I'm considering it."

This interview hadn't proceeded as she'd anticipated. No man had ever sat across a table from her, regarding her with expressionless eyes, returning minimal responses to her questions or statements. She'd all but ordered him to leave town, and he just sat there watching her like a cat with a cornered mouse.

"When are you going to leave?" she asked.

"Why is it so important to you?"

She bridled at the inference. "It isn't. I just wanted you to know you're free to go about your usual activities."

"Thank you." His smile was faint and ironic.

"Hans said you refused to keep the money Otto offered you. Why did you do that?"

"I hadn't done any work. It seemed unreasonable to keep the money."

"But you took it at first."

"Yes."

"Then you gave it back."

"Yes."

"Stop answering me in monosyllables!"

"Why?"

She'd never liked the idea of firing squads, but right now she'd have given half her dowery to see him standing before one. "Because it's rude."

"Why?"

Luke clearly had no respect for position in society, her status as a woman, or her as a person.

"I just came to let you know you were free to take other employment," she said, getting to her feet.

"I'm not sure I feel like working just now."

She turned to leave.

"Bonner seems like a nice little town. I think I'll stay for a while."

She turned back. "I would prefer that you leave."

"Give me a good reason why I should care what you prefer."

She saw traces of that ironic smile. She reminded herself this wasn't Belgravia, that he wasn't one of her subjects. Probably not one person in this entire, huge, endless country cared what she thought or what happened to her. That terrified her. Only the loyalty of her servants separated her from complete and helpless isolation. And what reason did they have to be loyal? Could money ensure the kind of loyalty she'd always taken for granted?

If she could only get to Rudolf's ranch. All her life she'd been protected by her prestige, her rank, the circle of people who orbited around the court. It had seemed so deep, so endless, so *permanent*, she'd never considered the possibility it might be taken away.

But it had been. Now she stood perched on the edge of a trackless wilderness with two old men who knew no more than she how to provide guidance and protection. She needed to get to Rudolf. Once she reached his ranch, everything would be all right again.

"Since you are no longer in my employ," she said, "I suppose there is no reason for you to care what I want. However, whether you stay or go, I would like you to remove your prohibition against anyone else serving as my guide."

His expression didn't change one iota. "I haven't prohibited anyone from accepting your offer."

"But Hans and Otto say they've been unable to hire anyone to take your place."

His look might as well have said, *No one can take my place*.

"I've offered a great deal of money," Otto said.

"Offer more," he said.

"I have, and they still won't take the job."

"Then I guess you'll have to find your own way," he said.

"None of my servants know anything about your country," Valeria said.

Mr. Attmore looked from Otto to Hans. "Do you consider yourselves servants?"

Otto sputtered.

"I consider myself in the service of the princess," Hans said.

"But not a servant?"

"I'm employed to advise her highness."

"So am I," Otto said.

Luke Attmore turned to Valeria. "Looks like you don't have any servants, ma'am, just advisers."

Valeria had known immediately she'd said something to upset this man. Now she knew what. She'd always referred to the people who worked for her as servants. The term didn't suggest anything demeaning. Apparently it meant something quite different in this country, something she would have to try to understand.

"My *advisers* know nothing about your country," she said, trying hard to remain pleasant in the face of his continued provocation.

Luke motioned to the man behind the counter to come over. "Sandoval," Luke said when the man reached him, "do you think Bob Wilson could guide the princess to a ranch above the Mogollon Rim?"

"Bob's tied up working for the stage company just now," Sandoval said. "Just took the job yesterday. He won't be done with that for I don't know how long."

"How about Abe Custis?"

"His cousin broke his leg yesterday. He's got to take over working his ranch until he can get back in the saddle."

"Surely Sam Prentiss could do it."

"Sam left to visit his mother in Alabama yesterday. It seems there's a senorita who claims Sam's the father of her baby. The senorita's father, four uncles, six brothers, and eleven cousins are anxious to talk with Sam."

"How about you, Sandoval?" Luke asked.

"I think the senorita should wait. Somebody will come."

Valeria hadn't failed to notice that all three incidents happened yesterday, *after* Otto had informed Luke his services were no longer required. Luke had boxed her in, and she couldn't do anything about it.

"How long would I have to wait?" she asked Sandoval.

"Can't say," the man said with his heavy accent. "A day. A month. Who can tell?"

"A month!" Otto exclaimed.

Sandoval shrugged. "It's possible." He returned to the bar, leaving Valeria to confront an innocent looking Luke Attmore.

"This is your doing."

"Do you think I could arrange all that?"

"Yes."

"Those are tough, dependable, knowledgeable men. They wouldn't care what I think."

"Miners are supposed to be tough men," Valeria shot back, "yet you frightened them into being quiet last night."

"I didn't frighten anybody," Luke said, his eyelids sinking a little lower. "I just told them we had a genuine princess staying at the hotel and that it would be plain old American courtesy to let her sleep."

"I was already awake," Valeria said, forcing herself to smile sweetly when she would much prefer hitting him hard enough to remove that self-satisfied smile from his face. "You know that. You saw me at the window."

"And a lovely sight you were," Luke said, "but I would advise against doing that again. In their condition, some of the men might misinterpret your reason for appearing at the window."

If it hadn't been for Hans's gasp, Valeria would have been at a loss to understand Luke's meaning. The idea that she could have been mistaken for a harlot would never have occurred to her.

"When a man is drunk and hasn't seen a pretty woman in months, maybe years, well . . ."

"It is a pity Americans are so prone to act like beasts. Your army should do something about that."

"They call America a melting pot," Luke said. "Most of the miners come from European stock. It's possible some immigrated from your own country."

"My countrymen would never behave so."

"Your countrymen behave better than anyone else in Europe, even when they're drunk? You must tell me how you managed that. Sometimes I'm hired to bring a town under control. It would be useful to know how to do it without having to kill so many."

Valeria had never dealt with a man who didn't hesitate to puncture her arguments or expose the folly of age-old custom.

She turned to Sandoval, who had returned to the bar. "If you learn of anyone capable and *willing*"—she glanced at Luke before turning back to Sandoval—"to act as my guide, would you please direct him to my hotel?"

"Si, senorita."

"Good day, Mr. Attmore."

"Good day."

He didn't stand when she got up to leave. He had no respect for her or the tradition she represented. She certainly didn't see why Hans should have thought him the person to guide her through the Arizona Territory.

But even as she strode toward the door, she couldn't rid herself of the suspicion that he was the best possible choice. She didn't believe for a moment Sandoval's stories about those other men. Luke Attmore had convinced them not to work for her. Just like he'd convinced the drunks to stop shouting and singing in the street. She didn't believe that nonsense about American courtesy, either. The farther west she went, the less she got. Until she met Luke Attmore.

Then she got none.

She left the cool, dark interior of the saloon and went out into the full brightness of the sun. And the heat. She would ruin her dress before she reached her hotel. Well, one dress didn't matter. She had others. And she wouldn't come out of her hotel again until Hans or Otto found a guide.

Which brought her thoughts back to Luke Attmore. She couldn't imagine what it was about this man that affected everyone so powerfully. She could understand his effect on women because she'd experienced it herself. Actually, *understand* wasn't exactly the right word. She didn't understand it at all. He was everything she disliked in a man. Well, that wasn't true, either. His looks were fabulous, or they would be if he bought some decent clothes, but he had a rotten personality. She doubted even his mother liked him.

She still hadn't gotten it quite right. She'd known men just as attractive, but she'd been virtually unaffected by their looks. There was something different about Luke, something she couldn't identify. She couldn't imagine why she should be so powerfully affected by a man without being able to explain why, but it was foolish to pretend she wasn't. Still, it wasn't a problem that needed solving. She'd never see him again.

"Keep looking for a guide," she said to Otto and Hans as she entered her hotel. "I don't believe everybody is suddenly busy."

"We've asked everyone," Otto said.

"Then ask again. Maybe one of them has changed his mind."

"Yes, your highness," Otto said.

"I think you ought to ask Mr. Attmore to take the job."

She spun around to face Hans. "I wouldn't beg him if he were the last man on earth."

"He may be the only man in Bonner who can do the job."

"Send a message to Rudolf. He'll come get me."

"Duke Rudolf won't leave his ranch for fear of assassination," Otto said.

"Then I'll wait until you can find a guide. Surely not every man in America is intimidated by Luke Attmore."

It seemed impossible to her that a single man without an army could exert such influence. She might have understood it if he'd been a king or a member of some royal family. Then his position, his birthright, would have commanded some influence, even with these disrespectful Americans. But Luke had nothing except his reputation as a gunman, and he seemed too lazy to use his weapon.

"What do you think about Mr. Attmore?" she asked Elvira over her shoulder as they climbed the stairs to her room.

"I think he is a very dangerous man," her maid replied. "I'm afraid of him."

That surprised Valeria so much she stopped on the landing and turned to face her maid. "Why would you say that?" She'd been a little afraid of Luke when she first saw him lurking outside her hotel. She actually felt more safe now knowing he was prowling about.

"Did you see his eyes?" Elvira asked, and shivered.

"Of course I saw his eyes," Valeria said, turning to continue up the stairs. "I couldn't help it with him staring straight at me." She'd never seen such blue eyes. They reminded her of huge sapphires, deep blue, hard, with light flashing from deep inside. Even now she could picture them as clearly as if he were sitting before her.

"He has hard eyes," Elvira said, "the eyes of a killer."

"Of course he's a killer. That's what he's paid to do."

"But a killer without conscience."

"I imagine a conscience would only get in the way of his job."

"That's why he frightens me," Elvira said. "I don't think he'd ever let anything get in the way of his job."

"Nothing's supposed to. That's why Hans hired him in the first place."

She stopped outside her door while Elvira unlocked it.

"I thought you wanted to know what I thought of him as a man," Elvira said as she opened the door and stepped back to allow Valeria to enter first.

"Why should you think that?" Valeria asked even as she realized that was exactly what she'd wanted. She doubted it was possible for a woman to think of Luke Attmore in any other terms. "Never mind. We won't speak of him again. Help me change into something cooler."

But as the long hours of the morning and afternoon crept slowly by, Valeria found that Luke Attmore continued to absorb her thoughts. The more she thought about him, the more confused she became. And the more angry. She didn't want to think about him. She didn't want to remember his eyes. Or his lips. Or anything else about his unforgettable face. Having nothing to do but entertain herself with thoughts centered around Luke made the empty hours still worse. She had no one to talk to, nowhere to go. And even if she did, the heat was intolerable.

"Where are my books?" she demanded of Elvira.

"You've read everything at least twice."

That was something else she had to do when she reached Rudolf's ranch. She hadn't been able to buy a book since she left England. As far as she could tell, people in the West—and they all seemed to be men—

didn't read. She couldn't imagine what they did with their time.

The last five days had been the most miserable and infuriating of Valeria's life. And she owed every crushingly boring minute of it to Luke Attmore. Neither Hans nor Otto had been able to find anyone who would agree to take them to Rudolf's ranch.

"You're going to have to ask Mr. Attmore to reconsider," Hans said.

"I will not beg that man to do anything for me."

"He merely wants you to ask," Hans said. "He said he won't take a job when the person he's supposed to protect doesn't want him."

"When did he say that?" Valeria asked. That put a different perspective on the situation. She supposed that not even Luke Attmore's armor of conceit would enable him to ignore a client who didn't want him around.

"Just after he was fired."

"What were you doing talking to him?" Otto demanded.

"I wanted him to reconsider. My research told me he was the best man for the job."

Valeria sensed the tension between the two men. She wished they wouldn't compete for her favor. She had complete confidence in both of them.

"We don't have anyone to take his place," Hans said, unnecessarily repeating that fact. "You'd better give me the money so I can rehire him."

"You can't rehire him," Otto said. "Her highness has to ask him."

Valeria knew she had no alternative, but the gall of defeat wasn't made any less bitter by necessity. Rudolf couldn't come to her, so she had to go to him. She had to ask Luke Attmore to escort her there whether she choked on her pride or not.

But then, she was a woman. No one expected her to have pride, certainly not the kind expected of a man. Men could fight wars, kill each other in duels, lose fortunes at the gambling table, and everything could be expected because of pride. Let a woman do anything similar, and everyone would call her a fool.

She sighed. "Ask him to come to my room."

"It's not proper for him to enter your room," Otto said.

"He was here when I arrived," she said, barely holding on to her temper. "I don't see that it matters if he's here once more."

"Duke Rudolf won't like it."

"Then don't tell him. Besides, he should have been the one to hire a guide for me. He would know how to deal with these men far better than any of us."

"I'll try to convince him to take my word that you've changed your mind," Hans said.

Valeria felt relieved and, much to her surprise, a bit disappointed. Rather than analyze this irrational response, she paced the floor, trying to decide what she would say in case Luke Attmore insisted upon a face-to-face meeting. She refused to beg, or sound like she was begging.

"I'll simply say, 'I want you to take me to Rudolf,' " she said to her maid. "Don't you think that's enough?"

Elvira didn't appear to have an opinion on the matter, at least not one she could state clearly. She seemed consumed with the fear that she would soon be in the same room with Luke Attmore.

"He won't hurt you," Valeria assured her. "He's just a man."

Even she didn't believe that, but neither did she fear him. She just hated that she had to *ask* him. Surely he wouldn't humiliate her by refusing. But the more she thought about it, the less sure she was about what he might do. He was a mystery to her, one she doubted she could solve. Rudolf wouldn't hire men like Luke. Once at the Ranch she would be surrounded by people who understood and valued her way of life. She would be comfortable.

A woman could feel safe with a man like Luke Attmore, but not comfortable. The possibility of an even closer relationship didn't bear thinking about. Apparently American women agreed with her. She hadn't asked—there was no reason she should—but she was certain he wasn't married. He didn't wear a ring.

When had she noticed that? She couldn't remember, but there was nothing domesticated about Luke Attmore. Despite that, she was certain he got everything he wanted from women. It would be so easy for a woman, wrapped in the sensual pleasure of his company, to forget that he was far more dangerous to her than anyone he might be expected to protect her from.

Valeria muttered a curse that would have brought a rebuke from her uncle. She was tired of thinking about Luke Attmore. The sooner she reached Rudolf's ranch, the sooner she could turn her back on him.

Hans returned alone.

"Where is Mr. Attmore?" Valeria asked.

"Gone to bed," Hans replied. "He said he wanted to leave at dawn. He said you were to go to bed, too."

Go to bed before eight o'clock! Leave at dawn! The man had to be crazy. She hadn't even had dinner. It would be impossible for her chef to prepare and serve breakfast before eight o'clock. She would have to talk to Mr. Attmore. She was willing to make some compromises, but this was preposterous.

Chapter Four

Valeria fought the call to wake up. It was winter, snow piled deep outside her window, and she was warm and cozy in her bed. She didn't want to get up and dress in a cold room. She didn't want to eat breakfast with her governess telling her not to gobble and to chew every mouthful thirty-two times.

"Go away," she mumbled. "I don't want to do my lessons."

She liked history and art, but she had math and natural science today. Her tutor made her seek nature where it could be found. That usually meant woods and swamps. She always came home wet and dirty.

Valeria felt her covers being stripped away. She opened her eyes to see Luke Attmore standing next to her bed.

"You've got exactly ten seconds to get out of bed and one minute to get dressed," he said, his eyes glinting hard as blue steel, his jaw rigid enough to support an entire building. "If you can't manage it in that time, I'll do it for you."

Valeria looked wildly about the room before she remembered she was in the tiny town of Bonner in the Arizona Territory and there were no footmen or armed soldiers to come to her aid, just her maid who was now cowering in the corner and looking frightened out of her wits.

"What are you doing in my room?" Valeria demanded. She reached automatically for something to cover herself, but Like had thrown all the bedding onto the floor.

"It'll soon be time to leave," Luke said.

Except for a solitary lamp, the room was in virtual darkness. Not a single ray of light entered through the windows. "It's still dark outside. Nobody travels in the middle of the night."

Luke reached out, took hold of her hand, and dragged her to the edge of the bed. "You do if you want me to take you to Rudolf. What do you want to wear? I'll find it."

"Don't touch my clothes!" she cried.

Luke paid no attention. He pulled one dress after another from the wardrobe and tossed each aside.

"Dozens of dresses and not a single sensible one. Stand up."

When shock prevented her from moving, he pulled her to her feet. "You're about five feet, four inches tall."

"Five-five," she corrected.

He put his hands around her waist. Before she could recover from the shock of having him touch her, he moved his hands up to her breasts. She froze, paralyzed, unable to move. No man had ever dared touch her. He would have died before the firing squad.

"Not bad," Luke said half to himself before his hands

moved down to run over her hips and buttocks. Valeria managed to recover herself enough to fling his hands away.

"I'll have you shot for this," she declared.

"Relax. I'm not trying to take advantage of you. I needed to take your measurements for a dress."

"I have plenty of dresses."

"None that won't give you heat stroke." He looked at her as if noticing for the first time that she was practically naked. "If you're going to stand here winding yourself up like a corkscrew, you might as well put something on." A knock sounded on the door. "That'll be your breakfast," Luke said. He picked up a sheet from the floor. "Wrap this around you. I don't want the cook to drop the tray."

"No one is allowed in my bedroom until my maid has finished dressing me."

"You'll have to get over that," Luke said as he crossed the room and opened the door. "There won't be much privacy on the trail."

Looking as stunned as Valeria felt, the chef entered the room, his gaze glued to the floor. Pants under a nightshirt indicated he'd been yanked out of bed and thrust directly into the kitchen.

"You've got one hour to dress, eat, and pack everything you mean to take," Luke said.

"It will take me longer than that to dress."

She felt pinned to the wall by Luke's gaze. "You leave this room in an hour with or without clothes on your back. What you haven't packed stays behind."

"Where are you going?" she demanded when he turned and walked through the open doorway.

"To see that the rest of the lazy fools in your entourage haven't gone to sleep standing up."

Valeria fought off the stupor that threatened to swallow

her. "I will not be hauled around like a sack of turnips. You're fired."

Luke crossed the room in the space of a single breath, his face, taut and angry, only inches from Valeria's. "We played that game once. Now you've got me whether you want me or not."

"I don't want you," Valeria said.

But she spoke to ambient air. Luke had left the room. She heard the sound of his boots on the stairs.

For a moment no one moved. Valeria felt weak, powerless. The chef stared at his feet, the breakfast tray still in his grasp. Elvira might as well have been a statue. She hadn't moved—or breathed, as far as Valeria could tell—while Luke had been in the room.

Then the enormity of what had happened swept over her. Luke had invaded her bedchamber, stripped the covers from her, and dragged her from the bed in her nightgown. He'd emptied half her wardrobe and strewn her clothes over the floor. But worst of all, he'd put his hands all over her as though he was studying the conformation of a horse he was about to buy. She checked the desire to hurl damning epithets down the stairs after him. She stifled the yearning to scream in helpless frustration.

"Don't stand there like a dolt," she snapped at Elvira. "Everything must be ready in an hour. Everything."

Elvira shuddered and came to life. "I locked the door," she said. "I don't know how he got in."

"There's nothing we can do about that now," Valeria said. "Just start packing."

"But you're not dressed."

"Forget me. My possessions are more important. All I have in the world—everything that can make life bearable in this wilderness—is with me. I don't want to leave any of it behind. Put that tray down," she said to the chef. "Find Otto and Hans and send them to me immediately."

"You can't see them dressed like that," Elvira protested.

"Luke has seen me like this," Valeria snapped. "Nothing can be worse than that."

But by the time Hans arrived, she had put on a dress and gotten the worst tangles out of her hair. She didn't look like a royal princess, but she wasn't half naked.

Hans looked as though he been dragged out of bed, aimed at his clothes, and thrust into the hall.

"I'm terribly sorry, your highness. I never—"

"What's done is done," Valeria said, cutting off his almost tearful apology. "I want you and Otto to make sure everything I brought is packed in one of the wagons and ready to go."

"The wagons are loaded," Hans said. "We're waiting only for your personal belongings."

Valeria didn't understand. Her possessions filled several train cars.

"He had men working all night," Hans said. "He said if he'd waited for us, it would be December before we got started."

"What men?" Valeria asked. There were no men in her entourage other than Otto, Hans, the chef, and his helpers.

"He emptied a saloon of miners and offered them free drinks if they didn't break anything."

Valeria thought of the priceless heirlooms she'd brought from Europe and her skin crawled. If he and his ruffians had ruined anything—well, she didn't know what she'd do, but she'd think of something. Her ancestors were famous for their dirty tricks. She must have inherited some of their ability.

* * *

Luke frowned at the six wagons lined up in the middle of the street, each loaded with enough stuff to furnish a house. He glanced at the sky, which was beginning to turn gray just above the horizon. The sun would be up in fifteen minutes. He wanted to be out of town before the residents began to stir out of doors.

The heavily loaded wagons cut tracks into the packed dirt of the street. It would be worse in the desert, impossible on ground softened by rain. Dishes. China. Flatware. It didn't matter what you called it, it was plates, cups, and saucers, literally thousands of them, packed in crates and barrels. The land above the Mogollon Rim was practically deserted. Valeria wouldn't find anyone to sit down at her table but rough cowboys who'd rather eat off a tin plate than one painted by hand and decorated in gold.

Then there was the furniture. He'd ordered most of it stored in Bonner. She had brought enough to furnish a small palace. He supposed that's what she expected to do with it. Instead she'd find a rough log house. She wouldn't have a staff of servants to clean and polish her silver, dust the priceless ornamental clocks, mirrors, statues, and whatever else she considered a necessary part of her life. She certainly wouldn't find any use for heavy dresses made to be worn in stone palaces in a cold climate. She should have gone to Canada, not Arizona!

She was either a stupid woman or very ill informed. Either way, she was remarkably stubborn. And he'd obligated himself to protect her!

He was the one who was remarkably stupid, and he couldn't blame it on any lack of information. He'd known what he was getting into from the moment she walked into that hotel room. He should have gotten on his horse and ridden as far and as fast as he could after she fired him. Instead he'd let an absurd little man convince him he'd forfeit his honor if he deserted this princess.

Princess! Who the hell did she think she was? Someone should have told her most Americans had left Europe to get away from that kind of nonsense. Nobody would consider her special just because some ancestor a thousand years ago had conquered the people in a tiny corner of Europe and set himself up as king. They were more likely to ostracize her.

Then there were the horses. Beautiful, hot-blooded horses. Why hadn't someone told her she might as well have dangled gold before a bunch of thieves!

Sandoval joined Luke. "You'll never get them wagons through the desert if it rains," he said.

"I'm more worried about her horses."

"You should be," Sandoval agreed. "They've been attracting attention ever since they arrived. And not the best kind, either."

Knowing that did nothing to improve Luke's mood.

"Everybody knows you haven't hired guards," Sandoval said. "They've been talking about it all morning. I give you two days before you're ambushed."

Out of the corner of his eye, Luke saw two horsemen appear around the corner of the bank. They paused, looked up and down the street, then turned their horses toward Luke's caravan.

"Maybe," Luke said, his mood lightening considerably, "but my chances just improved."

"You've decided to leave the horses here?"

Sandoval's expression lightened so much, Luke wondered if his friend had designs on Valeria's priceless mounts.

"See them?" Luke said, motioning with his head. "They're worth a dozen gunmen."

"Who are they?" Sandoval asked.

"You might say they're my brothers."

"The hell I would," Sandoval replied. "I ain't blind. One's a half-breed and the other is black."

"We were adopted."

Sandoval grinned. "And all this time I thought you was brought up by a mountain lion."

"I was sired by a mad coyote and nursed by a rabid bitch," Luke muttered. "A mountain lion would have been better."

Luke's irritation increased. He rarely spoke about his adopted family, but he *never* mentioned his true parents. He had done his best to erase all memory of them from his mind. It irritated him that he was so riled up about Valeria he'd spoken without thinking.

Which was another problem. He wasn't thinking clearly these days. He usually avoided jobs involving women. He liked clean, neat jobs he could walk away from without having to look over his shoulder. Nothing about women was easy. There was always some kind of complication. He'd only accepted this job because of the money. He'd considered the princess only a small part of the job. More fool he.

Still, that didn't account for his staying after he'd been fired. Otto had even paid him for his time and inconvenience. Yet despite Valeria's objections and the insanity of carrying so much useless stuff through the desert, Luke felt obligated to honor his promise.

He hoped honor had been the deciding factor. He didn't want his decision to have anything to do with Valeria.

"I wouldn't turn my back on them for five seconds," Sandoval said.

"You shouldn't," Luke said. "Zeke can kill you in two seconds. Hawk can do it in one."

Sandoval shuddered. "And you grew up sharing a bunkhouse with those two?"

"And seven others, including my real brother."

"It's a good thing you had somebody to watch your back."

Chet had always watched Luke's back. He'd become a gunfighter so he could continue looking after his younger brother. But Chet had given up guns seven years ago, gotten married, gone back to Texas, and bought himself a ranch next to Jake and Isabelle's place. Last Luke heard, Chet had two boys and Melody was expecting again. Luke hadn't seen his brother's kids. Respectable women didn't want a man like him around. He couldn't fault them for that. He didn't think much of respectable women, either.

"Glad you could make it," Luke said when Zeke and Hawk brought their horses to a halt.

"When did you start helping settlers?" Hawk asked. "And why in hell would they go into the Rim country? Those ranchers will burn them out."

"They're not settlers," Luke said. "I'm taking a woman to her future husband's ranch. She was a princess, but her people threw her out, and his people threw him out. They decided to settle in the Arizona Territory."

"They've got to be crazy," Hawk said.

"That's not my worry," Luke said. "I'm just supposed to get her there."

"Are those horses going with us?" Zeke said, indicating the six blooded thoroughbreds.

Luke nodded.

"You trying to get us killed? That's what's going to happen if we travel nearly four hundred miles with those horses."

"I expect they'll be something of a problem," Luke said, "but it wouldn't be any safer to leave them here."

"It would have been safer to have left them where they came from," Zeke snapped.

"It's a little late for that."

"It's not too late for Hawk and me to turn around and ride out."

Luke didn't respond to Zeke's burst of temper. Jake and Isabelle had pounded the same belief in honor and loyalty into Hawk and Zeke as they had into their other adopted sons. Once committed, Hawk and Zeke wouldn't turn back. Unlike him, they hadn't put a price on their honor. Luke wondered why Jake and Isabelle had failed with him.

"Get acquainted with the drivers," Luke said. "Maybe you'll feel a little better after that."

"Hired some of your gun-toting friends, did you?" Hawk asked.

"I found me a full-blooded Apache and a couple of half-breeds."

Hawk's black eyes glowed, but his face remained impassive. He turned his horse and walked it toward the wagons.

"Why the hell did you have to go and say something like that?" Zeke demanded.

"I want him mad. Nothing gets past him then."

"You made me mad, too."

"Good. You're a better fighter when you've got the prospect of spilling some white man's blood."

Zeke jerked his horse around and trotted after Hawk.

"You're crazy," Sandoval exclaimed, "baiting those men like that. They're liable to put a knife in you."

"They'd die before they'd let anything happen to me. Jake and Isabelle taught them nothing is more important than family."

"You ain't part of nobody's family," Sandoval said. "You're like a lone wolf. You'd eat your young if it would get you anything by it."

"They don't know that."

"They're liable to find out before this trip's over."

Hans, dressed exactly as he must have dressed for court in Belgravia, came out of the hotel and started toward Luke with mincing steps.

"What's he going to do up on the Rim?" Sandoval asked. "I'll bet you fifty dollars he can't stay on a horse more than ten minutes."

"I doubt any of them can ride worth a damn. I don't know why Valeria wanted to bring these horses."

"Maybe her husband wanted them, though I don't know what use he'll find for them on the Rim."

"Probably fox hunting," Luke said. "I expect somebody showed him a picture of a coyote."

Sandoval burst out laughing, glanced at Hans, and headed off to his saloon.

Luke pulled a watch from his vest pocket. "Your mistress has two minutes to be downstairs," Luke said when Hans toddled up.

"The princess is ready," Hans said. "Please get all these people off the street so she can enter her coach."

Luke jammed his watch back into his pocket. "Did she ask you to say that?"

"No, but she'll naturally expect it. It's nearly impossible to enter a carriage without exposing a limb to public view."

With a muttered curse, Luke headed toward Valeria's hotel. "I haven't got time for such foolishness," he said over his shoulder to Hans, who was practically running to keep up with him. "Before this journey is done, she'll expose more than that."

"She's a royal princess. She can't be expected to appear in public like an ordinary person."

"This is America," Luke said. "As far as people here are concerned, she *is* an ordinary person."

Luke reached the hotel and pushed through the doorway to find Valeria and her maid waiting in the lobby, luggage piled up behind her. She looked like a queen, regal and distant, waiting for her subjects.

"You've got about one minute to get yourself and all your belongings into the coach," Luke said. He turned to her maid. "Get some of the drivers to load this stuff. Now!" His imperative command caused Elvira to jump, and run from the hotel as through pursued by a dangerous animal.

"Don't shout at my maid," Valeria said.

"I expect I'll shout at everybody, including you, before this trip is over. Why are you standing here instead of getting into the coach?"

"I'm waiting for you to clear the street."

His temper stretched by the circumstances of this absurd journey and his being stupid enough to take responsibility for it, Luke had no tolerance left for this kind of arrogance. "This is a Western territory, not a medieval kingdom."

"Hans said—"

"It's desert," he said, interrupting her. "It's hot, dirty, and dangerous. Men kill each other for gold, silver, cows, horses, or a cup of water. Some kill just because they like it. If they see something they want, they take it. If anybody tries to stop them, they shoot the fool or put a knife in his heart. The only thing standing between your being raped and probably having your throat cut afterward is me and those two men outside."

Hans tried to insert his pudgy body between Luke and Valeria. "You can't talk to her highness like that." He was so upset he could hardly articulate the words.

Luke didn't bother looking down at him. He just picked him up and set him aside. "Now you either get into that coach on your own," he said to Valeria, "or I'll put you in it."

"In case it's of any interest to you—and I doubt it is since you appear to be interested only in your own opinions—it was not my idea to wait here," Valeria said. "I was quite prepared to climb into the coach in full view of everyone in this town. Hans stopped me, certain you'd be glad to accord me this sign of courtesy."

"I'll accord you courtesy when you earn a little," Luke said. "So far you've done nothing but sit back and wait for servants to do everything for you."

"If I had any such expectations of you, Mr. Attmore, I assure you I have them no longer. Now if you will remove yourself from my path, I would like to enter my coach. I don't want to be accused of being the one to hold up your departure."

Looking furious enough to use a knife herself, she started past him. Luke reached out and caught her by the arm. "Why aren't you wearing one of the dresses I bought you?"

"Because I despise them." She looked down at Luke's hand, apparently stunned he would do anything so shocking as take hold of her. "Release my arm."

Luke kept his grip. "Where are those dresses?"

She attempted to pull away but Luke tightened his grip.

"I asked you a question."

He thought for a moment Valeria would refuse to answer. He also thought Hans would expire of a heart attack on the spot.

"Elvira put them in the bottom of my truck," Valeria admitted grudgingly. "You can't make me wear them."

Luke glared at her for a moment longer before he released her. "I won't have to," he said, his voice dropping lower. "Before long you'll be begging me to let you wear one."

"I'll never—"

"Never make rash promises," Luke said, as he moved to one side to allow her to pass. "It's so much more difficult when you have to swallow them *and* your pride."

Valeria started to speak, changed her mind, and strode toward the door.

"Buck up, Hans," Luke said. "Arizona isn't like your fusty old court, but it's not half bad once you get used to it. You might even discover you have two thoughts in your head that have nothing to do with Valeria. It'll do her good to have to take care of herself. She's been indulged too—"

A scream from the street caused Luke to turn on his heel and race from the hotel.

Chapter Five

Luke found a white-faced Valeria supporting Elvira. The maid had fainted.

"It's those two men," Valeria said, indicating Zeke and Hawk.

"She ran smack dab into my chest," Zeke said, grinning. "She took one look at me and backed right into Hawk. That's when she fainted."

"Throw some water on her," Luke said.

"Don't you fancy ladies carry smelling salts?" Zeke asked. "My old mistress did."

"Everything is packed," Valeria said.

Luke delivered two sharp slaps to the maid's cheeks. She came out of her faint with a start. She looked from Luke to Hawk and Zeke. Her eyes got wide again.

"Don't faint," Luke said, "or I'll dunk you in the horse trough. These men are my brothers."

"B-brothers," the maid stammered.

"Obviously we're adopted," Luke said. "Now pull

yourself together and get into the coach. You've made us late."

"Have some compassion," Valeria said. "She still hasn't gotten used to your country. You can't know how different it is from ours."

"I've been to your country," Luke said. "I've seen your royal palace."

Valeria looked so skeptical, Luke laughed. "I'll describe it to you."

"I know what it looks like," she said.

"But you don't believe *I* know. I can see it in your eyes. Now get your maid in the coach. We can't afford to wait any longer."

Elvira didn't wait for Valeria's help. She practically flung herself into the coach, to escape Zeke and Hawk, Luke guessed.

When Luke had first accepted the job, he'd purchased an old mail coach, had it cleaned and the seats recovered. Valeria's elegance made it look shabby.

"You'll never get that woman out again," Zeke said with a laugh that sounded as mocking as it did lacking in sympathy.

"I'll let you take her food to her," Luke said.

He ignored Zeke's flash of anger. "Want me to help?" Luke asked Valeria when she paused, contemplating how to enter the coach. He could see she wanted to refuse, but he knew she'd never get inside without assistance. She probably didn't know how, especially not in those cumbersome skirts.

"You'll end up showing more than an ankle if you try it on your own," he said.

"Is that what you've been waiting for?"

"I'm in no hurry. I expect I'll see a great deal more than an ankle before this trip is over."

"And just what do you mean by that?"

If she hadn't looked so ridiculously overdressed, it would have been funny. Maybe ridiculous wasn't the right word. She'd made a very poor choice of what to wear, but she looked lovely. "A trip like this doesn't allow for privacy of the kind you're used to."

"Why not?"

"You'll soon find out. Now, do you want me to help you into the coach?"

"Please." The word sounded more like a curse.

"When I lift you, put both feet on that step. You'll be able to climb up on your own after that." He didn't wait for the protest he knew trembled on Valeria's lips. He stepped behind her, caught her under the arms, and lifted her into the air. He kept his hands on her back while she put a foot on the second step, then stepped up into the coach.

"Next time I'll wait for Hans or Otto," she said.

"Next time you'll have to," Luke said as he closed the door and turned his back. He didn't mean to get near her again unless he had to. Just looking at her disturbed him. Touching her upset his equilibrium, destroyed his feeling of detachment, and that threatened his ability to do his work. He couldn't have that. Luke didn't have anything he could point to with pride, except his work. He wouldn't allow anything to jeopardize it.

"I want you to stay with the horses," Luke said, turning back to Zeke. "Hawk will scout around for good camping places and keep a lookout for trouble. When we camp at night, I want you two to sleep on opposite sides of the camp."

"It sounds like you're expecting trouble."

"I'm certain of it."

"Then leave the horses behind."

"It's not the horses."

"The woman?"

Luke nodded.

"If I were looking to rob you, I'd settle for the horses or the wagons."

"I expect somebody will try," Luke said. "She should have left it all in New Orleans, but I guess she wants as much of her past around her as possible."

"She'll never survive."

"She's spoiled and temperamental, but she's tough."

Zeke's gaze narrowed. "You sound like you admire her."

"People like her have survived as heads of state in Europe for hundreds of years. When it comes to making decisions, there's not an ounce of sentiment in them. Their hearts would put a cash register to shame. She's like a snow-capped mountain, filled with fire deep inside, but cold enough to freeze anyone who tries to conquer her."

"And I was beginning to think you liked her."

Luke stopped. He hadn't realized he knew half the things he'd just told Zeke until the words were out of his mouth. That wasn't like him. To Luke, women were objects of desire, for companions for an evening to soothe his spirit and satisfy his body. He never bothered looking beneath the surface. Occasionally he might remember a name, but most of the time women were interchangeable.

But not Valeria. The moment she'd walked into that hotel—tired, irritable, imperious—he'd felt something inside him jump. A muscle twitch. A spasm. A sensitive nerve. He didn't know. He just knew he had a definite reaction to her, and that wasn't good. He needed to be immune to all women, unaffected by anything and anyone around him.

"Time to get moving," Luke said, "or we'll still be within sight of Bonner when we camp tonight."

"Move 'em out!" Zeke shouted, then headed toward his horse.

The call reminded Luke of the days when he lived with Jake and Isabelle, working the ranch with all the orphans, going on trail drives with the Randolph family. They had been good days, but all the boys had been filled with hate, anger, jealousy, distrust, a thirst for revenge, a desire to hurt someone because they'd been hurt so badly. For some, the anger gradually worked itself out and faded away. Others learned to keep it under control.

For Luke it remained just below the surface, festering, infecting everything he did, until he couldn't stand it any longer. One day he'd simply taken his guns and ridden out. Within a month he'd taken his first job, killed his first man. It was something he could do, something he did better than others. He kept on doing it until he became known as the best.

Now he didn't know how to do anything else.

Hans burst from the hotel, waving and shouting, "Wait for me."

The silly fool. He could get himself killed running in front of a wagon. "Get in the coach with the princess," Luke said.

"No one rides with the princess except her maid," he said. "It's not proper."

"You'll ride in the coach, or you'll walk," Luke said. "Now where the hell is Otto?"

"He and the landlord can't agree on the bill."

Luke uttered a volley of curses and headed toward the hotel. Inside he found Otto and the landlord shouting at each other. "How much does he owe you?" Luke asked the landlord.

"Two hundred and forty-seven dollars."

"This flea-infested hovel isn't worth seven dollars," Otta said.

"Give me your wallet," Luke said to Otto.

Otto clutched his coat protectively.

"Give it to me, or I'll take it from you." Luke drew his gun, gripped it by the barrel, and raised the butt in the direction of Otto's head. Otto quickly withdrew a wallet from inside his coat and handed it to Luke. Luke holstered his gun, opened the wallet, and pulled out three hundred dollars.

"Here," he said to the landlord. "Keep the extra. I'm sure you deserve it."

"Thank you." The landlord took the money and shoved it into his pocket. He made no attempt to hide his triumphant grin.

"That's robbery," Otto shouted.

"I'm sure you paid more than that for hotels in London and Paris," Luke said.

"But they were elegant."

"This is the most elegant hotel in Bonner. Now get in that coach. I won't wait for you any longer."

"I'm in charge of the princess," Otto said, swelling up like a blow toad. "I'll say when—"

Luke grabbed him by his shirt front and pulled him close until their noses were only inches apart. "You were in charge until you hired me. Now *I* decide when you get up, when you go to bed, when you eat, when you relieve yourself. You try my patience, and I'll leave you in the desert for the coyotes to pick your bones. If this isn't to your liking, stay here. Otherwise, shut the hell up and get in that coach."

Otto was so off balance when Luke released him, he nearly fell.

"I will speak to the Duke about this," Otto said, trying to maintain his dignity but sounding spiteful.

"Speak to anybody you want," Luke said. "But if you annoy me too much, I'll cut your tongue out."

Luke strode from the room, Otto's stunned reaction bringing a rare smile to his face.

Valeria had never spent a more miserable morning in her entire life. Luke had assured her the coach was one of the finest made, that its suspension was the best that could be had, that the seats rode on additional springs to absorb shock. If all that were true, she couldn't imagine the torture of riding in a normal coach. She had been jostled and tossed about until she wanted to scream. Every part of her body would be covered with bruises before nightfall.

But nothing could compare to the heat. They had opened the leather curtains earlier, but reluctantly gave up. The sun poured in, baking whoever was unfortunate enough to be in its path. The dust choked them.

"I'm so sorry, Your Highness," Hans said for the hundredth time. "If I had known things would be this bad, I'd never have brought you here."

"You had nothing to do with it," Otto said. "I'm in charge of the princess."

"For the time being, Mr. Attmore is in charge," Valeria said. "And I'm going to tell him to stop and let us rest for a while. I can't wait for a drink of cool water."

"Here, drink some of mine," Hans said, holding out a canteen.

Valeria recoiled at the idea of drinking from such a vessel. "Where did you get that thing?"

"At the hotel. The landlord said there would be no water in the desert, that we all ought to have canteens."

"There has to be water out here," Valeria said. "If I had needed a canteen, I'm certain Mr. Attmore would have said so. That looks exactly like the kind of thing he would take pleasure in forcing me to drink from."

Valeria lifted the leather curtain. After the dimness of

the interior, the sunlight nearly blinded her. She closed her eyes, then opened them gradually until they adjusted to the light. Distant mountains rose abruptly out of the flatness, almost as though God had punched his fist through the earth's surface without disturbing the surrounding land. They didn't form a chain but were scattered, breaking up this seemingly limitless, parched plain.

Nowhere did she see any sign of shade. They hadn't crossed a single stream, creek, or wash containing a drop of water. Nor did she see any sign of animal life. If the native animals had forsaken this part of the Arizona Territory, how were people supposed to survive?

She put her head out of the window and was able to see the wagons that went before and behind her coach, but not Luke. She pulled her head back inside and lowered the leather curtain.

"He must be on your side," she said to Elvira. "Exchange places with me."

Elvira stood up to allow Valeria to slide across the seat. The coach lurched, throwing Elvira into Hans's lap. Valeria couldn't decide who was more embarrassed—Hans, who blanched white, or Elvira, who plopped down in the seat next to her, red-faced, her gaze fixed on the floor of the coach.

Valeria raised the leather curtain and stuck her head out. The landscape looked remarkably similar, with one exception. A belt of lush green meandered across the plain only a few hundred feet away. She didn't know the name of the tall trees with deep green leaves that rustled in the light breeze, but she thought they were incredibly beautiful. Trees meant shade. And water. The grass grew thicker, the bushes taller. The sight of a bird appearing momentarily above the trees before diving back into the shady coolness cheered her considerably. She didn't see Luke.

"Stop the coach," she said to Hans. He pounded on the roof with his walking stick, but the coach continued to bump along. Repeated pounding did not good.

"How do you stop a coach in America?" Valeria asked.

"I don't know," Hans said.

But Valeria knew who could stop it. She stuck her head through the window. She didn't see Luke. "Mr. Attmore." He might be the most obnoxious man in the world, but she couldn't believe he'd abandoned them. "Mr. Attmore!" she called again, more imperatively. Still, he didn't appear.

She drew her head back inside. "He is the most insufferable man, forcing us on this horrible journey, then leaving us to others."

"I'm sure he's close by," Hans said. "I don't believe he's a man to take his obligations lightly."

"He takes the rest of us very lightly indeed," said Otto, still angry over Luke's overpaying the landlord.

Valeria sometimes wondered if the money Otto saved didn't manage to find its way into his pocket. "If he's here, I wish he would do me the courtesy of answering," she said.

She stuck her head through the window again and came practically nose to nose with a horse. She jumped back with such force she nearly knocked Elvira off the seat.

Luke leaned low in the saddle until the window framed his face. "Did you want something?"

Valeria struggled to regain her composure. Even though she'd nearly been kissed by his horse, she didn't want Luke to know it had upset her.

"Pull this coach into the shade of those trees," she said, pointing to the inviting belt of green. "We're hot and thirsty."

"We're all hot and thirsty," Luke said. "We'll stop for a short rest in a couple of hours."

His head disappeared from the window. His horse moved away from the coach. Valeria thrust her head out the window. "I want to stop now."

He didn't come back toward the coach or even turn around. "Not getting what you want will be good for you," he said. "It'll get you in shape for life on your husband's ranch."

It took a moment for what he'd said to penetrate. "You can't refuse to do what I ask!"

He turned toward her. "Look, woman, I know you're not stupid, so don't act like it."

"Don't you dare address me as *woman!* I am a princess."

"We don't have princesses in this country," Luke said. "Fortunately for you, we don't cut their heads off, either. We just strip them of their titles. What do you want me to call you?"

"You must address her as *your highness,*" Hans said.

"We don't do that, either. Do you want me to call you Valeria?"

"You wouldn't presume," Hans said.

Luke grinned. "You have no idea how much I can presume. How about Miss Badenberg?"

"The proper form of address would be *Your Highness, the Princess of Badenberg,*" Hans said.

"No more argument," Luke snapped. "I'm calling her Valeria. That's the end of it."

"Then I'll call you Luke."

"Good. If you're still thirsty, drink some of Hans's water. He was the only one sensible enough to come supplied with a canteen. If you'd looked out your train windows in Texas, New Mexico, or Arizona, you'd have known this place is as dry as a bone."

"But we're following a river," Valeria objected. "There's plenty of water there."

"You'd better hope so. With all these animals, we'll need barrels of it."

He dug his spurs into his horse's flanks and rode off toward the head of the column.

"He's not going to stop," she reported unnecessarily. "Apparently he doesn't consider our comfort of any importance."

"It must be even hotter riding in the sun," Hans observed.

"He's not human," Elvira said. "He can't be and have grown up with those savages."

"They were adopted," Valeria reminded her maid.

"I don't care. How could he go to sleep with them in the same room?"

"I wondered the same thing," Valeria said. "But then I remembered the people we saw in Bonner, all kinds mixed together, and nobody appearing to notice the difference."

"I would," Elvira insisted.

"But Mr. Attmore—Luke—wouldn't, not if he'd been raised with Indians and black people." It was a strange notion. That would never have happened in her country, but after giving it some thought, she decided it might not be such a bad idea. It was certainly better than being afraid of everybody who was different.

She doubted Rudolf would be as willing as Luke to accept people who weren't like him. She was curious to know how different people got along. Did most of them eat the same food, wear the same clothes? The people in Bonner hadn't eaten anything she could recognize. They certainly didn't dress like she did.

She had heard many different languages from her window. She recognized French, German, and Italian, but there were others. She wondered how people of so many different nationalities had all ended up in Arizona. There must be something here that attracted them, kept them here, but she couldn't see what it was. If she had known what Arizona was like, she'd never have agreed to marry Rudolf.

But then whom would she have married? There were no other men of suitable rank who weren't old, fat, and greedy for her money. There weren't any men like Luke Attmore in the aristocracy. There must have been back in the days when the ruling dynasties were no more than lusty young men dreaming of wealth and power. Over the centuries, that youthful vigor had been bred out of them, or bored out of them, or just drained away. There were no young men left who caused her heart to race, her blood to warm, her gaze to pause.

She'd been taught to consider herself part of a special class of people, a class of such pure blood, so privileged, it would be impossible to think of marrying out of its ranks. Those who rebelled were shunned. Those who followed the rules were rewarded with wealth, power, privilege, position, and the comforting belief that they were the most favored of God's creatures.

For a long time Valeria had accepted that belief without question. Even the revolution and the deaths of her parents hadn't entirely destroyed her faith in the system that had upheld her family for more than a hundred generations.

The first man to ask for her hand had been a drunk, a womanizer, a gambler, a liar, and completely incapable of inspiring anything but disgust in Valeria. She felt fortunate to be marrying Rudolf, even if it meant coming to America. At least he was young and attractive. She had had every hope she would learn to feel admiration for him, if not affection.

But that was before she met Luke Attmore.

Even though she'd disliked him immediately, she now understood that she had also recognized in him the kind of man the founders of the house of Badenberg must have been. Except for his looks. If all the gloomy portraits that adorned the walls of the various palaces where she'd grown up were any proof, no one in her family could claim half the looks Luke Attmore possessed. After their first encounter, Valeria had tried to tell herself looks didn't matter, that nothing could compensate for a personality as cold and rude as Luke Attmore's.

But she couldn't get him out of her mind.

He'd held an entire town in his control, yet no one appeared to be afraid of him. He hadn't killed anyone or raised his voice. What was it about this man that caused everyone to pay such attention to what he wanted?

The search for an answer plunged her so deep in thought she didn't notice that two hours had passed until the coach turned and headed toward the river. It came to a halt within a hundred feet of the dappled shade of those trees with the rustling leaves.

"You have thirty minutes to rest," Luke announced. "Don't waste it sitting in the coach."

Chapter Six

Valeria didn't have to wait for him to open the door. Hans practically fell out of the coach, then scrambled to his feet to offer his assistance.

"Next time you'd better let me do that," Luke said. "You're liable to break your leg. You wouldn't want me to have to set it for you."

Hans blanched.

Valeria knew Hans wasn't a man of physical strength or courage, but his loyalty was unquestionable. "At least he's a man of honor," she said to Luke.

"I yield to no one in my admiration for Hans," Luke replied.

Valeria didn't know what to make of that. As far as she could tell, Luke didn't respect or value anyone. "Please help Elvira down," she said to Hans. "She's suffering more than I am."

"Then I'd better get you both in the shade as soon as possible," Luke said.

Cactus unlike anything she'd seen until now and grass

thicker than she'd seen since her train rolled out of San Antonio filled the space separating them from the shade. She couldn't possibly drag her skirts through all of that.

"What are you waiting for?" Luke asked.

"I can't wade through all of that," she said, gesturing at the uneven ground and thorny vegetation.

"Unless you come down off your high horse, you won't be able to leave that ranch house until they carry you out in a coffin," Luke grumbled. Then, without warning, he swept her up in his arms and started toward the trees.

"Put me down!" Valeria cried.

He put her down right between a towering cactus with several upstretched arms and a big bush covered in tiny, greenish-gray leaves and an unbelievable number of thorns.

"I didn't mean here," she said.

"You said to put you down. I did."

"You shouldn't have picked me up."

"I thought you wanted to reach the shade."

"I do, but—"

He swept her up and headed off again. "You've got to learn to say what you want the first time. Not everybody is going to stand around while you dither."

"I suppose you mean yourself."

"You're paying me to stand around."

"I hadn't noticed you standing anywhere for more than a few seconds. Do you always snatch up women before they can make up their minds?"

"No, just ex-princesses who don't like it. Most women out here can't wait to be snatched up. They can be the devil to get rid of."

There was so much in that group of sentences to take exception to, she didn't know where to start. She waited too long and lost her advantage. They reached the trees, and he set her on her feet.

"If I were you, I'd unbutton that dress and try to cool off. You can wade in the water if you like, but drink first. It's not so good once you stir up the mud."

"I'm not going to drink that water," Valeria exclaimed.

"What water are you going to drink?"

Surely he couldn't expect her to drink from a river. The idea was revolting. "You must have a water barrel you filled before we left town."

"It's on one of the wagons."

She turned to look back across the tangle of thorns and rocks and saw Elvira being carried by Zeke. Elvira looked as white as he was black.

"Zeke won't harm her," Luke said. "But it would help if she didn't look so petrified."

"She's no more used to being picked up and carried by strange men than I am."

"But her fear is caused by prejudice. I saw how she looked at Hawk. He'll stay away from her, but Zeke will torment her. He was a slave. He hates all white women except Isabelle."

"Isabelle?"

"The woman who adopted us."

"All three of you?"

"There were ten of us."

"Poor woman."

"Nobody would cross Isabelle. She could be mighty tough when she wanted."

Valeria couldn't imagine a woman tough enough to handle these three men, even as boys. She watched, hardly daring to breathe, until Zeke set Elvira down.

"I'll be back for you in a little while," Zeke said, a big grin exposing white teeth.

Valeria thought Elvira would faint.

"I've got to check the wagons," Luke said.

Hans and Otto arrived as Luke left, Otto wiping his forehead with his handkerchief.

"I've never though I'd be thankful to sit in the woods," he said. He tottered over to a fallen tree and settled on the trunk. "You'd better sit while you can. We'll be back in that infernal oven soon enough."

But Valeria didn't want to sit. She made her way through the sparse undergrowth toward the water. She hated the West, but the creek beckoned to her. She knew it was supposed to be a river—Luke had said it was the San Pedro River—but the water didn't seem more than a few inches deep. If she hadn't seen a leaf float by, she wouldn't have been able to tell there was any current.

Maybe it was the profound stillness, but she didn't think she'd ever felt more at peace in her life. It was odd that such a feeling should settle over her in the heart of an alien and fiercely dangerous land. Even the birds seemed to have fallen quiet.

Moments later the mules crashed through the undergrowth about a hundred feet downstream, shattering the quiet. They waded into the water to drink.

"I told the men to water them downstream," Luke said.

Valeria nearly jumped out of her skin at the sound of his voice. "I appreciate that, but I don't want a drink."

He waded a short way into the river, squatted down, scooped up some water in his hands, and drank.

"It's good," he said, "the best you'll find until you reach the streams up on the Rim."

"Thank you, but I don't want any."

He scooped up more water and came toward her, water dripping from his hands.

"Here, taste it. You can't condemn what you don't know."

She backed away. "I don't want any."

"I thought you royal people were supposed to have courage and an adventurous spirit."

"We do, but—"

"You look like inept cowards to me. You get thrown out of your homes and have to run six thousand miles before you can stop. Then you're afraid to take a swallow of water. That's the definition of a rank coward if you ask me."

"I didn't run," Valeria snapped. "I was sent."

"Then what's your excuse for being afraid of everything around you?"

Talking to this man did no good. She either had to show him or save her breath. "I have the courage to do anything you do," she said.

She pulled his hands toward her and drank. She wouldn't have admitted it for the world, but it was the sweetest tasting water she'd swallowed in many a month.

She'd drunk most of the water before she realized her lips were touching the inside of Luke's palm. Then she became aware she was holding his hands. There was something intimate about her lips touching his skin. She hadn't intended it to happen—she'd been so angry, so goaded, she hadn't considered what she was doing—but what could be more intimate than holding a man's hands, her face lowered to drink the water caught in his palms?

She'd never had any discernable reaction to the casual touch of the many men who'd danced with her or held her hand. But Luke's touch, his presence, gave rise to a very strong feeling. She couldn't describe it exactly, but she did know it was an attraction. It would be hard for any woman not to be attracted to a man like him, but Valeria hadn't expected herself to feel this tug, this curiosity to know what it was like to touch him, to be near him, to be held in his arms. He was rude, rough, and completely lacking in any respect or consideration for her. His clothes showed signs of heavy wear and too much washing. But for everything about him that repelled her, something attracted her more strongly. And it was not just his provocative good looks.

She figured it must be the heat. Nothing else could cause her to feel so peculiar.

"Have another drink," Luke said. "We won't stop again until dark."

He withdrew his hands from her grasp and turned back to the river before she could reply. She felt abandoned. Stupid. No woman in her right mind could feel abandoned with the man practically within arms' reach. But it wasn't his physical nearness that affected her so strongly. He had brought her water. He had waded into the river, caught the water in his hands, and brought it to her. That might seem ordinary to other women, but it had never happened to her. Servants brought her food and water. No man of her rank had ever been concerned enough with her needs or wants to take care of them himself. Luke Attmore had, and he didn't even like her. These Americans were a strange breed.

"We're lucky the winter rains lasted longer than usual this year," Luke said as he returned, water dripping from his hands. "I didn't look forward to digging for water every night for the next hundred miles."

Valeria chose to drink rather than respond to Luke's statement. She felt like a peasant drinking from an ordinary man's hands, but she preferred it to water drunk from the finest teacup in her uncle's priceless collection. Which just went to show how desperate a person could be when thirsty. She preferred that explanation to the alternative.

That she was attracted to Luke Attmore.

She didn't want it to be true. She was a princess, he a hired gun. There was no common ground between them.

She finished drinking and looked up into a blinding smile.

"You've got water dripping from your chin," Luke said. "What would the secretary of royal etiquette say about that?"

Before she could look for a handkerchief, Luke touched her chin with his finger, brought it all the way up until it reached her lips. Shivers chased each other through her body until she felt her legs grow weak. When he put his finger to his lips and drank the drop of water, Valeria was certain her legs would go out from under her.

"Do you have a handkerchief?" he asked.

She couldn't answer, not even nod her head.

"It's a good thing I do."

He dug his hand into pants she had been certain were too tight to allow access to his pocket. He withdrew a handkerchief and wiped the moisture from her chin.

"We can't have a princess dripping water from her chin," he said. "What would the servants think?"

Anger flooded through her, and she slapped his hand away. He was making fun of her. "They wouldn't think anything," she snapped.

"American servants would."

"I didn't think you had servants in this country."

"We do, but we don't think of it as a profession, just being temporarily down on your luck."

"What's wrong with being a servant? It's a respectable calling."

"Maybe in your eyes, but enough people hated being subservient that they took the risk of coming to America to seek a better life."

"So they could hire servants of their own."

He surprised her by laughing.

"Probably. American women like being independent,

but they don't like to cook and clean if they can get someone else to do it for them."

"What do you mean independent?"

"They like controlling their own property, owning their own businesses. A few have become doctors and lawyers. And women in Wyoming will soon have the right to vote."

Everything else he said was overshadowed by one statement. "Do you mean American women can have control of their own money?"

"Of course. No woman wants to work all day just to hand her money over to some man."

"What about my money?"

"In this country you'd have control of it."

"Then I could marry who I wanted."

"As long as he wanted to marry you. It works both ways over here."

She'd never thought of anyone not wanting to marry a rich woman. She'd never met a man like that.

"It's time to get back to the coach," Luke said. "I want to make at least fifteen miles today."

Valeria started to tremble. Did Luke mean to carry her to the coach? She turned away from the river. She was certain the color had drained from her face. She didn't want him to know he had such a strong effect on her. She felt helpless enough already.

"I hope Zeke doesn't mean to terrify Elvira again," she said.

"Zeke and Hawk will treat her fine as long as she acts like she's got a little gumption. It's hard on a man to know a woman is petrified to be near him just because he's not the same color or race as she is."

"We've heard terrible stories about Indians."

"They're probably true. But they aren't half as terrible as stories I could tell you about what we did to them."

"Your country is very different from what Elvira and I are used to. I imagine we're going to do many things you don't like. I can assure you that you've done quite a few we neither like nor understand."

"Like carrying you from the coach?"

He'd cornered her. "That's one."

"You don't want me to carry you back?"

"It's very ungentlemanly of you to force me to answer that question. You know I can't pass through that brush on my own. But to ask you to carry me would sink me beneath reproach."

"Not in this country. Any woman who can get a man to carry her anywhere is likely to be greatly admired."

"Not by other women."

"Especially by other women."

Valeria gave up. If Americans were as Luke said, she'd never understand them.

"Hawk has come for Elvira," Luke said. "I can't wait to see how she acts when she sees him."

"You're cruel."

"You can't blame me. My parents didn't have any normal feelings to give me."

Valeria didn't know or care about the shortcomings of Luke's parents, but she did care about Elvira. "Are you a little cooler?" she asked when she reached her maid's side.

"How can she be?" Otto asked. "It's hot even under these trees."

"Not as hot as in the coach," Hans said.

"I do feel a little better," Elvira said.

"Good, but I'm afraid it's time to go back. One of Luke's brothers is already here to carry you back."

Elvira's hand gripped Valeria's arm with conclusive strength when she saw Hawk approaching.

"Luke said he likes Hawk the best of all his brothers."

Luke, of course, hadn't said any such thing. "He said he's kind and sweet tempered."

"He doesn't look like it," Elvira whispered.

"That's just the way Indians look. Both Hawk and Zeke are ordinary people. I want you to treat them just as you would Hans or Otto."

Elvira didn't shrink from Hawk, but she looked doubtful.

"Thank you for taking her back to the coach," Valeria said to Hawk. "Maybe there won't be so much brush the next time and we won't have to impose on you."

"I don't mind," Hawk said.

"Stand up, Elvira," Valeria said. "He can't pick you up if you're sitting down."

Casting an apprehensive look over her shoulder, Elvira stood. Hawk picked her up.

"You easy to carry," he said.

Valeria imagined that with arms as big as a horse's foreleg, he could pick up a woman two or three times as heavy as Elvira.

"That was well done," Luke said from behind her.

"We may be used to a tradition of service in my country, but the people who serve us become our friends, even part of the family."

"Sounds like you're overdoing it a bit, but I won't complain if Elvira doesn't."

It didn't matter what she did; the infuriating man managed to find a way to criticize her.

"You ready to go back?"

"No, but I take it you're ready to leave."

"Not giving an inch, are you?"

"I don't know what you're talking about."

"Yes, you do. You're royalty. You couldn't possibly be wrong."

"According to you, everything I do is wrong."

"Not everything."

"You're too generous."

"No I'm not. I think your class should have been done away with years ago. I don't see any reason for kings and princesses. Or dukes."

"Then you ought to be pleased they got rid of us."

"But you managed to keep your money."

"We deserve something for all the work we've done over the centuries."

"You mean stealing money from your countrymen and getting them killed in useless wars so you could stuff your pockets with more gold?"

"Not every ruler steals money or starts useless wars. Many men in my family died to protect our country."

"Not as many as the peasants."

"Of course not. You can't have everybody running the country."

"Of course you can. That's what we do here. Every man has a vote. In that way, we all have a hand in deciding what the government does."

She wanted to argue with him, but he kept cutting the ground out from under her, producing another piece of information she didn't know about.

"And if we don't like what they do, we can throw them out and vote for somebody else," Luke added.

"Do you like the people who run the government? Are they the ones you voted for?"

"I don't vote."

"Why not?" Here he was lecturing her on the advantages of the American system and he didn't believe in it enough to participate himself.

"I move around too much."

She was certain that wasn't the real reason, but she didn't get a chance to ask what it was. Without warning, he scooped her up and started toward the coach.

"Come on," he called to Otto. "We've lost too much time already."

Hans had already run ahead to hold the coach door for Elvira.

Otto got to his feet reluctantly, muttering irritably. "I don't know why we can't stay here longer."

"The longer we stay here, the longer before we reach Rudolf's ranch," Luke said. "And the longer we're on the road, the more likely someone will attack us."

"I'm sure there's no one after us," Otto said, tottering after Luke, still wiping his forehead with his handkerchief.

"I'm not talking about anybody from your country," Luke said. "We have plenty of people right here who would be only too happy to relieve you of your horses, not to mention all the silver and other valuables you've got packed in those coaches. Then there are the men who haven't seen a woman in weeks, maybe months. They'd be only too happy to take Valeria and Elvira."

Valeria's blood ran cold. She didn't know much about America, but European men had been stealing women for centuries, always for the same reason. She looked around at the barren waste that stretched for miles north and south along the river. There was nothing to impede her view, no concealment for anyone wanting to attack them.

"Then I'm glad you chose this route," she said to Luke.

"Why?"

"No one can attack without our seeing them from a long way off."

"There could be ten Indians between us and the coach, and you wouldn't see them until they attacked."

Valeria looked around her. Except for one tall cactus, she didn't see anything that could hide a man. "Where can they hide?"

"An Apache can be in full view and you won't see him."

"I don't believe you."

"Hundreds of soldiers used to feel that way. Most of them are dead now. The Apache have fought over this land for hundreds of years. They know it better than your uncle knows your country."

Valeria wanted to argue, but they'd reached the coach. Luke set her feet on the bottom step, then helped her inside.

"I'd keep the curtains open in spite of the dust," he advised. "It's going to get hotter."

Valeria couldn't see how that was possible.

"When do we eat?" Otto asked.

"Not until we stop tonight."

"But I always have lunch," Otto protested.

"You can have any meal you want as long as you bring your food with you," Luke said as he slammed the coach door shut. "Move out!" he called to the driver.

Otto opened his mouth to protest, but Valeria heard a whip crack and the coach lurched forward.

"He has to stop," Otto said, consulting his watch as the coach bumped over the rocky trail. "It'll soon be one o'clock. I always eat at one."

"You should have eaten more breakfast," Hans said, his tone unsympathetic.

"I don't eat breakfast," Otto informed him as though it were some sign of superiority.

"You've got enough fat around your waist to hold you until dinner," Hans said.

Valeria usually ignored their sniping, but she couldn't stand the prospect of being shut up in the intolerable heat listening to them going back and forth at each other.

"There's no point in arguing over it," Valeria said. "We're at Mr. Attmore's mercy until we reach Rudolf's ranch. We'll all have to eat more at breakfast."

"And bring your own canteen of water," Hans said, glaring at Otto.

"Aren't you hungry?" Otto asked Valeria.

"A little, but I can wait until evening. I'll have an even better appetite for dinner."

Chapter Seven

Luke sat just outside the ring of light. He'd never led a trip like this, if you could call what he was doing leading. He might as well have been a bird they were following for all the influence he had over their behavior.

He and his men had eaten more than an hour ago, but Valeria's chef had yet to set the first course on the table. Luke was familiar with European customs, but he'd never expected to see anybody hold court in the desert.

They had dressed for dinner!

They had tumbled out of that sweltering coach, waited impatiently while their servants set up the two enormous tents they'd brought and unloaded several trunks. Then they'd disappeared inside. Even when he saw the men begin setting up a table, he didn't suspect the full insanity of what they meant to do. He figured that out when he went to Valeria's tent to ask if she'd like to eat with the drivers. Elvira had informed him Valeria was dressing and would sit down to dinner at eight-thirty.

About a quarter past eight all four emerged from their

tents, Hans and Otto in white tie and swallowtail coats, Valeria and Elvira in gowns. They sipped wine while they waited for dinner. Luke had thought Valeria had more sense than to try to maintain European pomp in the desert. He changed his mind when the servants lighted candles and everyone sat down. The chef and his helpers served the first course with all the ceremony Valeria could have expected at home.

"What the hell are they doing?" Zeke asked.

"Having dinner," Luke replied.

"I can see that. I'm talking about the rest of it."

"They changed for dinner."

"Before, I thought they were crazy. Now I know it."

"Isabelle changes for dinner."

"Not on a cattle drive."

Luke remembered the early cattle drives to New Mexico. He used to complain about the heat, dirt, hard work, and the fact that Jake never paid them more than token wages. He swore he'd never work for less than top wages and never sweat doing it. Well, he got his top wages, but he was still sweating.

And not just because of the heat.

"Why did you take this job?" Zeke asked.

"The money."

"Is that all you ever think about?"

"What else is there?"

"That these fools could get us killed."

"Their world is dying, and it's scared them to death. They're trying to hold on as long as they can."

"When did you start getting sentimental?"

"I'm not. You can make a lot of money off people who're scared and rich."

"How? You planning to hold her for ransom?"

"It's a possibility."

"It'll put the law on your tail again."

"I can handle it."

"Chet can't."

"He shouldn't look for what he doesn't want to find."

Zeke cussed, got to his feet. "You don't deserve a brother like Chet."

"I didn't ask for one. Look, Zeke, I don't want anybody worrying about me. That includes Chet and Isabelle."

"You try and tell her that."

"There's no need to tell anybody anything."

"Why the hell did you ask Hawk and me to help you?"

"Because you two are the best."

"That's a lie. You wanted us because you knew we'd bust our asses for you."

"What's wrong with that?"

"Didn't Isabelle teach you anything?"

"What was I supposed to learn?"

"Nothing," Zeke said, then turned and stalked away. "Nothing at all."

Everybody expected him to be like his brother. Chet was perfect, or nearly so. He had inherited all the good qualities their parents had to give. When they got around to their second son, they had nothing left. He and Chet looked enough alike to be twins, but inside they were different. There was nothing inside Luke. He didn't feel love, hate, envy, or passion. Like a wild animal, he expected nothing, offered nothing, cared for nothing. It wasn't just that he didn't want to care. He couldn't. He didn't dare let himself.

That brought him back to Valeria.

It wasn't that he cared about her. How could he care about a silly woman who dined on gold plate in the desert? He was a realist. He never lay awake thinking of how he would change the world, never had attacks of conscience over things he'd done or things he'd left undone. He took life as it came, wrung out what he could for himself, and moved on. If the people around him got screwed, it was their fault for being stupid, cowardly, weak, whatever excuse they offered for their failure.

Which brought him back to Valeria.

In a few years her whole class would be gone. He ought to let them kill each other off. That would finish the job faster, make it easier for everyone. But he wouldn't let anybody kill her, and not just because he'd promised to protect her. This job had an entirely different feel about it, a difference that centered around Valeria. He'd let Hans convince him to wait, to make certain no one else would take the job. He'd even watched her hotel at night, convinced the miners to be quiet when they passed her window. He'd refused Otto's bribe as well.

He'd let Hans and Valeria get to him. How? Why?

Hawk came over to where Luke sat. "I don't like it," he said. "We got too much light. Banditos can see us from a hundred miles away."

Luke knew the light was bound to make people curious, but he doubted most people would attack such a large party. He had made certain the seven drivers were good, dependable men with guns. He could count on Valeria's party for additional help. They might be useless at most things, but aristocrats learned to handle guns practically at birth.

"They'll run out of fancy food, wine, and candles before we reach the Gila River," Luke said. "Then they'll eat the same as we do—beef, beans, and pork."

"Many people can hide in those mountains," Hawk said, indicating the mountains about thirty miles away.

"I've organized the drivers on one-hour watches," Luke said. "We'll sleep out from the camp."

He usually stayed in the camp, but this time he felt the need for separation. He would sleep the farthest out.

Hawk and Zeke were notoriously light sleepers. Luke had a sixth sense that warned him if anybody approached. They'd form a nearly impregnable perimeter.

"I still don't like it," Hawk said. "Indians could be in those mountains."

The Indian wars had ended a year earlier with the capture of Geronimo. The venerable chief had been sent to Oklahoma, others to Florida. Though some Indians remained in the area, they weren't likely to cause trouble. Luke was more worried about white men. Indians might steal the horses, but they would do it at night without waking anyone. White men wouldn't hesitate to kill to get what they wanted.

"I'm more worried about what'll happen after we cross the Gila," Luke said. "That's rough country."

"We got to get there first," Hawk said.

"We'll get there. You and Zeke find a good lookout."

"What about you?"

"I'll wait until they're done."

"You going to tuck them into bed?"

"Just make sure they don't stay up so late they keep the crickets awake."

He wanted to talk with Valeria. Or Hans. They needed to adapt to Arizona. Sitting down to a hot, heavy meal at eight-thirty wasn't the way to start.

"We leave at dawn tomorrow," Luke said.

Hawk looked at the group gathered at the table. "Do they know?"

"They will."

Still, he felt a reluctance to be hard on Valeria. She had been molded by a different culture, one that would make it difficult for her to understand the life that lay before her. She or her husband would squander their wealth in a fruitless effort to reproduce their former life. By the time they realized the impossibility of doing that, they'd have nothing left. Maybe he could talk with Hans. He knew Valeria wouldn't listen to him. She thought him beneath her.

He was.

Valeria put her fork down and leaned back in her chair. She'd eaten too much too fast. If she didn't stop now, she'd be awake half the night. She had made the same mistake as Otto and eaten almost nothing for breakfast. She'd compounded her error by having nothing at midday and no more water than absolutely necessary. She could hardly make herself swallow from Hans's canteen.

They hadn't reached the campsite Zeke had chosen until just before dark. She had been thinking of food for the last several hours, her tastebuds watering at the thought of the delicacies the chef would have prepared for her dinner. It came as a cruel surprise to find he hadn't started cooking when they arrived. He was in a rage about having to find his own wood, start his own fire, do without enough assistants under these harrowing conditions. He stated flatly it would be impossible to prepare a dessert.

Luke had invited her to eat with him and the drivers. She had refused. Partly out of pique, but mostly because she didn't trust herself to be able to swallow what Zeke was cooking in that great big pot. It looked disgusting with everything cooked together. Still, she had to admit it smelled good.

Nothing about dinner went smoothly. The men took much longer to set up the tent than she expected. By the time they finally managed to drive the stakes into the rocky ground and drag the necessary trunks from the wagons, Valeria had lost patience with everyone. Despite a thick canvas covering, the rocky ground made the floor of the tent so uneven she stumbled every time she tried to take more than a few steps.

Dressing for dinner proved no easier. She had too little space inside the tent and no way to press out the creases in her dress. She emerged looking as if she'd slept in her clothes. It didn't make her feel any better that Hans and Otto looked no better.

And she felt dirty. An entire day's collection of dust had settled onto her hair and skin. She'd removed as much as she could with a damp cloth, but she still felt unclean. She wanted a bath with lots of hot water in a tub deep enough to soak in.

Luke had said she could bathe in the river! As if she would do anything so shocking, even though there wasn't a living soul within ten miles. There were actually fish in that water. And frogs, too.

"I feel much better now," she said as she laid down her napkin.

Elvira had remained silent during the meal, her gaze continually searching the night. Valeria knew the poor girl was petrified of what might be out there. Valeria had never been afraid of the dark, but she'd never been out in it without dozens of men to protect her.

"A full stomach tends to give one a different perspective on life," Hans said. He continued to be nervous and jumpy, but he'd stopped responding to Otto's jibes.

"Mine's not full yet," Otto complained. "And I'm not used to doing without dessert."

"You've eaten enough for two people," Hans observed. "Maybe we ought to eat less. Our supplies won't last forever."

"I didn't expect they would," Otto said. "We will acquire fresh supplies every third day. Luke and his men may be content to eat that goulash, but I am not."

"When you speak to Luke, ask about the distance to

the next town," Valeria said. "I would love a bath." But she wasn't certain there would be a *next town* anytime soon. She remembered the vast, flat plains stretches of Texas when they had traveled hundreds of miles without seeing a living soul.

"We should have invited him to join us," Hans said. "He could have answered all our questions."

"When did you start inviting servants to join us at table?" Otto asked.

"I'm sure he wouldn't presume," Hans said.

"What do you expect him to do, stand quietly at the end of the table answering questions while we eat?"

Valeria laughed. "He'd be more likely to sit down and help himself to the best bits of everything."

"Exactly," Otto said.

"But we are depending on him to get us safely to Rudolf's ranch."

"We depend upon servants to attend to our safety all the time," Otto said, impatiently, "without asking them to sit at table with us. That's what we pay them for."

"Nevertheless, I think Hans is right," Valeria said. "Mr. Attmore is different."

"How?" Otto asked.

Valeria wasn't sure she wanted to answer that question. Her feelings for Luke disturbed her. He had the same ruthlessness, the same disregard for anything that got in his way, as her father and uncle, but there was something different about him. She couldn't explain it. Whenever she tried, she ended up deciding it didn't exist. But as soon as she did that, the feeling returned as strong as ever. Something about him struck an answering chord in her, touched a need. She was drawn to him as to no other man.

Could it be his disregard for her bloodlines, her title, her past? She didn't know why she should be attracted to a man who felt nothing but scorn for everything that had been her life up until a few months ago. It made her furious, but something about him still wouldn't let go of her consciousness.

"I guess because he's American and doesn't consider himself a servant," Valeria said, answering Otto. "In his eyes, we're all equal. Neither my title nor my money qualifies me for more consideration than anyone else."

"That's absurd. Nobody worships money more than these Americans."

"Maybe. I just know he thinks he's as good as we are."

"What else could you expect of a country that lets every man vote," Otto said.

"Women will be able to vote soon, too," Valeria said.

"Where?" Otto looked so scandalized, one would have thought someone had proposed that women in Belgravia be allowed to vote.

"I don't remember."

"I still don't see how that makes him our equal," Otto said.

"I want him to join us," Valeria said. "Hans, would you ask him?"

"I don't want to talk to him," Otto said.

"Then take your wine and go to your tent."

"I haven't finished eating." He served himself the last of the lamb and boiled potatoes. The other serving dishes were already empty.

"You can clear away and bring coffee and liqueurs," she said to one of the men hovering nearby.

"Yes, your highness."

"I guess you shouldn't call me that."

"Yes, your highness."

"Then how should we address you?" Elvira asked.

"Exactly as you've always done," Otto said. "Duke

Rudolf will expect his dignity, and that of his future wife, to be respected and preserved."

"But if no one else uses titles here, won't it seem rather awkward?" Valeria asked.

"You should leave that sort of decision to your husband," Otto said.

Luke might think she was a fool, but at least he encouraged her to think for herself. "I don't want to insist on being referred to by a title that will cause people to scorn me."

"Why should you be scorned?"

She looked up, surprised to find Luke standing practically at her elbow. "Otto said Rudolf would insist that people continue to use our titles. From what you've said, I thought that might be unwise."

"Would you have everybody calling you Valeria?" Otto asked.

"In America we refer to an unmarried lady by her family name," Luke said. "After she is married, she takes her husband's name."

"What would I be called?" Valeria asked.

"Probably Miss Badenberg."

Valeria had been addressed as *princess* or *your highness* for so long, she couldn't imagine anything else. Still, she liked the simplicity of his suggestion. With no title, she could become anonymous. That thought frightened her as much as it intrigued her. She'd always been a princess. She didn't know how to be anything else.

"What did you want?" Luke asked.

"To ask about provisions," Otto said. "The chef will need to replenish his larder in two days. Please take us to a town where suitable supplies can be obtained."

"The only way to do that would be to go back to Bonner," Luke said.

"Are you saying there are no towns ahead of us?" Otto asked.

"How far is the next town?" Valeria asked. It was obvious what Luke meant.

"It depends on how far we can travel each day," Luke replied. "If we were on horseback, we could be there in two days. With all these wagons, probably a week at a minimum."

"We will starve before then," Otto said.

"Can we get food when we get to this place?" Valeria asked.

"Yes, but not what you're used to." He pointed to the remains of their lamb. "Out here, if you want lamb, you have to buy it on the hoof and dress it out."

"That's absurd," Otto said.

"Well, it's not likely to be a problem," Luke said. But Otto enjoyed only a moment of relaxation. "I doubt you'll find any lamb to buy, on the hoof or otherwise."

"Goose," Otto said. "I would love a fat goose."

"You'll find salt pork and dried beef," Luke said. "Anything else will have to come in a can."

Otto looked horrified. Hans looked equally nonplussed.

"What can we eat if we run out of food?" Valeria asked.

"You're not going to like it," Luke warned.

"I haven't liked anything that has happened to me in the last year," Valeria snapped. "And not much that's happened to me during my whole life," she added as an afterthought.

"You have two choices," Luke said. "You can eat with us. I brought enough to last the trip for all of us."

"And the other choice?" Otto asked in a faint voice.

"You can go hunting," Luke said. "Your best bet is a mule deer. They generally don't go too far from the river. If you bag one, it ought to last you a few days. If you've got your heart set on sheep, you can climb any one of the mountains you see from here. If you're lucky, you might get a desert bighorn, though you might have a hell of a time getting to the kill before a mountain lion does."

Otto lost considerable color.

"If you're interested in pork, there's a piglike creature called a javelina. I don't like it myself, but some people think they're right tasty. You'll probably need three or four of those."

"I didn't hire you to be told I had to hunt for my food," Otto said. "I demand—"

"You didn't hire me," Luke replied, cutting off his angry explosion. "Hans did. And I was hired to take Valeria to Rudolf. When I asked about supplies, you said you would take care of your own."

"We expected to be able to buy what we needed."

"You could if there were anybody selling it."

"But there isn't," Otto nearly shouted.

"Now maybe we can start to deal with reality," Luke said.

"What does that mean?" Valeria asked.

"It means you make your food last as long as possible. It also means you'll have to get used to eating things you've never eaten before."

"I will not hunt for my food," Otto declared.

"I doubt you could," Luke said. "You're much too fat."

"How dare you—"

"You need to eat more at breakfast and less at dinner," Luke said, turning to Valeria. "If you want something at midday, ask your chef for some leftovers."

Valeria had never had leftovers. Everything that came to her uncle's table had been cooked fresh. "What should we ask for?"

"Meat, bread, cheese."

Valeria didn't know if her chef had anything like that.

Someone else had always ordered the food.

"It's clear we should have consulted you on that aspect of the trip before we set out," she said, determined to make the best of a difficult situation. She refused to apologize to him, but it would be foolish not to admit she needed help. "However, it's too late for that. In my country, it's not the custom for Hans, Otto, Elvira, or me to be involved in ordering provisions."

"Don't you know what you're going to eat?"

She sighed over her next admission. "Not until it reaches the table."

"People here generally take care of things themselves, or nothing gets done."

"I understand that," she said, trying hard to keep her voice steady. "I just need to know what you think we ought to do now."

"I need to talk to your cook. Go find him," he said to Elvira.

Valeria had to bite her tongue to keep from saying anything. Luke deplored her dependence on servants, yet he spoke to Elvira as if she were a slave. How could a man who kept talking about the importance of the individual act like people were of so little value?

Chapter Eight

Luke wondered why Europeans came to America thinking they could continue to behave as they had in the old country. Didn't they know anything about America? And the cook—Luke refused to call him a chef—had no concept of how to prepare anything except grand dishes. One of the drivers said he'd rescued enough leftovers from that night's meal to feed the whole party for two days.

"I don't care how you do it," Luke told the cook when he presented himself at the table. "You've got to do your work faster and make your food last longer."

It was nearly midnight, and they still hadn't finished cleaning up. Luke didn't know how he was going to get that many pots and pans washed when the river went underground and there was no surface water to be had without digging for it. There'd be a lot of dirty pots, pans, dishes, and glasses. Sorry, goblets. Royalty didn't drink from glasses.

"I cannot serve the princess ill-prepared food," the cook protested. "I would disgrace my profession."

"Fine. She can eat with us," Luke said.

"The princess cannot eat that *mélange* you call food," he said, turning up his nose with enough disdain to have been a member of royalty himself.

"Do what you want," Luke said. "Just remember we leave at dawn tomorrow."

"When is dawn?" Otto asked.

"About six o'clock."

"I'll have to be up at four!" the cook exclaimed. "The princess will have to be up at four to dress. We will both be too tired."

"Your wagon leaves whether you're in it or not. That goes for everybody else. You should have been in bed hours ago."

"I haven't finished my cognac," Otto said.

"By all means, finish your cognac," Luke said as he turned away.

"Mr. Attmore."

Luke didn't stop at the sound of Valeria's voice. He'd had just about all he could take. Though they came from a country where revolutions happened all the time, they didn't seem the slightest bit concerned about danger.

"Mr. Attmore!"

"What?" Luke whirled to find Valeria had followed him.

"You can't leave like that," she said. "You haven't told us what to do."

"I have, but you continue to ignore it. Apparently you can only learn by experience. Well, you're in luck. You're about to get more experience that you ever thought possible."

She drew herself up just like he was certain her royal ancestors had when about to announce someone was going to lose his head. "Why don't you like us?"

"There are too many of you for one answer."

Her back seemed to get a little stiffer, straighter. "Very well, I'll make it easier. Why don't you like *me?*"

He'd never expected her to ask that question. "Give me one reason why I should like you."

"I'm a woman, reasonably attractive, I'm told. I thought American men liked women."

"You got two things wrong. First, American men like *sex.* They don't much care about the woman as long as she isn't downright ugly."

If it were possible, she became even more stiff. "And the second thing I got wrong?"

"You're not reasonably attractive." He saw her prepare herself for the blow. "You're beautiful. Even a savage American can see that." It pleased him to know he'd surprised her.

"Then why are you so cruel to me?"

"I just gave you facts. Why should I waste time being cruel?"

"Because you don't like me, what I represent."

"I don't hold you responsible for what you represent, but I can hold you responsible for what you do."

"Then I can hold you responsible for what *you* are."

"And what am I?"

"You're rude, thoughtless, and you enjoy making fun of me. You resent the fact that you have no ancestors you can point to proudly, no history, no—"

Luke's patience snapped. "You got two out of four this time, a better average than before. I am rude and thoughtless. I'm hired for my ability, not my manners. I don't give a damn about your ancestors. You people don't think, you don't create. You're like a wind-up toy that does the same thing over and over again.

"You're right in saying I have no noble ancestry. I don't have hundreds of relatives with portraits on the wall prodding me to remember who I am, but you're wrong in thinking I want to remember my family. My father was an outcast from an old Southern family, my mother a barroom songstress. Their passion for each other burned out almost as quickly as it ignited. I'd hardly learned to walk when she ran off. My father dragged me from one high-stakes card game to another until a poor loser shot him in the back. My parents had nothing to leave me but their weaknesses. They're probably laughing right now, waiting for me to screw up, knowing I'll end up in Hell with them.

"My advice about the food and my plans for tomorrow still stand. It'll be a lot easier if you cooperate, but if you want to fight me, I'm game. Just remember I knew a hell of a lot more about fighting before I was five than you'll ever know."

Luke walked away, leaving Valeria in a state of shock. She felt nearly destroyed. He didn't hate her. He felt nothing at all.

"I don't think he means that."

She turned, startled to find Hans standing a few feet away, mortified to realize he had heard every word Luke uttered. In her world appearance was everything. That was why clothes, servants, palaces, and extravagant food served on costly silver or exquisite china were essential. That was the reason for the ritual, the pageantry, the enormous sums of money spent on show. Luke, and circumstances, had ripped all that away from her, and Hans had seen and heard every bit of it.

"I'm certain he does," she said. "From the first moment he set eyes on us, he's made no effort to disguise the fact that he despises me and everything I stand for."

"I don't think—"

"You heard him, Hans. It's not a matter of guesswork."

She was surprised to feel the tears start. Princesses weren't allowed to cry. Weakness wasn't tolerated.

Yet she was crying. She turned away to dash the tears from her eyes.

"I don't understand him," Hans said, "but I think he's a good man."

"He's not. He said so himself."

"He could have taken the money Otto offered him and disappeared, but he stayed. He also kept anybody else from taking his job. He's a proud man, your highness. I don't think anybody has ever fired him before."

"So being stubborn and full of pride is a good thing."

"It has to be. It's what has sustained your family for these past five hundred years."

Somehow it didn't look the same when she saw it in Luke. Was it the clothes, the palaces, the wars they won? Did all that wealth and power make it look admirable and worthwhile in her family but churlish and mean-spirited in him? "Are you sure?"

"My family has served your family for more than a hundred and fifty years," Hans said. "We know just about every mean, despicable, underhanded, traitorous deed your family has committed during that time. I can assure you that there are enough to make a man like Luke Attmore seem very good. He may not think much of himself, but he has a code of honor he will up hold at the peril—possibly even the expense—of his life. Your great-grandfather wouldn't have hesitated to sacrifice his entire family to keep his throne."

"How can you say such a thing?"

"He sacrificed a son."

"Who?"

"Your grandfather."

Valeria wanted to deny it, but her words died unsaid. There had always been a silence, a turning away of heads, when she asked about her grandfather. Even her father would say only that he died in a military operation.

"He wanted to lead the country toward democracy," Hans said. "He had met with opposition leaders. They were all killed at the direct orders of your great-grandfather. My grandfather delivered the orders."

Valeria had never pretended her ancestors were scrupulously honest or honorable. But she'd always glossed over their misdeeds, saying they had done what was necessary to preserve the government, keep the country safe and prosperous for the people. Could she still say that?

She longed to ask Hans more, to search until she found a reason to believe he was wrong, but she was afraid she would find even more that would shame her. "What does this have to do with Luke Attmore?"

"He will do what he must to see that you reach Duke Rudolf. It won't matter to him whether you like what he does or the way he does it. He will deliver you safely."

"Then what?"

"He'll move on to his next job."

"Just like that?"

"Why shouldn't he?"

She couldn't think of a reason, but she couldn't understand how he could just turn his back after being willing to risk his life for her. She didn't see how her life could be so important and his count for so little.

Then she understood. It wasn't her life at all. It was his reputation. His honor as a gunfighter. But having understood that only made her feel worse.

"You think we ought to do what he says?" she asked.

"I don't see that we have any choice."

Her laugh was humorless. "Nor do I. I expect we'd better get to bed. I intend to eat breakfast tomorrow."

"And I intend to see the chef finds something to feed Otto at noonday. If he's in the same mood tomorrow as today, I'll kill him before nightfall." He paused. "Aren't you coming to bed?"

"In a minute."

"Goodnight, your highness. Don't stay up too long."

It would probably be better if she stayed awake all night. Then she would sleep through some of the interminable day. When her family had gone on vacations to the Greek Islands, Marrakesh, or Tangiers, the native people had taken naps after luncheon to escape the heat of the day. Some people in Bonner did the same. It was probably a good idea.

Besides, she felt too full of food to go to sleep, and she wanted to enjoy the coolness of the evening. Being outside in the dark was a new experience for her, but she felt safe as long as she could see the light from the fires. The trees along the river looked dark and menacing, but bright moonlight bathed the plain, the foothills, and the mountains. It was an unfamiliar and forbidding landscape, but it didn't frighten her.

Luke was nearby.

She didn't want to think about him—he made her question too much—but she couldn't stop. Was her family as bad as his? Were they two sides of the same coin, one looking better only because of its setting? Disturbed by her thoughts, she tried to come up with ways to make the food last longer, ways to make the journey as quick and easy as possible, but she couldn't focus on anything but his comments about her family, about the things her family would have done—*had* done according to Hans—to preserve their throne. If he was no worse than she, then she had no right to question his advice or scorn his opinions.

Something inside whispered that her entire existence had been a sham. But she couldn't accept that. If she wasn't a princess, what was she? A figment of her own imagination. Could she exist without substance or purpose?

Everything inside her cried out against such an appraisal. She *was* somebody, she *did* have a purpose, she *wasn't* imaginary. She did exist.

But if she wasn't a princess anymore, *who* was she? What was her purpose?

Luke nearly bumped into Zeke.

"That was a clever way to handle them," Zeke said, sarcasm dripping from each word. "I'm sure they can hardly wait to cooperate."

"Shut up!" Luke snapped.

"I agree they're just about the most worthless human beings I've ever seen, but you can't keep carrion from rotting."

"I'm not trying to keep them from rotting. I'm just trying to keep them alive."

"You're doing more than that, brother."

"Don't call me brother."

"Adopted brother," he said, caressing the words in a way that made a mockery of their meaning.

"To hell with you!"

"Isabelle wouldn't like that."

Luke wanted to say *to hell with Isabelle!* but the words wouldn't come up as far as his throat. No matter how low he sank, that part of his life was too sacred to curse. "They're so caught up in their fantasy world, they can't see the reality around them. They're too afraid to admit things have changed, that nothing is the way it used to be."

"Otto's not afraid of anything," Zeke said. "Elvira is afraid of everything."

"She wouldn't be if you'd stop terrorizing her."

"I'll stop terrorizing her if you'll stop coddling the princess."

"Her name is Valeria. When have I coddled her?"

"I heard you got the miners to be quiet when they passed her window."

"I was trying to annoy her."

"That's a strange way to annoy someone."

"If you're trying to say something, spit it out and get to bed. Tomorrow will be worse than today."

"Don't let yourself go soft on her. Her kind will never see people like us as anything except servants."

"You mean slaves, don't you?"

Zeke's features hardened. "I know what it's like to be thought of as worth less than a good milk cow. To her we're peasants to work in the field, servants to fetch and carry, so much cannon fodder to die on the battlefield. She'd never consider marrying one of us."

Zeke's words blindsided Luke. The idea of marrying anyone, least of all someone like Valeria, was so preposterous his anger evaporated, and he laughed. "If that's what you think, you've been in the sun too long. Remind me to ask Valeria if she's got an extra parasol."

"Make a joke if you want," Zeke said, "but I've worked with you on more than one job. This one's different. Maybe you're not going sweet on her, but whatever it is will put us in danger if you don't watch out."

"I'll watch out. I don't want to lose my hide any more than you do."

"Sometimes I think that's exactly what you want," Zeke said. He turned and walked off.

Luke was at a loss to understand Zeke's meaning. He had done everything he could to make certain he had the edge on anyone who might come up against him. He took great pride in having been wounded only twice in his career, neither time seriously. He sometimes took chances that might seem overly dangerous to someone else, but he'd learned long ago that doing the unexpected was often the safest way out of a difficult situation.

He had an uneasy feeling that he would need all of his expertise on this trip. Valeria was the wrong kind of person for Arizona. He could see no logical reason why an ex-princess with her wealth would want to live in such an out-of-the-way place. He didn't know much about fine china, silver flatware, and crystal goblets—he'd been uninterested when Isabelle tried to teach the boys about such things—but he knew the money represented by her belongings would have supported a small town for several years.

His instincts had served him well over the years. The minute he'd set eyes on Valeria, they had told him this job didn't feel right. He should have kept going when he walked out of her hotel room. He could think of no reason why he'd let Hans talk him into staying. Or why he had talked three other men out of accepting Otto's offer. He could talk about pride and reputation all he wanted, but he knew what made this time different.

Valeria.

He should have been furious at her. And he was. He should have scorned everything she stood for. And he did. He should have lost patience with her ignorance and reluctance to make even minimal changes in her ritual. And he had. He should have turned his back, walked out, and left her high and dry.

He hadn't.

It would have been the same as abandoning children. They knew nothing about the new world they had entered. They were trying to live, act, and think as they always had. While that was understandable up to a point, anyone could see they would have to make substantial alternations in every aspect of their lives.

At times Luke wondered if it was fear that made them hold on to the past so grimly. They'd always been in control, but now that was the one thing they didn't have.

Hans accepted the fact that they'd lost their source of power, but he expected the old-world traditions to be perpetuated. Luke couldn't be sure what Otto thought. He figured he was one of the opportunists to be found about any court, clinging to the past because it provided him an opportunity to pluck rich rewards without having to break a sweat.

Then there was Valeria. In a way she was the most obvious and at the same time the most enigmatic. She'd been raised to provide her husband a loyal consort, to bear his children, to be an ornament to his position, and to accept all of that without question. No thinking required. Individuality discouraged. Conformity rewarded.

Yet Luke was certain she'd inwardly disliked being treated like a priceless jewel to be taken out for display and tucked safely away when she wasn't needed. Now she'd been cast out of her familiar setting without any preparation for her new life.

It was as if she'd been kept in the dark her whole life and was suddenly brought into blinding light. No wonder she couldn't see clearly. Even familiar things would have a new meaning. She must feel fear, a reluctance to venture too far. At the same time she would feel curiosity, a desire to explore the uncharted.

Valeria was an innocent standing on the edge of great discovery. Great care had to be exercised to make certain she didn't fall and do permanent injury before she had a chance to run.

Nice, idealistic, altruistic. Isabelle would have loved it. It was just the kind of thing she'd tried to pound into the boys during the few years they'd all been at the ranch. Apparently she'd been successful. All but three of them were back in Texas, living within a day's ride of each other, raising families, becoming the solid citizens Isabelle had envisioned when she started out from Austin to find homes for eight incorrigible orphans.

Luke's brother, Chet, had believed. Maybe it worked for him. Luke didn't know. He hadn't been back to the ranch since he'd left more than fifteen years ago. Chet had been able to escape the curse of their blood. Luke hadn't.

Which didn't explain why he should suddenly want to save a woman who'd lived an equally useless and selfish life. Valeria used other people without regard for their feelings or well-being. She lived off the toil of others and considered herself more praiseworthy because of it. At least he only used people. He knew he was worse than they were.

He didn't understand why he should care about this woman's fate. She was beautiful, but he could have all the beautiful women he wanted. He hadn't seen any fine inner character to preserve and liberate. No great intellect, no grand passion to accomplish something, no enduring love lost and longed for. No reason why he should treat her any different from any other woman.

But he had. He could only assume it was a quirk. Maybe one of Isabelle's lessons was trying to take hold. Yet it didn't really matter why he was acting so uncharacteristically. The job would come to an end and he would leave Valeria to her fate. He would have nothing to do with whether she changed or remained the same.

Yet he knew that if she didn't change, he would be disappointed. And that in itself was strange. He was never disappointed in people because he never expected anything of them.

"They've finally stopped washing those damned dishes," Zeke called. "Now we can get some sleep."

"You shouldn't be close enough to be bothered by the noise," Luke called back.

"An army troop could ambush us under cover of that racket," Zeke replied.

Valeria felt as though she hadn't slept at all. She'd asked Elvira to wake her at four o'clock. She'd expected to need at least an hour to get dressed, and it had taken every minute of that time. Bathing from a basin had been difficult enough, but it had been nearly impossible to see anything in the dim light of the one oil lamp Luke allowed them. At home sunlight pouring in through tall windows was supplemented by banks of gaslights, which she preferred to the new electric lights other rulers were putting in their homes.

The tent had no windows. The air felt heavy and muggy. By the time Elvira had finished helping her dress, Valeria was hot. She was relieved to be able to go outside. The coolness of the night still lingered.

She laughed to herself when she saw Otto, appearing far from his usually impeccably attired self, hovering impatiently near the table set for breakfast. He caught sight of her and came forward.

"The chef is furious," he said. "He's threatening to leave."

"Why?"

"There was a rattlesnake in one of his pots this morning, and a creature in his shoe that looks something like a shrimp but is called a scorpion and is very poisonous. The driver said it happens all the time. He said we ought to check our shoes every morning before we put them on."

Another reason to dislike this new land. She knew about snakes. She hadn't known about scorpions.

Hans emerged looking as nervous and ill put together as Otto. Valeria wondered if he calmed down even during his sleep. He seemed about to jump out of his skin.

"I'm glad it's almost too dark to see one's hand in front of one's face, your highness," he said to Valeria. "I have no doubt I make as sad an appearance as Otto."

"I couldn't even shave," Otto complained. "There wasn't enough hot water, and I couldn't see well enough to keep from cutting myself."

"You'll have plenty of light when we stop at midday," Luke said. "And plenty of water if the river doesn't go underground."

Valeria jumped. She disliked his habit of seeming to appear out of nowhere. She didn't know how he could walk on this rough ground without making a sound. She had trouble just keeping her feet under her.

"How can it do that?" she asked. She had made up her mind to learn everything she could about this new country. It was going to be her home, so she might as well get used to it.

"The riverbed is made up of loose gravel. When there's not much water, there's not enough to fill up all the holes below the surface."

"Then how do you get water?" Otto asked.

"You dig for it."

"Like a well," Valeria said. She knew about wells. There had been an old one in one of the castle gardens.

"Something like that," Luke said. "Now I suggest you eat your breakfast. Your cook has to wash up and pack everything before he can follow."

"Why don't you have breakfast with us?" Valeria asked Luke.

"I've already eaten."

"What?" Otto asked.

"Salt pork with biscuits and jam."

Valeria could tell Otto was about to say that wasn't

decent food for anyone, even an American. She'd had enough arguing, especially about things that couldn't be changed. "Then you can have some coffee with us," she said. "And answer our questions."

Chapter Nine

"I can't stay long."

Valeria could tell Luke would have preferred to refuse her invitation. He acted as if he'd accepted as a way to get an unpleasant job done more quickly. Regardless of what might be in his mind, it wasn't flattering. Because of her position and wealth, she was used to having men practically fall over each other to please her. She had been spoiled by attention her whole life.

"Didn't your cook listen when I said to cut back until he could buy more?" Luke asked.

"Of course he did," Otto said. "This is barely half what he usually serves."

The meal consisted of coffee, rolls with butter and jam, eggs cooked with bits of bacon, a goulash made of beef and potatoes, sausages, big chunks of bread, and cheese. To Valeria, whose uncle insisted upon a table loaded with several hot and cold meat dishes, and hot and cold fruit, this looked almost Spartan. "You said we couldn't eat again until evening."

"Do you plan to eat everything on this table?" Luke asked.

Valeria wasn't sure what he was asking. It was obvious they couldn't eat it all.

"The chef prepares food in such quantities that everyone can eat as much as he or she wants of any particular dish," Otto said.

"But you can leave a dish untouched if you've had enough?" Luke asked.

"Well, yes."

"Starting tonight, your cook can prepare what he likes, but there'll only be as much as will be eaten at that meal."

Hans held Valeria's chair. She sat down with what was perilously close to a plop. "Please be seated," she said. "You, too," she added when Luke appeared to hold back.

"Don't force him," Otto said. "He probably feels uncomfortable because he's not dressed."

The fact that he left off the word *properly* didn't take any sting out of the remark. Valeria's gaze flew from Otto to Luke.

He surprised her yet again. "I'd be delighted to join you," he said, pulling up a chair next to Otto. "I hope my dirt and stink doesn't put anyone off his food. I didn't bathe this morning. But then it's not unusual for me to go more than a week without taking a bath or changing my clothes."

Valeria realized he was saying this for Otto, who reacted with horror and disgust just as Luke must have expected. Elvira looked at him as though were some kind of wild animal momentarily allowed to roam among civilized people but who might at any moment revert to his natural state and savage them all. Hans regarded Luke with a kind of wonder Valeria couldn't interpret.

She wondered how much of what Luke said she could

believe. Most of it, probably, but she wouldn't put it past him to enjoy mocking their ignorance and prejudices. And her midnight decision to look at everything American in a different light told her that much of her attitude toward America and Americans was built on ignorance and prejudice.

"It's not a good idea to shave and splash yourself with perfumed water when you're sleeping out," Luke added. "It attracts insects. They love the sweet smell. You'll be covered with bites. Then there's the wild animals, especially the big ones."

"What *big ones?*" Otto asked.

"Coyotes, wolves sometimes. But it's the cats I worry about."

"Cats?"

"Mountain lions," Luke explained. "They mostly live on deer and mountain bighorns, but they love the smell of perfume. It's like a drug. They can hardly keep from coming up to take a sniff or two."

Valeria knew Luke was deliberately trying to frighten them. He had succeeded with Elvira, who had turned white. She didn't know about Hans. His expression hadn't changed. Otto fidgeted uncomfortably. He doused himself daily with nearly as much scent as a woman.

"Don't these animals bother you or your brothers?" Valeria asked.

"Naw. After a couple of days, they're careful to stay upwind of us."

She couldn't resist. "Should we do the same?" She was so used to anger and scorn from him, the slow rise of one ironic eyebrow surprised her.

"That's probably a good idea," he said.

He was daring her not to be afraid of him.

Determined to test his invitation, she said, "Elvira said

one of the drivers told her it's customary for ranch hands to eat at the same table as the owner."

"Duke Rudolf would never allow that," Otto assured her.

"That's the custom on most ranches," Luke said, watching Valeria carefully. "Some of the wealthy ranchers have a separate cook and kitchen."

"I told you," Otto said, relieved that his faith in the absent Duke Rudolf had been restored.

"Do they bathe regularly?" Valeria asked.

"No, ma'am. There's not enough water most times. Besides, you get used to the smell after a while."

The eyebrow rose again, and Valeria repressed a smile. "What's it like to live on a ranch?"

"For you or the cowhands?" Luke asked.

She felt herself blush. "Both, I guess."

"It depends on whether you live on the ranch or live in San Francisco and let a foreman run it."

"Assume I have to live on it."

"Are you going to have servants?"

Valeria hadn't expected that question. Servants had always been part of her life. She couldn't imagine life without them.

"Naturally her highness will have a full staff," Hans said. "You can't expect her to do her own cooking."

It had never occurred to her to wonder what she would do if she were on her own. Nothing about her situation had made that a likely problem. Even deposed royalty had servants. "What would I do if I didn't have servants?"

"Cook, clean, wash clothes, iron, mend, and do all the ordering of supplies for the household. Probably for the ranch hands, too."

She didn't know how to do any of that.

"Maybe make your own clothes."

She'd never repaired a rip or replaced a button. "What about the men?" she asked. "Where do they live?"

"In a bunkhouse. It's a lot like military barracks."

"What do they do?"

"They spend most of their time away from the ranch looking after the cows. In the spring they round up the new calves and brand them. During the summer they make sure the cows can find food and water, doctor them against disease and insects, and try to keep lions and wolves from getting too many calves. In the fall they round up the steers they mean to sell. During the winter they do pretty much what they did during the summer."

"That sounds a lot like the herders in our country who take the cattle to the mountains for the summer," Hans said.

"They don't get to come back to the ranch very often," Luke said. "They sleep in the open, do their own cooking over a campfire, and wear the same clothes until they come back to the bunkhouse."

"You'll have nothing to do with any of that," Otto assured Valeria.

But she thought she probably would have more to do with it than any of them expected.

"It'll be dawn shortly," Luke said, getting to his feet. "I've got to talk to your cook." They'd eaten less than half the food on the table. "If he cooks this much food again, I'll have the drivers eat with you. There won't be anything left then."

He left before Otto could swallow his food and lodge a protest. "You were a fool to hire that man," he said, turning to Hans. "You were an even bigger fool to rehire him."

"If I hadn't, we'd still be sitting in Bonner."

"At least we wouldn't be faced with starvation or being pushed about by a petty tyrant."

"He's doing what he thinks is best for us," Valeria said.

"Then he's got a peculiar idea of what that is. I'll have to set him straight."

"Don't say anything," Valeria said. "He dislikes us enough as it is."

"He's a servant, your highness," Otto objected. "He has no *right* to dislike you or disapprove of anything you choose to do. If we were in Belgravia, I'd have him before the firing squad."

"Maybe that's one of the reasons we're no longer the rulers of Belgravia; people like you and my uncle put too many people in front of the firing squad."

"We didn't send enough," Otto replied. "Next time—"

"There won't be a next time. We're fortunate to have enough money to reestablish ourselves. We should begin to learn American ways, to forget our old life."

"I can never forget it," Otto said.

Valeria was afraid she couldn't, either. But she could do many things in America she couldn't do in Belgravia. Maybe she wouldn't miss her old life so much after all.

A deep, male voice dragged Valeria from a sound sleep. She couldn't imagine who it might be. And no one, man or woman, would have dared to rouse her with a peremptory call to, "Wake up! You've got one hour to get dressed!" Nor would anyone have spoken to her like she was a kitchen maid. She had to be dreaming.

Then she came fully awake. The heat and the stuffiness, the smell of bodies too closely confined, told her immediately she wasn't in her spacious bedchamber at home but in a tent in the middle of the hostile Arizona desert, traveling to a destination equally unfamiliar. Luke Attmore stood outside her tent demanding in his mocking voice that she get ready in a hurry so she wouldn't hold him up. She considered reminding him that *she* was the one whose arrival was of importance. If she didn't mind a leisurely journey, he shouldn't.

But she didn't. Luke had made it abundantly clear that while he was responsible for her safety, he made the rules.

Valeria threw back the covers. "Wake up, Elvira," she called. "Mr. Attmore is on the prowl again."

Elvira had compared him to a caged lion, always pacing back and forth, unhappy with his bondage but unable to leave. She decided it was an apt description. There was something of the lion about him—his blond hair, powerful shoulders, athletic body. His roar of disapproval.

"What time is it?" Elvira moaned.

"It doesn't matter. We've got to get dressed." She got out of bed, fumbled in the dark for the lamp, a match to light it.

"I'll do that," Elvira said, sounding sleepy and guilty for not performing her duties.

"It's time I started doing things for myself," Valeria said.

"Duke Rudolf would never allow it," Elvira said, scrambling to lay out Valeria's clothes.

Valeria doubted Rudolf could change the habits of a whole country no matter how much he wanted to.

Valeria looked at the dress Elvira had taken out for her to wear. "Don't I have something less elaborate? Something like one of your dresses."

"No, your highness."

"Not even a day dress?"

"You gave those away after your uncle announced your engagement."

Her uncle had wanted her to look splendid at all times.

"How about one of your dresses? We're about the same size."

"Your uncle would be scandalized."

"My uncle won't know, and I'm tired of being so hot. Besides, if I wear all my best clothes in this dirt and heat, they'll be ruined before I reach the ranch." They agreed that for the rest of journey, they would share clothes. Valeria also reduced her petticoats by three. "I'm no longer in a palace. It's not necessary that I wear enough petticoats to fill a doorway."

She saved more time by adopting a simple hairstyle that required only brushing before pinning her hair on top of her head. "Anything to get it off my shoulders."

She left the tent in thirty minutes, half the time she'd taken the day before. She felt rushed and thrown together, uncertain whether her appearance would be acceptable or incite laughter. She had her reward in Luke's look of surprise.

"Did Elvira throw you out?" he asked.

The man had a peculiar sense of humor. Maids didn't throw princesses out of their own bedchambers. Even if that bedchamber was nothing but a tent.

"I don't want to be guilty of wasting your time," she said. "I intend to learn to dress as quickly as you."

"Then you'll have to sleep in your clothes."

Valeria didn't think she could do that, not even to earn a smile like the one he gave her now. Which was just as well considering how silly she was being. She started casting about in her mind for more ways to make him smile, ways to get dressed faster, eat less, anything to earn his approval.

She told herself not to be foolish, that a princess didn't seek the approval of ordinary people, but she didn't feel Luke was in the least ordinary. She felt he had been created on a grander scale than anyone she knew. She was the one who felt inferior, and that was an unfamiliar and unsettling sensation.

"Would you like to have breakfast with us?"

There was no sign of the table or of her breakfast.

"Your cook doesn't seem to be able to get himself organized as quickly as you."

Valeria hadn't thought of that. She was used to everything being ready when she was.

"Then I'll take a walk."

"Where?"

"Down to the river. Maybe over to one of those hills. I imagine the view from there is wonderful."

"You're welcome to walk to the river, but watch out for animals coming down for their morning drink. You can't walk to that hill. It's about eight miles away. Your clothes would be torn to ribbons, your shoes cut to pieces."

"Then I'll ride."

"I don't have time to take you, and I can't spare anyone."

"I can go by myself. I won't get lost. I can see the camp from there."

"When are you going to realize this is dangerous country? Mountain lions live in those hills. And if anyone is following us, that would be like handing you over to them."

"Do you mean I'm confined to that coach for the entire trip?"

"Until I feel sure we're not being followed and are reasonably safe from attack."

Her satisfaction in getting dressed in half the usual time faded. She still had no control over her life, and Luke thought she was an idiot. "No one's trying to kidnap me. I'm not of value to anyone."

The look he gave her—it lasted for only a fraction of

a second—caused her to come vibrantly alert. It said she was of value. *To him!*

It was gone quickly, but a princess learned to be expert at interpreting brief glances. His glance said he cared. Being of value to Luke would be different from being important to Rudolf or her uncle. For them, her value would be inextricably interwoven with her position as a princess, with her inheritance. If Luke valued her at all, it would be for herself.

As a woman.

"I have to assume you're in danger," Luke said. "If you want to be helpful, get Hans and Otto to dress as quickly as you."

He turned, started to move away, then turned back. "Thanks for getting ready so quickly. The boys and I appreciate it." He flashed a quick, almost impersonal smile, then was gone.

"That's the rudest man in the world," Elvira said. She'd come out of the tent in time to hear the last exchange.

"By our standards, he probably is," Valeria replied. "By his standards, I think he just apologized."

Luke settled the deer more securely over his saddle, smoked a cigarette, and let his anger simmer quietly. He'd never had a more frustrating four days. He'd barely made eight miles a day, and then only because he drove everybody to the brink of rebellion. Valeria's people declared they were doing everything as fast as possible, but it seemed they got slower each day. A rattlesnake bit one of the cook's assistants. He'd survived but was laid up in one of the wagons, his leg black and swollen with the poison. Another man had broken his arm foolishly trying to convince one of the mules it didn't want to sample Valeria's dinner.

Now Luke had had to go hunting for meat.

Otto and the others had continued to eat as though there was no end to their food, and as Luke predicted, they ran out of meat. He could have sent Zeke after a deer. He should have sent Hawk, but he had gone himself. Given his present mood, he figured he'd be better off away from everybody for a few hours.

He had no intention of handing the deer over to the cook. He'd probably cook all the best pieces tonight, serve what remained for breakfast tomorrow, and throw the rest away. There were twenty adults in this group. Luke, Hawk, Zeke, and seven drivers made up one half. Valeria, Hans, Otto, Elvira, the cook and five servants made up the other half. Valeria's half consumed three-fourths of the food and did none of the work. They spent all their time setting up and taking down tents, cooking and cleaning up after sumptuous meals.

But he couldn't blame Valeria for his difficulties. She had started to wakeup before he called. She was dressed and outside her tent long before Otto or Hans appeared. She still refused to wear any of the clothes he'd bought her, but she no longer complained of the heat. She said she had stripped her table down to bare essentials, but she simply had no idea how bare essentials could be.

Despite their continuing disagreement, he had begun to think of her less as a beautiful remnant of a useless and outdated society and more as a woman struggling to adapt to a new and unfamiliar environment. Zeke treated her like an ex–slave owner. Hawk ignored her.

Luke wished he could do the same.

Instead, he kept finding excuses for her mistakes. He paid no attention to Zeke's absurd accusation that he was going soft on her. Having lived in Europe, he understood more of what she was going through. That made it easier to keep from losing his temper when she demanded that extra water be heated so she could wash her hair. It enabled him to understand why she continued the ritual of sitting down to a table set with priceless china and crystal. She wasn't emphasizing the distinction between herself and those around her. She was holding on to a piece of the only life she understood.

Coming to America must have been as frightening for her as being put into an orphanage had been for him and Chet. If they hadn't stuck together, fighting to protect each other, they wouldn't have survived. They'd felt almost as fearful when Jake and Isabelle adopted them, treated them with fairness, showed them love. It was a foreign world, but Chet had finally understood and wanted it for himself.

Luke couldn't accept it. He'd stayed outside the circle. He—

The sound of rifle shots brought Luke out of his abstraction. He immediately whipped his horse into a gallop toward the camp.

Wild thoughts chased each other through his head. Somebody was after the horses, the mules, the gold and silver, silks and velvets—Valeria. He raked his mount's flanks with his spurs, but the horse couldn't run any faster over the treacherous ground.

Before Luke came into rifle range, he saw Indians circling the wagons. Even as he raised his rifle to this shoulder, he realized the scene made no sense. All the Indians in the area had been moved to reservations.

He started firing even though only the greatest stroke of luck would enable him to hit anyone from this distance. His horse galloped over rocks, around a towering saguaro cactus, through a chest-high tangle of mesquite. Luke kept up a steady rat-a-tat-tat of rifle fire even when his shots were deflected by branches of paloverde, cottonwood, or willow. He'd be lucky if he didn't fall out of the saddle, but the attackers would know someone was firing on them from behind. Maybe that would drive them off before they could hurt anyone.

It did.

By the time Luke threw himself from the saddle in front of Valeria's tent, the Indians had gone. He rushed forward, threw aside the flap, and looked inside. Valeria and Elvira sat huddled on the floor propped up against the bed. For a moment neither of them moved, and Luke had the horrible feeling he had arrived too late.

As he started forward, Valeria lifted her head, turned a face with fearful eyes toward him. The look of relief, thankfulness, welcome—so many emotions were packed into that one glance—was unlike any that had ever come his way before. No woman had ever looked at him like he was the answer to her prayers, a hero come to rescue her, her savior in denim and scuffed boots.

Chapter Ten

"Are you hurt?" Luke hurried forward, dropped to one knee.

"No, but I can't get Elvira to move."

Luke tore his gaze from Valeria and directed his attention to the white-faced maid. He put his hand next to the side of her throat. He felt a pulse, weak but steady. He saw no sign of blood. He lifted her up, checked her back and sides, ran his hand over her body with the thoroughness of a physician.

"She's not wounded," Luke said, a weight lifted from his shoulders. "She's just fainted again."

He heard the tent flap being thrown back and turned, expecting to see Hawk or Zeke. Instead Hans entered the tent, his nervous body clad only in a pair of trousers.

"Your highness," he whispered, his voice hoarse with fear, "are you all right?"

"I'm fine," Valeria said.

"Elvira . . . is she . . ."

"She fainted," Luke said. "Where are your smelling

salts?" he asked Valeria. She dug though one of the boxes in her trunk until she found an elegant, cut glass and silver-gilt bottle, which she held out to Luke.

"Take the top off and hand it to me while I hold her up," Luke said.

During this, Otto stumbled into the tent. He had managed to put on his shirt, but he didn't look nearly as upset as Hans. Luke suspected him of being far more loyal to his own safety than his employer's.

"Is she hurt?" he asked.

"She fainted," Hans explained. "Luke is going to revive her with smelling salts."

"I can see that," Otto snapped.

Luke waved the smelling salts beneath Elvira's nose. It took a moment before she revived with a violent jerk.

"Thank goodness," Valeria said.

"W-what happened?" Elvira asked.

"You fainted," Luke said.

"It's understandable," Hans said, shifting his weight from foot to foot, looking more nervous and upset than usual. "It's like the civil war all over again."

His words caused everyone to fall silent.

"It's your fault," Hans said, surprising Luke by his anger. "You weren't here when the princess needed you."

"He was hunting food for our table," Otto reminded him.

"He should have sent someone else," Hans said. "His job was to protect her highness."

"You're right," Luke said over Valeria's protest. "It was a stupid mistake, and I'm ashamed of it. I won't leave Valeria again. I'll sleep inside the tent tonight, right there." He pointed to a spot on the floor next to Valeria's bed.

"You'll do no such thing," Valeria said. "Elvira would

never get a moment's rest with you—a man—inside the tent."

Luke wasn't happy to know he'd tensed the moment he made the offer, that his body relaxed at Valeria's prompt refusal. He couldn't be sure it wasn't from disappointment rather than relief.

"Then I'll sleep outside the door. Isn't that what your guards did in Belgravia?" He hadn't meant to be snide, just to cover his reaction to his own feelings. He had to stop letting Valeria affect him like this. It might have been a long time since he'd had a woman, but he'd never been desperate before. Finding that Elvira could sit up on her own, Luke got to his feet. "I've got to see if anybody else is hurt. Stay here until I let you know it's safe to go outside."

"We can't stay in her highness's private tent," Hans said. "It's not proper."

"You can go," Luke said. "Nobody's trying to shoot you or Otto."

"How do you know?" Otto demanded.

"I don't. But if I thought they were, I'd be tempted to throw you outside so they could have a second chance."

Outside, confusion reigned. Luke heard groans, one man yelling, presumably in pain. "Anybody hit?" he asked Zeke.

"Just a couple of the cook's helpers, but they deserved it. If I'd been here, I'd have shot them for stupidity. Instead of dropping to the ground when the attack started, they ran out into the open, directly into the field of fire. They're lucky they only got flesh wounds."

"Are they bad?"

"I don't know. I left the cook taking care of them."

Luke found the cook bandaging one man's arm; a second man was chattering away in a language Luke didn't understand.

"Do you need any medical supplies?" Luke asked.

"In the kitchen we have accidents all the time," the cook said. "I have everything."

"Did anybody manage to hit one of the Indians?" Luke asked Zeke.

"I don't know. I was down at the river with the horses when they attacked. By the time I got back they had gone."

"That seems awfully quick."

"Maybe the drivers ran them off too soon. As soon as they heard the first shot, they were on their bellies under the wagons firing as fast as they could. If those foreign fools hadn't gotten in the way, they might have killed a couple."

"We didn't have much chance to get any of them," one of the drivers said. "They were gone by the time I was able to work around my wagon, find my rifle, and get into position."

"You didn't see or hear them coming."

"I wasn't paying no attention," the driver said. "I thought you was taking care of that. I had my hands full trying to harness up these stubborn mules."

Luke supposed the man meant to make him feel guilty for not doing his job. He did, but he didn't have time for self-recrimination now. "Where did they come from? What direction?"

"Northwest," Zeke said. "That's what you saw?" he asked the driver.

"Pretty much. They ran off in that direction, too."

"Where's Hawk?" Luke asked.

He wasn't worried that anything had happened to Hawk. The man was more Indian than white, but Luke had expected him to head into camp as soon as he heard the first shot.

"Somewhere off to the south."

Luke had gone northwest, so he wouldn't have seen the attackers even if he hadn't been on the other side of the river. "I shouldn't have left," he said.

"You had to, unless you wanted us to starve," Zeke said. "I hope you got a deer."

"It's across my saddle. I'll get Hawk to dress it out as soon as he gets back."

If he gets back. He didn't know why that thought should bedevil him. Hawk had gone in nearly the opposite direction from the attackers. He couldn't possibly have been hurt. The orphans didn't always like to acknowledge the bond between them, but Hawk would never stay away if he thought one of them was in trouble.

"They were Indians," one of the drivers said.

"It looked that way," Luke said. "Do you know what kind?"

"No. I can't tell one Indian from another. They all look the same to me."

"You'd better not say that around Hawk," Zeke warned.

"I don't say nothing around him," the driver said. "I like my hair where it is."

"Hawk wouldn't scalp anybody," Luke said, disgusted anybody would think he might.

"He'll just cut your liver out," Zeke said, then laughed.

"Shut up," Luke said. "You scare them off, you find replacements."

"Where?" Zeke said, looking around at the empty desert and hills. "There's not a living soul within fifty miles of us."

"Except those Indians," the driver said.

"They was Chiricahuas," a boyish driver said. He had coal-black hair and cheeks as downy as a peach.

That didn't make sense to Luke. The Chiricahua had been banished to the San Carlos Reservation in 1876. The closest part of that reservation was more than a hundred miles away. A few renegade braves had terrorized the area under Geronimo, but they'd been sent to Florida in 1886. There wouldn't be enough fugitives in the area to mount such an attack.

"Are you sure?" Luke asked.

"I used to live in Douglas," the young driver said. "I saw them Indians all the time. He was a Chiricahua."

"Have you seen Hawk?" Luke asked.

"I ain't seen him since he went out of here heading south," the boy said, returning to the job of harnessing his team of four mules. "That was over an hour ago."

Luke scanned the hills and desert to the south, but he didn't see any sign of Hawk.

"There he is," one of the drivers called.

"Where?" Luke asked.

"Over there, where those Indians disappeared."

It took Luke a moment before he could distinguish Hawk from several blooming yucca plants. A surprisingly strong feeling of relief swept over him. He'd hate to be the one to write Isabelle that Hawk had died because he hadn't attended to his responsibilities. Luke couldn't forget the passionate warmth Isabelle showered on her adopted family. He had stayed away because he didn't know how to return it. It would be easier if they just forgot about him.

Zeke pointed out the obvious. "Hawk's leading a horse with a body thrown across the saddle."

Hawk had apparently heard the attack, ridden to intercept the attackers, and killed one of them before they got away.

"We might as well get ready to pull out," Luke said to the drivers. "Everybody get your teams hitched up. Lend me a hand with this deer," he said to Zeke.

Luke figured it was probably safe for Valeria to come

out of her tent, but he wanted to hear what Hawk had found out first.

"You think this attack has to do with her?" Zeke asked, nodding his head in the direction of Valeria's tent.

"I don't know," Luke replied. "They didn't appear to be looking for her tent."

"They couldn't have missed it. It's big enough for a king."

"She's a king's daughter," Luke pointed out.

"A fact I hope you remember."

"I will. Now stop sticking your nose in my business and help with this deer."

They had the deer skinned and half the meat butchered, wrapped, and out of the heat by the time Hawk rode up.

"Where did they go?" Luke asked.

"Toward the mountains," Hawk answered as he slid from the saddle.

"A driver said they were Chiricahuas," Luke said.

"This one is a white man." Hawk grabbed the dead man by the hair and lifted his head until Luke could see his face. "White man," Hawk said.

The man had dressed himself as an Indian, but there wasn't enough makeup in the world to make him look like an Indian.

"I know him," one of the drivers said. "He goes by the name of Sam Lewis."

"Where did you meet him?" Luke asked.

"When I was doing some freighting over near Benson. They threw him out of one of the saloons for coming on too hard with one of the girls. He swore he'd come back and kill 'em all."

"Well, now you can go over to Benson and tell them they're safe," a fellow driver said.

"Not me. I don't want nobody thinking I'm a friend to that coyote."

"The one I saw was a Chiricahua," the young driver said. "I couldn't mistake something like that."

It didn't make any sense to Luke. A group of a half-dozen men, at least one real Indian and at least one fake, attacks the camp, doesn't take anything, doesn't kill anybody, and breaks and runs after less than a minute.

"Does anyone have an idea what they could have been after?" Luke asked the gathered drivers.

"They didn't try to get anything," one said. "They just fired off a lot of shots and rode off again."

"Maybe they were after the horses," another volunteered. "When they didn't see them, they rode off."

"We have twenty-four mules worth a fortune," Luke pointed out. "Why didn't they take those?"

"We all had our teams near our wagons," a driver said. "They couldn't have gotten the mules without getting shot."

"Then why didn't they come earlier when the mules and horses were still staked out?" Luke asked. "That's what Indians usually do. Kill any guard and make off with the livestock before anybody knows what's happening."

No one had an answer.

"Why should this man be dressed up like an Indian?" one driver asked.

"So the raid would be blamed on Indians," Hawk said.

"But they didn't take anything. Why get yourself in trouble and not take anything?"

Which was exactly the question Luke wanted answered.

"Who is that man?"

Luke hadn't heard Valeria approach. The men stood back to allow her to step forward.

"I told you to stay in your tent," he said. She looked composed, but he could tell from the continual movement of her eyes, the incident had upset her a great deal.

"I waited, but you never came back."

"I wanted to find out what Hawk had discovered."

"If you had told me, I wouldn't have worried."

"Worried about what?"

"About the men I heard moaning," she said. "I was on my way to see if I could help, but Hans told me the chef had already taken care of them."

"What could you do?" It never occurred to him that she would think of anyone but herself.

"Elvira and I worked in the hospital during the war."

That surprised him even more.

"I'll remember that next time."

"Do you think there'll be a next time?"

He didn't know how much of the truth he wanted her to know. "You never can tell. It's always best to be prepared."

She looked at the man on the horse.

"He's an Indian," she said. That appeared to relieve her mind.

"No. A white man dressed up to look like an Indian."

The worry returned. "Why would he do that?"

"That's what we're trying to figure out. Does it make any sense to you?"

"No."

"I told you we would be in danger," Hans said. He'd forced his way into the bystanders, followed by Otto. Luke groaned inwardly. All he needed now was Elvira, and the group would be complete.

"There's always danger when you travel through open country," Luke said. "You've got more wealth here than most men can dream of. That's why I made sure all the drivers are expert gunmen."

"Is that why the attackers left so quickly?" Valeria asked.

"I hope so." He felt certain the attack had something to do with Valeria, but he was at a loss to say how. "We can't stand 'round talking. Tell your cook to get breakfast ready."

"But we've been attacked," Hans said.

"All the more reason to leave," Luke said. "If they come again, they'll have to look for us. You can be sure I won't be out hunting."

"Did you find some meat?" Otto asked.

"A deer."

"I love a venison roast. I'll talk to the chef right away."

The fool was more concerned about his appetite than his safety.

"It won't last long with twenty people to feed," Zeke said.

"That's our deer," Otto said, apparently never considering the possibility Luke would share the meat with the drivers.

"Any meat I kill belongs to everybody," Luke said. "There'll be no more cooking three times what you can eat. Nor," he said before Otto could protest, "will I allow you to eat three times as much at a sitting as one of my drivers."

"You can't give us orders." Otto seemed more shocked than fearful of going hungry.

"If you want more to eat, go kill it yourself."

"I can't ride."

It was Luke's turn to be surprised.

"Then you'd better trim your appetite."

Otto made a sputtering noise.

"We'll all have to make changes in the way we do things," Valeria said. "It really doesn't make sense to serve more food than we can eat."

"But I can eat my share," Otto protested.

"Maybe you shouldn't," Hans said. "A slimming diet

would prolong the life of your coat buttons."

Luke had no intention of standing around while these men took potshots at each other. "Hawk, get some of the drivers to help you bury that man. Zeke and I will finish dressing the meat."

Valeria followed him.

"You don't want to watch," he said.

"Why not?"

"It's not a sight suitable for a woman of your type."

"And what is my type?"

He refused to let her put him on the spot.

"I'm certain you've never had to dress the meat you ate."

She looked at the deer. "Is that the kind of food I'll be expected to eat at Rudolf's ranch?"

"Maybe."

"Then I'll watch. I expect I'll have to learn to butcher, too."

Luke studied her expression for a moment, trying to determine if she was serious. He hoped she wasn't. She was a spoiled, silly woman, and no man in his right mind would consider having anything to do with her, even temporarily, even if it was only physical.

But then women like her didn't have merely physical relationships. Nor were they temporary. They had only marriages governed by contracts. It would be like becoming part of a government. No emotion involved. None desired. Arrange the politics and the money, and the people fell into line. He wasn't the least bit sentimental, but he was glad such an inhumane system was being pushed into oblivion.

Her wanting to change was a good sign, but he wasn't sure about her sudden determination to learn all she could about living in Arizona. He didn't want her to be sincere. He didn't want a reason to admire her. That could be more dangerous than being physically attracted to her. He hadn't wanted to admire Isabelle when she adopted him and his brother, when she gave them unconditional love whether they wanted it or not, when she enfolded them into a family that was warm and comforting despite the years of hurt and anger each carried with him. He hadn't wanted to admire Jake when he taught them to do an honest day's work, when he tried to instill in them a sense of right and wrong, when he gave them understanding without demanding less from them.

Yet his memory of his adoptive parents remained as strong and clear as the day he rode away from their ranch. Nor could he forget their teachings, the memories of a life he'd enjoyed for five years. That's what came with respect and admiration. No matter what he did, where he went, they'd be looking over his shoulder for the rest of his life.

He didn't want that to happen with Valeria. He might start thinking of her all the time.

Valeria couldn't sleep. The attack had stunned, frightened, and confused her. She hadn't really believed anybody wanted to kill her. She couldn't think of any reason why someone should. She didn't have any power, and her uncle and future husband would control her money.

Rebellions and changes of government in her country had always been understandable. Battles took place on neatly confined battlefields. The men of her family died in combat or in their beds. No attempt had ever been made to harm the women and children. There was a much greater chance she'd die in childbirth than at the hands of an assassin.

But if she was to believe Luke and Hans, she was the reason for the attack. She didn't know the man dressed up like an Indian, had no reason to feel sympathetic, but no one had ever died because of her. It made her feel guilty, as though it was her fault. For the first time she felt the weight of her heritage, of being able to cause men to die. She didn't like it. She wanted to hide, to do anything she could to keep from feeling guilty for that man's death.

She heard the rustle of covers, the creak of a bed. "What's wrong, Elvira?"

"Nothing."

"Can't you sleep?"

"No."

"Neither can I."

The attack had made them late leaving that morning, and Luke had driven them hard all day to make up the lost time. Valeria decided he cared more about the loss of time than he did about the death of the stranger or the injuries to her servants. Valeria tried to tell him that palace servants weren't used to being attacked by Indians. Zeke had said anyone stupid enough to run into the path of a bullet ought to get shot. If they hadn't had different colored skin, Valeria could have believed Luke and Zeke were blood brothers.

"Is Luke still outside the tent?" Valeria asked.

"He said he would be," Elvira replied.

"Go look."

Despite the attack, the most powerful image in her mind was that of Luke sleeping on the ground in front of her tent. She knew there was a wall of canvas and several feet of space between them, but it felt like he was so near she could reach out and touch him.

And he could touch her.

"Don't light the lamp," Valeria warned Elvira. "I don't want him to think we're spying on him."

Spying wasn't quite the way to put it. She didn't want him to know she was even thinking of him. He never hesitated to take advantage of his experience and knowledge to make her look vain and foolish. If he thought she had any personal interest in him, he'd probably make her life miserable.

"I can't see him," Elvira whispered.

Even though she had argued on three separate occasions during the day against his sleeping outside her tent, Valeria felt hurt and disappointed that he hadn't thought her safety important enough to keep his promise.

"Open the tent and look out," Valeria said.

"I can't."

"Why?"

"I'm scared."

It wasn't fair to make Elvira look for Luke. If Valeria wanted to know where he was, she ought to have the courage to look for herself.

"Never mind," Valeria said. "Get back in bed."

Elvira scurried across the tent so quickly, Valeria couldn't help smiling. She got out of bed and reached for a dressing gown.

"I don't think you ought to go outside," Elvira asked.

"I'm not. I'll just stick my head out. It'll only take a second."

She opened the flap, stuck her head out, then stifled a scream. She found herself practically nose to nose with Luke.

Chapter Eleven

"Do you need to take care of nature's call?" Luke asked.

Valeria couldn't answer. Other than jerking back instinctively when she found herself face-to-face with Luke, she couldn't move. Not even the incredible, inconceivable, ridiculous notion that she should seek relief among the grass and thorns had the power to unlock her tongue.

"You can't go wandering off by yourself," Luke said. "No telling what kind of critter you might stumble over."

It was impossible even to consider discussing such an eventuality with a man.

"Oh, God, you're sleepwalking," Luke exclaimed. "You're about to go wandering around in the middle of the Arizona desert without knowing what the hell you're doing. I'll slit Hans's throat. He didn't breathe a word about this."

Luke took her by the shoulders, turned her around, and gave her a tiny push. She stumbled forward.

"Elvira, put her to bed," Luke hissed, "and don't let her get up again."

Luke withdrew his head and closed the flap on the tent.

Valeria felt the tension leave her body so completely, she wasn't sure she had the strength to make it to her bed. She stumbled forward and collapsed with a sigh of relief. Luke hadn't ignored her. He hadn't gone back on his promise. He'd been so vigilant he'd known the instant she opened the tent flap.

As she pulled the covers over her and settled back into bed, a smile curved her lips.

"There's nothing I can do but take the wheel apart and rebuild it," the driver said.

Luke had spent the last half hour airing his entire lexicon of curses. He'd even invented a few. But nothing could change the fact that the wagon's wheel was broken, and it would take most of the day to fix it. They'd left camp barely an hour earlier and traveled less than a mile. Their day was over. They'd eat more from their dwindling stores of food and exhaust more of his patience without getting a mile closer to their goal.

"The rest of you might as well pull your wagons under the trees," Luke told the gathered drivers. "It'll be hot today."

"It's hot every day," Otto said. He'd complained about the inferior quality of American wagons, the fact that there didn't appear to be a single proper road in the entire country, said he hadn't been this hot when he lived in Egypt.

Luke ignored Otto. "Hawk, you want to see if you can find a deer?"

Hawk nodded.

"That means all of us have to be extra watchful," Luke

said. "The only time we were attacked was when one of us went out hunting."

"Do you think they're watching?" Otto asked. He seemed almost hopeful.

"No," Luke said, "but I don't intend to be caught off guard again."

It didn't take long to pull the wagons down to the river and unhitch the mules. They could use a day's rest. They were big, strong animals, but the extremely difficult terrain and the heavy wagons had taken a toll on their strength. If it had been up to Luke, he'd have dumped half that stuff days ago.

He watched as Valeria's servants set up her tent in the shade of the cottonwoods. He wondered how a woman used to having a whole palace to herself could accustom herself to a tent, but she had adapted much more quickly than her maid. Hans tried, but the little man struggled with the heat, the strangeness of the situation, and his fear of something happening to his beloved princess. He simply didn't have a mind that could stretch far enough to envision a social system different from the one he'd been born into. Valeria would always be a royal princess to him, worthy of devotion, obedience, and reverence. Luke couldn't figure out what Valeria or her family could have done to warrant such devotion.

His thoughts broke off when Valeria, after looking over her shoulder and noticing him looking her way, said something to Elvira and started toward him. He was tempted to turn away, but that would have been an admission of weakness he wasn't ready to make even to himself.

"Are we definitely going to be here all day?" Valeria asked when she reached him.

"It looks that way."

"I want to ride to that mountain," she said, pointing to

one of the sky mountains that rose straight up from the desert floor.

"The closest one is at least ten miles away."

"How long would it take to get there?"

"Maybe two hours with another hour or so to climb high enough to notice a difference in the temperature."

"We've got all day."

"It's a very exhausting ride, and I couldn't allow you to go alone."

"I wasn't planning on going alone. I was hoping you would take me."

He didn't want to take her anywhere. He certainly didn't want to spend an entire day alone with her.

"You don't have a suitable horse."

"She's not using my horse," Zeke said, "even if I am going to be stuck here all day."

"I have my own horses," Valeria said.

"They're not used to the desert."

"They're used to mountains," Valeria said. "That's about all we have in my country."

"I shouldn't leave the camp," Luke said.

"Your job is to protect me. Since I'll be with you, you can still do your job."

"Such a trip will expose you to danger."

"Does that mean you're unable to protect me without all these men to help you?"

Zeke let out a crack of laughter. Several of the drivers grinned. Luke acted as if he didn't see them. "I don't need anyone's help to do my job."

"Good. The land looks flat," she said. "We can see anyone coming from miles away."

"There are lots of breaks in the land—dry washes, ravines, low hills—"

"Do you dislike me that much, or are you afraid to ride with me?"

Luke felt all eyes focus on him. "No."

"Good, because I'm going for a ride."

Valeria had never been so hot in her life. If Luke had made the slightest attempt to be friendly, she'd have admitted her mistake and asked him to take her back to camp and the coolness of the cottonwoods. She even considered turning around and starting back by herself. It was impossible to miss the San Pedro River. It formed the only ribbon of green in the desert landscape.

But she wouldn't turn back if she fainted or her nose burned so badly it peeled. He'd been rude, talked as little as possible, and made it abundantly clear he'd rather be almost anywhere than by her side. Besides, they'd been climbing for the last hour and she'd finally begun to notice a drop in the temperature.

"The mountains in our country are more beautiful than these." She'd said as much before but had received little more than a grunt for her trouble. "They're covered with pine and fir trees that give the woods a wonderful scent. They have beautiful meadows filled with wildflowers in the spring."

"We have mountains in Colorado like that," he said.

"Where's Colorado?"

"North of here."

That was good. Anything north sounded cooler. "Is it very far?"

"Five or six hundred miles, depending on where you want to go."

Her entire country was less than thirty miles from one end to the other. She could barely conceive of a country big enough to have all these states and each one so large.

"We have snow on our mountains in winter."

"There are snow-covered mountains in any one of a dozen states."

"We can ice skate on the ponds and rivers." It had been unbearably hot every step of the way from New Orleans to San Antonio and El Paso to Arizona. She couldn't imagine any place in America getting cold enough to freeze ponds and rivers.

"We have lakes bigger than your whole country that freeze up for the winter."

She really didn't want to hear any more about the geography of America, its flora and fauna. That was all Luke would talk about except for saying that her horse seemed remarkably surefooted for a hot-blooded animal.

"He's a thoroughbred," she'd explained.

"They're fast but high strung," he said. "They wouldn't be any good on treacherous mountain trails or around cougars."

Then he'd gone right back to talking about cactus, poisonous snakes, and the Indians that used to roam the area.

"Why did you go to Europe?" she asked, interrupting a monologue on the various kinds of plants found at different altitudes.

"I went there to work."

"Guarding people?"

"To fight."

"In the infantry?"

"I was an officer."

"A mercenary."

"Yes."

No one liked mercenaries. They were foreigners, cold-blooded, and often cruel. They fought for money alone, not ideals, principles, or the people.

"Where did you fight?"

"Everywhere."

"Why didn't you stay?"

"I didn't like the people who hired me."

At least he had a conscience somewhere inside him, even if he kept it well out of sight.

"Which side did you fight for?"

"The one that paid the most money."

"That means you fought for some king. I thought you said you hated kings."

"I do."

"But you'll fight for the person who pays you the most money."

"That's right."

"Regardless of what the fight is about."

"Yes."

"Don't you care about the people in the conflict?"

"No."

They had just left an area of oak, juniper, and manzanita. Squirrels and chipmunks scampered across the rocky ground while jays and hawks called noisily from above. She half-expected Luke to shoot one of the white-tailed deer they spotted, but he didn't appear to notice the inquisitive animals.

She welcomed the drop in temperature that came when they entered a forest of ponderosa pine. She was delighted by a pair of turkeys ambling through the dappled light of the forest floor, their new chicks running ahead of them, eager to explore every aspect of their new world. It was beginning to look more like her own country. Luke had said Rudolf's ranch was in mountainous country full of trees. She hoped it would look like this.

The narrow trail forced them to ride single file. She had a prolonged view of his broad back, the powerful hindquarters of his horse as they rose and fell. She liked her sleek, racy mount, but she liked the look of Luke's more powerfully muscled horse. She'd ask him to let her ride it one day.

"How long does the trail stay like this?" she called out.

"I don't know."

That startled her. "You mean you don't know this road?"

"There are far too many trails in the West for any one man to know. You learn to trust your instincts."

"And your instincts say this trail is safe?"

"It's been worn smooth by wild animals. That means it's a good route to somewhere."

"Where?"

"Wherever they go for food or shelter."

The forest had changed to pine, aspen, and fir. A thick carpet of needles muffled the sound of their horses' hooves, and Valeria became more aware of the sounds around her, the squawk of goshawks calling among the treetops, the chatter of squirrels, the scratching of some animal as it dug under the straw for grubs, the whirr of hummingbird wings among flowers that had sprung up in every opening between the trees. It reminded her of her youth when she'd been allowed to take long rides in the forest or go on picnics and long walks. All that had ceased when she reached marriageable age. She'd forgotten how much she enjoyed the freedom to wander through the outdoors, unconcerned about the safety of her clothes or her skin.

"We'd better stop here," Luke said. "We'll have to start back soon."

They'd reached a small, blessedly cool section of the pine forest, the first time Valeria could remember being truly comfortable since she reached New Orleans. She knew there was no point in asking Luke to let them camp here for a few nights. It would have been impossible to bring the wagons up that trail.

Luke dismounted and dropped his reins. She expected to see his horse wander, but the animal stood perfectly still.

"Why doesn't he run away?" she asked.

"He's ground hitched."

She'd never heard such a thing. Her mount would wander off at the first opportunity. Luke walked toward an opening in the forest. When he realized she wasn't following, he turned around.

"You'd better get down," he said. "Give your muscles a chance to relax."

"I can't dismount by myself."

She had ridden sidesaddle, the only way she knew, and couldn't dismount without help or a set of steps.

"Just unhook your leg and slide out of the saddle," Luke said.

"I can't. You have to lift me down."

He glared at her for a moment, his expression hard and unfriendly. "If I'd known that, I wouldn't have suggested we stop."

"Well, we have, and I'd like to get down."

He hesitated so long she thought he might refuse. Then he stalked toward her.

"Stop!" she exclaimed when he seemed about to wrench her from the saddle. "You can't snatch me off like a sack of grain. You have to hold me while I unhook my leg."

Again he paused. She didn't understand his reluctance. He might not like royalty, but he didn't have to act as if touching her would infect him with some incurable disease. As though making a sudden resolution, he placed his hands on her waist and lifted her out of the saddle.

"Can you free your leg now?" he asked.

"Yes." He'd lifted her straight up off the horn. "You can let me down now."

But he didn't. He continued to hold her in the air as if she weighed hardly anything.

"Let me down."

"I just wanted to show you what it's like not to feel in control of your life."

"I've never been in control," she said, "not from the first breath I took. Now please let me down."

He lowered her slowly. Again the effort seemed to cost him nothing.

"Come over here," he said, indicating a break in the trees. "You can see where you've been."

Valeria gathered her composure as best she could. She refused to be overwhelmed just because the man was strong. That was foolish. An ox was strong and she had absolutely no admiration for an ox. But she couldn't deny that she had come perilously close to being dazzled by Luke Attmore. He said he'd never had much effect on women. His indifference to people in general had probably kept him from seeing it. And women, recognizing his remoteness, had probably done their best to get over him as quickly as possible. The best way for her to do that would be not to see him again.

But she had to see him every day for the duration of this trip, and could watch him without interruption for hours on end. Since he was the primary topic of conversation among Elvira, Hans, and Otto, there was little chance she'd be allowed to put thoughts of him out of her mind.

It shouldn't have been that hard. All her life she'd disciplined herself to think only of acceptable things. But everything had changed. She'd been away from her uncle for several months, and though Otto and Hans were in charge of her journey, she had some real freedom for the first time. Not that it did her much good. Luke controlled her just as absolutely as her uncle ever had. Still, the sense of being out from under her uncle's control and the responsibilities of her position as princess was real. Being around Luke only made that feeling more acute. He made her question things she'd taken for granted, things she'd done because she was *supposed* to do them, because a princess of Belgravia had *always* done them.

But the idea of being completely free was worrisome. As a princess she knew who she was, what to do, that she was safe and sheltered. Freedom took away that support, that protection. As tantalizing is it seemed, it frightened her. But she probably didn't need to worry. She would soon be married, and though she might have to learn what foods to have the chef prepare and what clothes to wear, Rudolf would take care of everything else.

That left her feeling dissatisfied.

"Are you afraid of heights?" Luke asked.

"No. Why do you ask?"

"You've been standing there with this slightly startled look on your face."

She started forward and reached for his outstretched hand. "I was just thinking."

"You can do that in the coach."

Luke took her hand, and suddenly she had to concentrate on walking. She'd danced with many men in her life, taken their hands to mount a horse, climb stairs, walk in the garden. Luke's touch was entirely different.

She felt his strength, sensed his steely determination, felt infused with the energy that flowed through him like a turbulent stream during the spring thaw. Like a rock thrown into the serene pool of her life, he disturbed her calm, sending ripples fanning out to every corner. She told herself not to be fanciful, but the feeling grew stronger.

Luke drew her onto a huge slab of rock that extended out into space. She felt as if she were suspended in midair, looking down at the world she'd just traveled. The view was breathtaking.

Below she saw where the mountain fell away into the tangle of oak and juniper. One could almost have drawn a line separating it from the saguaro cactus, ocotillo, and mesquite that marked the beginning of the desert. Then there was the almost barren strip that merged with the verdant band bordering each side of the San Pedro River. On the other side of the river, the pattern reversed itself as the land climbed toward a distant mountain.

"You'd never know from up here that it was so hot and miserable down there," she said.

"That's pretty much what it's like being a princess. You're so far above the ordinary world, you have no concept of what it's like to live down there."

It angered her that he should ruin a lovely moment by taking up his favorite litany.

"My father and my uncle devoted their lives to improving the condition of our people."

"Then why were they overthrown?"

Why? She didn't know. No one had bothered to teach her how the government worked. Or why it might fail. When she asked, she was told such things were unsuitable for a woman to ask, especially a princess. She had asked her servants, but they were insulated from the general population by the same system that kept her in a virtual cocoon. "I don't know," she admitted. "My uncle said it was outside subversives, mercenaries like yourself."

"And you believe that?"

She'd always been told what to do, what to believe. Luke's relentless questioning made her realize she'd given up trying to think long ago. "Why shouldn't I?" she asked.

"Look down there," Luke said, pointing to the desert several thousand feet below. "What can you see?"

"Trees, bushes, cactus."

"Do you see any birds, mice, or squirrels?"

"You know I can't see anything that small from up here."

"That's exactly how it was in your country. You were so high you couldn't see the people below. You had no idea who they were, what their lives were like. They could have been starving, living in abject fear, and you'd never have known."

"Things couldn't have been that bad without my knowing," she protested.

Without warning, he grabbed her and kissed her hard on the mouth. It shocked Valeria so much, she couldn't breathe. No coherent thought emerged from the jumble whirling about in her head. Everything about her simply came to a dead stop.

Just as abruptly, Luke broke the kiss and held her at arm's length from him. "Did you like that? Did you want me to do it? Could you stop me from doing it again?"

Exclamations of surprise, words of protest, and pleas for explanation stumbled over each other in her mind.

He wrapped his arms about her, pulled her tight against his chest. "You're helpless, aren't you? You can't run away and you can't fight me."

She could if she could get over the shock. She had never been held in such an intimate embrace. Not even when dancing in public would a man have dared let his body touch hers. The sensation was enormous, disabling.

"Imagine you are a peasant woman," Luke said. "You sell flowers on the street. You have six children, cook three meals a day, do the laundry, clean the house, satisfy your husband at night. You have less money to spend in a whole year than you now spend on one dress. Can you imagine what your life would be like?"

Try as she might, she couldn't think of anything except Luke's body pressed against the length of her own. She could feel his warmth, the curve of his muscles, but she felt no give in them.

Two opposing feelings succeeded her initial shock—anger that he would treat her with such contempt, and a desire that he never let her go. Since she could hardly breathe, she didn't understand that at all. She'd known for some time that Luke aroused strange and unruly longings within her, but she'd never realized until now just how intense they were. She wanted to throw aside everything she'd ever learned, and fling her arms around his neck.

"I have no idea what her life might be like," she said, abandoning any attempt to understand Luke or her conflicting emotions.

"You say you have no control over your life, but there's a legion of servants to see to your comfort, an army of soldiers ready to give their lives to protect you. Suppose a soldier came to her flower stand—or a mercenary like myself—who liked what he saw. Supposed he drew her to him"—Luke's arms tightened around her still more—"and kissed her ruthlessly."

He kissed her again.

No other man had ever kissed her on the lips. She had no way to differentiate ruthless from enthusiastic . . . or impassioned . . . or heedless. Her mind told her she ought to be furious, insulted, violated, even frightened. Her body pleaded with her to give in to Luke's embrace.

She felt herself responding to him, leaning into his caress, returning his kiss. Somewhere in a corner of her brain, the sudden tenderness in her breasts registered. She'd think about that later when she wasn't wrapped in a whirlwind of sensations that narrowed her focus to Luke's body.

She felt the shape of him as he pressed against her, the curve and power of his leg, the hardness and breadth of his chest, the softness and warmth of his lips enveloping her like a tidal wave, nearly suffocating her with the intensity of his kiss.

Luke released her and stepped back.

The shock was immense. She felt deprived of energy, of the strength to stand. Her knees trembled and she reached for his arm to steady herself. It was as hard as an iron balustrade and just as immovable. It took a moment before her strength returned. She looked up at him, questioning, hoping for an explanation of what had happened to her.

One look told her Luke had been nearly as unprepared for what had happened between them. His expression combined surprise, confusion, and fear. She couldn't understand why he should be surprised or confused. He had kissed her. She might be inexperienced, but she could tell he'd done it many times before. What could he possibly have to fear from her? She was helpless. He'd said so himself.

"There would be no one to help you," Luke continued. "Anyone who interfered would be beaten senseless." He appeared to be having difficulty making his words form coherent sentences. "Or bayoneted and thrown into the river."

How could he expect her to think logically when her entire well-ordered way of thinking had just come tumbling down? Suddenly she didn't know what she wanted or how to go about finding out. She just knew that in some way this man was the key to everything, and he couldn't talk about anything but peasants and mercenaries.

"Peasant women, especially the pretty ones, have to worry about being caught out alone. Men of your class take advantage of them, then discard them when they lose their appeal. You've never had to think of your safety, but that thought never leaves the mind of a peasant woman. Not even marriage can protect her from soldiers like me."

"Why?" She didn't know why she asked. She didn't want to know.

"There's no limit to what I might do to you—*with* you—now," Luke said. "And there isn't anyone to stop me."

He came two steps toward her. All the confusion had left his expression. His face had assumed a hard, uncompromising mask. She had sensed danger in him from the beginning. It had seemed exciting, alluring, but now she wasn't so sure about it. She took a step back.

"I am not a peasant woman."

"It doesn't matter. You've lost your army and your servants are miles away."

"You wouldn't dishonor me."

"Why?"

"You're not that kind of man."

She didn't like his smile, or the laugh that followed. "You don't know what kind of man I am."

"You've been hired to protect me."

"I've been hired to deliver you to your future husband. I made no promises about anything else."

"You said women had rights in your country."

"They do, but men like me have no honor and no loyalty, not even to ourselves. We don't live long and seldom die in our beds, so we take what we can while we have the chance."

Valeria had never thought she would be frightened of Luke. Or even careful around him. He didn't like her, despised what she represented, but he cared passionately about his reputation. She couldn't believe he'd jeopardize it to teach her a lesson. And that was what this seemed like, a lesson to make her understand that everything had changed, that she could no longer take her safety for granted. He certainly didn't act like a man carried away by emotion, even lust. She might not be in control of her life, but Luke rigidly controlled everything about his.

She backed into a boulder, tried to move around it, but Luke placed his hands on either side of her. When she tried to duck under his arms, he grabbed her and pulled her hard against him.

"I've been without a woman for a long time," he said. "I've spent four hours bringing you up here. It'll take four hours to get back. I think I deserve a little something for that, don't you?"

Chapter Twelve

Valeria didn't know what to do or say. Despite war, revolution, and being driven from her own country, her physical safety had never been threatened. If her father were still on the throne, Luke would have been hanged for even talking about what he'd just done. But she was alone, miles away from anyone, pinned against a rock, helpless against Luke's superior strength.

"You've made your point. I'm not safe anymore. I'm not as strong as a man."

"Is that what you think I'm doing, making a point?"

The slight pause before he spoke gave him away. "Aren't you?"

"You could look at it that way, but we could both have some fun with it."

She didn't like the sound of his mocking laugh. It made her angry that he would treat her this way just to prove a point. It made her even angrier that her body would respond to him.

"I'll fight."

"That will make it more exciting," he said. He pressed his body more tightly against her. He moved his face closer and closer until she could look nowhere but directly into his ice-cold blue eyes. "I like it when a woman fights back. It heats my blood, and I like everything better when my blood is hot."

The words issued from his mouth on a moist cloud that seemed to scald her cheek. She thought of going limp in his arms, but *her* blood was up, and she couldn't be passive if she wanted to.

She attempted to duck under his arms. He just moved his hands closer to her sides, pinning her body against the rock with his own.

"It wouldn't do any good to escape," he whispered. "Even if you could outrun me, where would you go?"

"My horse is faster than yours."

"You can't mount without my help."

She wasn't as strong as he was. She couldn't run as fast. She couldn't mount her horse alone. She would have to defend herself by her wits, hot blood or not. She had nothing else.

"You don't want to do this."

"Why not? You're a woman. A beautiful woman at that. What more could a man want?"

"I've never done this before. I wouldn't be very good at it. When we got back to the camp, I'd accuse you in front of everyone."

"I've been accused of worse."

She couldn't imagine what could be worse. "I'll keep on accusing you until your men cringe at the sound of my voice. I'll make the men so miserable they'll quit."

He moved a little bit closer. "You're making me very warm."

She didn't want to make him warm. She wanted to cool him off.

"I'll lie still. I won't help you. It'll be like making love to a corpse."

The very idea made her skin crawl. She hoped it would have an equally chilling effect on Luke.

"Beggars can't be choosers."

She couldn't believe she'd misjudged him. Could he really mean to assault her? If so, why didn't she feel frightened? Why was she afraid she might like his lesson too much to lie still?

"I bet you'll be a pretty hot number once I thaw a little of that royal ice in your veins," he said, his lips almost touching hers. "I hear blue-blooded females like jumping from one bed to another after marriage. Just consider this your initiation. You couldn't have a better teacher. I've had lots of experience."

She could believe that. As handsome as he was, he probably had half the females in the West panting after him. She'd been on the verge of doing the same thing until she realized he didn't have a heart. She wondered how many other women had made the same mistake.

He kissed her. He simply took her mouth captive. She tried to resist, but she couldn't move. She could barely summon the will to resist. His lips were warm, soft, and very persuasive. It was inconceivable to her that he could make her a willing participant in this *lesson*, and yet she felt her anger fading, the rigidity leaving her muscles. Any moment now, she'd start kissing him back.

She jerked her head to one side, breaking their kiss. "Stop," she said.

When he ignored her plea, she tried to bring her hands up to scratch his face. Anticipating her intent, he grabbed her wrists, and pinned them to her sides. "You wouldn't want to ruin my face. Think of all the women who'd be disappointed."

"I'd be thrilled," but she wouldn't. He had a wonderfully handsome face. She would have enjoyed kissing him if he'd wanted to kiss her for who she was. Knowing he was teaching her a lesson took all the pleasure out of it. She struggled to break his hold on her, but it was useless. His strength made a mockery of all her attempts.

So did his kisses.

And his closeness.

She felt the heat of desire coiling sinuously within her, lazily and languidly, like the smoke from burning incense. It flowed through her body, sapping her physical strength, her willpower, her desire to resist. She felt scorched by the pressure of his body against hers. Her breasts had become so tender the material of her dress felt rough against her nipples. But it was his knee, thrust between her legs, that most affected her. Never had her body felt like it did now.

She felt so alive, she thought she would jump out of her skin.

She'd never thought of herself as a sensual person. She'd been taught duty and decorum all her life. Love and sensuality were for the common people. In less than five minutes, Luke Attmore had been able to destroy both illusions. She didn't care that she had promised to marry another man. She could think only of the man who held her in his embrace, who ignited her body with his kisses.

She reveled in Luke's touch, in the feel of him pressed hard against her, in the wild sensations that whirled through her body as his lips scorched trails of liquid heat over her mouth, throat, shoulders. Nothing mattered any longer except—

With paralyzing suddenness, Luke released her and stepped back. She stared at him, unable to comprehend why she should feel as she did—lost, abandoned, and terribly hurt.

"I never intended to hurt you," Luke said, his voice

rough, his hands balled into fists at his sides. "I just wanted to show you everything is different now, that you can't go on living like you always have, that you can't depend on the same people and institutions to protect you."

He sounded as if he was giving a prepared speech. He looked as stiff and wooden as he had been hot and aggressive only seconds before.

"We'll start back immediately."

He walked away so quickly, Valeria expected to see him break into a run.

For a few moments she couldn't move. The shock that held her immobile was quickly succeeded by mortification. If Luke hadn't stopped at that very moment, she would have turned his lesson into something quite different. She even *wanted* to give in to him. She couldn't imagine how such a thing could have happened, how she, Valeria Badenberg, a princess of the royal blood, would willingly have allowed herself to be ravished *on the ground* like a common slut.

Her entire body shivered with revulsion. At least she hoped it was revulsion. She feared it was from the shock of plummeting from the heights of passion to the depths of deprivation. No, she didn't feel repulsed. She felt deprived. Embarrassed. Mortified. Humiliated. She didn't know how she could face Luke after this. His behavior was dishonorable, but hers had been no better. Regardless of the words she'd uttered, despite her struggles to escape from him, deep down she had wanted him to make love to her.

Make love!

That was an insane thought. Love didn't come into it on either side. This longing was nothing but pure lust. She'd been taught her entire life to expect that kind of reaction from men, but she'd never expected to experience it herself. She would bear her husband heirs because it was her duty, but nothing about Luke's embrace felt like a duty. She'd felt excited. The anticipation of what was to come had heated her blood to a boil. She had lusted as much as Luke.

Valeria was anxious to return to the wagons. No one there would know what had passed between her and Luke, what she'd thought and felt. The presence of others would help return her disordered thoughts to normal, shield her from the assault of these new confusing emotions. But she couldn't hide from the knowledge that something of enormous importance had taken place. She'd had an experience that made her a different person. No, that wasn't it. It was an experience that exposed a part of the person who'd existed inside her all these years without her knowledge.

Her future was unknown, unfamiliar, uncontrolled. She'd been depending on Luke to help her learn how to live in this dangerous country. Now she'd learned that she herself was part of the danger she faced.

That was the most frightening thought of all.

"You have to be careful going down," Luke warned. "It's easier for the horses to climb on loose rock than to descend."

He was relieved they had to travel single file. That way he didn't have to look directly at Valeria, to pretend nothing of any consequence had happened.

"My horse is surefooted," she replied.

She'd been snapping at him since they'd left the clearing. He couldn't blame her. He might have taught her a valuable lesson, but he had done it at the expense of her pride, and he wasn't unfeeling enough to think pride unimportant. Pride in his work, in his success, was all he had. He'd stopped wanting more. He had a terrible feeling Valeria had started him hoping again.

That would be the worst mistake of his life.

"He's an outstanding horse. So are the rest of your horses. I can see why you wanted to bring them with you." He kept talking, trying not to think, but it didn't work.

He couldn't forget one moment of what he'd done on that mountain top, what he'd made happen in his arrogant assumption that he knew what he was doing and had both himself and Valeria under control. He'd started out to frighten her a little, to make her aware she had to be more careful, less trusting, that she couldn't just head off on a long ride with a man she didn't know because she was bored. But his laudable intention of teaching her a lesson had turned into something quite different.

"I have more horses," she said. "Otto insisted I leave the mares in New Orleans. Several were about to drop their foals."

"How many did you bring?"

"Seventeen."

That was a perfect example of what he meant. No sensible woman would travel halfway around the world, burdened not only with incredible quantities of furniture and china, but with in-foal mares. And this was a woman he wanted to make love to.

Okay, it wasn't love. He'd never been in love. He couldn't love. He didn't want to love. But the emotions between him and Valeria were unlike anything he'd experienced with the dozens of women he'd known. He felt confused and he was never confused about anything. His feelings were always straightforward and uncomplicated.

Not this time.

"I hope you don't intend to hire me to bring the rest

of your belongings to Rudolf's ranch after you're married."

"I don't know what I'll do, but you can be certain I won't hire you to do it."

Good. He would have refused anyway, if she'd asked. "I don't know anything about Rudolf's house, but I doubt most of it will be suitable."

That was part of the problem. *He felt sorry for her.* She might be a silly, vain woman, but she was what the men around her had made her. Then they'd thrust her into a world she knew nothing about and left her to survive on her own. Isabelle and Drew could take care of themselves under just about any circumstances, but Jake would never have let them head off across several thousand miles alone. If he couldn't go himself, he'd have made sure at least two of the orphans went along.

Yet Valeria had been practically abandoned by an uncle who knew somebody was trying to kill her. For all he knew, her future husband was no better. Luke might not have any real feeling for his adopted brothers, but he'd never ignore somebody trying to kill them. He had a little honor left.

Maybe that was why he felt protective toward Valeria.

"How much longer will it be before we reach Rudolf's ranch?" she asked.

"At least two weeks."

"Are you sure it won't be sooner?"

"It'll probably take longer."

That worried him more than it apparently worried Valeria. He'd started kissing her to prove a point. He'd kept kissing her because he wanted to. And not just because he wanted to make love to her. Because he wanted her *to want* to make love to him.

This wasn't just sex. That's what scared Luke.

A long time ago he'd decided he wasn't worth much.

His parents might still have been a little bit in love when they conceived Chet. But by the time they got around to Luke, they'd felt nothing but loathing and disgust for each other. It had spilled into their relationships with him. Not even Jake and Isabelle had been able to dissolve the feeling of worthlessness that had hardened and crystallized around his heart before he was able to think well enough to know what was happening.

That was why he'd become a professional gunman. It was the perfect profession for a man who felt nothing, wanted nothing, expected nothing. He was accustomed to living without love. He'd cut himself off from feelings.

Yet a tiny flicker of hope remained alive. Against all reason, Valeria's presence had caused that flicker to grow stronger. Valeria, of all people. She was as empty as he, a pretty, decorative vessel representing an outmoded way of life. She saw the rest of the world only as it related to her. Such a woman could never truly love anyone, certainly not anyone like Luke. They were too much alike, each taking, using, and casting aside.

"Do you plan to bring your horses to the ranch?" Luke asked. He had to do something to keep from thinking.

"Yes. I was hoping to breed them for sale."

"They're too light-boned for ranch work. You need something like my horse."

"I realize that. I'm planning to look around for suitable stock to mate with my animals. Maybe I'll start a new breed."

"Don't you mean *your husband* will start a new breed?"

"Rudolf has no interest in horses. I've planned the matings of every horse I brought with me."

Luke wasn't sure he believed that. Other than wanting to ride, she hadn't shown an overwhelming interest in her horses. He supposed it was different when you were a princess. You didn't muck out stalls, shoes horses, deliver foals, make poultices. Servants did all that. All the more reason for him to snuff out that foolish flicker of feeling as quickly as possible.

He'd always been a sensible man, able to think and act rationally in any situation. But he had begun to worry that he couldn't control himself when it came to Valeria. He ought to make sure he wasn't around her any more than necessary. If he wasn't careful, he would do something very stupid.

Worse, the drivers would know he'd done something stupid, and he couldn't stand that. He had to maintain the upper hand. He couldn't be vulnerable. That would threaten his position, and he couldn't allow anything to do that, especially not Valeria. He shuddered at the thought of people's reaction to the news that flint-hearted Luke Attmore had fallen in love with a princess. Men would laugh over their whiskey in fifteen states and territories. They'd trade versions at every bar and saloon in the West. They'd stop each other on trails to exchange the news for extra laughs.

No, he had to stay away from Valeria, and he had to start tonight.

Valeria was thoroughly irritated. She'd spent half the night awake, thinking about what had happened between her and Luke on that mountain. It hadn't taken long to stop blaming everything on Luke. He'd chosen a very crude method to illustrate the dangers of her new world, but it was her feelings about the kiss that kept her awake.

Something beyond good looks and physical attraction, though they were dangerous enough, fascinated her about Luke Attmore, and she had to find out why. She had gotten up early, had her breakfast before Otto and Hans had emerged from their tents, and supervised the saddling of one of her horses. She meant to ride with Luke today. She intended to keep riding with him until she figured out what it was about him that appealed to her so strongly.

"Luke rode out an hour ago," Zeke had just told her. "He's switching jobs with Hawk."

"What job?" she'd asked.

"Hawk usually rides ahead, checking out the trail, looking for a good spot to camp, keeping a lookout for danger."

"But Luke promised not to leave my side."

"He figures I'm just as good," Zeke had said.

He might be, but he wasn't Luke, and that was all that mattered.

"You sure you don't want to ride in the coach?" Zeke asked about every fifteen minutes. He refused to ride next to her. Every time she tried to come abreast with him, he spurred his horse forward. She'd accepted that she'd have to talk to his back if she wanted to talk to him at all. They were riding in the middle of the caravan, her coach in front of them. He rode about a dozen feet off to the side to avoid the dust kicked up by the mules' hooves. It had rained a little during the night, but not enough to keep the dust down.

"I'm quite sure," Valeria replied. "If I'm going to die of the heat, I don't want to do it closed up inside that coach. It's too much like a coffin."

"Nobody ever died of the heat who acted sensible."

Her clothes were too hot, but at least she had a hat with a brim wide enough to keep the sun from beating directly down on her.

"I'm trying to learn to act sensibly," she said, "but it'll take a while."

"Maybe you should have stayed where you were."

Zeke disliked her and everything she represented more

even than Luke. She'd never considered herself or her family evil, but nearly everybody in America acted as though they were criminals.

"I had no a choice," she said. "My countrymen decided they didn't want us around anymore."

"We don't want you around either."

"You can get rid of me by going back to Bonner," she snapped.

He looked around at her, his big black eyes a little wider than usual. "You learning to snap?"

"If I don't, I'll get trampled."

"Your kind will get trampled anyway."

She didn't need to ask what he meant by *your kind.* She'd heard more than enough of his opinion of women, especially white women, most particularly European white women. "I intend to learn everything I can so I won't get trampled," she said. "I wanted to talk to Luke about that today."

"If you're counting on Luke to bring you up to the mark, you'll wait a long time."

"Why? He's lived here all his life. He knows the country better than anyone else."

"Even me?"

"Even you."

She had no idea what Zeke knew, but she was tired of his bullying.

"I can tell you anything he can," Zeke said.

"Will you?"

"No."

"That's why I want to talk to Luke."

"Luke doesn't like women like you."

She wondered what Zeke would say if he knew what had happened yesterday. She couldn't be certain Luke felt anything more for her than physical attraction and mild interest, but he did feel something. And if her intuition was right, that interest was behind his decision to change jobs with Hawk.

"Maybe I should talk with Hawk."

"He won't say anything. Hawk hates white women, too."

"I thought his mother was a white woman."

"He doesn't hate his mother."

"Since neither you nor Hawk will talk to me, I suppose I'll have to ask the drivers."

"Luke won't let you talk to the drivers."

"Since he's not here, he can't stop me."

"I'll stop you for him."

She didn't know any of the drivers well enough to feel comfortable asking them questions, but it angered her that Luke and Zeke thought they could stop her from talking to anybody. "I suppose there's a reason for this."

"You'll have to ask Luke."

At that moment she saw a rider top a ridge several miles ahead.

"I think I will," she said and put her horse into a gallop.

Zeke shouted and started after her, but she was riding her favorite thoroughbred today. There wasn't a horse in Arizona that could keep up with him once he reached full stride. She just hoped he didn't stumble on the rough terrain.

And she hoped the man in the distance was Luke.

Chapter Thirteen

An uneasy feeling settled in the pit of Luke's stomach when he saw a rider galloping toward him. He couldn't think of any reason for Zeke or Hawk to leave the wagons unless something had gone wrong. But he'd heard no gunfire, seen no signs that anyone had been in the area since the rain.

It didn't take long before he knew the rider was neither Hawk nor Zeke. That enormous hat indicated a woman, and no one but Valeria would be foolish enough to ride a horse at a gallop over unfamiliar ground.

He'd planned to stay away from the wagons, but he waited for her. Obviously Zeke couldn't control her. He smiled when he saw Zeke's horse falling steadily farther behind. It had been bred to work cows and couldn't match the sustained speed or stamina of a thoroughbred. He was certain Valeria knew that, too.

Luke wasn't fool enough to try to deny the pleasure that surged through him. If you didn't like something, you faced it and dealt with it. If you couldn't conquer it, you made a compromise. At this point he planned to conquer it. He liked compromise only slightly less than defeat.

He just had to make certain he didn't do anything foolish, like think there could be something between him and Valeria. There was no question in his mind that she responded to him physically, no question his response to her was just as strong. But he had promised to do a job, and that didn't—*couldn't*—include any relationship with Valeria, regardless of its nature or duration.

It bothered him that such a possibility had entered his mind. He was certain it hadn't entered Valeria's. She was probably bored, looking for some excitement. It would be nothing but a game to her. When all was said and done, she was still a princess.

And he was still a hired gun.

"Do you make a habit of racing your expensive horses over rough terrain?" Luke asked when Valeria pulled her mount to a halt before him.

She looked uncertain about her reception but was flushed with pride at having outmaneuvered Zeke. He reluctantly admitted that victory looked good on her.

"Do you make a habit of running away?" she asked.

He hadn't expected a frontal attack. But if she wanted to dispense with pretense, he'd oblige her.

"It's not good for us to be around each other. I promised to deliver you to Rudolf in the condition in which I received you."

"I'm not a package to be wrapped in brown paper and tied with string."

"You'd be a damned sight easier to deal with if you were."

Zeke's horse pounded to a stop, spraying gravel in all directions. "I tried to keep her with the wagons," he said, anger distorting his words, "but she's crazy. I'm not messing with her anymore."

"I would have stayed with you," Valeria fired back, "but you refused to talk to me. You said Hawk wouldn't talk with me either."

"He wouldn't."

"Then I could see no reason to accede to your wishes."

"You *accede* to her wishes if you want," Zeke snapped at Luke. "I'm done with her."

He turned his horse and started back. Luke knew there was no point in asking Zeke to take Valeria back with him. He wouldn't do it even if she'd been willing to go. "You know you'd be safer with the wagons."

"Of course I don't. I don't know anything about the West, as you've gone to great pains to point out."

Now they were getting to the heart of the issue. "So you're mad at me."

"I was yesterday, but I'm not today. You could have made your point some other way, but that's done. I don't mean to speak of it again."

"Then why did you come after me?"

"I want you to teach me about America, about the West," she said. "You said we'd be on the trail about two more weeks. I don't see why I should spend all that time roasting in the coach. By the time we reach Rudolf's ranch, I could know as much as a real American."

Valeria would never be able to act like a real American, not if she questioned him for the next ten years. But it was only fair that he do what he could to help her learn to survive. There was more to her than he'd assumed. If she was *really* willing to learn, she had a chance of making a decent life for herself in this country.

As long as her husband wasn't a fool.

"Okay, ask away. What do you want to know?"

"Tell me about American women," she said. "I want

to know why you think they're better than I am."

She continued to surprise him. He'd accused her of expecting to remain safe in her gilded cage for the rest of her life. But once she climbed out of her cage, she left all pretense behind and looked him straight in the eye.

He touched his heels to his mount's side, and the horse moved forward. He had a job to do. He'd have to watch, think, and talk at the same time.

"I'll begin by saying I don't know you very well," he said. "I thought I did, but I don't. I don't think you know yourself very well, either."

Valeria had brought her horse alongside his. "That's ridiculous. I—"

Their gazes locked.

"Do you want to know what I think, or do you want to argue?"

She obviously didn't like that, but she nodded. "Tell me what you think."

He almost smiled. She wasn't used to hearing things she didn't like. It must have cost her a lot to swallow her protests.

"I don't like hereditary monarchs or people with titles. I don't like people who think being born to a particular set of parents makes them better than everyone else, gives them more rights and privileges, entitles them to more wealth and happiness." He waited for her to interrupt, but she remained quiet. "I especially don't like people who think everyone else should work so they don't have to."

"I don't think that," Valeria protested. "My family worked very hard."

"Deciding what to wear, who to marry, so you could perpetuate your life of power and luxury."

"That's a pretty harsh judgment."

"I don't think much of women who've never cooked a meal, or nursed their own children."

"A woman shouldn't have to be a drudge to be admired."

"I don't consider preparing food for your family or taking care of your own children drudgery. Isabelle liked doing it, and she was raised rich."

He'd been telling himself for years that Jake and Isabelle hadn't had much influence on his thinking or his values. It startled him to realize he'd been comparing women to Isabelle all his life. He wondered how many other things he'd been doing without realizing it.

"I judged you because of your birth," Luke said. "You were a princess, and you acted like the world owed you a living. I didn't think you were capable of being anything else. Now I'm not so sure."

"Why?"

He shouldn't be spending this much time thinking about Valeria. The more he understood her, the more he wanted to think about her, which defeated his purpose in trying to stay away.

"You've never screamed, fainted, or ordered Otto to shoot me when I touched your royal body. You didn't like it at first—"

"I never liked it!"

"But you figured out I really wasn't threatening you." He turned until their gazes met. "And you do like it. It scares you to death, but you want me to do it again."

It pleased him to see her flush with embarrassment. He refused to let her hide behind her royal trappings to protect herself from facing an uncomfortable truth.

"I don't agree with you, but go on."

"You've learned to get ready in the morning without all your old rigamarole. You eat more sensibly, and you don't complain of the heat. I wish you'd wear the clothes I bought you, but I guess I've got to be thankful for every little bit of progress."

"You're generous," she said sarcastically.

"I'm never generous," he said. "I never give people the benefit of the doubt, and I always assume they'll make the worst possible choices."

They reached a low saddle between two ridges. Luke scanned the horizon. He didn't see anybody, but then he didn't expect locating possible attackers would be that easy. The people who'd attacked them two days ago had gone to a great deal of trouble to make it look like rogue Indians had staged the attack. He couldn't be sure of their purpose, but he was certain that wasn't the end of it.

"Are there any other incidents that have served to moderate your opinion of me?" Valeria asked. "I'm not asking for praise, just trying to understand the way you Americans think. I'd rather you didn't dislike me."

"You've got spunk," Luke said, "and a streak of common sense. You don't like me, and you don't like Arizona, but you know you've got to learn to get along and you know I can help. So you're willing to pull in your horns long enough to pump me for what I know."

"Do you always have to state everything in the most unflattering manner?"

"I state things as I see them."

"Then you've got a very dim view of people."

"People are selfish, narrow-minded, willing to sell their souls to get what they want."

"And what have you sold your soul for? Notice I didn't say what would you be *willing* to sell it for."

He laughed. "You keep giving as good as you get, and I might actually learn to like you."

"I'm not sure I understand you."

"And you're half right. I don't have a soul, but I didn't sell it. I never had one."

"Everybody has a soul."

"My brother does. Even Zeke and Hawk do, though Zeke tries to deny it. I don't."

"I don't believe you."

"I protected a man once because his father paid me to. The very day I quit, I killed him."

"What did he do?"

Her reaction surprised him. He'd expected shock, horror, even claims that he was a monster. Maybe she was so used to her father and uncle killing anybody who opposed them, it didn't seem important to her. After all, what was the death of a few peasants now and again?

"What makes you think he did anything?"

"You've got a strange code of honor, but it's absolutely inflexible."

If he hadn't been riding into the sun, he'd have sworn he felt a flush of embarrassment.

"I don't understand you half of the time," she said, "but I know you wouldn't kill anyone without a good reason."

"Or without being well paid."

"You didn't mention pay. You did this on your own. Why?"

He'd underestimated her. She could see around corners. He wondered if it was that kind of talent that had kept her family in power for more than five hundred years. "I killed him because he ambushed my brother."

"I thought you had nothing to do with your family."

"When I left the ranch, Chet insisted on following me, trying to protect my back, even though I was much better with a gun."

"So you repaid him by protecting him."

Luke shrugged. "I was there."

Her gaze made him uneasy. He spurred his horse forward. A dry wash cut through the desert a little way ahead. He'd have to find an easy crossing for the wagons.

The sand in these washes tended to be soft. If the wagons got stuck, it would cost them several hours to get them free.

"What happened to your brother?" she asked.

"He got married and went back to Texas. I think he has two boys. Last I heard they were expecting another child."

"Haven't you seen his family?"

"No."

"Don't you want to?"

"No."

"Why?"

He didn't like all these questions. Answering them would force him to reconsider aspects of his life he'd sealed shut years ago. It didn't go any good to keep agonizing over a decision. It was best to make it, move on, and not look back.

"I thought you wanted to learn about Arizona?"

"I do. It's not just the land and the customs that are strange to me. The people are different. Maybe if I learn to understand you, I'll understand others better."

If she believed he was anything like other men, she wasn't nearly as perceptive as he thought. "Stick with the land and the customs." he said.

She looked hurt, but she was badly mistaken if she thought wanting to learn about Arizona entitled her to poke about inside him like he was a musty closet. He didn't pretend his life was perfect, but he'd molded it to suit himself, and he wasn't about to let some dispossessed princess go rummaging about, knocking things out of kilter.

"Okay, tell me about the country where Rudolf has his ranch. You said it was completely unlike this desert."

Valeria listened to Luke's descriptions of the Mogollon Rim country with only half her mind. Knowing they were headed toward mountainous country covered with pine forests was a relief. She didn't think she could ever learn to like the desert. She had no desire to know anything about cows, but she allowed him to ramble on about how best to raise cattle. If she hadn't known better, she'd have sworn he wanted a ranch of his own.

She noticed that everything around her looked fresh and clean. It had rained the night before. The layers of dust had disappeared. The wilting tree limbs had revived, and the air smelled crisp and clean. She had never smelled the air before, only aromas *on* the air, food, perfume, the piney scent of the forest. There was nothing here to cover the scent. Nothing false.

"Tell me about the women," she asked when she thought she couldn't stand another word about branding irons and doctoring for screw worms.

"What about the women?"

"You told me they could control their own lives. How?"

"They can choose their own husbands."

No women in her country chose their own husbands. Parents arranged all marriages. "Why would they want to do that?" she asked.

"Because they don't want to be sold to the highest bidder. They want to marry someone they love."

Love was never mentioned in her country in connection with marriage. No one expected it. Maybe a man loved his mistress, or a woman her lover, but emotions were fickle, and those arrangements never endured. Marriages lasted forever. The continuation of society, even the survival of the state, depended on them.

"Do you know anybody who married for love?"

"Jake and Isabelle were always crazy about each other, though they came from different backgrounds and fought all the time."

"Do they still fight?"

"Probably. But nothing they argue over is as important as their love for each other. They always manage to find a way around any problem."

"What did they argue about?"

"Everything. How to bring us up, how to run the ranch, where to spend the money."

"And other people do this, too?" It didn't seem possible. In her country, wives did not argue with their husbands. A woman might have an allowance for clothes and personal things, but everything else was taken care of by her husband.

"My brother and his wife," Luke continued. "They each have a ranch which they run together."

"But that's just two couples."

"Not every marriage works out. If it fails, a woman can get a divorce and try again."

"But that would take an act of state."

Luke laughed. "Only in your country. Over here it only takes a judge."

"I could get a divorce from Rudolf?"

"Yes. And your cook could get a divorce. The dancer in the saloon can get a divorce. The farmer's wife, too. *Everybody* can get a divorce. No one has to be stuck in a loveless marriage."

"But how would a divorced woman live?"

"She could get a job, work to support herself. If she were rich, she could live off her own money."

"It really doesn't belong to the husband?"

"Not unless you give it to him. If you work, you can keep your money. If you inherit a fortune, you can keep that, too."

"Suppose he wants it."

"You can refuse to give it to him."

Valeria wasn't sure just how much more she could

absorb in one day. It was obvious there was a great deal about this country her uncle hadn't told her. She hadn't read the marriage contract—women in her country weren't supposed to be interested in such things—but she was certain her money passed directly from her uncle's control into Rudolf's. She didn't even know how much money she had, where it came from, whether it was in land or cash. The last thing she could imagine would be refusing to give Rudolf access to it. He wouldn't even ask.

"Not everything's easy," Luke said. "American women have a lot more freedom, but they have to work hard for it."

She couldn't imagine a woman who wouldn't be willing to work for the right to control her life. Immediately she realized she was wrong. She knew many women who would be willing give up any rights they might have for the comfort of knowing they would enjoy luxury and privilege for the rest of their lives. She didn't have a clear idea of what Luke meant when he said American women had to work for their freedom. It was entirely possible she wouldn't be able to do what was required, wouldn't be able to match these seemingly remarkable women.

"Tell me more about these freedoms."

Luke might say he had spent most of his life as a lonely gunfighter, but from all he said, Valeria decided he knew half the women in the West. He came up with dozens of examples. He probably knew more women than she did.

She didn't want to ask how she compared. She knew what he thought. Once a useless princess, always useless, whether she remained a princess or not. But she was not useless. She was determined to be just as good as these American women.

She figured life in America was pretty much what you

made of it. There were lots of freedoms and opportunities, but if you didn't work for them, you didn't get them. But while the idea of all these freedoms was exciting, they seemed out of reach. She didn't have any skills. She'd never had to *do* anything. She'd just had to be, and Luke had made it clear that just being wasn't enough.

"You can be almost anything you want," Luke said. "You just have to work at it."

"But how do you learn to work at it? How did Isabelle work at it? How did she start?" He didn't seem to know how to respond.

"She just did it," he said. "She wanted to help some orphans, so she talked the authorities into letting her find homes for us. When that didn't work out, she talked Jake into taking all of us so a few of us could help him with his cattle drive. When that was over, she married him and talked him into adopting us. She said she loved us dearly, but if she had to wash, cook, and clean for eleven men, we had to help. Before she was done, every one of us could do for himself."

Valeria had spent her life talking people into doing what she wanted, so maybe she wasn't completely ill-equipped to survive on her own. As for the organization, she'd have to start paying attention to Luke. He had the whole train organized and functioning smoothly. Everything seemed to happen without his having to do anything, but she knew it wasn't that simple.

She knew one very important ingredient to success was leadership. People worked hard for Luke because they respected his ability to make them successful. It worked the same way with kings and princesses. She would start on that right away.

But she wanted to get back to this concept of a woman's marrying for love. According to Luke's examples, nearly all the really successful women were single, widowed, or divorced. That didn't appeal to her.

"You said a woman is allowed to marry a man because she loves him," Valeria said. "How does she know when she loves a man enough to want to marry him?"

She wasn't even entirely sure of the feelings involved in falling in love. In her country, adult women considered love a childish emotion. All the women who'd offered her advice had said love was a dangerous state of mind that should be avoided at all costs. "Have you ever loved anybody?" she asked Luke.

"Not the way you mean. Certainly not so I'd want to marry them."

It seemed Luke was better at explaining actions than emotions. He looked like he didn't know the answer any more than she did.

"According to Isabelle, you've got to want to be with that person," he said, "more than anybody else in the world."

"More than family?"

"More than anybody."

She wasn't sure about that. She'd never met anybody who'd made her want to leave her uncle, Hans, and Elvira.

"You've got to want to do things for them, to make them happy."

She understood that. People were always doing things to make her happy. In all honesty, she had to admit she hadn't done much of that herself.

"Isabelle says you've got to want to make them happy even if it makes you unhappy."

That was a bit too much for Valeria. She couldn't understand how it would work. When her uncle was unhappy, *everybody* was unhappy.

"Isabelle says you've got to be happier giving in to someone you love than getting your own way."

She'd spent her whole life giving in to what people wanted her to do, but she wasn't enthusiastic about it. And now it seemed that just as she was on the verge of getting all these freedoms, Rudolf would insist she give them up to make him happy.

"Jake says you've got to love your wife so much you think she's the most beautiful woman in the world, that no matter who you see, she's not as attractive to you as your wife."

That was something else hard to understand. She didn't know a single man who had any difficulty deciding if a woman he was looking at was more beautiful than his wife.

"And you've got to be faithful to her. Always. Jake says nothing destroys love faster than infidelity. Isabelle says she'd kill Jake if he even wanted to touch another woman."

Valeria decided this kind of love was an impossible dream. She'd never heard of a man being faithful to his wife. She'd been told Nature constructed men so they were incapable of limiting themselves to one woman. As long as a man publicly honored his wife, supported his household, and conducted his affairs discreetly, he was considered an ideal husband.

"What else do you have to do to be in love?"

"You have to be willing to change, to give up almost anything to make your husband happy."

"Do men change to make their wives happy?"

"Yes."

But she noticed his answer was a bit less emphatic. That didn't surprise her. Apparently even in America, women were expected to give up more than men. "Could you ever feel this way about a woman?" she asked.

Chapter Fourteen

Luke had assumed every woman knew what love was and was only waiting for the chance to be allowed to express herself. If he interpreted Valeria's questions and blank looks correctly, she didn't have any idea what it was. "No."

"Why not?"

He wasn't about to answer personal questions. Just because she didn't know the answers to things everybody else understood practically from birth that didn't mean he had to expose his inner feelings and secrets. He didn't mind being helpful, but he didn't owe her his life story.

"I just haven't."

"Don't you believe in love?"

"Yes."

"Then you've got to believe you could fall in love."

"Look, love's not for everybody. Just like being faithful to your wife isn't for everybody. Or being a banker, or liking children. Some people can do some things, others do other things. Being in love is just not something I want to do."

The statement was barely out of his mouth before he realized it was a lie. He had cut off his feelings for so long, he didn't think he could love. He didn't think anybody *ought* to love him, but he did *want* somebody to love him. He'd just been telling himself he didn't because it made not being loved easier to take.

"Could you love somebody back if they loved you?"

"No."

He didn't need the startled look on Valeria's face to know his answer had come too fast. "Not everybody's made to love."

"You've never met anybody you could love?"

"No."

That at least was an honest answer.

"Has anybody loved you?"

"I hope not. I wouldn't make a very good husband."

"Do women love only good husbands?"

"No. A lot of women, and men, love the worst possible person."

"Then it seems it would be better if their parents arranged marriages for them."

"It probably would, but that's not the way we do it. Everybody wants a chance at happiness."

"Don't you want to be happy?"

"I am happy."

"But you're not married."

"You don't have to be married to be happy."

"But I thought you said—"

"I was just talking about the people who want to get married."

He'd let himself wade too far into this murky pool. He didn't know anything about love. He was only repeating things he'd heard. He ought to be talking about horses or guns or traveling through rough country, things he understood.

He suspected men couldn't love as deeply and truly as women, that it just wasn't in them. They were always going back on their word, lying, cheating, catting around, doing all the things they swore on bended knee they'd never do.

And that was another thing. No man would ever have thought to get down on his knees to ask a woman to marry him. That was too humiliating. It was too much like begging. It was obviously something some woman had thought up and talked some weak-minded man into doing, setting a bad example for other men. Like going to church and rocking the baby.

That started him wondering if Chet went to church or rocked his own babies. He remembered when Jake and Isabelle's only child, Erin, was born. Some of the boys couldn't wait to hold her. He'd kept his distance, but he couldn't remember what Chet had done. He wondered if it was different when you had your own babies.

It hadn't been for his parents.

"I think I would like to be married," Valeria said.

"That's a good thing, since I'm escorting you to your future husband."

But he could tell from her expression Valeria hadn't been thinking of Rudolf. That didn't surprise him. There was bound to be some young man in her past who had touched her heart. A rich, beautiful, young princess would certainly have been courted by some of the most handsome men in the world.

What did surprise him, and anger him as well, was his own reaction. He could tell from his quickened pulse, his shallow breathing, that he was hoping she'd been thinking of him. He could hardly have done anything more stupid if he'd tried. He'd discovered long ago he couldn't inspire love in the heart of a good woman. He'd accepted that because he didn't know any good woman he could stand to be around for more than a few hours at a time. Yet though he told himself it was impossible, that he wouldn't like being married, that he wouldn't make a good husband, he hadn't given up hope that somewhere, somehow, he'd find a woman who could learn to love him.

That was foolish in itself, but it was the height of folly to think that Valeria could be that woman. She was a princess, for God's sake. They couldn't possibly find any common ground. She thought of him as a servant, a man hired to work for her like dozens of others. If she could learn to love—and he wasn't sure anyone in her class could—she certainly wouldn't be interested in a man who sold his gun and honor to the highest bidder.

Despite all that and the many arguments he advanced during the rest of the day, that was, nonetheless, exactly what he did hope.

"Did you enjoy your ride?" Otto asked Valeria.

He sounded out of sorts. Valeria was glad she hadn't been closed up in the carriage with him all day. "Very much."

"Are you sure you didn't get too hot?" Hans asked.

"Yes, I'm sure."

"It was very warm in the coach," Elvira volunteered.

"It was hotter than hell in that coach," Otto said. "If I had known what this country was like, I'd never have let your uncle talk me into accompanying you on this trip."

He patted his forehead with his handkerchief, but the perspiration continued to pop out on his skin like drops of rain.

"Maybe it'll rain again tonight," Valeria said. "It

makes things cooler for a little while at least."

They were seated at the table, eating a light dinner. That was part of the reason for Otto's foul mood. He was convinced he would starve before they reached Rudolf's ranch. The chef made up the menu, but Luke controlled the quantities prepared.

"I hope we reach a town soon," Otto complained. "I don't know how much longer I can exist on game."

"I find the change in diet invigorating," Hans said.

"Then why don't you help your guide bring down tomorrow's dinner?" Otto snapped. "After all, you were the one who hired him."

"I'm quite pleased with my choice."

"Pleased with a tyrant who forces us to swelter in this oven while being bounced to death over rocks all day! I was more comfortable and better fed when I was in the army."

"You only have to endure this until we reach Duke Rudolf's ranch," Hans said. "I'm sure you'll find things there more to your liking."

Valeria wished the two men would stop arguing. They had never gotten along, but their duties in Belgravia hadn't brought them together very often. Here, closed up in a coach under miserable conditions, even the most good-natured men would have been cross from time to time. It would be a relief to reach Rudolf's ranch and be able to get away from them.

But Valeria found herself feeling less and less anxious to reach her future husband's home. She had spent a lot of time thinking of what Luke had told her. The most important conclusion she'd reached was that she didn't love Rudolf and most likely never would. She realized he was domineering, austere, completely uninterested in women except to satisfy his physical needs, a man who would expect complete and unquestioning obedience.

As soon as Luke had told her American women had choices, Valeria knew she wanted a husband as different from Rudolf as night from day. Visions, hopes, and dreams had formed in endless bursts during that memorable day. She'd never known she had so many ideas that were contrary to the future she'd expected for herself. It was almost as though she had been asleep, and Luke had awakened the real Valeria.

She hadn't known herself at all.

"I think I'll go for a short walk before bed," she said.

Hans and Otto got to their feet. "I'll come with you," Hans said. "It's not safe to wander around in the dark."

"I thought your perfect guide was keeping all of us safe," Otto sneered.

"Elvira can come with me," Valeria said. "You two finish eating."

"There's nothing left," Otto moaned.

It was too dark to walk under the trees by the river, and the surrounding desert was full of thorns that would tear at her clothes. Valeria chose to circle the wagons that had been pulled up to the fire.

"Are you going to ride in the coach tomorrow?" Elvira asked.

Valeria heard the apprehension in her voice. "Why do you ask? Did Hans or Otto say something?"

"No. I worry that you won't be safe."

They passed close to a wagon where three drivers were talking quietly.

"Evening, princess," one said. The others echoed his greeting.

"Good evening," Valeria replied.

"Did you enjoy your ride?" the first man asked.

"Very much. I'm looking forward to riding again tomorrow."

"Must you ride again?" Elvira asked.

"No, but I want to. There's no need to worry about my safety. Luke can protect me."

"But he's a stranger."

Now Valeria understood. Elvira thought it improper for her mistress to be in the presence of a stranger without a chaperon.

"Things are different in this country, Elvira. We have to learn a whole new way of thinking."

"Why?" She sounded frightened.

"So we can belong here."

"I want everything to be like it always was."

Valeria opened her mouth to say she did, too, then closed it again. Part of her clung to the past because it was familiar, but another part looked forward, however nervously, to a future she could shape to fit her talents and desires. She had never thought of herself as a rebel, but she had been given a vision of freedom too precious to turn her back on. No matter what the cost, she would not go back.

Valeria jerked the hem of her dress loose from some kind of thorny plant—there seemed to be an endless number of them—and exchanged greetings with another driver. She stopped in her tracks and turned to face Elvira. "If you could marry any man you wanted, what would you do?"

"I've never thought of marriage," Elvira exclaimed. "I hope to serve you my whole life."

"But suppose you didn't have to serve me. Suppose you could choose your husband, marry, have children, manage your own household."

Valeria had clearly gone further than Elvira could follow.

"Is that what you talked about with Mr. Attmore?" she asked.

"That and a great many other things. He says that in

America women don't have to marry if they don't want to. They can earn their own living, keep their money, divorce their husbands if they no longer want to be married to them."

"Please, can't we go back home?" Elvira pleaded. "I don't like it here. It's strange and frightening. Just like Mr. Attmore."

"Luke's not frightening."

"He scares me so badly I can hardly breathe. And those other men!"

Valeria knew she referred to Hawk and Zeke.

"I was uneasy at first," Valeria said. "I hope it's not this hot and thorny in the rest of America, but I find it exciting."

Valeria saw Luke now, standing just outside the light, talking to his brothers. She guessed they were talking about the next day's plans. She wanted to ask him to share them with her, but she could tell from the glances cast her way that though many men had accepted the new status of women in America, Luke's brothers preferred that women keep their distance.

"But you will marry Duke Rudolf," Elvira said. "Once he has your fortune, he will take you back to Europe and we can live in a palace like always."

The notion of Rudolf getting her money set Valeria's teeth on edge. She found herself on the verge of declaring that no one would control her fortune but herself. She paused, wondering how such a change could have come about so quickly. All her life she'd accepted that her fortune would go to her husband. "Maybe I won't marry Rudolf," Valeria said.

"What!"

"I said I might decide not to marry Rudolf."

"What would you do?"

"I don't know. Maybe buy my own ranch and breed horses."

Her own words surprised her, but no sooner had she uttered them than she knew that was something she wanted to do. She didn't know *everything* she wanted. She hadn't had time to think, but Luke's words had given rise to a tremendous feeling of excitement. She felt as though she were a boiling pot that threatened to blow its lid any moment. She looked forward to the explosion. She was certain that with that eruption the real Valeria would finally emerge.

"But you have to marry Duke Rudolf," Elvira said. "The marriage contracts are signed."

Valeria felt hope plummet. She'd forgotten about the contracts. A sudden feeling of claustrophobia assailed her. A breathlessness, a quickened pulse, a queasy feeling in her stomach.

She had begun the journey perfectly content with her future marriage. Now, in the space of a few days, she looked upon this marriage as something like a death sentence.

How could her feelings have changed so drastically?

She had no definite plans for her future, only a hazy idea of what freedom of choice would mean. Only an idea that she wanted breeding horses to be part of her future, that being in love sounded wonderful, that she could depend on Luke to guide her through the confusion of learning how to make the most of these freedoms.

She would ask Luke. Surely a country that allowed a woman to divorce her husband wouldn't honor such contracts. He would help her. He wouldn't let—

It hit her like a double whiff of smelling salts. Luke was the reason she didn't want to marry Rudolf! Did that mean she loved him?

No, she couldn't love a man that harsh. And angry. He

gave the appearance of being calm and in control. He probably was in external matters, but inside, he was very angry about something.

"I'll worry about the contracts some other time," Valeria said. "It's time to go to bed."

"Are you're going to ride with Luke tomorrow?"

"Yes."

She had a lot of questions that needed answering, and Luke was the only one who could answer them. That in itself was probably a sign of something very important, but it didn't dismay her any longer. From this point on, everything in her life was going to be new and important. On the whole, she liked that idea very much.

"You going to scout again tomorrow?" Zeke asked Luke.

"I haven't decided. Why?"

Luke had watched Valeria out of the corner of his eye. He hadn't seen her for several minutes now, so he assumed she had gone to bed. He was glad for the cover of night. He hoped the dark hid the fact that his gaze had strayed to the women more than to either of his brothers.

"I think you ought to stay with the wagons," Zeke said. "We can protect that woman better."

"Who said she's going to ride again tomorrow?"

"I could see it in her eyes."

"She doesn't like being closed up in that coach," Hawk said.

"Do either of you want to scout ahead?" Luke asked.

"I don't care what I do," Hawk said.

"Me, neither," Zeke said, "but I think you ought to stay away from that woman. She's trouble."

"What do you propose I do, lock her in the coach?"

"No, but if she's got to ride, she can ride with me."

"We tried that today."

"Let Hawk give it a try," Zeke suggested.

Hawk's grunt implied that he didn't think much of the idea.

"I'd rather do it myself than have her hanging on your neck," Zeke said.

"She's not hanging on my neck. But even if she were, what is it you're afraid she'll do?"

"If she didn't do any more than take your mind off your work, she'd be dangerous."

"And what else do you think she might be able to do?"

"Seems to me you'd know the answer a whole lot better than Hawk and me. You're the one who's spent the last two days in her company."

"I've spent weeks in the company of females at one time or another, and I've always managed to keep my mind on my work."

"This one's different."

Luke couldn't deny it, and it had nothing to do with her being a princess. In fact, being a princess was just about the biggest strike against her. There were more drawbacks, all of them substantial, but they didn't seem to make any difference.

"She's richer and more beautiful," Luke said. "She's also a lot more trouble."

"That's not what I mean," Zeke said.

"Then spit it out. I've never known you to be coy about saying what you felt."

"Zeke thinks you're sweet on her," Hawk said. "Me, too."

"You're sweet on her, too?" Luke said, deliberately misunderstanding Hawk. "I can't wait to see her reaction when I tell her."

"Anybody ever tell you that you can be a real bastard sometimes?" Zeke said.

"A time or two," Luke said, "but it never stopped anyone from wanting the protection of my gun."

"Well, Hawk and I don't need your protection. We're just trying to look out for you."

"I don't need anybody looking out for me, especially not a half-breed and an ex-slave."

Zeke's fist caught him under the chin and sent him flying through the air. It hurt like hell when he landed on the rocky ground.

Luke sat up and rubbed his chin. His jaw felt like it ought to be broken, but it still worked. "I guess I deserved that."

"If I gave you what you deserved, you'd be dead," Zeke growled. He stood over Luke, ready to knock him down again if he attempted to get up.

"Okay, we've established that I'm a bastard. What do you want me to do, start saying my prayers and going to church on Sunday?"

"It wouldn't be a bad beginning," Zeke said. "You wouldn't mean a word of it, but anything that rubs off on you has got to be better than all that hate rotting away your insides."

Luke stood.

"I don't hate anybody or anything," Luke said wearily. "It's too much trouble."

"The way I see it, you hate just about everybody, yourself most of all."

Luke wasn't about to argue with Zeke. He could think what he wanted. It wouldn't change anything. "You're not worried I'm going soft on Valeria," Luke said. "What's really bothering you?"

"You're a stubborn son of a bitch," Zeke said.

"At least you got the parentage part right."

"That's exactly what I mean."

"What?" Luke was tired of this discussion. He needed some rest. Tomorrow wouldn't be any easier than today, especially if Valeria insisted on riding with him.

"You hate your parents."

"Hell, yes, I hate them." His voice had risen to a near shout. He brought it back down again. "Even Chet cusses when anybody mentions them. That's old news."

"Old news doing more damage each day."

"Okay, have it your way. Now if you've got nothing else to say, it's time—"

"I promised your brother I'd keep an eye on you," Hawk said.

"Me, too," Zeke said.

That surprised Luke. And it made him angry. Years ago he'd put up with Chet following him about, but he'd be damned if he'd put up with Zeke and Hawk doing it. "Anybody else in on this conspiracy?"

"Isabelle's worried about you. She says it's time you found a nice girl and stopped trying to get yourself killed."

Next thing he knew, they'd have the entire clan after him. He wouldn't put it past them to bring the kids, just to make him really feel like a heel.

"Let's get this straight once and for all," Luke said. "I'm not trying to get myself killed."

"Then why do you keep accepting the most dangerous jobs?"

"Because they pay the most money. Besides, if I am trying to get myself killed, it's my own damned business."

"There's a bunch of people back in Texas who think otherwise."

"I can't help what other people think. I've done my best to make them forget me."

"It beats the hell out of me why we can't," Zeke said. "I blame it on Isabelle."

Luke decided that if Zeke mentioned Isabelle one more

time, he was going to hit him. "I'm not going nuts over Valeria and neglecting my job. She's got a lot of questions about living in this country. I answer the ones I can."

"She'll soon have a husband," Zeke said. "Let him answer them for her."

Luke couldn't argue with that logic, but he didn't trust Rudolf to tell his future wife she didn't have to marry him if she didn't want to, didn't have to turn over her fortune to him, didn't have to obey his every command regardless of how stupid or selfish. Even an honorable man would have difficulty telling a future wife of all the advantages she could keep for herself by not marrying him, especially a wife who'd make him a wealthy man. "I imagine there are a few things the duke might want to keep to himself."

"Maybe, but that's none of your business."

"And what I do is none of your business," Luke said. "Now let's not argue about it anymore."

Luke turned and walked toward the river before Zeke or Hawk could reply. He wasn't in the mood for a walk in the moonlight, but Zeke had stretched his patience to the limit. He had to get away before he did something he'd regret. He'd give them ten or fifteen minutes to get to bed, then he'd go back.

He welcomed the dark under the trees. He always felt better alone and in the dark. It was the only time he could be himself. He used to be sure what that was. Then Valeria came along and everything got all mixed up. Despite the fact that she came to him with her questions, it was folly to think she could possibly be interested in him. She depended on him to help widen her horizons, to tell her of her possibilities in America. It was only natural that she should continue to turn to him.

Until she reached her future husband's ranch.

Then she'd turn to him, and Luke would be right back where he was before the trip started. Well, not exactly. He would have let down a barrier, allowed himself to hope, and he would probably become more bitter and angry when that hope died, just as he'd known from the very beginning it would.

If a guy's parents couldn't love him, he had to be unlovable. A perpetual outcast. But Luke didn't like being an outcast. He didn't like carrying this hate for himself all balled up inside. He didn't need Zeke to tell him it was eating away at him. He'd known it for years. That was why he had hoped to find someone who *could* love him, who *could* help him stop hating.

Jake and Isabelle had tried, but that ball of self-loathing was so big it got in the way of everything they tried. It even came between him and Chet. He knew Chet loved him, and he came as close to loving Chet as he could to loving anybody, but it wasn't enough to dissolve the ball of bitter hate, to break the tension that kept him perpetually on edge.

He'd left Jake and Isabelle's ranch because he knew he wouldn't find peace there. During those first years he'd moved from one place to another, hopeful he would find it. But the years had gone by until hope faded to a faint ember. The anger and bitterness made him strike out at people trying to help him, but he couldn't stop himself.

Nor had he been able to stop himself from feeling that somehow Valeria could provide the missing pieces. Advice from his friends hadn't helped. He couldn't stay away from her. Even now he couldn't stop thinking about her. He could see the ebony hair falling on her shoulders, her dark-brown eyes watching him closely. He still wondered which of her ancestors had bequeathed her that exotic look, an almost Mediterranean sultriness. He could smell the heavy perfume she always wore, the—

Gunfire shattered the silence of the night.

Chapter Fifteen

Luke knew immediately this was no fake attack. Though the attackers were again dressed up as Indians, this was no lightning horseback raid. These men had crept up to the camp on foot under cover of night and taken up defensive positions. They meant to stay until they achieved their objective.

Luke was certain that objective was Valeria's death.

Though he berated himself for letting his preoccupation with Valeria drive him into the dark along the river, he knew it would prove a considerable advantage. These men hadn't thought to secure protection from a rear or flank attack. As long as his ammunition held out, he could catch them in a crossfire.

His first gunshot startled the gunmen, but when they didn't scatter and run, Luke knew he faced a group of hardened professionals. He would have given anything to have had his rifle with him. He could have picked them off with deadly accuracy. Driving off a half dozen determined killers with handguns wouldn't be easy.

Luke dropped to the ground and crawled forward on his hands and knees. He had to keep very low. He was in almost as much danger from the bullets coming from the circle of wagons as he was from those being fired by the gunmen. At the same time he had to be careful his bullets didn't hit one of his men.

Or Valeria.

He kept moving, using any cover he could find from cactus to sagebrush to grass. He hit one gunman but not seriously. He heard the man cussing vigorously. He shot a man hiding behind a cactus. The man went down with a loud groan.

A bullet hit the ground in front of Luke, throwing dust into his eyes and blinding him. He rolled to the side and blinked rapidly to cleanse his eyes. His vision cleared just in time to see a man coming toward him through a patch of tall grass, crouched low to avoid being seen. Luke fired off two quick shots.

The man sank out of sight. Luke saw no signs of movement.

That broke the attack. The men retreated through the sparse cover, their withdrawal hastened by the barrage of gunfire from the wagons.

"Hold your fire," Luke shouted. "I'm coming in."

Zeke met him at the wagons. "It's a damned good thing that woman's got you tied in knots," he said. "They were settled in to stay."

"Where is Valeria?" Luke asked, not bothering to argue with Zeke's assessment.

"In her tent, I reckon. Nobody's had a chance to check on her."

Luke sensed something was wrong before he reached the tent. Sounds of a struggle could be heard from several feet away. He burst inside to find Hans and Otto struggling with each other, and Valeria and Elvira smeared with blood, huddled in a corner. He crossed quickly to Valeria and knelt down.

"Are you hurt? Did a bullet hit you?'

"He tried to kill me," she said, looking toward the battling men. "He took out a pistol and pointed it directly at me."

"Where did he hit you?"

"He's killing Hans!" Valeria screamed.

Luke turned to find Otto stabbing the fallen Hans. Luke pulled his gun and fired twice. The impact of the bullets knocked Otto away from Han's body.

"I'm all right," Valeria said. "Please help Hans. Otto would have killed me if Hans hadn't stopped him."

Luke was reluctant to leave Valeria until he could be sure her wound wasn't serious, but she was pushing him too hard toward Hans to be seriously wounded. He moved to the wounded man's side. A cursory glance told him Otto was dead.

Zeke burst into the tent. "What's going on?"

"Otto tried to kill Valeria," Luke said without looking up from Hans's body. "Hans stopped him."

A single glance told Luke that Otto's knife had inflicted a mortal wound. Hans's face was contorted with pain, his face drained of color. Luke was certain his lungs were filling with blood. He had only minutes to live.

Valeria crawled to Han's side. She smoothed his brow with her hand. Hans's eyelids fluttered, then opened.

"Why did you do it?" Valeria asked, her words barely understandable through the tears.

"You're my princess," Hans said. "I'd give my life for you." He frowned. "You're hurt."

"I'm fine," Valeria said. "You kept him from killing me."

"Why didn't you tell me?" Luke asked, angry over the death of a man whose integrity and courage he admired.

"I only suspected," Hans managed to say. "How could I tell anyone her own uncle wanted her dead so he could claim her inheritance?"

Valeria's face registered shock, disbelief.

"But her money goes to her husband."

"If she dies before the marriage, it goes to her uncle," Hans said.

"What does he want the money for?" Luke asked.

"To help win back the throne of Belgravia."

Luke cursed vigorously. "He'd kill his own niece for a throne?"

"One of our kings killed his own son," Hans managed to say before a cough shook his body.

Luke knew he wouldn't last much longer.

"You should have come to me," he said.

A faint smile curved Hans's lips. "My family has always protected the princess of Belgravia."

"But you're a soft little bureaucrat," Luke said, too angry to be polite. "You're not fit to fight."

"I saved the princess," Hans said. His eyelids began to sink.

"But it's cost you your life."

"The princess is all that matters," Hans said. "That and my family's honor. I have not disgraced them. Now she's your responsibility. You must promise to keep her safe. I wasn't good enough. I should have been stronger."

"You were strong enough," Luke said softly. "No one could have done better."

His expression relaxed. He seemed relieved of a great worry. "You'll guard her with your life?"

"Yes."

"Promise?"

"On my honor."

Hans smiled. "Then I know she'll be safe."

His eyelids closed, his body shuddered, and then he lay still.

Luke's renewed and invigorated cursing broke the silence. Then Valeria started to weep. Luke put his arm around her and drew her close. He wanted to shout and curse at the death of this little man who'd had more honor and courage than the whole damned house of Badenberg. He wanted to console Valeria as well. She had lost a beloved friend. And her uncle, her only relative in the world as far as Luke knew, had ordered her killed for her money. Luke's parents were rotten, but they hadn't sunk that low.

"Why didn't he tell me?" Valeria sobbed.

"Because none of us would have believed him," Luke said. "Otto was paying very generously for your protection. The worst that could be said of him was that he was a snob and a glutton." Luke paused. "He was probably supposed to kill you under cover of the attacks and blame it on Indians. Only someone forgot to tell your uncle the Indians in this area were sent to Florida years ago."

"I can't believe Uncle Matthais would do this," Victoria sobbed. "Hans must have been wrong. Uncle Matthais didn't want me to leave Belgravia, but when it became clear we all had to leave, we had long discussions about what to do to make sure I was safe."

Luke figured her uncle had probably wanted to keep her in Belgravia so he could poison her or have her die from some mysterious wasting disease. When she had to leave, he entered into discussions for her safety so he would better know how to arrange her death. Clever and ruthless tactics.

"What do you want done with these bodies?" Zeke asked.

"You can throw Otto into the desert," Luke snapped.

"Let the coyotes tear him to pieces. Put Hans in his tent. I'll see to his burial."

"We've got another casualty," Zeke said.

"Who?" Luke asked.

"One of the cook's helpers. Shot right through the brisket."

Valeria cried harder.

"Anything else?" Luke asked.

"Nothing important. Your coming up from behind did the trick. One of the attackers is dead."

"I know," Luke said. "Now get these bodies out of here."

For the first time since Luke had known him, Hans didn't look nervous or jumpy. He looked at peace, as though having done his job, he could rest at last. Despite his own cynicism, Luke envied him that death, the feeling that his life had been worthwhile, that he'd given it in a cause he believed in with all his being.

Luke reined in his thoughts. He'd never allowed himself to be swayed by sentiment. This was no time to start.

"I want him buried in Belgravia," Valeria said.

It was on Luke's tongue to say that was impossible, but the words died unsaid. Hans deserved to be buried with honor, not left in a grave that would soon be swallowed by the desert. "We'll have to bury him here, but as soon as I can, I'll send his body back to Belgravia. Does he have a wife or children?"

"No, he always said my family was his family." She started to cry all over again.

"He was a brave man," Luke said. "A bigger man than I gave him credit for."

A moan from the corner reminded him of Elvira. Apparently she'd fainted. She couldn't be of any use to Valeria if she fainted every time there was a crisis. Then he remembered the blood on Valeria's clothes. If it didn't belong to Elvira, it must belong to Valeria. "Where did he shoot you?" he asked.

"It's nothing," Valeria said.

"It needs taking care of. It could become infected."

"He just grazed my arm."

Luke saw the small hole in Valeria's sleeve. He pushed the sleeve up on her shoulder. The bullet had gone through the fleshy part of Valeria's arm. It wasn't a bad injury and wouldn't disable her, but it would hurt and take some time to heal. He waited until two of the drivers had removed Hans's body.

"Are you recovered now?" he asked Elvira. She seemed on the verge of fainting again. "Can you sit with Valeria till I get back?"

She nodded, but Luke had the feeling it would be the other way around. He met Hawk when he left the tent.

"Get rid of Otto and the man I killed. I don't care where."

"You don't want the other one buried?" Hawk asked.

"Yes, but I've promised Valeria I'll send his body back to Belgravia. Bury him where animals won't get to him and mark the grave so you can find it again."

"Me!"

"Yes. As soon as you get these wagons to the ranch, have them build a coffin. Then come back, get the body, and ship it to Belgravia."

Unlike Zeke, Hawk's expression rarely changed. Luke could hardly ever tell what he was thinking. "What?" Luke said, impatiently, when Hawk just stood there.

"Zeke was right."

"I don't know what Zeke is right about, but Valeria wants Hans buried with his family. Since he lost his life defending her, that doesn't seem too much to ask."

"You bury him with honor?" Hawk said.

"As much as I can get."

"That's good. I liked him."

Luke had admired him. He hadn't known how much until too late.

"I'm going for my saddlebags. Otto shot Valeria in the arm."

"Bad?"

"Just a flesh wound, but I'm sure she's never been hurt before."

But as Luke went to retrieve his saddlebags, he realized Valeria hadn't cried, complained, or even mentioned her wound. And she hadn't appeared the slightest bit faint.

He grabbed up his saddlebags and strode back to her tent.

She had a right to be more than shocked. She'd been shot, seen the man who'd saved her life stabbed to death, and learned her uncle wanted her dead. She should have been the one who'd fainted, not that useless maid. He still didn't approve of royalty, but if this was an example of their courage and fortitude, Luke had greatly underestimated them.

When he reentered the tent, Valeria and Elvira still sat where he'd left them. He dropped his saddlebags next to the bed. "Let me help you up," he said to Valeria.

She looked for a moment like she was still too stunned to move, but she held out her hands. He pulled her to her feet and led her over to the bed.

"The wound looks pretty clean already," he said, "but it's better to be safe." He reached inside his saddlebags to get the bottle of whiskey he kept for such occasions.

"You can't take care of the princess," Elvira protested.

"What do you suggest I do?" Luke asked without slowing his preparations. "Leave her wound to heal itself?"

"She needs a physician."

"We're in the middle of a desert, Elvira," Valeria said.

"I doubt there's a doctor within ten miles."

"More like fifty," Luke said. "And he'd do exactly what I'm about to do. Grit your teeth. This will burn."

He poured a liberal amount of the whiskey directly into the raw wound. Valeria's swift intake of breath and the stiffening of her body told him more about her pain than the fleeting expression that crossed her features. Her body remained rigid for at least ten seconds before it began to relax again. "Good girl," he said. "You do your ancestors proud."

"You despise my ancestors."

"I despise monarchy. I don't necessarily despise the monarchs."

"Isn't that a rather fine distinction?"

"Yes, but it's a valid one. I don't despise you. In fact, I admire your courage."

He didn't look up, but he could tell that caught her by surprise. Him, too. He wasn't used to praising women, even those who deserved it. He opened a tin of ointment and spread a liberal amount over the wound.

"What's that?" Elvira asked.

"An ointment," Luke replied.

"It doesn't look very good."

The salve looked like old grease.

"It'll have to serve until I can get her to a doctor," Luke said.

"You must send for one immediately," Elvira said.

"He wouldn't come for a simple flesh wound," Luke said.

"But she's a princess," Elvira said.

"Not in this country," Valeria told her maid. "I'm like everybody else. A doctor would come for you just as quickly as he'd come for me."

That appeared to be a concept beyond Elvira's understanding. Luke was surprised it wasn't beyond Valeria's as well.

"That is true, isn't it?" she asked.

"Yes. Now I have to bandage your arm. Let me know if I get it too tight."

Valeria made no protest, and he soon had the wound safely bandaged.

"Do you have anything to help Valeria sleep?" Luke asked Elvira.

"Yes."

"I don't want to be doped," Valeria said.

"Give her a mild dose," Luke said to Elvira. "I want her asleep before the wound begins to throb." He looked around the tent. It was in shambles. "And straighten up as much as you can. It'll make it easier for her to forget what happened."

"I'll never forget," Valeria said.

Luke was certain she wouldn't. "Get as much sleep as you can."

"Are those men gone?" she asked.

He'd been so preoccupied with Hans's death and Valeria's wound, he'd forgotten about the attack. "Yes, they're gone. I'll post guards to make sure they don't return. You don't have to worry. No one is going to hurt you again."

But it hadn't been the gunmen who'd shot her. It had been Otto, a trusted retainer. Her sense of betrayal must have made her feel doubly insecure. He took her by the hand and pulled her to her feet. Then he drew back the covers on her bed.

"I want you to lie down and get some sleep. You're tired and—"

"Don't treat me like an imbecile!" she snapped. "I'm not tired. I'm frightened and upset and sick to my stomach that I should have been the cause of Hans's death.

You may be used to killing people all the time—you killed two tonight and don't appear to have given it a second thought—but I'm not a paid killer. I can't even treat Otto's death as though it's of no consequence."

Luke knew what he was. He'd accepted it years ago, but Valeria's words felt like poison-tipped arrows piercing the thick protective armor he'd built around himself. He felt himself flinch.

"People have to kill to protect princesses. You ought to be damned glad I'm the one who did the killing. If Hans hadn't begged me to wait until you changed your mind, you'd be dead by now. Remember that before you make snap judgments about people. Get some sleep. Starting tomorrow, everything's going to be different."

He turned and left the tent before he could say anything more. He didn't know if he'd ever been more angry, but it was the hurt that surprised him. He hadn't realized Valeria's good opinion was so important to him. It was obvious a woman like her could never understand a man like him. He was a fool to care, a stupid fool to let it hurt.

"Don't go to sleep," he rapped out to Zeke and Hawk. "I'm going to read everything in Hans's and Otto's letter cases. Then I'll decide what to do about the princess."

"He must really have it bad," Zeke muttered as Luke entered the other tent. "I never heard him call her *the princess* before."

The canopy of stars twinkled against the deep blue of the night sky. The cool air that occasionally wafted up from under the trees by the river felt good against skin heated by Zeke's cook fire. Luke held Valeria's marriage contract in his hands. "This is the key to the whole situation," he was saying to Hawk and Zeke. "Money."

"It's always about money," Zeke said. "What did you expect?"

"According to this, if Valeria dies before her marriage, her entire inheritance reverts to her uncle."

"So what's the problem? Otto's dead and we'll deliver her to this Rudolf in a couple of weeks. Then she'll be off our hands."

"I'm not so sure about that."

Luke had spent a large part of the night in Otto's tent, going over the papers in his and Hans's carrying cases. He'd learned something about the minds of the men who were the hereditary leaders of one small European country. They would do anything to retain their power, including betraying allies, destroying friends, even sacrificing family.

"What's wrong now?" Hawk asked.

"These people care about only one thing, their power as rulers. I found papers in Otto's carrying case that prove Rudolf is planning to raise an army to reclaim his throne."

Duke Rudolf was such a man, and nothing stood between him and restoration to his ancestral throne but the money to raise an army. Valeria's dowry would provide him with that money. The minute the marriage was final he would have no reason to keep a wife who objected to his spending her fortune that way. Living in the remote country of the Mogollon Rim, Rudolf could dispose of Valeria without anyone knowing.

"That doesn't concern us," Hawk said.

"He's planning to use Valeria's dowry."

"So?"

"Suppose she doesn't want him to use her money to raise an army."

"They can fight it out like married couples."

"People like Rudolf don't *fight it out* with their wives.

They issue orders which they expect to be obeyed."

"I still don't—"

"Suppose she decides she doesn't want to marry him."

"What are you getting at?" Zeke asked.

"If she doesn't do what he wants, there's nothing to stop him from locking her up and taking her money. Or worse."

"You mean killing her."

"Who's to stop him?"

"We're supposed to deliver her to this Rudolf," Zeke said. "What happens after that is none of our concern."

That had been Luke's attitude when he took the job, but everything had changed. He hadn't expected to like the woman he had come to know since then.

And he hadn't expected Hans to die trying to keep her safe.

He wasn't a sentimental man. Death was part of his world, his work. He accepted that, rarely thought of it afterward. But Hans's death had touched him. That nervous little man had left his home, traveled to a strange country he didn't understand, all the while knowing he faced death. He'd hired Luke to protect Valeria, begged him to stay on the job after Valeria fired him, because he thought Luke was the man most capable of getting her to her future husband safely.

He had died happy knowing he'd saved Valeria.

Before that, he'd passed the torch to Luke. And whether Luke wanted it or not, despite the fact it went against his policy, he couldn't refuse it now. No dying man had ever handed off a commission to him, at least not a man he admired. He couldn't let Hans down.

"I promised Hans I'd keep her safe," Luke said. "That makes it my business."

"That's bullshit," Zeke said.

"What do you think might happen?" Hawk asked.

"I don't know, but I'm going to hang around until I find out."

"So what's different?" Zeke asked. "We take her to this Rudolf, stay for the wedding, then leave."

"Maybe."

"I don't like this *maybe*," Hawk said.

"You can't marry her," Zeke said. "She's already promised to someone else."

"I don't want to marry her."

"Okay, you're in love with her, but she's still promised to someone else."

"I'm not in love with her."

"Infatuated."

"I'm not—"

"The hell you aren't!" Zeke shouted. "I've never seen you act like this."

"Act like what?"

Luke turned to see Valeria come out of her tent and walk toward them. "What are you doing up?" Luke asked. "I wanted you to sleep."

"No one can sleep with you three arguing. Since it's about me, I thought I ought to know what you've decided."

"He thinks this Rudolf wants your money to raise an army to get back his throne," Zeke said.

"Rudolf gave up any idea of regaining his throne when he came to this country," Valeria said.

"Not according to information I found in Otto's carrying case," Luke said. "I had to look though his things," he said when Valeria looked at him as if he'd done something unpardonable. "I had to know who to notify, who to tell of any unfinished business."

"I agreed to marry him if he didn't get involved in any more wars," Valeria said.

"Your uncle had proof Rudolf is making plans to raise an army and do it with your money."

"Then why would my uncle have agreed for me to marry Rudolf?"

"He didn't plan to let that happen," Luke said, his voice softer. "He planned to keep your money for himself."

He hated to cause Valeria any more pain, but the sooner she accepted her uncle's treachery, the better.

"So what do you plan to do?" she asked.

"First, I'm going to tear up the marriage contracts." Before anyone could register an objection, Luke ripped the contracts in half and threw them on the fire.

"What the hell did you do that for?" Zeke demanded.

"Valeria is safe from her uncle at least for a few days. She's also safe from Rudolf."

"But she has nowhere to go."

"Yes, she does. The ranch is hers."

"If you thought she wasn't safe before, she's really in danger now," Zeke said. "You're taking away everything this Rudolf has."

"Harming her won't gain him anything," Luke says. "And now she won't have to marry him."

"He'll force her."

"I'll be there to see that he doesn't."

"We'll all be there," Zeke said.

"No, we won't," Luke said. "You and Hawk are going to take the wagons ahead, along with the message that I destroyed the contracts, that the ranch belongs to Valeria, and that she's not going to marry Rudolf unless she wants to."

"Who asked you to interfere in their affairs?" Zeke demanded.

"Hans made me vow to keep Valeria safe."

"That doesn't include messing about with marriage contracts."

"I think it does. Besides, I don't think Valeria wants to marry him anymore."

"Do you want to marry this duke fella?" Zeke demanded, turning to Valeria. She hesitated, looked from one man to the other.

"Forget the contracts," Luke said. "You can always marry him later once you get to know him. Do you want to marry him now regardless?"

"No." She looked relieved to have finally decided, committed herself.

Zeke turned to Luke. "You got the answer you wanted. Now what are you going to do?"

"I can protect Valeria better if it's just the two of us. We're leaving the train."

Chapter Sixteen

It was inconceivable to Valeria that she would go off alone with a man. She might not be able to find anyone to marry her after that, not even with her money. And what about her safety? If a member of her family could want to kill her for her money, wouldn't a stranger be even more likely to see her as a means of getting rich?

The answers to all those questions were straightforward and unequivocal. It was impossible for her to go into the desert alone with Luke.

Yet that was exactly what she wanted to do.

She could hardly believe she wanted to do anything so absurd, but apparently her feelings had nothing to do with logic or self-preservation. The thought of being alone with Luke caused her heart to race. No man had ever excited her the way he did. Even before he'd grabbed her, kissed her, practically possessed her with his body, he'd fascinated her. She told herself he was rough, rude, incapable of love, but she couldn't stop thinking about him. She insisted she hated him, but she couldn't stop remembering his every touch, his look, the sight of his body sitting erect and powerful in the saddle.

She told herself she was a princess betrothed to a duke, that Luke was possibly a lawless criminal, but she dreamed of Luke rather than of Rudolf. When she had questions, she thought of him. When she was in danger, she thought of him. When she thought of the future, she imagined he would be there. It seemed impossible that her world could exist without him.

"I can't go," she said. "It would be totally inappropriate."

"Is getting killed more appropriate?" Luke asked.

"That's not the question."

"What is?"

"You're supposed to take me, Elvira, and my horses to Rudolf's ranch."

But she didn't want to get to Rudolf's ranch. If anyone would know Rudolf was planning to use her money to raise an army, it would be her uncle. She vehemently opposed starting a war to regain his throne. It would only lead to another war to drive him out.

But it was more than that. The things Luke had told her about America had fired her imagination, opened up a world of possibilities she hadn't known existed. She knew marrying Rudolf would close that door just as firmly as if she had never left Belgravia. She didn't yet know what she could do, but she wanted the freedom to explore the possibilities.

The most exciting idea was that she could marry for love. She wasn't exactly sure what love was all about, but she was certain it had a lot more to do with the excitement generated by being around Luke than the tepid liking she'd had for Rudolf. She also wanted to know more about what a woman could do if she didn't want to marry anyone at all. The possibility that she could make her own decisions, control the activities that filled her days, was too exciting to be ignored.

"I'll have a better chance of getting you to Rudolf's ranch if I don't have to worry about these wagons," Luke said. "I don't know what kind of deal Otto made with the men who attacked us. They may continue to attack until you're dead. It's obvious they were trying to place the blame on renegade Indians so no one would suspect your uncle."

"Nevertheless—"

"I don't have time to argue," Luke said. "You're coming with me. Don't pack more than you can carry in your saddlebags."

When she didn't move, Luke reached out and took her by the arm.

Hawk intervened. "We talk," he said.

"No," Luke said. "I want to be out of here before daylight."

"She doesn't want to go," Zeke pointed out.

"That doesn't matter."

"I think it does," Zeke retorted.

"Me, too," Hawk said.

Luke looked ready to take them both on. Valeria didn't understand the relationships among these men, especially their combativeness, but she didn't want to be responsible for anybody else being hurt. Han's death still hung over her like a pall.

"Tell me why you think I ought to go with you," she said. "If your brothers agree with your argument, I'll go along."

Luke looked ready to fight anyway.

"You told me women in America had the right to choose their husbands," Valeria said. "If that's so, then surely I have the right to choose whether to go off with you."

"She's got you there," Zeke said.

"I've already given you my reasons," Luke said, his face still tight with anger. He might say Americans were tolerant and understanding, but he expected blind obedience, just like her uncle.

"But how do I know you won't take advantage of me?" she asked. "You've already demonstrated how vulnerable I am."

"What does she mean by that?" Zeke asked.

"You have only my word," Luke said, ignoring Zeke. "I've known a lot of women, but you won't find a single one who'll say I forced her." He suddenly flashed a shameless smile. "Though you'll find quite a few who'll complain because they wanted more."

"That's the God's honest truth," Zeke muttered. "He's as mean as a snake, but females fall all over him. I'll never understand it."

Valeria understood all too well. It should have scared her away. It only made her want him more.

"Where will we go?" she asked.

"There are several canyons between here and the rim. Two people can get lost in them. A group of wagons has a choice of only two routes. We'd be sitting ducks."

"Won't your brothers need your protection?"

"Who the hell needs him!" Zeke exploded.

"They'll probably be safer without us," Luke said. "They won't have to worry about protecting you or fighting off the people who want you dead."

"We just have to worry about the thieves who want her horses, her fancy dishes, all that silver I saw on the table, and the other stuff women are so crazy about. Somebody could make a whole lot more money by selling this junk than by killing her."

Valeria decided she was tired of being talked about like a commodity, equated with her dowry, her possessions, or Rudolf's chance to regain his throne. She was a person. She had an identity, a personality, and even though she hardly knew who she was, she was determined to make other people know that she had thoughts, opinions, and feelings.

"Don't worry about that," she said to Zeke. "If anybody attacks you, abandon the wagons, but save my horses." She took a deep breath and turned to Luke. "This may be the most foolish thing I've ever done, but I'll go with you."

Valeria knew she would die from exhaustion. And the heat. She thought of her relatively comfortable coach following at least a semblance of a trail as it ambled along the nearly flat San Pedro River valley. She thought of her comfortable bed that would be set up tonight for Elvira. She thought of the wonderful dinner the chef would serve during the cool of the evening. She thought of the comfortable companionship, and nearly cried. She couldn't remember being more miserable.

Luke had forced her to leave before dawn. He'd also made her leave nearly everything she owned behind. Including her clothes.

"You'll wear the dresses I bought," he'd said. "Your clothes would be ruined before we reach the ranch."

She wasn't worried about ruining a few gowns, but Luke refused to let her take more than those three dresses. She used to wear three outfits in the course of a day.

She'd never been forced to wear anything so unattractive. One dress was dark blue with white spots all over it. A second was excessively simple, yellow-and-white stripes. The third was a dull brown. There was no beautifully patterned material, no overskirt, no lace at the elbows, no ruffles. All three were made of thin cotton and closely resembled a chemise.

He had insisted that waiting for breakfast would make them late. He wanted to reach the cover of the oak, juniper, and manzanita woodlands before dawn. After an arduous hour's ride, they'd stopped to eat. Valeria's anticipation had been high, the experience itself demoralizing. They ate sitting on the ground, holding tin plates in their laps. The food consisted of beans, bacon, bread and coffee. It tasted awful, and the coffee was strong enough to peel the leather off her saddle. Luke had encouraged her to eat up. "We won't eat again until after dark."

Valeria decided she wouldn't have to worry about her money or her freedom. She would die before she reached Rudolf's ranch.

They climbed up one ridge only to go down the other side. They entered canyons so narrow and bounded by such steep walls, they could only get through by riding down the creek bed. She had been attacked by at least a dozen different kinds of insects whose sole purpose appeared to be to deprive her of as much blood as possible and to leave large, itching bumps as a reminder of their visit. Even the branches of trees and bushes took swipes at her as she passed.

Luke rode just ahead of her, apparently impervious to insects and ill-tempered branches. She'd remained in the saddle only by telling herself they would stop as soon as they rounded the next bend or topped the next rise. She knew she lied, but it was the only way she could keep from begging Luke to have mercy on her miserably unfit body. She made up her mind that she would die in the saddle before she uttered one word, but she was practically at the end of her endurance when he finally pulled his mount to a stop.

"I think we'll camp here for the night," he said.

It didn't matter that there was no flat ground in sight.

It didn't matter that they seemed to have left civilization at least a thousand miles behind. It didn't matter that mountain lions were probably watching her at this very moment, licking their chops in anticipation. She could get off this horse. She'd worry about how to keep from being some big cat's dinner later.

Luke dismounted and stripped the saddle from his horse. The tired animal walked to the creek, waded in, and drank. Valeria remained in the saddle.

"Do you need help getting down?"

He knew she couldn't dismount without help. What he didn't know was that her muscles were so cramped she couldn't move. She'd ridden all her life, but she'd never been in the saddle from before dawn until after dusk.

"Please."

She knew she was exhausted when she felt little more than a tremor of excitement as Luke lifted her from the saddle. She didn't know how he had the strength to lift her after such a long day, but she'd stopped being surprised at his physical strength. He wasn't overly big, but he was tall and well muscled. Apparently being a hired gunman required more than just ability with a gun.

And the willingness to bully helpless females.

"Unsaddle and water your horse while I collect wood for a fire," Luke said.

Fortunately he didn't just set her on the ground and turn away. He put her on her feet and waited.

"Are you all right?" he asked when her legs gave way under her weight.

"It'll take a minute before my muscles loosen up," she said. "I haven't been riding much lately." Not even princesses found occasion to go horseback riding during a seven-thousand-mile trip using a succession of trains and ships to cross two continents and an ocean.

"Stretch your muscles," Luke said. "I'll hold you."

Having Luke's hands around her waist, his thumbs perilously close to her breasts, awakened sensations that had nothing to do with fatigue. The memory of his kisses on the mountain top came rushing back, causing her cheeks to burn and adrenaline to course through her body. She had found the perfect antidote to fatigue—Luke's touch.

"I need to walk," she said.

"I'll hold on to you."

He put one arm around her and pulled her against his side. She stumbled along, unsure whether she stumbled due to the uneven ground, her weakened muscles, or the effects of his arm around her.

They made two circuits of the small clearing before Valeria felt able to walk on her own. Luke unsaddled her horse. She would never have managed it without losing her balance. Besides, she'd never saddled or unsaddled a horse. She expected that was something she would have to learn before morning.

"Don't fall in the creek," Luke warned when she led her horse to drink. It was a useless warning. The water occasionally formed pools, but it barely came above her ankles. The oppressive heat made it too warm to be refreshing.

After watering her horse, Valeria had nothing to do except sit down on her saddle and wait for Luke to cook dinner. This shouldn't have bothered her. She never had anything to do except wait for others to do things for her, but tonight it felt wrong.

"Can I help?" she asked. "I can get the water," she said, stung by the sardonic look Luke tossed her way. Luke handed her two pots.

"Wade out to the middle of the stream to make sure you don't get any silt."

"I haven't seen any dirt since I got to Arizona," she muttered as she took the pots and walked to the stream.

"I don't know how anything grows in this place."

"There's plenty of dirt," Luke said. "It's just the same color as the rocks."

She didn't understand that. Belgravia's soil was wonderfully black. She reached the creek and found herself facing another dilemma. She couldn't wade into the stream without getting her dress wet and water in her riding boots. Unlike Luke's boots, hers laced up. Coming to a sudden and uncharacteristic decision, she set the pots down, seated herself on a small boulder, and proceeded to take off her boots. Then holding her skirt up with one hand, she waded into the stream.

The rocks hurt her feet, but going barefoot felt wonderful. She decided to return the first pot before filling the second. Luke's look when he noticed her bare feet was a mixture of amusement and disbelief.

"Aren't you afraid of rattlesnakes?" he asked.

Leave it to Luke to ruin her fun.

"No," she said, looking about in case he'd spotted one of the disgusting reptiles. That was another thing. Belgravia was practically free of poisonous snakes.

She filled the second pot, but she couldn't enjoy wading in the water. She kept expecting a snake to slither out from under a rock and head straight for her exposed ankles. She put her boots back on.

"That's probably a good idea," Luke said without stopping his preparations for dinner. "Scorpions like to hide in empty boots. And in bedding."

"Are you trying to frighten me?"

"No."

"Well, you're doing it anyway. Why do you have so many disagreeable creatures in Arizona?"

He grinned. He didn't do it very often, but when he did, he looked devastatingly handsome. She could understand why women threw themselves at him.

"I suppose they're just trying to survive."

"Well, I'm trying to survive, too, but I don't go around biting everything within reach. And I would never think of crawling into a boot."

His crack of laughter surprised her. She couldn't tell whether he was laughing with her or at her. "What's so funny?"

"You."

That's what she'd been afraid he'd say. "I can't help it if I don't understand your country."

"It's not that. I'd just never thought of everything in Arizona biting everything else, but I guess it's true."

She felt a little better. "What are you cooking?" She still felt she ought to help, but common sense told her she'd be more of a hindrance.

"A stew made from dried beef and vegetables."

If that dish had been served at her table in Belgravia, she'd have been horrified. Right now it sounded delicious.

"Teach me how to cook," she said. "I can't let you do all the work."

There was that look again, the one that made her feel like a parasite. "I'm aware that in your eyes I'm a totally useless human being, that there is absolutely no reason for my existence, but I do exist. I'm also intelligent enough to realize everything in my life has changed and that I have to change with it."

His look didn't alter.

"I didn't understand that at first, but I don't want to be a burden on everybody around me. I want to learn to do things for myself, and the first thing I need to know is how to cook. If you get hurt, I wouldn't be able to feed you. Tomorrow you can teach me how to saddle my horse."

He continued to stare at her while he stirred his stew.

"Stop looking at me like that!" she exclaimed. "Don't you think anybody can change?"

"I didn't think you could."

"Well, I can. I have. My uncle would have had a stroke if he'd seen me wading in a stream."

"Pity he didn't. That would have solved half your problem."

She didn't like being reminded that her uncle had tried to have her killed. "What's the other half of my problem?" she asked.

"Rudolf."

"How do you mean?"

Luke stopped stirring the stew and looked up. She didn't understand how it was possible for a man to have a day's growth of beard, be dressed in dust-covered clothes, and still be so handsome her heart fluttered every time he looked up at her. Fatigue must have caused her vision to blur, her brain to create a human mirage, her heart to turn Luke into the man of her dreams.

Only she'd never had a man of her dreams. She'd always known she would marry for reasons of state, that someone else would chose her husband, that it would be her duty to be a good wife. She'd kept her mind free of fanciful images. Now she found Luke had taken up residence, and she doubted she could dislodge him.

Worse, she didn't want to.

"Rudolf is only marrying you so he can use your money to regain his throne. No telling what he'll do with you after that."

"I will be his consort," Valeria replied.

Luke looked down as he ladled some of the stew into a tin cup. "Is that what you want?"

"It's the role I've been preparing for my whole life."

His eyes bored into her as he handed her the stew. "That's not what I asked." He poured some coffee and handed it to her. It looked as black as the soil of Belgravia.

"I tore up the marriage contracts. You're free to do what you want."

She turned away from the challenge in his gaze. Was she capable of handling freedom? She'd never been allowed to make choices. Now she needed to make a great many. She didn't know where to start.

"What do you think I ought to do?"

Luke settled back to eat his own stew. "What do *you* want to do?"

"I'd like to raise my own horses."

"Where?"

It was very difficult to imagine owning a ranch, particularly since she wasn't sure what a ranch looked like or how it worked. This was all wishful thinking, so she might as well go for broke. "I'd want my own ranch."

"You already have one. The ranch Rudolf is living on is yours until you marry."

She'd forgotten that. She'd never owned anything. "Do you know what it's like living on a ranch?"

"Sure."

"Tell me about it."

She tried to listen carefully at first, but she soon got lost in the description of the various kinds of cows she could raise. It seemed that the kind of grass depended on where you had your ranch, and the kind of grass determined the kind of cows. Then there was something about heat and surviving in the wild. After that she got totally confused over the differences between a Texas ranch and one in the Arizona Rim country.

Valeria decided she really didn't want to run a ranch, not if she had to learn all that stuff. She'd have to find someone like Luke to run it for her. That idea startled her so much she interrupted him by saying, "Would you run it for me?"

His expression went blank.

"My ranch," she explained, thinking he hadn't understood her question. "I don't know any of the stuff you're talking about. Would you run it for me?"

"No."

The answer was so sharp, his expression so angry, she figured she must have insulted him somehow. "Is there something wrong about offering a gunfighter a job managing a ranch?"

He finished his stew and poured more coffee before he answered. "I like to keep moving."

She couldn't figure out why he wouldn't tell her the real reason. He seemed excruciatingly truthful about everything else.

"Well, when you decide it's time to settle down, would you consider it?"

"Men like me don't settle down."

"Why not?"

She held out her cup for more stew. It was delicious. She'd have to get used to the coffee, however.

"For the same reason men like Rudolf and your uncle can't stop fighting to keep their thrones. It's in our blood."

"You'll have to settle down when you get married."

"I'll never get married."

"Everybody gets married."

"Not me."

"Why? I know," she said when he frowned, "it's not in your blood. My uncle says even the most restless soldiers settle down after a while. You're still young. In a few years you'll—"

"I'm thirty-four. I'm as settled as I'm going to get."

"Do you think Zeke or Hawk would be willing to run my ranch?"

"Why would you want a black man or a half breed?"

She didn't understand his ambivalence toward his adopted brothers. They seemed loyal to him, but he lashed out at them every now and then, almost as though he wanted to keep them from getting too close.

Or from allowing himself to feel close to them.

"That doesn't sound like something Isabelle would have taught you."

She'd said it without thinking, but his reaction was startling.

"You don't know Isabelle," he said, his tone brutally harsh. "You don't know what she would have said. You've been closed up in a palace your whole life. You don't know anything about ordinary people."

"I know enough to know any woman who would adopt ten boys wouldn't want them making slighting comments about each other."

He'd made her angry, and she'd answered him in an angry voice, but he seemed not to notice. For a moment he appeared to have left her, to be revisiting somewhere only he could see. His expression was haunted. For the first time she saw naked wanting. Only she had no idea what he was remembering, what he wanted so badly.

Then it was gone, as quickly as it had come.

"Let's have a look at your wound," he said. "It's been worrying me all day."

Chapter Seventeen

Luke knew better than to let himself remember. It started him wanting what he knew he could never find. There was no woman alive who could love him enough, trust in him with such unwavering faith, that he could actually start to believe he was worth saving. Isabelle and Jake had tried, but no one could make him into something he wasn't. He was irritated that Valeria, the most unsuitable person in the world, should start him remembering and hoping.

He got to his feet. "Does your arm hurt?"

It surprised him that she hadn't complained of it during the day.

"All of me hurts," she said with a failed effort to smile. "I couldn't notice anything as minor as a flesh wound."

"Wounds can become infected. Roll up your sleeve. I'll take a look at it."

He didn't like what he saw. The wound itself didn't look bad, but the flesh surrounding it had turned an angry red. "Are you sure this doesn't hurt?"

"Of course it hurts, but it's not unbearable."

"I didn't ask you that."

"It hurts. There, are you satisfied?"

"No. I don't like the way it looks."

"What's wrong?"

"It looks red and raw."

"I got shot. How's it supposed to look?"

Red and raw. He didn't want to tell himself he wouldn't have been so worried if the wound had belonged to someone else. Still, while it didn't look bad, it didn't look good.

"I'll clean it again," he said.

"With whiskey?"

"It's all I've got."

"It's going to burn, isn't it?"

"Probably."

He didn't ask if she'd faint. She hadn't yet, and he was positive she'd endured more this last week than in her whole life. She looked at him, her gaze open and curious. Trusting.

"Have you ever been hurt before?"

"Bruises and scrapes."

"Gunshot wounds sometimes take a while to heal. It varies from person to person."

"How about you?"

"I heal very quickly."

"I thought you would."

"Why?"

"You like it out here. You wouldn't if you were forever trying to recover from some kind of hurt."

"I don't get hurt."

"I guess that would help."

Maybe discomfort made her sharp-tongued. Maybe she would develop enough backbone to survive. Now if he could just convince her not to marry Rudolf.

He took the top off the whiskey bottle and poured a generous amount over the wound. Valeria's sharp intake of breath told him it still hurt.

"You don't have to hold back," he said. "You can scream if you want. There's nobody out here to hear you."

"I don't want to scream."

He could see it took a lot of self-control to speak calmly. The whiskey must have burned badly.

"I'd rather not announce my presence to every mountain lion within five miles. If they're going to have me for dinner, I intend to make them work for it."

He felt proud of her determination to keep things from getting too serious. "Don't worry. They're more afraid of you than you are of them."

"I don't see how that's possible. They have claws and teeth. I don't even have a riding crop."

"I'll protect you."

"You'll be asleep."

"The horses will let us know if any lions are around."

"I'd prefer not to rely on a horse for my safety."

"He'll be thinking more about his safety than yours."

"That may be a comfort to you, but it doesn't do much for me."

He finished bandaging her arm. She hadn't cringed, whimpered, or jerked away when he rubbed salve into the wound. If this trip lasted long enough, she'd be more than a match for Rudolf.

"Do you sleep outside often?" Valeria looked around her as she asked the question.

The sun had dropped below the canyon walls long ago. The shadows had assumed a deep blue hue. Orange and purple streaked the sky above the canyon.

"Before this trip," Valeria continued, "I'd never slept anywhere without guards outside the gates, footmen in the hall, a maid in the adjacent room. My bed was piled high with down mattresses and sheets of perfumed silk."

Again she looked around at the canyon. Shadows of the darkest night lurked under the branches of the willows and cottonwoods that lined the creek. Not a breath of air stirred. The scratching sounds of many tiny animals reached their ears. The rocks radiated heat absorbed during the day.

"Now you expect me to sleep on rocks under an open sky with nothing to protect me from wild animals." She shivered. "I probably won't get a wink of sleep."

"I can take care of that," Luke said.

"What are you doing to do?" she asked when he got up and came toward her.

"I'm going to rub some of the kinks out of your muscles."

She looked nervous.

"All my muscles are fine," she said.

"I'll be the judge of that. Hand me your bedroll."

"What does it look like?"

"Like a blanket rolled up. You're leaning against it."

"Is this all I'll have between me and the rocks?"

"It's plenty." He spread the bedroll out and opened it up. "Crawl inside."

"I can't get up."

He'd suspected as much. "Give me your hand." He helped her to her feet. Her grimace told him all her muscles had gone stiff again. "Now lie down on your stomach." She knelt on the bedroll and gradually extended her limbs. She turned her head to one side, trying to look up at him. "What are you going to do?"

"Work the kinks out of your muscles. I'll start with your calves." Her muscles were hard as rock. He rubbed them gently until he felt them begin to relax. "Don't look so nervous. I'm not going to hurt you."

"I'm nervous because I can't see you."

"Don't you trust me?"

"I don't know."

After what he'd done to her on the mountain, he deserved that. "I gave Hans my promise I'd get you safely to your ranch. There isn't much I haven't done at one time or another, but I've never gone back on a promise."

"Everybody breaks a promise at one time or another," she said.

"My word is all I have," he said. "If I break it, I have nothing."

"I don't understand."

He couldn't explain. Even his brother didn't understand.

"I'll massage your thighs now," he said, knowing it was likely to make her extremely uneasy. "Try to stay relaxed. The looser you are, the sooner I'll be done."

Luke tried to tell himself he was performing an ordinary task of no particular significance. It worked for a short while, but touching Valeria's thighs shattered the illusion. He might fool himself into thinking her calves were no different from anybody else's, but her thighs were a whole different proposition. They were soft, rounded, and uncomfortably close to her buttocks. There was no way Luke could pretend there was anything ordinary about Valeria's bottom. He could pretend she was a useless ornament, but she was a beautifully crafted ornament, every detail of her body having been fashioned with meticulous care.

Luke tried to concentrate on the stiff muscles, to focus his attention on the gradual release of tension in her body, but his gaze kept straying to the rise of her bottom. His body began to swell. The tightness of his jeans, especially in the kneeling position, made that extremely uncomfortable.

"Are your shoulders tight?" he asked. He had to think of something else, or his hands were liable to wander a little too far north.

"I think so."

He shifted position. It was more difficult to loosen the muscles in her shoulders, but it was safer. "You're tight as a water barrel."

"I'm not used to riding so much."

She sounded sleepy. Apparently exhaustion had overcome her fear of sleeping in the open. He gradually reduced the pressure on her muscles until he was barely touching her. In a few moments he was rewarded with the sound of her soft, regular breathing. He leaned back on his heels.

She was asleep.

He moved away quickly. He poured himself a cup of coffee and faced reality. He was interested in this woman, and it wasn't his usual kind of interest. He felt protective. Not because he'd been paid a very large sum of money to protect her. Not because he'd made a promise. Not because she was a woman and he was a man and men were supposed to protect women. Certainly not because she was a princess in search of a safe place to lay her royal head.

He was interested in her the way every other man was interested in that special woman when—and if—she came into his life. She touched something in him, brought a part of him alive he'd thought dead. She made him care, something he'd thought impossible.

But he didn't want to care, certainly not enough so he could be hurt. His parents hadn't been able to love him. No one else could.

Valeria awoke to the sound of a man speaking her name from a distance. She couldn't figure out why it should be a man's voice. No man was allowed to enter her suite until she had breakfasted and dressed. She knew that hadn't happened because she was still in bed, though it was the most uncomfortable bed she'd ever slept in. Maybe that accounted for the feeling of stiffness in her body. She felt like she'd been made out of papier-mâché.

"Valeria, wake up. Breakfast is ready."

She jerked awake. She remembered. That was Luke's voice. They had left the wagons and gone off by themselves. She tried to move and found her body was so stiff she couldn't sit up.

And she'd slept in her clothes! Nothing like this had ever happened. She changed her clothes from the skin out at least once every day. Everything she wore was washed or cleaned after a single use, even if she'd only worn it for a few hours. The thought of wearing clothes for a second day made her skin crawl.

"Are you awake?" Luke asked.

"Yes."

"You can't get up, can you?"

"No."

"Can you move anything?"

Her fingers and toes worked just fine. So did her feet. She could turn her head to one side, but the muscles in her shoulders, back, thighs, and calves were immobile. "Not enough to get up."

"It won't take me more than a few minutes to work out the stiffness," Luke said.

She remembered how he'd massaged her muscles last night. She'd fallen asleep in the middle of it! She didn't understand how she could have gone to sleep with a man's hands touching her body. Surely there wasn't enough fatigue in the world to justify that, but it must have been fatigue. It certainly wasn't indifference.

She nearly groaned aloud when he began to knead the muscles in her shoulders and neck. She awakened with a cramp one morning as a little girl, but she didn't remember it hurting as much as this.

"This will hurt," Luke said.

His warning came late. She cringed.

"You shouldn't let yourself get so out of shape," Luke said. Her shoulders didn't hurt quite as much now. "You'll have plenty of opportunity to ride at the ranch."

At the moment, she found the notion of never getting on a horse again appealing.

"Why didn't you tell me you were so miserable? I would have stopped to give you a chance to get down and work out the cramps."

"No, you wouldn't have," she managed to say through the pain. He'd moved to her back. She'd never known she had so many muscles there. "You'd have said I was a useless parasite and I should have been ready to ride fourteen hours over impossible country at the drop of hat."

She thought he laughed. She couldn't be sure through the haze of pain.

"I probably would have, but I won't today."

She doubted he'd be happy about breaking his trip once he got under way. "I think I'll walk the rest of the way," she muttered.

"It's not that bad. You'll be feeling fine in a few minutes."

He'd reached her thighs. The muscles ached, her nerves tingled like needles, and her skin had been chafed until it was sore. There was no way in this world she was going of be fine anytime soon. If ever.

He didn't spend very long on her calves before he said, "Now you can stand up."

She didn't have to fall on her face to know she wasn't

ready. "You'll have to give me a hand," she said.

"Sure."

"Go slowly," she said, but he had already brought her to her feet in one swift movement. Every muscle in her body screamed in protest.

So did she.

It seemed all the wildlife in the canyon had gathered near their camp. A flock of birds flew up from the trees, squawking in protest. A doe and two fawns scampered up the far bank of the creek and disappeared. Dozens of little animals scurried around in the underbrush, probably snatching their young into dens for fear she would trample them in her desperate efforts to get her feet under her. She hoped any snakes or mountain lions were off doing other things. They'd know at a glance she was helpless to defend herself.

"Did that hurt?" Luke asked.

"No. I just screamed to clear the underbrush. I don't like being watched while I'm suffering the agonies of the damned."

Luke's lips twitched. "That bad?"

"I've never been damned before," Valeria said, "but I don't think it can get any worse."

"Remind me to tell you about a few Apache tortures."

She intended to forget that reminder. If Luke thought what the Apaches did was bad, it must be truly inhuman.

"I hope breakfast isn't overcooked," he said.

She found herself a boulder, hoped nothing disgusting was hiding under or behind it, and leaned against it. "You go ahead and eat," she said. "I'll stay here."

"I'll bring your breakfast to you."

"I don't want anything."

"We won't stop to eat again until nightfall."

She wasn't sure she could force herself to eat anything, but she was sensible enough to know she had to eat to keep up her strength. "I'll be all right in a few minutes. Maybe I'll have some coffee."

"You'll have a full breakfast if I have to force it down you. I won't have you so weak from hunger, you fall out of the saddle before noon."

The old Luke was back. In all probability he'd never left. She'd just interpreted acts of necessity as acts of kindness. She'd be careful not to do that again. She pushed off from the boulder and took a tentative step. Her muscles burned, but she didn't collapse. If she could just keep putting one foot in front of the other, maybe she could learn to walk again.

"Be careful or you'll stumble over a rock."

He probably didn't want to have to haul her to her feet.

"I'll manage. Give me some coffee."

Despite being stronger than she liked, the coffee tasted good. The morning was mercifully cool. Her muscles gradually grew more pliant, the burning lessened, and she could walk without limping about. She ate her breakfast standing up. It tasted a lot better than she'd expected, but it still looked awful. She would ask her chef to teach these Americans something about food presentation. She could see no reason why her meals had to look like something that should have been thrown out.

She watched disbelievingly when Luke cleaned the dishes with sand. "Wouldn't water work better?"

"It won't get rid of the grease," Luke said. "Now I have to look at your wound before we leave."

He'd doused the fire, and it was still dark. He struck a match after he removed the bandage. Then he struck a second match.

"I don't like the way it's healing," he said.

"It's probably doing fine." It had started to hurt so much it had awakened her twice during the night. That hadn't frightened her. She expected a gunshot wound to hurt, but Luke's worry robbed her of that comfort. He didn't have to tell her they were beyond the reach of medical attention, and she knew enough about wounds to realize people could die of them.

"I see signs of infection."

He poured whiskey over it again. The burning pain convinced her maybe it wasn't doing as well as she'd thought.

"I'll check again tonight," he said.

"What if it's worse?" She didn't know what he could do. She couldn't imagine why a competent doctor would want to live west of San Antonio.

He began saddling the horses. "I'll have to do something about it."

Probably amputate her arm. It was just the kind of pragmatic solution a man like Luke Attmore would think of. He hadn't an ounce of sentiment in him. If something went wrong, he'd fix it in the quickest, most efficient way and move on. She supposed that was the smart thing to do. Her uncle would have done the same thing.

Her parents had been killed in a freak accident while she was still an infant. She had no idea what either of them had been like. It was odd that she should miss them now for the first time in years. She never thought of herself as an orphan. She'd been surrounded all her life by people anxious to take care of her, to cater to her every whim, but no one said much about love, not even her uncle's wife. It was all duty and responsibility. Personal emotion had to be set aside for the sake of the family or the state.

But Luke's ruthless attitude didn't come from a sense of duty. It probably came from a totally utilitarian approach to problems. Drain the situation of all emotion, all prejudice, all preference, then do what works the best.

Valeria conceded that she ought to admire such an attitude, but she didn't. She'd been denied emotions her whole life. Now that she discovered she actually had likes and dislikes, could admit the presence of emotion, she'd decided she liked it.

She had no intention of letting Luke amputate her arm. It would certainly be scarred, but she wanted to keep it.

"Time to mount up," Luke said.

Valeria couldn't recall when she'd ever heard more ominous words. Her body ached at the mere thought of what was in store. But she was determined not to let Luke know how much she dreaded what lay ahead. She supposed she'd developed a cynical attitude, but she still had her pride. She might be a deposed princess, but she was still a princess. She was going to act like one if it killed her.

Faced with the prospect of getting into that saddle, she figured it probably would. "How about another cup of coffee?" she asked.

"You hate my coffee."

"I never said that."

"When you acted like you'd swallowed alum water, I figured it out."

"It's just that it's so strong."

"You could have put some water in it."

She would have if she had been able to get used to the idea that she and the horses drank from the same stream. That shouldn't have bothered her. Luke's coffee was strong enough to kill and dissolve the bodies of any critters that might be in the water.

"I'll learn to drink it your way. It's probably the only way anybody in Arizona knows how to make it."

"It's time to stop stalling and mount up. It'll soon be daylight."

Maybe he considered that barely perceptible lightening

in the deep blue velvet overhead a sign dawn was on its way, but as far as she was concerned a single candle could have been responsible for it.

Luke put his hands around her waist. "Wait!" she cried, but it was too late. She was in the air and settled on the saddle before the sound of her plea finished echoing down the canyon. Every muscle from the bottom of her feet to the back of her neck screamed its objection, but Luke had handed her the reins and walked over to his horse. He had already packed up the food and cooking pots.

"We have a long day ahead of us," he said as he swung into the saddle. "I was serious when I said I want you to let me know when you need to stop. If you're this sore when we stop tonight, you'll never get the saddle tomorrow."

That thought gladdened her soul until she realized Luke would probably leave her. No, he'd said he'd get her to Rudolf's ranch one way or the other. She wondered if that could include being slung over the saddle like a sack of flour. She didn't know where the ranch might be, but she wasn't going to set one foot off the property until Rudolf built a proper road to town. A couple more days of this, and a war would be a welcome relief.

She had landed in an incomprehensible, uncomfortable, uncompromising world. She still didn't know if she liked it, but she did know she didn't want to go back to Rudolf's kingdom or to Belgravia. She found it hard to believe, but this new land appealed to her.

She hoped Zeke didn't forget to tell Rudolf she didn't want to marry him. She really *didn't* want to marry Rudolf. Only Luke interested her, but that seemed like a recipe for disaster. Or hurt. He didn't want to get married.

He didn't even like her. He thought she was an idiot, a useless ornament.

She would prove him wrong even if it was the last thing she did.

Which was probably the reason she didn't tell him to stop until she fell out of the saddle.

Chapter Eighteen

Luke cussed long and loud. Only pure luck caused him to turn in time to see Valeria swaying in the saddle. He practically had to throw himself off his horse to catch her before she fell. Why hadn't she asked him to stop? He'd told her to before they left camp. He looked for a flat, shady place to lay her down. They had left the canyon to climb a series of low hills east of the San Pedro River. The midday sun was directly overhead. The best he could do was rocky ground and the partial shade of a juniper.

He didn't know much about a woman's constitution, but he thought Valeria looked sick rather than exhausted. Maybe she'd had a heat stroke. She couldn't be used to riding in heat above a hundred degrees. It never got above the middle eighties in her mountain country. Dammit, why hadn't she asked him to stop!

He removed his bandana, soaked it with water from his canteen, and bathed her forehead. She didn't respond. He put his hand inside her dress to make sure her heart was still beating. The feel of his hand on her bare skin caused his body to swell. He cussed himself. What kind of man was he when even his concern for Valeria's life couldn't outstrip his lust for her body? A man who'd lost his usual control and didn't know how to get it back.

He bathed her face and neck. When she still didn't stir, he opened her dress and bathed her chest and the tops of her breasts. He did his best to concentrate on figuring out what to do for her, but the sight of her soft, white skin made a mockery of his control. He couldn't stop imagining what it would be like to caress that soft flesh, to taste it with his mouth, with his tongue.

Much more of this, and he'd be the one having a heat stroke.

Fortunately, Valeria groaned and opened her eyes. "What happened?" she asked, her words slurred.

"You fainted?"

"Did I fall?"

"No. I managed to catch you."

She looked directly into his eyes and smiled. "I should have known you would."

He wasn't sure what she meant by that, but he did know its effect on him was unwelcome. His heart beat so fast he felt breathless. He attempted to counter the effect with anger. "Why didn't you tell me you needed to rest?"

She averted her gaze. "I didn't feel tired."

"You're lying. You looked so awful I thought for a minute you were dead."

Her gaze swung back. "Thanks for telling me. You don't know how much better than makes me feel."

He'd known he had said the wrong thing the minute he opened his mouth, but he wasn't used to watching his tongue when he was upset, and he was definitely upset. "I'm not very good with words."

"So far you've managed to express yourself very

well." She tried to sit up, but her strength failed her.

"Don't move. You need rest."

"No, I don't."

"Yes, you do."

"Very well, I do, but how am I going to get it in this sweltering sun?"

He didn't want to take her back to the canyon. They would lose practically a whole day. Besides, it was miserably hot in the canyon, even in the shade.

"I can use the horses to help block the sun."

"They're liable to step on me."

"Then I'll shade you."

"You'd do that?"

She sounded surprised. He wasn't one to mollycoddle people, but he didn't hold back when they really needed help.

"I promised to get you to your ranch."

"I forgot your pride." She sounded slightly angry. "You couldn't possibly let anything jeopardize your unbroken record of success. If you failed even once, you might actually have to admit you're human."

He hated thinking his record of success was meaningless. It was his measure of a man, of who he was, of his proof he was the best. But a woman who'd never had to *do* anything couldn't understand something like that. "What would a pampered princess know about being human?" he demanded.

"Not much when I started this journey, but I've learned a great deal since I met you."

"I asked you to tell me when you needed rest," he said. "Why didn't you?"

"Do you want the truth?"

"Of course I want the truth. It's a waste of time to lie." There were times he didn't understand her at all.

"I'm tired of being treated like a pampered, useless,

weak, stupid female. I wanted to prove I could stay in the saddle as long as you could."

"But you're not a man."

"You can't blame that on my being a princess."

"I didn't mean it like that. Besides, you're not used to the desert."

Her defiance seemed to collapse. "I probably never will be."

"You can get used to anything. Now let me make you more comfortable."

But the moment he touched her wounded arm, she grimaced. "Is your arm hurting more?"

She looked at him as though weighing every word. "I don't know."

"Why can't you give me a straight answer?"

"Because I never know what you're going to do."

He didn't understand her. The harder he tried to consider her feelings, the more angry she became. He wished Isabelle were here. She could tell him what to do.

"Are you afraid of me?" he asked as he removed her bandage. It was obvious she didn't want to answer. "Come on, I'm not going to beat you."

"There are worse things than a beating."

How could she know? Probably nothing worse than missing dessert had ever happened to her. At least until the last week. "Maybe, but are you afraid of me?"

"Yes."

He wouldn't have cared if it had come from another woman, but from Valeria it bothered him. "Why?"

"Because you're always angry with me."

"I'm not."

"Yes, you are."

"No, I'm not!"

"See, you're shouting. You're angry at me."

He forced himself to speak in a level voice. "I'm frustrated. That's not the same."

"It sounds the same."

It obviously wouldn't do any good to tell her she was wrong. "Why do you think I'm angry with you?"

He didn't like what he saw once he removed the bandage. The wound was still angry and red. He couldn't get rid of the fear that somehow gangrene might set in. Obviously his whiskey treatment wasn't sufficient.

"You act like I'm so useless I'm a waste of your time. You've made it abundantly clear you think all royalty ought to be eliminated. You've also made it very clear you think I'm the worst example of my class you've ever encountered. If not the worst female ever. I'm surprised you bothered to stop Otto from killing me. Oh, I forgot your precious record of unbroken success. You couldn't let the elimination of someone as worthless as myself endanger your reputation."

He was angry that she'd misjudged him so badly. He'd gone against his better judgment in accepting this job. He'd spent hours trying to explain America to her, what she had to learn to survive. He'd never spent that much time with any woman, never cared so much about any woman's well-being.

And that didn't take into account the effect she had on him physically. He didn't know if that would please her or insult her, but he'd be damned if he'd give her the pleasure of knowing she had him in knots.

"I've never heard such nonsense in my whole life," he said as he started to replace the bandage. "You're obviously delirious. I'm taking you to a doctor. I don't like the looks of that wound."

"How many days will that take? I'll probably be dead before we get there."

"It won't take more than a few hours. There's a town about thirty miles from here."

"Where?"

"Beyond those ridges."

"But there's nothing here."

"We're close to the Gila River. There are at least a dozen towns along it."

She seemed to swell up like a puff toad. "Do you mean there are towns all around here, and you've been dragging me through the hottest, most uncomfortable places you could find?"

"I didn't want to take a chance on anyone trying to kill you."

That took the steam out of her.

"Can you stand up?" he asked.

"Of course."

She couldn't. She could barely keep her feet under her with him holding her up.

"We'll have to ride double," he said.

"How can we do that?"

"We'll manage. Can you stay in the saddle for a few seconds without me holding you?"

"Of course."

That was what she'd said about standing up, but he'd have to hope she was right this time. He brought their horses close together. "Hang on," he said as he lifted her into the saddle. She blanched, but managed to hold on. Luke mounted immediately. "Now I'm going to lift you out of your saddle onto my lap."

"That's impossible."

"Probably, but like you said, I have no intention of letting you ruin my record. Here goes."

It wasn't easy to lift a woman out of the saddle when you were astride another horse. He had no leverage. He grunted when he lifted Valeria. There was nothing graceful about it as he dragged her into his lap.

She looked appalled to find herself in his arms. "Relax. I'm not going to teach you any more lessons about being alone with strange men."

"I didn't think you would. Once you give your word, I'm sure nothing can induce you to break it. It's how you feel about me that I don't like."

He had an almost irresistible urge to tell her how he really felt, but he doubted she would believe him. More important, *he* didn't want to believe it.

If he did, what could he do to keep himself safe?

"Bring her right in," Mrs. Alice Brightman said. "I'll put her straight to bed while you fetch the doctor."

"I don't need to go to bed," Valeria said. "I just need to get out of the sun."

"Nonsense," Mrs. Brightman said. "You look worn to a frazzle. After the doctor sees you, I'll give you some cold chicken and tuck you into bed."

By the time they reached the little community of Ogden, Valeria expected to faint again at any moment. Luckily Mrs. Brightman took her inside immediately. Valeria didn't want to be treated like an invalid—it wouldn't help her campaign to make Luke respect her—but she felt too tired to resist. She'd be strong and independent tomorrow. Tonight she simply wanted to go to sleep and forget this nightmarish journey.

"Fetch the doctor," Mrs. Brightman said when Luke laid Valeria down on the bed. "I can take care of her for now."

"I'm worried about the wound," Luke said.

"I'll clean it," Mrs. Brightman said. "Go on," she said when Luke seemed reluctant to leave. "You can trust me to take care of her."

"He's not worried about me," Valeria said after the door closed behind Luke. "He's worried about his precious reputation."

Mrs. Brightman laughed easily. "I've never known him to be indifferent to a beautiful woman."

"Maybe, but he has a particularly strong dislike for me."

She sounded like a jealous woman. If she'd had any doubt about it, Mrs. Brightman's reaction would have eliminated it. Her eyes opened a little wider, became a little brighter, and her expression become positively eager. "Now why would he have that?"

Valeria had allowed her feelings to run away with her, something she never did. Now she had to offer some explanation and hope it didn't lead to more curiosity. "I was born into a privileged position," Valeria explained, "and Mr. Attmore doesn't approve of privilege."

Mrs. Brightman gently pushed Valeria's shoulders down until she lay on the bed. She drew a sheet over her. "Luke wouldn't care about that, only what a person can do."

"That's the whole problem. I can't *do* anything. He thinks I'm a useless ornament."

And he was right. Looking back on her life from her new vantage point, she had to concede she hadn't been raised to do anything that could actually contribute to the well-being of anyone, even herself.

"I'm sure you'll learn," Mrs. Brightman said, cheerfully. "It'll be a whole lot easier once your arm's well."

"That's not as much of a problem as the rest of me."

"How do you mean?"

"I'm quite a capable rider, but I'm not used to riding from dawn until dusk. My entire body aches. It hurts to sit in the saddle."

"Let me see," Mrs. Brightman said. She wasn't shy

about lifting Valeria's skirts and pulling down her undergarments. "Merciful heavens!" she exclaimed. "I don't see how you can sit down without screaming."

Valeria was so glad to have someone sympathize with her, she pretended it didn't hurt as much as it did. "It's not that bad, but it is hard to enjoy the scenery."

"There's no scenery in this part of the territory worth looking at," Mrs. Brightman declared, "but I wouldn't notice a stampeding herd of antelope if my bottom looked like yours. I'll rub some ointment on it immediately."

Mrs. Brightman rubbed every part of her from the underside of her knees to the curve of her bottom until she felt her skin sting from friction.

"There," Mrs. Brightman said after she'd righted Valeria's clothes and pulled the sheet over her again, "that will feel better in a little bit."

"Thank you," Valeria said, but she didn't feel any better.

"Let me get this wound cleaned up. I don't know what Luke was doing. I've never known him to get a woman shot before."

"He kept me from being killed," Valeria said.

"His mind couldn't have been on his job. Everybody knows no killer gets past Luke. You sure he hasn't taken a shine to you?"

Valeria didn't understand the words, but she understood their meaning. "Luke doesn't like me at all. And the killer didn't get past him. My uncle hired one of my trusted advisers to kill me."

"I always did say nobody makes a worse enemy than kin," Mrs. Brightman said. "Did he do this to you?" She had unwrapped the wound.

"Yes."

"Then you don't have much to worry about. He can't be a good shot."

"I don't have to worry about him at all. Luke killed him."

"Better late than never," Mrs. Brightman observed. "Now let me get this cleaned up. The doctor will be here soon, and I won't have him thinking I left a wound looking like this."

"Luke cleaned it with whiskey," Valeria said. She didn't want Mrs. Brightman to think Luke hadn't attempted to take care of her.

"I bet it burned like the devil."

"Worse," Valeria said with a weak laugh. "I kept wishing he'd leave it alone."

"Whiskey medicine is fine for men," Mrs. Brightman said, her tone rather reproving. "Most of them don't have any feelings anyway, but it's a right cruel way to care for a woman."

Once more Valeria found herself wanting to defend Luke. "He didn't have anything else. He said he'd take me to a doctor if it didn't get well quickly."

"Luke's a good man. As men go, he's probably one of the best, but he hasn't figured out yet that you're supposed to treat a woman different from a man."

"Have you known Luke a long time?" Valeria asked. She'd love for someone to tell her something about him. He wouldn't say anything about himself.

"A long time, but not well," Mrs. Brightman said as she gently dabbed the wound clean with a soft cloth. "He travels all over doing I don't know what, but he drops in every now and then since my husband was killed." She laughed easily. "I guess the boy thinks I can't take care of myself."

Valeria found it difficult to think of Luke as a *boy*. She didn't see how Mrs. Brightman could, either. "How old are you?"

The look Mrs. Brightman gave her caused heat to flood Valeria's face.

"It just sounded strange to hear you call him a boy."

"I guess it comes from being married for so long. You just tend to think of unmarried men as boys."

Valeria felt certain she could be married a hundred years without thinking of Luke as a boy.

"I guess it's the way they act," Mrs. Brightman said. "Married men settle fast. They treat women nice but not real special. The unmarried kind, if they're decent in the first place, put most women on a kind of pedestal. They treat you like you're one of them painted dolls made out of porcelain. It's foolish, of course. We're just as tough as they are, but it's kinda nice all the same."

"Luke isn't like that, at least not with me. He hated me from the moment we met."

Mrs. Brightman inspected her work. "That's not the way I see it," she said as she patted the wound dry with a second soft cloth. "I got the feeling he was sweet on you."

"You mean you think he likes me?"

"Yes." It was a long, drawn-out syllable accompanied by a searching glance.

"Well, you're quite wrong. He's made it very plain he dislikes me and everything I represent."

"I can't imagine you representing anything terrible enough to cause Luke Attmore to turn up his nose. It's never been turned up at much as far as I can tell."

Valeria wanted to explore that statement further, but the sound of the front door opening indicated the doctor had arrived.

"Don't let the doctor's looks put you off," Mrs. Brightman said as she rose, set her pan of water on a table against the wall, and walked to the door to wait for the doctor. "He came out here to get over tuberculosis."

The doctor entered almost immediately, followed by Luke.

All the doctors Valeria knew had been portly, florid, jovial gentleman obviously well-supplied with the necessities of life. This man looked as though he'd been diagnosed as incurable and left for dead. He was so thin his clothes hung on him in folds. His face and hands appeared to be nothing but skin and bones, the flesh having wasted away. Only his eyes, rich brown orbs that scanned her face with abundant nervous energy, showed signs of the inner life that activated this skeleton.

"Looks to me like Luke's gotten mighty careless," the doctor said as he came toward Valeria. "Can't remember that he ever brought a female to me before." He looked at her wound. "Mighty careless indeed. What kind of man would let a pretty woman like you get shot? I'm Reed Felkner. I'll have you fixed up in a trice. Let me know if I hurt you."

Finally a man who didn't look upon pain as a sign of weakness.

"This doesn't look too bad," he said. "Was the man a bad shot, or did Luke manage to bring up the cavalry just in time?"

Valeria was having a difficult time understanding what he meant. Nobody talked like this in Belgravia. "He shot the man who was trying to kill me," she said, hoping she'd interpreted his words correctly.

"Good. We won't tell anybody about this close scrape. Wouldn't want to ruin his reputation."

Valeria couldn't understand everybody's obsession with Luke's reputation. It seemed nothing else mattered. "No, of course not," she said.

The doctor dusted her wound with a white powder. "You're healing well," he said. "All you need is some rest. Leave that to Mrs. Brightman. She'll take very good care of you."

"We have to leave tomorrow," Luke said.

"It would be better for her to rest a day or two," the doctor said, "but there's no reason she can't travel if you take care to keep the wound clean."

"I'll give you a reason she can't travel," Mrs. Brightman said, a look of determination on her kindly face. "Her backside looks like you scraped the skin right off."

"You a horsewoman?" the doctor asked Valeria.

"Yes," she replied.

"But you haven't been riding much lately?"

"Not for several months."

He turned to Luke.

"I'm being paid to protect her," Luke said, "not to worry about her bottom."

"I know you don't remember much about being a human being, Luke Attmore, but you do remember a person's bottom is attached to the rest of them, don't you?" Mrs. Brightman said.

"I remember."

"Well, it don't look like it." She threw back the sheet. "See for yourself, Reed."

"Turn over, young woman," Dr. Felkner said, as though it was of no consequence that he intended to inspect Valeria's bare bottom in the presence of two other people.

"You're going to have to turn over," the doctor said when Valeria didn't move. "I can't guess at the condition of your bottom."

Valeria decided no one in America had any sensitivity. No doctor in Belgravia would have made such a request without profuse apologies and forcing everyone else to leave the room. Her gaze settled on Luke.

"I'm not leaving," he said, understanding immediately

what she meant. "I can't decide what to do unless I know what I'm up against."

"You could leave me here and tell Rudolf where to find me," she said.

"I promised to take you to that ranch, and—"

"You never break a promise," Valeria finished for him. "It's clear my humiliation means less to you than your promise."

"Would it humiliate you to have me see your bottom?"

"Yes, you dense man. It would humiliate any woman."

Luke turned to Mrs. Brightman.

"I wouldn't let you see my bottom even if you were to hold a gun on me," she said.

Luke turned to the doctor.

"Even husbands leave the room at times like this."

Luke's expression made it clear he didn't like this advice. "You'll tell me exactly what it looks like?" he asked the doctor.

"Exactly."

Wearing an even deeper scowl, he left the room. Valeria felt the tension flow from her muscles. She hadn't realized she was so edgy.

"I've never seen him so worried about anybody," the doctor said, his eyes sparkling with interest. "Don't tell me you've managed to snag his interest. I can't tell you how many women have tried."

"He's not interested in me," Valeria said, "only in his promise to deliver me safe and sound."

"Luke is fond of his reputation, but—"

"Look at her bottom, Reed," Mrs. Brightman said. "Luke'll be back any minute now. He's not one to wait long."

Valeria turned over and buried her face in the pillow. She accepted the necessity of letting the doctor see her abrasions, but she couldn't look him in the face. The heat flamed in her face when he pulled her petticoats aside.

He whistled sharply. "What did you put in that saddle—cactus? Your bottom looks like a piece of raw meat. You can't possibly ride for at least two days."

Though Valeria greeted with relief the doctor's announcement that she didn't have to climb back into the saddle immediately, she didn't appreciate being compared to raw meat. She remembered what the butchered deer looked like.

"I'll give Mrs. Brightman a stronger salve," the doctor said. "I want you to let her rub it in tonight and again tomorrow morning. I'll come by tomorrow afternoon." He pulled Valeria's petticoats back in place.

"Tell Luke to come in," he said to Mrs. Brightman. "If he cares for this young woman, he'll hire a wagon to take her the rest of the way."

Chapter Nineteen

"I don't know how she stayed in the saddle without screaming," Dr. Felkner said to Luke.

"I told her to let me know when she wanted to stop."

"Just sitting in the saddle must have been pure agony."

Mrs. Brightman had insisted Luke and the doctor stay for coffee. They sat in her small, neat parlor while Valeria rested. Mrs. Brightman had wallpapered the room with white paper covered with pink and red flowers and vivid green foliage. She had made the cotton slip covers on her furniture of similarly bright, cool material to combat the perpetual heat. She had decorated the very feminine room with small pillows, lace-framed pictures, and crocheted doilies. She poured coffee from a cream-colored pot and served it in white porcelain cups adorned with a floral design.

"Valeria never said anything," Luke said.

"She doesn't want you to think badly of her," Mrs. Brightman said. "She thinks you hate her."

Luke didn't understand how Valeria could think that.

He'd gone to more trouble for her than for any female. Ever. "I don't hate her."

"How do you feel about her?" Mrs. Brightman asked.

That was one question Luke didn't mean to answer. "This is just another job. I—"

"Don't you dare say a word about your reputation," Mrs. Brightman said. "She thinks that's more important to you than she is."

Why shouldn't it be? If he lost his reputation, he'd be the nonentity his parents thought him. "You can't balance people's lives against a reputation," he said.

The words had hardly left his mouth when he knew that wasn't the way he would have answered a few days ago. It was what Isabelle would have said. What had made her words come out of his mouth? That hadn't happened in years. He started to speak again, to change his statement, but couldn't. He wasn't sure how he felt, and that surprised him just as much.

"I'm glad to hear you say that," Mrs. Brightman said. "Valeria's right sweet on you. Maybe it's time you thought about settling down and getting married."

Luke hated the arch look that came with Alice Brightman's words. Why did every woman think a man couldn't be happy, that his life couldn't be complete, until he married and saddled himself with a passel of kids? But the absolute dumbest thing she could have thought was that he and Valeria could develop such a relationship.

"My job is to take her to the man who's supposed to be her husband" Luke said. "They signed some contract."

"Contract?" Mrs. Brightman asked, not understanding.

"She's a princess from a tiny European country," Luke said. "They sign contracts instead of falling in love."

"Does she want to marry this man?"

"She says she doesn't."

"If she's signed a contract, she won't have any choice."

"I tore it up."

Both Mrs. Brightman and the doctor's looks demanded explanation.

"She's rich," Luke began. "Her money goes to her uncle if she dies before she's married and to Rudolf afterward. I tore up the contracts so she won't be forced to marry Rudolf, but that doesn't protect her from her uncle, who's already tried to kill her. I don't know who coordinated the attacks, and I don't know when they'll strike again. That's why we can't go by wagon and can't use the trails."

"Do you think you can get her safely to the ranch?"

"I can if she's able to ride."

"She'll be able to ride in a couple of days," the doctor said, "but you'll have to take it easy at first."

"You said she doesn't want to marry this Rudolf." Mrs. Brightman said.

Luke had known for some time he didn't want Valeria to marry Rudolf. He kept telling himself he'd torn the contacts up for no reason except her safety, but he'd told Zeke to notify Rudolf about the destroyed contracts as soon as he reached the ranch. He'd reminded him three times. He'd accepted his attraction to Valeria. He'd even stopped pretending it was just physical. But he'd kept himself under control by repeating over and over that Valeria didn't like him.

No one could love him. If his parents couldn't do it, how could anyone else? But as stupid as it was—and he told himself constantly that it was very stupid—he couldn't get the idea out of his head that somehow Valeria could. "My job ends the moment she sets foot on that ranch."

"But you can't leave her there if she doesn't want to marry him."

"What do you suggest I do?"

"Take her somewhere like Phoenix and help her find a job."

"She's a princess. She can't take care of herself."

"Then you'll have to take care of her until she learns."

That was something else he refused to think about. His responsibility ceased as soon as they arrived at her ranch. If she decided not to marry Rudolf, she could work it out herself.

"She's rich. She can hire someone to take care of her."

But he knew he was just trying to avoid what he had to do, what he wanted to do. She had no experience, no knowledge of the world. She wouldn't know where to start to find a job, how to protect herself from chiselers and fortune hunters.

But there was no point in thinking about any of this. She would probably marry Rudolf. She'd spent her whole life doing what she was told. Faced with momentous change, she'd cling to the familiar.

But if she didn't marry Rudolf . . .

"I don't know what she'll do," Luke said. "But if she doesn't marry Rudolf, I'm the last person she'll ask for advice."

"Why?" Mrs. Brightman asked.

"Because she thinks I represent everything that's bad about this country." He puts his coffee cup down and rose. "Now I have to see to the horses and find myself a room."

"You're not staying here?" the doctor asked.

"I don't have any extra rooms," Mrs. Brightman said. "I had to give Valeria my own bedroom."

"I appreciate your making room for her," Luke said.

Mrs. Brightman smiled. "I couldn't think of turning

her away. How many women can say they've had a real princess sleep in their bed?"

"None, I would expect," said the doctor. "That ought to make your boardinghouse the most popular in town."

And that, in a nutshell, was what was wrong with the notion of his caring for Valeria. She would always be a princess, and he would always be a gunman.

He needed to get out of Alice Brightman's fancy boardinghouse. He needed the heat, the stench of sweat and manure, the noise and odors of a saloon to remind him of his reality. It was becoming all too easy to imagine something quite different.

"Have you always run a boardinghouse?" Valeria asked Mrs. Brightman.

They were in the kitchen, Mrs. Brightman and her daughters fixing dinner for twelve men, Valeria doing her best to stay out of the way. She'd started by standing in the middle of the room. But after Mrs. Brightman politely walked around her—her twin daughters weren't so circumspect about letting her know she was in the way—Valeria took her coffee and found a place against the wall. She reminded herself she was no longer a princess surrounded by people whose sole aim was to minister to her comfort.

"Only since my husband died," Mrs. Brightman replied.

"Was he a gunman?" Valeria asked.

Mrs. Brightman laughed. "Nothing so exciting. He managed one of the mines. He got killed during a robbery. Be careful with that dough, Sue. You know the men like their biscuits fluffy."

Valeria didn't know the age of Mrs. Brightman's daughters, but she guessed they couldn't be more than eleven or twelve. She found it incredible that anyone so young could actually make biscuits.

"Weren't you afraid?" Valeria asked.

"Afraid of what?" Mrs. Brightman replied.

"Of everything, I guess."

Mrs. Brightman tasted the beef stew, decided it needed more of something, and added a dash from one of the many bottles of herbs and spices that filled one shelf. "I wasn't afraid of anything except being married to the wrong man," she said. "Besides, after my Horace, I wasn't sure I wanted to be married again."

"Was he that mean to you?"

Mrs. Brightman stopped stirring her stew and turned to Valeria. "He was that good. Built me this big house when he had to haul the wood from a hundred miles away. He paid to have all my mother's furniture brought west after she died. I know he was disappointed I couldn't give him a son, but he always acted like no man could have wanted more than his two daughters."

Valeria knew about the need for a son. Her father had stopped speaking to her mother after she failed to produce a son. Only an occasion of state brought them to gether the day they were killed.

"But how did you know what to do?" Valeria asked.

"What's there to know?" Mrs. Brightman asked. "All a man wants is a soft bed with clean sheets and a good dinner. As long as you can supply that, you'll have boarders lining up at your door. Come to think of it, that's a pretty good formula for keeping a husband, too."

Valeria wondered what it would take to keep Luke happy. He appeared to be satisfied with food cooked over a campfire and a bedroll spread on the ground. What else would such a man want?

A woman.

Valeria felt herself blush. She never used to think

about the physical side of marriage, but being around Luke had changed that. Just being near him, just looking at him, caused her to have hot and cold flashes, to feel unfamiliar stirrings deep in her belly. She was uncomfortably aware of his body, his arms, his legs, his rear. This was no polite or casual awareness. It was hot, intense, and kept her watching him long after she knew she should turn away.

She knew men placed great importance on their physical relationships with women, but no one ever explained why it was so important for men and not for women. Valeria wondered if it might not be the same with some females. If so, the way she reacted around Luke made her wonder if she might not be one of those females.

"Do you ever feel afraid, being here by yourself?" Valeria asked.

She had never been alone. She couldn't imagine what it would be like to be responsible for running a boardinghouse, preparing the meals, and taking care of two daughters.

"Goodness, no," Mrs. Brightman replied. "If any boarder gets unruly, I tell him to leave."

"Suppose he doesn't want to leave?"

"The business end of my shotgun would take care of that."

"Mama shot a bear last winter," one of the daughters said.

"And a prospector last summer," the other added.

"He was trying to get one of my girls around the corner," Mrs. Brightman said, "and I couldn't have that."

Valeria felt a bubble of happiness forming inside her. Listening to Mrs. Brightman and her daughters made her want to laugh. She couldn't explain it, but just being in the same room with them made her feel better.

"Are you looking for a husband?" she asked Mrs. Brightman.

"No."

"Would you marry again if somebody asked you?"

Satisfied her stew was up to her standards, Mrs. Brightman tasted a pot of beans. "Maybe," she said. She added some pepper and covered the pot again. "He'd have to be pretty persuasive though. I'm used to doing things my way. I'm not sure I like the idea of changing to please some man. He'd have to go a long way toward making it worth my while."

"How would he do that?"

Mrs. Brightman looked straight at Valeria. "You don't know?"

"Luke will tell you princesses are useless, that we live off the efforts of others. I guess that's true. I know how to dress, how to behave at parties, how to talk to men, but I don't know much beyond that." Valeria remembered the way she felt when she was around Luke. "Do you mean the physical relationship between a man and a woman?"

Mrs. Brightman smiled. "You know more than you give yourself credit for."

"My aunt said women aren't supposed to like that."

"Maybe you aunt didn't, but I know a lot of women who like it very much." She turned back to her pots. "Sometimes it's all that makes it worth putting up with a man."

A thousand questions flooded Valeria's mind, but she didn't even know how to ask them. "I wouldn't know about that," she said.

"Well, I can't talk about it now, not with long ears listening," Mrs. Brightman said, nodding in the direction of her daughters.

"We know all about boys, Mama," one of the girls said.

"You'd better not know too much."

"We don't have time to get into trouble if we wanted to," the other twin complained. "There's always beds to make, sheets to wash—"

"Dinners to fix and clean up after," finished her sister.

"Do you want to have a boardinghouse when you grow up?" Valeria asked.

"No!" the twins answered in unison.

"I want to sing and dance on a stage in front of a lot of people," one said.

"I want to marry a rich man and have lots of jewels and furs," the other said.

"I've had the jewels and furs," Valeria said. "It's not as much fun as you might think."

"Tell us about it."

"You'd better pay attention to your work, or you'll spend your evening scrubbing burned food off the bottom of those pots," their mother said.

They had none of the hundreds of things Valeria had grown up thinking essential. But Valeria could tell that in spite of the large amount of work that needed doing, Mrs. Brightman and her daughters were quite happy.

Valeria was not.

"You feel up to taking dinner with the boarders?" Mrs. Brightman asked Valeria.

Valeria almost said she'd rather eat in her room when she realized that would be a lot more work for Mrs. Brightman and her girls. "Of course."

"You sure you can sit down?"

"I'll try if you promise not to let Luke toss me into a saddle first thing in the morning." She hated to appear weak, but this was the first time she'd been remotely comfortable since leaving Bonner.

Valeria knew she needed time to let her chafed skin heal before she got in the saddle again, but she also wanted time to study Mrs. Brightman. This woman had been a wife, was a mother capable of running a boardinghouse patronized entirely by men. This was the kind of woman Valeria wanted to be. Then maybe Luke wouldn't despise her.

"Time to take up," Mrs. Brightman announced. "Ring the dinner bell." One of the twins ran out of the room. Moments later the sound of a loudly rung bell sounded through the house.

"That man is back," the twin announced when she returned. "Did you set a place for him?"

"What man?" her mother asked.

"The man who brought her," she said, pointing to Valeria.

Valeria felt herself stand a little taller. She no longer felt quite so tired or so unsure of herself. Luke had come back. He must be concerned about her.

She longed to check her looks in a mirror, but it would depress her spirits. She lacked the clothes, jewels, and beautifully arranged hair she'd always depended on to make herself attractive. She had the plain, brown dress Luke had bought her and a pendant necklace she never took off. She had brushed her near-black hair back and tied it with a ribbon. Elvira probably wouldn't recognize her.

Her spirits plunged, then lifted slightly. Because she had none of those things, she had nothing to remind Luke she was a princess. Maybe he could see her as she was, as a woman.

Her spirits plunged again. If she just a woman, she was useless. She didn't know how to do the things Mrs. Brightman's daughters could do without thinking. She had no idea how to make a biscuit, keep vegetables from burning, or season a stew.

"I know who he's come to see," Mrs. Brightman said and winked at Valeria.

Valeria didn't misinterpret that look. "He's worried about his reputation. He's probably come to find out how long before I'll be ready to ride again."

"I know something about men," Mrs. Brightman said. "And Luke is interested in more than your bottom."

They both realized what she'd said at the same time. Valeria blushed. Mrs. Brightman laughed.

"That's not quite what I meant," she assured Valeria.

"I know, but you're wrong. He despises me."

"He does not!" Mrs. Brightman stated in a manner that brooked no contradiction. "He may not know it yet, but he likes you."

"I'm quite sure you're wrong," Valeria said. "But if you aren't, you've got to promise to help me."

"Do what?" Mrs. Brightman asked.

"Help make him fall in love with me."

Valeria was shocked by her words. How could she want anything so ridiculous, so absurd, so impossible? Had coming to American caused her brain to stop functioning altogether? She couldn't want to marry Luke. The idea was insane. She didn't even like him. He was . . . he was . . . he was the only man who made her feel alive, who caused her to think of him all the time, to weave endless scenarios by which he came to adore her. She didn't fully understand her feelings for him, but she knew they were powerful and true. She also knew that if Luke did fall in love with her, he'd love her for herself, not her money or her crown. That was the most wonderful feeling of all.

"Are you sure?"

"I haven't been sure of anything since I set foot in this

country. But I am sure no man has ever caused me to feel the way Luke makes me feel."

"How's that?" one of the twins asked.

"You're too young to know," her mother said. "Take the vegetables into the dining room and keep a still tongue in your heads."

"Have you considered what kind of man he is?" Mrs. Brightman asked after her daughters left the room. "He's a gunman, a professional killer."

Valeria laughed, but the sound lacked humor. "That exactly describes the men in my family for the last five hundred years. How else do you think they managed to stay on the throne of a country that didn't want them?"

Valeria didn't know what Luke had done to make Mrs. Brightman think he liked her, but she could see no sign of it. He sat directly across from her at the table, but he hardly glanced in her direction. Nor did he take part in the conversation. Since Mrs. Brightman and her daughters served the meal, it was left to her boarders and the men who paid for the privilege of taking their meals at her table to carry on the discussion.

"Are you certain there's no immediate danger of war in Europe?" Bill Tierney asked. He sat at the head of the table and had been grilling Valeria about European politics ever since he discovered she came from Belgravia. She had begged Mrs. Brightman to introduce her as Valeria Badenberg. Mr. Tierney didn't appear to know it was the name of the exiled royal family.

"You can never be certain about war," Valeria told him, "especially in the Balkans. Some of these people have hated each other for hundreds of years."

She'd been subjected to endless political talk her entire life. There wasn't much about European politics in the last ten years she didn't know.

"No one could hate you. You're much too pretty."

That was Fred Dample, the man on her right. Valeria had been told he sold harnesses, but she wouldn't have bought anything from a man so given to flattery. She'd been subjected to it her entire life but hadn't realized until now just how much she disliked it.

"Looks don't affect political decisions," she said.

"You could have a real powerful influence on me."

"Have some more stew, Fred," Mrs. Brightman said, forcing herself between Valeria and Fred Dample.

"I have an acquaintance in Germany," Bill Tierney said. "He tells me Queen Victoria won't let anybody start a war."

"Wars are most often started by a single person hungry for power," Valeria said, "or some madman willing to sacrifice his life for an ideal."

"I wouldn't sacrifice my life for you," Fred said, laying his hand on Valeria's arm, "but you sure do make me hungry."

"Then I suggest you get your hand off Miss Badenberg and eat your stew," Luke said.

"It ain't a food kind of hunger," Fred said, glaring at Luke.

"Food's a hell of a lot safer," Luke replied. "Now get your hand off the lady before I take it off for you."

Valeria moved away from Fred. She didn't like him, she especially didn't like his touching her, but she hadn't expected Luke to threaten the man. It was nice to be on the right side of his temper for a change.

"What's your interest here?" Fred demanded of Luke.

"The lady is trying to discuss politics," Luke said, "and you're interrupting her."

"Who cares about Europe?" Fred asked.

A man down from Luke spoke up. "I do. I have family

back in Poland. Every time there is a war in Europe, somebody attacks Poland."

"Where the hell is Poland?" Fred demanded.

"It used to be between Prussia and Russia," Valeria said. "But a hundred years ago Prussia, Russia, and Austria divided it up among themselves."

"Then we don't have to talk about it anymore."

"But that's exactly the kind of thing that can lead to war," Bill Tierney said. "People like the Poles will do a lot to get their own country back. I'm surprised the Austro-Hungarian Empire hasn't collapsed."

"Nobody gives a damn about any of that," Fred said, "not in this country, anyway. We're worried about free silver."

"It won't do you any good to worry about it," Luke said. "It'll be decided in Washington, not the Arizona Territory."

"Why is free silver so important?" Valeria asked. If this was going to be her country, she needed to know about the important issues.

"It's about whether the price of silver will stay high enough to keep the mines open," Fred said.

Valeria soon lost interest in Fred's explanation of the problems with the gold and silver standard. She looked at Luke. When he smiled at her, her heart nearly turned over in her chest. She didn't know what she'd done to please him, but she was determined to find out so she could do it again. She made up her mind that if women in America were allowed to choose their husbands, she was going to choose Luke. She just didn't know how she was going to go about convincing him to choose her. He was the most hardheaded, stubborn, iron-willed man she'd ever met, absolutely determined to keep his distance.

She would have to ask Mrs. Brightman how to attract

a man like Luke. He wasn't like the men she'd known in Belgravia. She also had to learn how to be an independent woman. She had only one more day. She was certain Luke wouldn't stay here a minute after the doctor said she could travel.

"A pretty girl like you has got to be bored by all this political talk," Fred said.

"Not at all," Valeria said, ashamed she'd paid so little attention to their argument. "I want to learn everything I can about America."

Fred's smile turned to a leer. "You've come to the right man, baby. I can teach you anything you want to know."

"I don't think Miss Badenberg has *come to you* at all," Luke said, his voice low and deliberate. "And if you were half the gentleman you think yourself to be, you wouldn't refer to a lady as *baby*."

"What are you, some sort of guard dog?" Fred burst out.

"I'm—"

"Well she don't need you baring your teeth as long as she's got me around. You hang with me, baby. I'll teach you things you never dreamed about."

"You mean you'll take me inside a silver mine?" Valeria asked.

Fred's laugh was positively lecherous. "The little lady has a liking for the dark. We can fix that right after dinner. There'll soon be plenty of dark outside."

Valeria's eyes widened in disbelief, but there could be no question about it. Fred had put his hand on her leg.

"What's wrong?" Luke asked, his body suddenly tense.

Valeria was embarrassed and angry. She tried to push Fred's hand aside without letting anyone know, but she couldn't.

"I thought you said you liked the dark," Fred said, a teasing tone in his voice.

"You misunderstood me."

"Valeria, what's wrong?" Luke said.

"He has his hand on my leg," she said, still unable to push it aside.

Suddenly glasses and dishes went flying across the room, spilling their contents on diners, the carpet, and the wall before crashing to the floor.

Luke had thrown himself across the table at Fred, his hands around the man's throat.

Chapter Twenty

Valeria was too shocked to scream, but Mrs. Brightman's daughters filled the gap. Squealing and jumping about like they were perched atop a hot stove, they gleefully pointed fingers at the two men pummeling each other on the floor of their mother's normally quiet, always clean and neat dining room. If Valeria hadn't been too stunned to be aware of any but her own feelings, she'd have realized they were delighted with the fight.

It didn't last long. In a short and brutal exchange, Luke pounded Fred's head against the floor until the man's eyes glazed over. Then he dragged Fred's limp, unprotesting body out of the room, down the hallway, through the doorway, and across the front porch. Luke tossed him into the street, closed the front door, and returned to the dining room.

"Are you all right?" he asked Valeria.

She was unable to utter a sound, so she nodded her head. She still couldn't get over the shock that he'd fought for her. She'd been surrounded by an army of men her whole life, but this wasn't a paid employee doing a job. Luke could have ordered Fred to remove his hand, could have pulled a gun on him. Instead his rage had caused him to fling himself across the table. Maybe Mrs. Brightman was right. Maybe Luke really did care for her.

"Sorry for the ruckus, ma'am," Luke said to Mrs. Brightman, "but some men don't know how to behave around a lady. The food was mighty good. I'll be back in the morning to check on Valeria's progress." He paused briefly, seeming to become aware for the first time of the damage to Mrs. Brightman's table and crockery. "Add everything up, and I'll pay for it in the morning."

He stood there, totally unmoved by the dozen pairs of eyes staring intently at him. He didn't look ruffled or out of breath. Except for the gravy that streaked his clothes from vest to pantleg and the blond hair falling over his forehead, it would have been difficult to tell he'd just been in a fight.

He didn't look the least bit like the men in the portraits that lined the walls of the royal palace in Belgravia. He didn't have a military uniform. He wasn't in court dress, and he hadn't decorated his chest with dozens of medals to prove his heroism. He wore a pair of plain gray pants, a white shirt, string tie, black vest, and black coat. He looked like any one of a dozen Western men she'd seen.

Valeria thought he looked more magnificent than any hero in her family's long history.

"You can't destroy my dining room, then offer to pay for it like it's an everyday occurrence," Mrs. Brightman exclaimed, finally able to regain her speech.

"Since I can't put it back the way it was, what else do you want me to do?" he asked.

Despite her shock, Valeria nearly laughed. How like Luke to dismiss the emotional and focus on the practical.

He had no concept of the emotional shock he'd just caused to Mrs. Brightman or Valeria.

"You'll ruin the reputation of my boardinghouse," Mrs. Brightman sputtered, unable to counter Luke's commonsense reply.

"You'll have more customers than you can serve, at least for a few weeks. They'll all be anxious to see where the fight took place."

Luke's reply outraged Mrs. Brightman. "If you think I want a reputation as a woman who allows fights to take place in her dining room, you're sadly mistaken."

"I'll be sure to let everyone know you threw me out right behind Fred Dample."

"You needn't bother. *I'll* make certain everyone knows it."

"If you need anything, send one of the girls for me," Luke said to Valeria. "I'll be staying at the Golden Horse."

"I'm not in the habit of sending for men in the middle of the night," Mrs. Brightman said, clearly incensed, "nor of letting my daughters go anywhere near the Golden Horse."

"I'll see you in the morning."

"You're crazy," Mrs. Brightman said as she followed Luke out of the dining room and down the hall. "You're not to come to my house ever again."

"Night, ma'am," Luke said as he opened the front door. "That stew was especially good this evening." He glanced down at the gravy on his clothes. "I'm glad I got the chance to take some of it with me."

Mrs. Brightman slammed the door behind him and turned back toward the dining room with a *harrumph* that seemed to say, "good riddance to bad rubbish." An arrested expression indicated that a new thought had occurred to her. She smiled, chuckled to herself, then reverted to her angry frown.

"I don't like to hurry you, gentlemen," she said when she returned to the room, "but eat up. It'll take me half the night to clean up this mess, and I want to get started."

The men wolfed down the remainder of their meals. Mrs. Brightman shooed them out of the dining room with food practically still on their forks.

"I told you that man was sweet on you," she said to Valeria the minute she closed the door behind her last guest. "My guess is he's dotty."

"Dotty?" Valeria wished these Americans would use ordinary words. She couldn't understand them half the time.

"Crazy about you," Mrs. Brightman said.

"Crazy?" This conversation was getting more and more difficult to follow.

"You been speaking English long?" Mrs. Brightman asked.

"All my life."

"Who'd you learn it from?"

"I had an English nurse who—"

"That explains it," Mrs. Brightman said. "Them people don't know how to talk like normal folks. I'm saying Luke likes you a lot, so much he might even want to marry you."

Valeria could only repeat what she'd said so many times before. "He hates me and everything I represent."

"Nonsense. It's just his way of not letting you know he can't think about anybody but you."

"If that's true, why wouldn't he want me to know?"

"Men are like that," Mrs. Brightman said as she started to sweep up the mess on the floor while her daughters cleared the table. "They think loving a woman makes them seem weak."

"Why?"

"I don't know. Well, actually I do. Men are peculiar beasts. They've got to appear strong enough to handle any situation, no matter how tough. If other men think they're weak, they'll try to take advantage of them. Luke's got a reputation for being ruthless. He shoots first, and if he worries about the consequences at all, he does it later."

"Don't gunfighters get married?"

"Most die young. There's always some stupid kid gunning for a quick reputation. If he kills someone like Luke, he becomes a feared gunhand overnight."

"Will Luke tell me he likes me?" Valeria asked.

"Not unless you force it out of him." Mrs. Brightman dumped a dustpan full of broken crockery into a bucket and began to sweep up some more.

"How can I do that?" Valeria began to gather and stack the plates the way she saw the girls doing it. It was a novel experience. She'd never removed a used plate in her entire life.

Mrs. Brightman looked up from the floor. "Take those plates into the kitchen, girls, and fix some hot, soapy water. This floor needs a good mopping. You'll be on the trail alone with him for several days," Mrs. Brightman said after her girls left the room. "You can get to him then."

"How?"

"Don't you know anything about men?" Mrs. Brightman asked.

"I know a great deal," Valeria replied, affronted. "I've helped my uncle entertain at parties and—"

"I'm not talking about parties, girl. I'm talking about seduction."

"I've always been warned to be on my guard to keep men from seducing me."

"You would ordinarily, but you'll practically have to hogtie Luke if you want him to marry you."

"Forgive me for disagreeing with you, but I have every reason to believe Luke has known a great many women."

Mrs. Brightman laughed. "He practically has to fight them off. But you're different."

"I don't understand."

"What did they teach you in that country of yours?"

"Nothing that has been of any use since I arrived in America," Valeria replied with some asperity.

"Those other women didn't mean a thing to Luke. He could bed 'em and leave 'em without a second thought. You're different. He hasn't laid a hand on you, yet he nearly killed Fred for putting his hand on your leg."

"Which means he like me?"

"Yes."

"So he ought to want to tell me so."

"No. It means he'll do everything he can to keep you from knowing."

"I think you must make men different in this country. I don't understand them at all."

"It's just Western men. Luke knows you're a danger to his independence, his image of himself as a hard nut to crack."

Valeria felt herself losing the sense of the conversation. "Do you mean he thinks telling a woman he's attracted to her, that he loves her, makes him less of a man?"

"Yes. That's exactly what I mean."

"But that's crazy." She was learning to talk like Mrs. Brightman.

"Of course it's crazy, but that's men all over. There's not a sensible woman in the world who'd do half the things they do. But you wouldn't want them sane. That would take away half the fun."

Valeria was fairly certain she didn't agree with that

sentiment, but she let it pass. She was more concerned with learning how she could prompt Luke to reveal the true nature and extent of his feelings for her. "So what am I supposed to do?"

"You're supposed to use his body against him."

The twins returned with two mops and a bucket of soapy water. "Make sure you get the hallway, too," their mother said. "I wouldn't be surprised if they got gravy on the front porch." She suddenly burst out laughing. "You could have knocked me over with a feather when Luke pitched himself across that table. I didn't believe my own eyes." She shook her head and picked up her bucket. "Come into the kitchen. I don't want long ears to hear what I have to say."

"Oh, Mama!" the girls said in unison, but their mother only smiled and preceded Valeria to the kitchen.

"Men like Luke Attmore have more willpower than is good for them," she said as she set the bucket of broken crockery on the back porch. "When it's a matter of their honor, you can't move them at all. You can torture them, and they won't budge. But when it comes to women, they're made of clay. It may take a little doing to undermine the foundation, but once you do that, the tower comes tumbling down in a hurry."

Valeria thought she understood, but she needed clarification. "How do I go about undermining his foundation?"

"Get close to him. That ought to be easy to do when you're out there by yourselves." She shivered. "I'd be so close to him he'd think I was his second skin."

Valeria understood that. "I've been that close, and all he said was not to let myself get caught alone with a man I didn't know."

Mrs. Brightman frowned. "That's downright discouraging. He might be harder to crack than I thought. Still, he did try to kill Fred for you."

He had killed Otto, but he'd done that to protect his reputation. Could he have attacked Fred for the same reason? If so, she had no chance at all.

"You've got to get him to kiss you," Mrs. Brightman said. "As pretty as you are, that shouldn't be hard."

"He's already kissed me."

Mrs. Brightman's interest flared. "When?"

"When he was proving to me that going off with a strange man was very dangerous.

"Hmmmm. I'm not sure how to take that."

Valeria was sure. Luke was so uninterested he could kiss her and not be tempted to do anything more.

"On the whole, I think that's a good sign, though it's liable to make it still harder to break through his barriers."

"I don't see how that's possible." Valeria didn't need discouragement. She had enough of that already.

"I'm working on the assumption he's really hooked," Mrs. Brightman said, "that he can't stand the thought of another man touching you. He scared you to make you wary of other men while letting you know you could trust him."

"Wouldn't it be easier just to tell me?"

"Nothing is ever easy for men like Luke. You've got to keep picking at their defenses until they defeat themselves. How brazen are you?"

Valeria had never been asked a question like that. She didn't know what to answer.

"Are you bold enough to kiss him first?" Mrs. Brightman asked.

"I don't know."

"Make him take you in his arms?"

"How do I do that?"

"Girl, if I have to explain everything to you, you don't deserve Luke. That man is hiding out, but behind the wall he's built is a man just begging to be loved."

Suddenly Valeria understood. She'd been placed behind a wall, too. Only she'd never been told about the possibility of love. She didn't know any more than Luke what to do about it. She was just as afraid of failure, of rejection. She'd hidden behind her role as a princess all her life because a princess wasn't supposed to feel, to love, to care. She was just supposed to do her job.

That was Luke. He had to preserve his reputation as the roughest, toughest gunman in the West. He felt locked into his role, unable to find a way out. She would have felt exactly the same if she'd stayed in Belgravia. When she'd been exiled, all the barriers and restraints came tumbling down, and she had to become a new person. That was what she had to do for Luke, knock him so far out of his rut, he could never go back to it again.

She had to destroy his reputation.

"You've figured it out."

"What?" Valeria asked.

"You're grinning."

Valeria hadn't been aware of her expression, just the feeling of relief that she finally knew what to do.

"Don't tell me what it is," Mrs. Brightman said. "I'll answer your questions if you've got any, but it's better you don't tell anybody."

"That's okay. You can't help me now. This is something I have to figure out on my own."

They had been back in the saddle for most of the day. Luke asked Valeria at least once every hour if she was tired, if she wanted to rest, but she always insisted they go on. He'd stopped twice anyway. He hadn't forgotten

Mrs. Brightman saying Valeria didn't want him to think badly of her.

After the way he'd attacked Fred Dample, he was surprised everybody didn't know he was about to go crazy keeping his distance. It didn't help that every time he looked back, she smiled invitingly. If the trail hadn't become too narrow to ride two abreast, he'd have been jumping out of his saddle hours ago. He knew he needed women more frequently than most men, but never before had his craving come so close to tearing him apart.

When it came time to stop for the night, he wouldn't be able to escape looking at her. Temptation would stare him in the face every minute until she crawled into her bedroll. Even then he'd know she was just an arm's length away, that all he had to do was reach out and—

"This looks like a good place to stop for the night," he said, desperate to keep from completing the image. He could have found a better spot, but not without getting closer to the mining town a few miles over the ridge. He didn't want Valeria to know it was there any more than he wanted the townsfolk to know Valeria was here.

He dismounted and led both horses to a spot with a sparse covering of grass. Valeria remained in the saddle, waiting for him to lift her down. Feeling particularly vulnerable, he would have moved away immediately after helping her down, but she clung to him.

"My legs are a little unsteady. Let me hold on to your arm a minute or two."

Instead she put his arm around her waist and leaned against him. He didn't dare release her, but his body chose that moment to betray him. In about thirty seconds it was going to be obvious to anyone who wasn't blind just what was on his mind.

"I thought you said you didn't need any rest," he said.

"I don't. I just need a couple of minutes to get my muscles used to bearing my weight."

She hadn't needed to do that before. He forced himself to think of what he would fix to eat, of looking under rocks for snakes and scorpions. He even tried to decide whether the horses could find enough food in the clearing or whether he would need to move them during the night.

"You're very quiet," she said.

"I'm thinking."

"You do a lot of that."

"There are a lot of things to think about." Even more to avoid thinking about.

"My muscles are awfully tight. Do you think you could massage them like you did before?"

His temperature shot up about five degrees. While she was staying at Mrs. Brightman's house, he had forgotten how difficult it was to be alone with her.

"Try walking around the camp. That ought to loosen you up."

She looked hurt. He longed to tell her he wasn't rejecting her, just restraining himself, but he didn't dare put that into words. If he once voiced his weakness, he'd have no reason to hold onto his pride. Without that, he didn't know if he could control himself.

"I will. But if I'm still stiff . . ."

She left her sentence unfinished, but he had no trouble filling in the missing words. Luke busied himself unsaddling the horses, building the fire, making coffee, frying a piece of ham he'd gotten from Mrs. Brightman. "Time to eat," he called when everything was done.

Valeria had been walking in circles around the campsite, smiling at him every time he looked up. He felt like a complete coward, but he finally kept his gaze on his work. Valeria came up to the campfire, but she didn't sit down.

"You'll have to help me," she said. "I'm so stiff I'm afraid I might fall."

She didn't look stiff to him. She looked supple and so damned enticing he could hardly keep his breathing and heartbeat from escalating further.

Her hand was warm, her skin soft, her touch gentle. He wanted to pull her to him and kiss her until he lost himself so deeply in his need for her, he could forget his iron will, his fear that she would never be able to give him the love he needed. He told himself he ought to give in long enough to prove to himself there was no hope. Then maybe he could treat her like any other woman.

But he knew he would never forget her.

"Thank you," she said when she was seated. He handed her a plate of food. "I know I'm a lot of trouble," she said as she took it. "You're probably can't wait to hand me over to Rudolf."

"I don't think you ought to marry Rudolf." The words were out before he could shut them off.

"Why not?"

He'd already put his foot in it. There was no reason to refuse to answer. "I tore up the contract, so you're free to do what you want, go where you like, marry a man of your own choosing."

She put a bite of ham in her mouth and chewed slowly. "I'm not going to marry Rudolf," she said after she swallowed. His expression must have told her he was surprised. "I decided that at Mrs. Brightman's. But I don't know where to go, what to do, how to find a man I can trust to help me. Would you consider the job?"

His thoughts were in chaos. Every possibility he'd tried so hard to deny was now alive and well. "You can't trust me."

"Of course I can. You've had me at your mercy, but

you've always protected me. Now that you've stopped hating me, you're the perfect person."

"I never hated you." He had to stop speaking his thoughts. There was no telling what he'd say next.

"Yes, you did. But after you attacked Fred, I knew you liked me."

Luke's food stuck in his throat. It would be foolish to deny that his feelings had changed. It would be foolhardy to tell her how much. "I wouldn't be doing my job if I let some jerk like Fred put his hands all over you."

She smiled. "You could have told him to stop. Or pulled a gun on him."

"Alice Brightman doesn't allow guns in her dining room."

Her smile didn't waver. "I didn't know it was possible for a man to jump across a table that wide. It made me think of a lion protecting its mate."

What was she playing at? Valeria had never acted like she was trying to seduce him. She just sat there, smiling, putting bits of food between her luscious lips, chewing with slow deliberation, her gaze never leaving him. He felt the blood stir in his groin. His cramped position was uncomfortable now, but he couldn't move to release the pressure without disclosing his condition.

She put her plate down, her meal unfinished. "If you're ready, I'd like that massage now."

She practically purred. When has she changed from a stiff, demanding princess into a siren? She spread her bedroll out and lay down on her stomach.

"It's not as bad as before," she said. "It won't take nearly so long."

Even a second's contact would be too much. He considered refusing, but he went like a lamb to the slaughter. He decided to start with her shoulders; they were the least likely part of her body to push him over the edge.

Just touching her was enough to arouse every nerve. Talk. Maybe if he could carry on a conversation he could last until her damned, lovely, sweet muscles were relaxed.

"Was today a better day in the saddle?" he asked.

"Much better. My bottom doesn't hurt nearly so much."

Already they were headed in the wrong direction. His gaze was drawn toward her bottom, to the swell that rose gently from the small of her waist and fell in a beautifully rounded curve until it joined her thigh. A shudder of desire ran through him.

"Is something wrong?" she asked, looking up at him with genuine concern.

"No."

"You're shaking."

"I put my knee down on a sharp rock."

He moved his hands down to her back. He knew the muscles that got the tightest from holding the reins all day ran down and across the back. But in order to massage all of them, his fingertips would come perilously close to her breasts. This wasn't at all like the time on the mountain when he was trying to teach her a lesson. There was no anger or frustration to protect him. He was filled with a raging desire that burned through his body like a fever.

He worked over the muscles in her back quickly, then sat back. "It's getting late. You ought to turn in early. We have a long day ahead of us tomorrow."

"Aren't you going to massage my thighs?" she asked.

"They're stiff, too?"

"More than anything else."

He couldn't be mistaken, not even in the fading light. Hers was a flirtatious, provocative smile. He'd seen enough of them to know.

When he touched her thighs, he felt all control fall away. He was at the mercy of his physical wants. And his physical self demanded prolonged contact with Valeria. He massaged her thighs in a kind of trance, up and down, up and down. He moved to her calves, then back to her thighs. His hands reached the curve of her buttock when—

"I feel relaxed enough to sleep now."

He felt something pop, and he came out of the trance. He didn't know how long he'd been massaging her thighs. Judging from the depth of the darkness and the dying embers of the fire, he'd spent at least twice as long as needed.

Valeria sat up. He started to move away, but she took hold of his arm. "I know I shouldn't have asked—you've got to be as tired as I am—but I appreciate what you did. It was very sweet."

Then she leaned forward and kissed him.

He was lost. He grabbed Valeria and kissed her with a ruthlessness equal to the effort he'd exerted to keep away from her. He pushed her back down on the bedroll, devoured her mouth with the hunger of a starving man. He felt like he was mad, crazed, incapable of getting enough of her to satisfy the hunger that raged in him.

His hands, so recently denied their goal, covered her breasts. The thin material of her dress did little to shield him from her softness. A low, guttural moan escaped him. He deserted her mouth for her neck and shoulder. But that wasn't enough. He'd been kept from his obsession for too long. His hand plunged into her bodice to cup her breast.

Valeria's gasp of surprise restored him to sanity.

Luke practically threw himself from her, horrified he'd completely lost control of himself. It had never happened before. He'd taken pride in that fact. Yet now he'd acted like an animal, a ravening beast.

He got to his feet, moved away. "I shouldn't have done that," he said, his voice tight with the effort to speak. "I promised you'd be safe, and I broke my promise."

"I'm safe." Valeria looked a little bemused, but she didn't look frightened or angry.

"You wouldn't have been in about three minutes. I'll go water the horses. It would be best if you were asleep by the time I get back."

"You didn't do anything so terrible."

"I broke my word. I've never done that before."

He left without giving her a chance to say anything that could enable him to excuse himself. What he'd done was inexcusable. It didn't matter that probably no one else would ever know. He knew and that was what counted.

The iron-shod hooves of the horses striking stones sent occasional sparks shooting into the night. Just like him and Valeria. They couldn't come together without sparks. He'd known that the day he met her in the hotel room. When she sent Otto to tell him she'd fired him. When he talked other guides into being unavailable. When he convinced the miners to be quiet. He'd never had more obvious signs of trouble ahead. Yet he'd let Hans talk him into waiting until she was forced to ask him to come back.

And he had.

Zeke's knowing he'd made a mistake should have been a dead giveaway. What Zeke knew about women would evaporate in a thimble. What the hell was it about Valeria that made it impossible for him to put her out of his mind?

It wasn't just her looks. Beautiful, raven-haired princesses weren't exactly common, but he'd had his share of beautiful women. It wasn't her figure. Nice as it was, it wasn't spectacular. It certainly wasn't the fact she was rich or a princess. Those were the two most compelling reasons to have nothing to do with her. Certainly it wasn't her pleasing manner. She hadn't shown any liking for him in the beginning.

Then what the hell was it?

He'd reached the tiny trickle of water that passed for a creek. The horses walked into the creek bed, searching for a small pool from which to drink. Luke sat down on a boulder next to a willow tree to wait until they had drunk their fill.

The moon bathed the canyon in its soft light. The soft gurgle of water flowing around rocks, the peaceful solitude, should have worked to soothe Luke's troubled spirit.

But they didn't.

He hadn't lost his honor, but he'd compromised the one thing he'd held onto from the day he'd left Jake and Isabelle's ranch. His reputation was no longer beyond question. He couldn't be depended on to do what he said, regardless of the risks. His own feelings had gotten out of control. What if she decided to marry Rudolf after all?

He'd have to kill him.

Suppose she wanted to run the ranch on her own?

He'd have to stay and help her.

He was a fool! She'd go to New York and make a big splash in society. That's where an ex-princess belonged. He didn't know people in New York. He couldn't help her there. They would have to separate.

So that's what he ought to encourage her to do.

But no sooner had he reached that conclusion than he started to worry about the sharks who would try to strip of her of her money, the rakes anxious to take her honor, the hangers-on willing to flatter and praise until the money ran out, men swearing eternal love and devotion who only wanted her for her title. She couldn't have any instincts for self-preservation, not if she would trust him.

Where would she be safe?

Her uncle still wanted to kill her, and getting married was no guarantee she'd be safe. Luke knew of more than one wife who'd died mysteriously, leaving her husband the sole beneficiary to her fortune.

Luke told himself it wasn't his problem, that once he delivered her to the ranch his responsibility would be over. But he couldn't turn his back on her. He'd been responsible for telling her about the opportunities in America, whetting her appetite for freedoms she'd never enjoyed. She hadn't been thinking of duty tonight when she'd kissed him.

She had developed a whole new way of looking at men, and he was responsible for it. Now that he'd ruined her for her old life, it was his responsibility to see her safely settled into a new one. It didn't matter that staying away from her would be the hardest thing he'd ever done. He had to do it. It was the only way he could reclaim his honor.

But how could he help her?

Luke went through several possible plans in exhaustive detail, going backward and forward as he discovered problems and worked toward possible solutions. He didn't know how long he might have remained there, absorbed in thought, if a horned owl hadn't captured a wood rat practically under his feet. The fluttering of wings and the squeak of the rat brought him out of his musings. He looked up. The horses had left the stream and were searching the slope for grass.

Luke got to his feet. Valeria had surely gone to sleep long ago. He hoped that would be enough to keep him on his side of the campfire. If he could just get through these next few days, he'd be okay. If she refused to marry Rudolf and didn't want to stay at the ranch, he could take her to a city, hire a companion or maid, and settle her in a boardinghouse with some woman like Mrs. Brightman to take care of her.

He'd be safe then.

He didn't allow himself to look in Valeria's direction when he reached camp. He busied himself with the horses. He gathered extra wood for the fire. But as he laid the limbs on the still-glowing coals, he couldn't resist any longer. He raised his gaze to Valeria's bedroll.

It was empty.

That was so unexpected that for a moment he didn't know what to think. She couldn't have gotten mad and gone off in a huff. There was nowhere to go. She wouldn't be hiding from him. She was afraid of wild animals. She couldn't have run away because he had both horses.

Luke searched behind boulders, under trees, along the creek more than a hundred yards in both directions, thinking she might have wanted to take a bath in private, but he couldn't find her.

Valeria had disappeared.

Chapter Twenty-one

Valeria had begun to wonder about the wisdom of her strategy long before she saw the lights of the small town nestled in the bottom of the valley. She breathed a sigh of relief. At least she wouldn't be devoured by a mountain lion before Luke found her. She had assumed he would follow her quickly, but he hadn't. She had tried waiting, but the innumerable tiny sounds that filled the night made her too nervous to remain still. As long as she walked, she made enough noise to cover other sounds.

She didn't know how long she'd been gone. Her feet told her it had been an eternity. Her boots weren't made for walking on rocky, uneven ground. Her feet were hot and sweaty. She was certain she had blisters forming on both. Where was Luke? Even if he didn't love her—and from the intensity of his kisses, she had every reason to believe he did—his unending worry over his reputation should have sent him chasing after her the minute he knew she had gone.

Valeria stumbled down the hillside and onto a rough track that served as a road to the small town. She wondered why Luke hadn't mentioned it. He probably didn't want to force her to sleep in a warm, soft bed when he knew she'd be much happier sleeping on rocks, wondering if she'd be sharing her bed with rattlesnakes and scorpions before the morning. She was determined to learn how to live in this country regardless of the discomforts—and there did seem to be a great number of them—but she didn't understand why they couldn't avail themselves of a few comforts now and then, especially when they didn't know what kind of animals might be prowling around their campsite. She didn't have much faith in horses as a first line of defense.

She had to bend her mind to deciding what to do when she reached town. She'd love to find a boardinghouse like Mrs. Brightman's, but she didn't know if all towns had boardinghouses. This one looked a lot smaller than Oxford. It had only one street with about a dozen buildings on one side, fewer on the other. None of them looked very large or very nice.

That didn't matter. She'd only be here as long as it took Luke to find her. She expected him to come hurtling down the hillside any minute. In the meantime, she was thirsty. And hungry. She hadn't eaten more than a few bites of her dinner.

The closer she came to the town, the more uneasy she became. She didn't see any houses with yards and flowers. She didn't see a church or anything that resembled a school. The decent businesses had closed for the night. At least half of the buildings appeared to be saloons, all open with lights in the windows. But it wasn't the abundant light of open, cheerful saloons welcoming passersby in for a drink. It was a dull, subdued, sullen light that offered little cheer.

Valeria stopped and looked behind her. Luke was nowhere in sight. What if he wasn't coming?

She couldn't believe that. She didn't know what had happened, but sooner or later Luke would come after her. The question was, what to do in the meantime. She couldn't continue to stand in the middle of the road. She was tired and thirsty. She would examine all of the saloons, then choose the one that appeared to be the cleanest and most genteel.

She rejected the first saloon with no more than a glance. The stench of whiskey, tobacco, coal oil, and human sweat that poured through the open door nearly made her gag. The second and third saloons were only marginally better. The next saloon had a second floor. It appeared to be a combination of saloon, restaurant, and hotel. But Valeria didn't see any women inside. She continued down the street, rejecting each saloon as she passed.

She crossed the street.

Most of the buildings on this side were dark, closed. One was a law office. Another, an assay office. A third, a barbershop. A fourth, a laundry. The fifth, another saloon. Valeria saw a brightly dressed woman inside. Her momentary hope was dashed when she saw a man fondle her as she laughed and teased him by tickling him under the chin with an egret feather.

Music came from the next saloon, but since the men were dancing with each other, Valeria assumed there were no women inside. She had no intention of being the first. As she stood there, trying to make up her mind, two men stumbled out of the first saloon. Valeria moved back into the shadow of a doorway.

They stopped at the steps going down from the boardwalk to the street. One grabbed onto a pole to steady himself. The other leaned against a post and lit a cigarette. "I can't wait to get out of this place," he said to the other man. "What's the use of getting rich if we ain't got any women to spend it on?"

"We ain't rich, not by a long shot."

Drink slurred their speech, but Valeria could understand every word.

"I got twice as much money in my pocket right now as my brother back in Alabama makes in a year, and I got nothing to do with it."

"You can spend it on Squirrel Annie."

"That woman is uglier than a swamp hog. She'd have to pay *me* to spend an hour with her." He leaned back and blew smoke rings into the hot night air.

"Probably just as well, since there ain't no nice looking women about. We wouldn't know what to do with them."

"I would, too."

"Neely, you ain't nothing but a dumb dirt farmer from Alabama. You ain't even started shaving regular. A real woman would scare you to death."

"I'd still know what to do."

"And just what would that be?"

When Neely elaborated, Valeria could feel the heat all the way down to her toes.

"Well, there ain't no point in getting yourself all worked up," the other boy said. "There ain't no women around here, so we might as well go off to bed. Tomorrow ain't going to be no easier just because you're horny tonight."

Neely tossed his cigarette into the street. "I'm horny every night."

"Don't think about it," his friend advised.

"I can't stop thinking about it."

"Well, I'm going off to bed. You coming now, or you going to have another beer?"

"I ain't going back in there," Neely said. "Any more

needling about my pretty face, and I'm going to smash Navez right in the nose."

"Yeah, and get beat to rat bait."

"I ain't afraid of him."

"If you had good sense you would be. Come on, I'm worn to the bone."

They started down the boardwalk toward Valeria. She pulled farther back into the doorway, hoping they'd pass without noticing her. They did, only Neely changed his mind and decided he wanted another beer. When he turned around, he saw Valeria.

He turned white, looked like he had come face-to-face with an apparition.

"Gawd Almighty!"

The exclamation startled Valeria into darting from the safety of the doorway.

"She's real," Neely exclaimed. "I ain't seeing things, Albie."

Albie appeared beyond speech. Neely started toward Valeria, his hand outstretched as though he had to touch her to believe what he saw.

"She's beautiful," Albie whispered reverently, "purtier than any angel."

"Shush!" Neely said. "Don't talk so loud. Somebody might hear you. I want her all to myself."

"Me, too," Albie said. "Don't forget me."

"What's your name?" Neely asked. Valeria backed farther away. "We won't hurt you."

"We just want to have some fun."

"Shut up, you fool. You're scaring her."

"I ain't the one trying to grab hold of her."

Neely looked at his hand as though he hadn't been aware of what it was doing. He dropped it to his side. "You're mighty pretty," he said. "I ain't never seen a girl as pretty as you. Want me to buy you a beer?"

Valeria shook her head.

"Maybe she wants whiskey," Albie suggested.

Valeria shook her head more vigorously.

"You ought to know a pretty girl like her wouldn't want none of that rotgut," Neely said. "She'll want something fancy."

"Like what?" Albie asked.

Neely clearly wasn't able to think of a drink he considered fancy enough. "What would you like?" he asked Valeria. He rattled the coins in his pocket. "I'll buy you anything you want."

"I'd like some water," Valeria said.

"Water!"

Now that she could see how young they were, she didn't feel frightened.

"And something to eat," Valeria added. "I'm hungry."

She realized as soon as the words were out of her mouth that she didn't have money to pay for food. She wasn't naive enough to think these boys would pay for her dinner without expecting something in return. And Neely had been kind enough to explain exactly what that was.

"But I don't have to eat," she added quickly. "Just some water."

"You come with me, babe," Neely said, trying to act like an older and more experienced man. "We got plenty of water in our room."

"Why don't we go to a saloon?" Valeria said, pointing to the saloon she remembered as being part restaurant.

"You don't want to do that," Neely said. "It's full of men who'll grab at you. You come on with us. We'll be real nice to you."

"I'm not the kind of woman you think," Valeria said. "My guide is camped over that hill. He's taking me to a ranch in the Rim country."

Both boys looked taken aback, but Neely recovered quickly. "You don't need to haggle over price. We'll pay you real good."

"But I don't want to go with you," Valeria said backing away. "I really am going to the Rim country."

"Yeah, and you've got a handsome cowboy who'll come riding to the rescue. Look, you and I know there ain't no female within ten miles of this place what doesn't wear her price painted on her chest. Whatever it is, Albie and me will pay it."

Albie nodded enthusiastically as Neely reached out and took hold of Valeria's wrist.

Valeria backed away. She had a notion the men in the saloon might be very much like Neely said, but they wouldn't do anything to her in public. If Neely and his friend got her into their room, she was quite certain what would happen. She wrenched her arm from his grasp and darted off the boardwalk into the street.

"You go up the street and I'll go down," Neely told Albie. "We'll cut her off."

The young men were faster than Valeria. Though she ran first one way and then another, she couldn't get around them. She could either stay here until they caught her and dragged her into their room, or she could run into the saloon and depend upon the public nature of the place to be her protection.

With a single backward glance toward the hills and a silent plea to Luke to come quickly, she turned and headed toward the saloon.

"Don't go in there!" Neely called when he saw what she intended to do. "Please, lady, don't go in there."

But Valeria had already stepped inside the door.

"Now look what you've done," she heard Albie say.

"I didn't mean to."

"We have to go after her."

"You sure?"

"Yeah."

Valeria hadn't gone two steps into the saloon before every eye in the place was on her. She'd spent her entire life on public display, but never like this. There was admiration in the gazes all around her. There was also hunger and lust that didn't hide behind polite smiles, well-rehearsed compliments, or hooded gazes. Here it was in the open, naked, raw, and unrestrained.

She was aware of a low sound that gradually filled the room, settling into corners and behind tables. It sounded unnervingly like the growl of a hungry animal when it sights food.

Keeping her gaze straight ahead, Valeria approached the bar, where a man was serving drinks. No one moved to give her room, so she went to an empty space at the end.

The bartender looked at her for several seconds before he moved in her direction, a look of disbelief on his face. "What do you want?" he asked.

"I'd like a glass of water."

The growl stopped. For an instant, the room was completely silent.

"Okay," the bartender said, disbelief turning to a sneer. "You want a glass with some water in it."

Valeria took an instant dislike to him. "Thank you."

"Now what do you want in it, and which one of these men are you going to con into paying for it?"

"You charge for water?" Valeria asked.

"I charge for whiskey."

"I don't want any whiskey. I want water."

"I don't serve water."

"But that's all I want."

"Give the lady her water."

Valeria turned to see a huge man get up from one of

the tables and come toward her. She wondered why she thought there was something familiar about him, then realized he was a miner. He looked like the men she'd seen in Bonner.

"You gonna buy some whiskey, Soderman?" the bartender asked. "I don't run this place to serve up water."

"Sure, I'll have a whiskey," Soderman said. "Make it a bottle. I might be able to talk the little lady into changing her mind."

"Thank you, but water is all I want. I have to get back to my camp."

Soderman's smile made Valeria uneasy. One missing and one broken tooth made him look dangerous.

"No use playing games, girl. We know there's nothing in those hills but snakes and scorpions."

"My guide is out there," Valeria said.

"I just can't figure where you come from," Soderman said, ignoring her words. "There's no way this lousy town could hide a beauty like you."

"She came with me." Neely strolled into the saloon with a show of bravado. A less courageous Albie followed.

Soderman took one look at Neely and broke out laughing. "No woman with her looks would settle for a kid like you. I bet she ran away 'cause she wanted a man."

Neely walked up and grabbed Valeria's hand. "I'm man enough. Me and Albie is more than enough for any female."

Valeria didn't trust Neely, but he was obviously trying to protect her. She'd go with him and worry about his intentions later.

But she didn't get a chance. Soderman backhanded Neely and sent the boy stumbling halfway across the room into Albie, both of them going down in a heap.

"Nobody gets between me and a woman I got my eye on."

Valeria had been frightened nearly out of her mind, but Soderman's hitting Neely replaced fear with fury. She pushed past him to where Neely lay on the floor, blood dripping from his mouth. "Are you all right? Do you need a doctor?"

"He don't need no doctor for a little blood," Soderman said. "He needs one for being stupid."

Valeria strode past Soderman without even looking at him. "I want my water," she said to the barman.

"I don't see—"

"Now!" The authority of twenty-five generations of imperious kings resonated in that single word. She picked up the glass handed to her and turned to face the men in the room. "Does anyone have a handkerchief?"

The man closest to Neely offered his.

"Thank you." She knelt down, soaked the handkerchief in water, and began to clean the blood from Neely's mouth.

"Don't waste time on me," Neely muttered. "Get out of here while you can. Albie will help you."

Valeria shook her head just as Soderman grabbed her by the shoulder and jerked her to her feet. "Stop wasting your time on that kid."

"Get your hands off me," Valeria said, icy disdain dripping from each word. Soderman stared at her, apparently uncertain how to react to her regal disdain. "I said, remove your hand." Maybe it was all her ancestors standing behind her, but Soderman released her.

Valeria jerked her arm away and turned back to Neely. "Can you get up if Albie helps you?"

"Yeah."

"You'd better take him straight to his room," she said

to Albie. "If you'll tell me where I can find the doctor, I'll—"

"You're not leaving!" Soderman roared.

He had recovered from his momentary hesitation.

"He needs a doctor."

"He can have all the doctors he wants, but you're coming with me."

Valeria drew back from him. It infuriated her that he would assume that just because he wanted her, she had to go with him.

"I don't know you," Valeria said. "But even if I did, I wouldn't go with you for the purpose that you—" she didn't know how to put her meaning into words.

"You came into this saloon."

"I was told America was a free country. I assumed that referred to women as well as men."

"I don't give a damn about freedom. I—"

"I come from a country where I had no freedom at all. It's very important to me."

"You were free to go to any town in the territory," Soderman said, "but you came here. The only women who come here are whores. And a whore is exactly what I want, especially when she's as pretty as you."

"I'm not a—" She couldn't make herself say the word. "I'm not what you think."

"I'm tired of all this talking," Soderman thundered. "You're coming with me."

He grabbed for Valeria, but she darted around a nearby table. She started toward the door, but Soderman blocked her path.

"These men won't let you abduct me," she said.

"Ain't nobody in this room going to stop me."

Valeria had to run around another table to keep out of his reach. Soderman was huge and powerful, but he was slow. "Are you going to let him do this?" Valeria said to the men who'd been watching in awed silence.

"Ain't nobody going to do nothing."

Neely struggled to his feet. "I got you into this mess, ma'am. I guess it's up to me to get you out."

That got Valeria madder than ever. "Are you men going to sit there and let this boy do what you won't?"

"He ain't doing nothing," Soderman said. With that his fist shot out, catching Neely square in the face. Neely dropped like a rock and lay on the floor, unmoving.

"I've waited as long as I'm going to," Soderman said. He waded through the room pushing men, chairs, and tables aside with the strength of a bull. He cornered Valeria. She fought with all her strength, but she could do nothing.

She prayed Luke would miraculously appear, but she'd given up hope. He'd warned her what could happen, but she'd felt so safe with him she hadn't taken him seriously. She hadn't thought of anything except pushing him past the breaking point.

"When I'm done with her, anyone else who wants can have her," Soderman announced.

He started toward the door. He stopped when a horse came through the doors into the saloon.

"Luke!" Valeria screamed, so relieved to see him she didn't remember that a princess of the royal blood never raises her voice.

A shot rang out, and Soderman lurched to one side. He lost his hold on Valeria, and she ran to Luke. Luke had shot Soderman in the leg. He looked around the room. The fire in his eyes could have set the place ablaze.

"I ought to put a bullet in every one of you for letting that piece of carrion put his hands on her." He pointed his gun at the man closest to the door. "Lift her into the saddle." His gaze turned ferocious. "And you'd better remember she's a lady."

Only then did Valeria realize Luke had brought a second horse. Her mount had stuck its head inside the saloon.

"You've got to help Neely," Valeria said, pointing to the boy still lying unconscious. "He and Albie tried to protect me."

Luke's mount had driven Albie up against the bar. The boy looked ready to join his friend on the floor.

"Look out!" someone shouted.

Almost instantly two shots filled the saloon with a deafening roar. A huge knife slipped from Soderman's hand as his body sank to the floor. There was a small hole in his forehead just above the bridge of his nose. The sound of agonizing moans caused Valeria to turn to the bar. The bartender had staggered back against the bar, his hand a bloody mess. A shotgun lay across the bar where he'd dropped it.

"Anybody else who wants to try me is welcome," Luke said, "but be warned, I'll shoot to kill. You two get this boy to a doctor," Luke said pointing to two men at random. They got to their feet, lifted Neely by his feet and arms, and carried him out.

"You his friend?" Luke asked Albie.

The petrified boy nodded.

"You want to get out of this cesspool?"

He nodded again.

"As soon as he's able to travel, get yourselves down to Bonner. I'll be going through there in about a week. You going to lift her into the saddle, or do I have to put a bullet in you too?" Luke said to the man he'd told to help Valeria.

The man jumped to his feet and gingerly lifted her to the sidesaddle. He was a big man, plenty strong, but he held her so lightly she almost slipped out of his grasp.

"If I ever have to come back to this town, I'll burn it

to the ground," Luke said. He turned his horse, took Valeria's mount by the bridle, and rode out of the saloon.

No air had ever smelled so sweet, no cloak of night been so welcome. Valeria took her first full breath in what felt like hours. She hadn't realized until she had to hold onto the reins that her muscles had been so tense they hurt. But though some of the tension began to flow from her body as they rode down the street and out of town, another kind of tension started to build. Guilt. As furious as Luke had been at Soderman, he was going to be more furious at her. She'd risked his life as well as her own because of a silly game.

Why hadn't she just told Luke she liked him?

. Because she hadn't thought of it until now. Such a thing was unimaginable in Belgravia, but it was too late. The last thing Luke would want to hear was that she'd risked their lives because she wanted to know if he could stop hating her long enough to fall in love with her.

That sounded silly even to her. Some women might go straight from disgust to love—she had—but she was sure men didn't. If they hated a woman, they hated her forever.

Luke didn't hate her, but she didn't know if his liking was just the kind of lust Neely had outlined to his friend. Valeria blushed as she recalled some of the things Neely had said.

She wondered if Luke wanted to do the same things. The women at court said men reserved anything of that sort for their mistresses. Valeria didn't know exactly what she wanted her husband to do, but she was certain she didn't want him to do anything with a mistress.

But she was no longer the naive and unquestioning Princess Valeria of Belgravia. She was plain Valeria Badenberg, free to fall in love, free to demand fidelity from the man of her choice. And her choice was Luke Attmore.

At the moment, however, he was so angry he wouldn't even speak to her.

"Thank you for offering to give Neely and Albie jobs," she said, finally unable to stand the silence any longer. "It was brave of them to try to defend me against Soderman."

Luke didn't speak, but she could see his shoulders draw together and rise slightly from tension. She would never tell him Neely had wanted to do pretty much what Soderman intended to do. He'd more than made up for it by trying to defend her.

"I hope he wasn't hurt badly. Soderman was very strong."

It surprised her that she didn't feel regret or guilt over Soderman's death. She felt nothing but relief that a man who would rape her, then offer her to every man in that saloon was no longer alive to prey on women. She supposed she was more like her ancestors than she'd thought. She didn't mourn the death of her enemies any more than her ancestors had mourned the deaths of theirs.

"I never did learn if there was a doctor in that town. It's not very large."

The only sound that came back to her was the squeak of Luke's saddle as his mount ascended the ridge leading to their camp. Okay, so she'd done a stupid thing, but she'd never been in love before. She didn't *know* how a woman was supposed to show a man she loved him. She wasn't even certain it was love. Maybe she was just holding onto the strongest, most dependable man she knew in this crazy country. Maybe she was projecting onto Luke the characteristics of the heros in her mind, men who led armies, conquered countries, men who were afraid of no one and nothing.

No, Luke *was* a natural leader, a man unafraid of anyone and anything. That was part of the reason she had been attracted to him in the first place. He was an old-world hero. Yet he was totally modern and had insisted she become modern, too.

"Would it make you feel any better if I said I was sorry, that I did a very foolish thing, that I never meant to risk anybody's life?"

Apparently not.

"I know you told me what would happen if I trusted strange men, but I was thirsty. I thought if I could just get a drink of water—"

"Water!" Luke turned his horse, then drove the animal hard up against Valeria's mount. "You entered that den of snakes for a drink of water?"

"I was thirsty."

He muttered something under his breath. She didn't know what. She didn't even recognize the language.

"That man would have killed you," Luke said. "Or he'd have made you wish you were dead."

"Surely it couldn't have been that bad. He—"

"If you're determined to ruin yourself, you could have at least turned to me."

Chapter Twenty-two

Valeria couldn't believe her ears. Luke hadn't said one nice thing to her. He couldn't even speak to her without looking like he had indigestion. "But you hate me."

He started their horses forward, but he stayed by her side. "I never hated you."

She might have been raised in a make-believe world, but she knew hate and anger when she saw it. "You told me I was useless, a parasite, a—"

"I told you the institution of monarchy was useless. I never meant you were useless."

"Yes, you did. You went out of your way to prove I didn't know anything, couldn't do anything."

He turned to face her. "That's because I couldn't stand to see you so ignorant."

Valeria began to wonder if she had heard Luke correctly. Maybe this was something else they did differently in America. She admitted she had only an imperfect knowledge of what love was like, but that knowledge was instinctive, and instinct told her a man who loved a woman wouldn't treat her like she was a plague on the Western world.

They were descending the west side of the low hill, riding toward the camp she'd left such a short time ago, returning to the isolation she had thought was total. She realized she felt safer *away* from people, safe in isolation that would have frightened her only a few weeks earlier. Coming to Arizona had changed her beyond all recognition.

"Why didn't you tell me how you felt?" she asked.

"Because you don't like me."

She knew that wasn't the reason. "But I do."

He pulled their horses to an abrupt stop. "When did that happen?" He didn't appear excited, happy, pleased. He didn't even seem to care.

"I don't know. I realized it when you took me to Mrs. Brightman's house."

He started the horses forward again. "Why would a woman like you care for a man like me?"

She couldn't answer that question. She didn't understand herself. She just knew she felt safe with Luke, that she admired his physical strength, his knowledge, his leadership. His looks. One glance, and no woman would need to ask why she'd fallen in love with Luke. He was tall, well-muscled, absolutely the best looking man she'd ever seen.

Maybe his temper, his black moods, his obsession with his reputation, should have given her pause, but those were characteristics of men who were leaders, who accomplished what they set out to do. Maybe it came from being a princess, from spending most of her life with one kind of man, but she admired a man who could take command of a situation, could convince others to follow him even when they disagreed with what he was doing, who never failed to do what he said he'd do.

But there was a softer side to Luke. He might not see it, but he'd been protective of her from the first. He'd been hard on her, but he'd also done his best to make sure she learned quickly that life in America was not at all like it was in Belgravia. And no matter how rude and ungrateful she'd been, he'd never deserted her.

She didn't believe he loved her yet. His change of heart had come too suddenly, but she did believe he liked her. He wouldn't allow himself to love anyone. She was certain he saw it as a weakness, possibly a fatal one. She couldn't remember a single general in Belgravia's entire history who was supposed to have felt great love for any woman. It might be very hard for a man like Luke to learn to love, but surely it wasn't impossible.

"Why shouldn't I care for you, even love you?" she asked.

"Women don't love men like me."

He couldn't have been more wrong. What did he think all those women in his past had been doing, using him for rehearsal?

"Women love all kinds of men." Even a princess knew that. "You're exactly the kind a woman falls in love with practically at first sight."

His laugh was harsh. "I know all about lust," he said. "I suffer from a big dose of that myself."

"I don't know about lust. I just know any woman would count herself fortunate to be loved by a man such as you."

When he turned back, the harshness of his expression shocked her. "Women want something very different from what I am."

"What are you that's so terrible?"

"Nothing good."

He turned back, put their horses into a canter. Considering the number of times he'd warned her about riding too fast on rocky ground in daylight, she knew he had to be upset. She just didn't understand why.

"A woman likes a little bit of the beast in her man," she said when he slowed the horses to a walk again. "It makes her feel he's capable of protecting her."

"There's a lot more to marriage than that."

"Like what?"

She'd been taught marriage was about doing your duty to your husband and country, being a credit to your station in life, and producing an heir. Leave it to these Americans to complicate things.

"You ought to ask a woman that question," he said.

"But marriage can't be just for the woman, not if two people marry because they're in love."

"Why not?"

"Because men have needs, too. I'm not sure what they are, but in Belgravia the men all had mistresses. That must mean they were missing something in marriage."

"Men in America have mistresses, too."

If a man married for love, why should he want—need—a mistress?

"Do you have a mistress?"

"No."

That lifted a weight from her heart. A man used to having a mistress wasn't likely to give up the privilege.

"Have you ever had one?"

"I never wanted to be tied down. Besides, no woman wants a man like me for very long."

"Why?"

"They just don't."

They'd reached the camp. She saw her bedroll where she'd left it, the coffeepot sitting on dead coals, the supper dishes left where they had been dropped. Oddly enough she felt more at home than she had in Mrs. Brightman's house. It was just her and Luke, alone.

It felt right, like that was the way it ought to be.

She started to slide out of the saddle. Instead she waited. He would have to touch her if he lifted her. And she wanted to feel his touch. His presence might be enough assurance for her mind, but her heart and soul needed something more concrete. She also intended to find out if he meant what he said. Considering his iron self-control, she doubted she could tempt him unless he touched her, even kissed her, committed himself so far even his restraint couldn't overcome his need for her.

So she waited.

He dismounted, walked over, and lifted her from the saddle. She didn't release her hold on his arms when he set her feet on the ground. She gazed up into his eyes, turned his face back when he would have looked aside. "I'm truly sorry for the trouble I caused, but when you left me alone, I thought you disliked me."

"How could you think that after the way I kissed you?"

"You said a man could lust after any woman, but he could only love someone he thought special." He hadn't really said that, but she'd deduced it from some of the things he had said. "I wanted to be that somebody special."

His body seemed to freeze. His eyes burned brighter, watching her with unnerving intensity. "You're promised to someone else."

"Not anymore. I don't want to marry Rudolf. I don't love him. I never did. I want to be like the American women you told me about. I want to marry for love."

"Where are you going to find a man to love out here?"

"I already have."

If it were possible, he seemed to grow even more still. "You can't love me, not like I need to be loved." He whispered the words, as though he were telling her a secret.

"Why not?"

"Because no woman can."

She was a princess. No one was going to tell her she was incapable of anything. She'd been in training her whole life to do what *had to be done*. Now that the time had come, she didn't intend to fail. But she could see it wouldn't be easy to convince Luke. She didn't know why he was so convinced no woman could love him, but she intended to make him believe no man was beyond the reach of love, that no woman in the world could love stronger and longer than an exiled princess.

He attempted to back away, but she didn't relax her hold on him. "You're afraid."

"Yes."

"Why?"

"Because I might start to hope you won't fail."

Valeria needed nothing more to convince her that no matter how much Luke resisted, no matter how thoroughly convinced he was that no woman could love him, he had never really given up hope. She reached up to pull him down to her. He resisted for so long, she thought he would refuse. Then, abruptly, his resistance collapsed, and he engulfed her in a tempestuous embrace that took her breath away.

In Belgravia, relations between a man and a woman were governed by strict, stylized rules of etiquette. There was nothing stylized about Luke's kisses. They were savage, hungry, demanding, hard, and she welcomed every one of them. After so many years of being treated as though she were a precious object, it was thrilling to be held so tightly by a man. It was wonderful to be touched, enfolded, crushed to him, to feel her body from her breasts to her thighs pressed against Luke's hard muscles. It made her feel more real, more *alive*, than ever before.

But it was her desire to kiss him back that had the

greatest effect on Valeria. It was as though some wall came crashing down to liberate feelings stifled by a world where the performance of her duty and the preservation of her family's position were the only things that mattered. Her feelings for Luke owed nothing to duty. Her desire to kiss him just as passionately as he kissed her owed nothing to preservation of the royal house. It was grounded in her need to be wanted for herself.

Luke scorned her title, position, and fortune. Anything he felt for her was for her alone. Knowing that made Valeria's heart sing. He might not love her yet, but he cared a great deal. And for the time being, that was enough. There was plenty of time for love to develop. She wouldn't leave his side until he believed she could love him fully as much as he needed to be loved.

Luke broke the kiss. "I shouldn't have done that."

"You promised to teach me to feel things I never thought were possible," she said. "Can you do that without touching me?"

"You don't know what you're asking."

"Then show me."

"You're a virgin."

"Every woman is a virgin until she gives herself to the man she loves."

"Don't say you love me!"

"Does it frighten you to think you might be loved?"

"Yes."

"Why?"

"Because I can't love. There's nothing inside here." He struck his chest. "And nothing can make it come alive again."

"You'll never know until you try."

"Valeria, this isn't like a summer outing. You can't start out, then turn back when you decide you don't like it anymore."

"Never in my life have I been able to turn around. I've always been forced to go forward."

"Loss of innocence is permanent."

"It has to happen sometime. I'd rather it happen with a man I love."

"Stop saying that!" He shook her so hard she thought her brain bounced around inside her skull.

"Do you want me to lie about the way I feel?"

"Yes."

"If I'm strong enough to face coming to a new country, learning new customs, trusting a man who has done everything possible to make me distrust him, why can't you trust your feelings?"

"Because I know feelings can lie. And they can change."

"If you loved me, would you change?"

His whole body shuddered. "No. That's why I can't take the chance."

"You don't think I can love you?"

He took a deep breath. "You don't know what it's like to be in love. You've never been allowed to find out. You don't know me or what it would be like to love a man like me."

"Then teach me. Do it for me if not for yourself. You said you stayed because you wanted to help me learn to survive in this country. My education isn't finished. You can't leave until it's done."

"No."

She needed something to push him just a little bit more. "Rudolf would teach me, but I doubt he'd want me to know too much. Then there's Neely. He's probably not very experienced, but he has a kind heart. He'd probably be willing—"

"Stop! If you're determined to ruin yourself, choose me." He seemed to lose some of the violent energy behind his outburst. "At least it will keep me from having to kill the man who does."

She didn't understand how he could be so fiercely protective of her yet keep his distance. If she could feel that intensely about anyone—and she knew she must or she never could love Luke the way he needed to be loved—she'd never want to let him go. "Teach me," she said. "Teach me now."

"I'm breaking my word," he said.

She felt guilty about taking away something so vitally important to him, but she knew that until he lost his honor, at least the way he defined it, he could never have something much more important to both of them.

Love. Family. A life that revolved around more than a fast gun.

"Isn't the chance for love worth sacrifice? Which do you want more, to be loved or feared?"

She watched the battle inside him as it was reflected in his eyes, his face. She had asked him to give up what he had, what he'd worked years to gain, in exchange for something as hard to capture and define as the breeze that rustled the cottonwood and willow leaves. That must be very difficult for a man who'd defined himself by action. Yet she knew action would never be enough for Luke. He wanted more. She wanted to give it to him. He had to have the courage to accept it. Odd that a man who faced death fearlessly each day should tremble in fear of love. She wasn't the only one who had a lot to learn.

Luke appeared to struggle, and then the tension left him. He rubbed the back of his fingers gently against her cheek. "I've wanted to make love to you from the moment I saw you," he said.

"You loathed me."

"You were cold and distant, but I knew under that veneer beat the soul of a passionate woman. But I didn't think you'd run me to ground like a coyote runs a rabbit to his burrow."

"You might not like my background, but I come from a long line of warriors who are willing to fight for what we want."

"I come from a short line who take what we want, use it, and discard it when we're through."

"You're only an amateur compared to an absolute monarch. Now stop trying to make me change my mind."

"I don't think I could let you." He pulled her to him. "You're in my blood."

Valeria slipped her arms around his waist, squeezed tight as she pressed her head against his chest. "I want to invade every part of your heart, soul, mind, and spirit."

Luke folded her in his embrace. "You already have." He planted a kiss on the top of her head. "I dreamed about you that first night."

Valeria looked up. "I thought you spent the night standing outside my hotel room."

"Only part of it."

"That's when I knew you weren't what you pretended to be."

Luke responded by kissing her into silence. Valeria didn't mind. Nor did she mind when they sank to the bedroll, Luke pulling her into his lap. She liked his being so much taller than she, but it was easier to kiss him sitting down. It was especially nice to do so sitting in his lap. The informality, the intimacy made her feel ordinary for the first time in her life. It made her feel valued just for herself. As a woman.

She didn't know that sitting in Luke's lap would cause unfamiliar warmth to gradually pervade her body. With it came excitement, tension, a feeling of being on the verge of discovering something wonderful. She'd barely gotten comfortable when Luke laid her down on the bedroll, then lay down beside her, leaning over her, looking down at her with an expression she couldn't fathom.

"You're beautiful," he said softly.

How could he say that? She wore a plain dress, no jewelry or cosmetics, and her hair was a mess. It would have taken Elvira a full day to get her ready to be seen.

"You look real, not someone to be bowed or curtsied to. I like you better this way."

She wanted to believe him. She'd learned a lot since coming to America, but she hadn't quite learned to separate her attractiveness from the way she dressed.

"Is this what you say to other women?"

She knew right away she'd asked the wrong question, but she had to know. How could she believe him if he said the same thing to everyone?

"I've never felt this way about another woman," Luke said. "That makes everything I say different, even if I sometimes use the same words."

That wasn't the answer she'd been hoping for.

"Doesn't every man who meets you use the same words to tell you you're beautiful, to compliment you?"

"Yes."

"When you meet a man you love, wouldn't you hear the same words but know they're different this time?"

She couldn't help but smile. "You should have been a diplomat. You're very smooth with words."

"Only because I mean them. You don't need extravagant gowns, fabulous jewels, or your hair twisted and curled and loaded with flowers or bird feathers to be beautiful. You don't need palaces. You're beautiful lying on a bedroll in the desert under a night sky. You're beautiful enough to make me jealous of every man who sets eyes on you."

Valeria had spent her whole life preparing to be seen, to make an impression by her appearance. To be valued in and of herself, devoid of her public image, was difficult to grasp. Could any man love her that much?

"Do you think you could be happy living like an ordinary woman?"

"I don't know what an ordinary woman's life is really like. The only one I've ever met is Mrs. Brightman. I'm sure I have a great deal to learn, but I think I would like running my own home, taking care of my children, having a husband I don't have to share with a mistress."

Luke chuckled. "You're turning into an American woman real fast."

"I could never go back to Belgravia, not even if my uncle regained his throne."

"He might insist that you return."

"I would tell him that I couldn't leave my husband and children. Even in Belgravia, a woman is expected to stay with her family."

"But you're not married, and you don't have any children."

"You told me in America women can choose their husbands. Well, I intend to choose mine."

"And what will you do if he doesn't choose you?"

"A wise woman never chooses a man who hasn't already chosen her."

That sobered him up. "That doesn't prevent her from choosing the wrong man."

"There was always the possibility I'd be the wife of some ruler, no matter how small the country, so I was taught how to judge character. I'll make certain the man I choose is perfect for me."

He seemed to draw back. "Then you've chosen the wrong man to take your innocence."

"I've chosen the perfect man." She pulled him down until their lips met.

Her body had recognized him the moment she met

him. So had her instincts. Only her mind failed to see that though Luke appeared to be different, he was very much the kind of man she'd been used to most of her life, a man determined to succeed regardless of the cost to himself or others.

Only with him there was a difference. A small, essential part, well hidden and probably never acknowledged, hoped for something better. It was that tiny part that had caused him to wait until Valeria rehired him, prompted him to teach her what it would be like to live in America.

He had tried to tell her he wasn't the man for her, but she knew better. His kisses had become warm and gentle. She missed the power, the sense of being overwhelmed by his intensity, but she welcomed the tenderness. Being overwhelmed made her feel safe and protected. Tenderness made her feel valued and loved. The two together were wonderful.

Contact with Luke's body caused her skin to tingle with pinpricks of sensation. Luke's arms were around her, his body looming above her, his chest brushing against her breasts. A tingling sensation sprang up in her breasts, concentrating in her nipples until she found it difficult to remain still.

Luke forced her teeth apart, and his tongue invaded her mouth. A new set of nerve endings came to life. If she had married Rudolf, she would never have expected him to thrust his tongue into her mouth, would probably have rejected any attempts from him to do so. With Luke, it seemed like one more example of the ways in which America was different from Belgravia, a difference she decided she liked once she recovered from the shock.

A sense of adventure surged through her, encouraging her to counter Luke's invasion with one of her own. But what began as an assault quickly turned into a sensual duel, Luke's tongue wrapping itself around hers. She escaped and tried to dart around and into his mouth. Their tongues engaged in a thrust and parry, then a sinuous dance followed by a chase that left Valeria panting for breath. She broke their kiss and fell back, emotionally exhausted.

Luke was made of sterner stuff. Without pause he spread kisses over her mouth, her cheeks, eyes, nose, eyelids, forehead, even her ears. That nearly caused Valeria to rise straight up off the ground. He nibbled her earlobe, nipped it with his teeth, traced its outer edge with the tip of his tongue. In less than a minute he reduced her to a helpless, quivering mass.

But not so helpless she didn't know when his hand covered her breast. Nor did her concentration falter when his lips returned to tease her mouth once more. The feel of his hand cupping her breast caused sensations to concentrate in that part of her body. Her nipple turned as hard as a pebble. The muscles in her back tightened and caused her shoulders to arch, pressing her harder and deeper into his palm, making the pleasure still more intense.

Luke scattered kisses on the side of her neck and across her shoulders, leaving her body in an uproar of heat and delicious sensations. These intensified when he unbuttoned her dress and lowered his lips to the tops of her breasts. Unable to lie still, she writhed on the bedroll, turning first to him, then away, drawn to the feast of pleasure and retreating to recover her breath before indulging herself once more.

All of which proved a mere prelude to the moment his lips touched her nipples.

Valeria's body went still, then stiff, then it arched in pure, incredible pleasure. She had never imagined anything would feel quite so spectacularly wonderful. So unbelievably extraordinary. So unlike anything she'd ever experienced. His tongue slowly circled her nipple, creating a ring of fire that made her skin feel so hot, she was afraid it would burn Luke's tongue.

When he took her nipple between his teeth, she gasped. When he nipped at it, she cried out. When he suckled it gently, she moaned in ecstasy. When he uncovered her other breast and allowed his fingertip to torture her second nipple, she was certain she couldn't stand so much pleasure. She quivered and writhed under Luke's assault. Yet she placed her hands on the back of his head and pressed him against her. The turmoil left her only a sliver of attention to give to the hand that played down her side and across her belly to undo the last buttons of her dress.

Yet when that same hand moved across her pelvis, around her hip, and down her thigh, she became aware of a center of warmth that had formed deep in her belly. It wasn't nearly as tempestuous as the riot of sensation that rocked the rest of her body, but the warmth became intense and spread like a heavy liquid, flooding all in its path.

Then, almost without her knowing what he was about, Luke slipped her dress and her chemise from her body. An extra moment to remove her boots and socks, and she lay naked before him.

"You're so beautiful," Luke murmured as he ran his hands over her body, touching every part once, twice, and once again as though he wanted to memorize her. "Your skin is like ivory in the moonlight."

Valeria felt his warmth banish a momentary chill. She loved Luke. She trusted him. There was nothing to fear, no reason to hold back.

She wanted to touch him, to run her hands over his body, but every thought flew out of her head when Luke touched her between her legs. Her breath caught, her body turned rigid.

"I won't hurt you," Luke whispered. "Relax and open for me."

Doing as he asked required the greatest act of faith in her life. She kept telling herself she wanted him to make love to her, that she wanted to give her body to him, yet she couldn't entirely banish the fear of the unknown. Doctors had touched her there as part of the arrangements for her marriage to Rudolf. It had been a time of pain, terror, and shame.

Luke's gentle touch reassured her. His fingertips feathered over her belly, her thighs, the insides of her legs, increasing the pool of liquid warmth in her belly. Finally, Valeria relaxed. Her body tensed again when she felt Luke's finger enter her. He stroked gently, waiting until the muscles relaxed before probing deeper. Still she couldn't entirely relax, couldn't be entirely sure discomfort wouldn't follow. Then he touched a spot that caused a wave of pleasure to shoot through her with the impact of a lightning bolt. She gasped for breath as he continued to rub the sensitive spot, causing the waves to radiate into larger and larger circles until they encompassed her entire body.

Valeria grabbed hold of Luke, gripped him with all her strength, as moan after moan ripped from her body until she thought she would scream. Then the ecstasy crested and released, seemed to flow from her body like an ebbing tide of rippling heat.

Valeria's muscles gave way, and she collapsed onto the bedroll, her breath coming in huge gulps. "I never knew anything could feel like that," she gasped.

"It only gets better," Luke said as he shed the last of his clothes.

Valeria felt wrung out, exhausted. She was certain she was incapable of feeling anything more.

She was wrong.

Luke rose above her, his body suspended on powerful arms and legs. "This may be a little uncomfortable at first, but it won't last long."

Valeria tried to tell herself this had nothing to do with the doctors, but the fear wouldn't go away. When she felt something large and hot begin to enter her, she was certain she'd been right to be fearful.

"Relax," Luke said softly. "You've got to make room for me."

Valeria didn't think she could. His fingers hadn't prepared her for the size of him. But Luke entered her slowly, withdrawing and penetrating a little more deeply each time, allowing her muscles to relax, her fears to calm. Then a sudden, swift entry and sharp pain startled her.

"That's it," Luke said. "From now on it's nothing but pure pleasure."

Valeria couldn't understand how he could fill her so full, but as the waves began to wash over her again, all memory of the pain receded, leaving her incapable of thinking of anything except what Luke was doing to her at that very moment. He seemed to be trying to do everything at once. He was kissing her lips, eyelids, neck, every part of her that was within his reach.

The heat in her belly continued to spread through her body until it engulfed all of her in agonizingly sweet torture. She dug her nails into Luke as moans of ecstasy poured from her. She moved her body in rhythm with his, trying to drive him faster, deeper, harder, anything to bring an end to the exquisite agony.

But not until his breath became labored, started to come in uneven gasps, did he respond to her urging. Then he took over, driving them both into a headlong rush toward some approaching precipice. As she neared the edge, could see the abyss beneath her feet, Luke's body stiffened and shuddered.

Then they plunged into the abyss together.

But the fall was nothing to fear. It was surrender. It was union.

It was bliss.

Chapter Twenty-three

"There's nothing I want at the ranch," Valeria said. "It's pointless to go there."

They had left the desert and entered a forest of ponderosa pine, piñon, and oak. The sheer towers of the Mogollon Rim seemed to rise up out of the desert to block the lower third of the sky. Soft white clouds decorated a sky so clear and baby blue she could see eagles floating on updrafts a mile away.

"You can't decide what to do until you see Rudolf," Luke said.

Except for this same argument, the last week had been unbelievably wonderful for Luke. Having broken his word to himself, he had made love to Valeria every night and every morning. They'd even made love once during the heat of the day in a cottonwood thicket along the sluggish Verde River. She was as eager to learn as he was to share everything he knew.

There would have been a second argument if Luke hadn't refused to take part. Valeria insisted she loved him and that she was going to marry him. After saying once that marriage between them was impossible, Luke had refused to discuss the subject. That, however, hadn't stopped Valeria from trying to change his mind. Neither his efforts to tell her more about living in America, his description of the ever-changing landscape, nor his description of what life on the ranch would be could divert her from the subject.

"I don't know why you're so stubborn," she said. "You know I don't want to marry Rudolf."

"That's not the reason I'm taking you to the ranch."

"I know, it's your reputation. Is that all you ever think about?"

He hadn't thought about his reputation nearly as much as he thought about Valeria. That was only a small part of the reason he couldn't marry her. What kind of life could he offer her? Hell, she was a princess. He was a gunfighter, a killer. He had no home, no friends.

"The land above the Rim is beautiful country, some of the best in the Territory," Luke said. "It would be perfect for raising horses. You could settle down, send for the rest of your horses, and grow rich."

"I don't want money. I want a husband and a family."

"You wouldn't have to stay at the ranch all the time. You could go to Phoenix, Santa Fe, San Francisco, New—"

"I don't want to do that."

"There are hundreds of fine young men from good families who'd make you a perfect husband. They could give you the kind of life you deserve."

"I thought you told me women in America could marry for love?"

"I did."

"I love you, so I choose you."

"I'm not going to get married, Valeria. Not to you or anybody else."

"Why not?"

It did no good to ignore her questions. She just kept asking until she wore him down. "I'm not the kind of man any woman should have for a husband."

"Don't you think I ought to be allowed to make that decision?"

"This kind of decision requires that two people agree. When they don't, the marriage won't work."

"But—"

"Let's not talk about it anymore. It's time you decided what you're going to do once you reach the ranch."

"I don't have to do anything. Zeke will have already told Rudolf I don't want to marry him."

"I doubt he'll believe it until he hears the words from you."

"Well, I'll tell him; then he'll leave."

"Where will he go?"

"I don't know."

"Does he have any money?"

"I don't know."

"Then I don't expect he'll leave without a fight."

"Why?"

"Because he loses a home and the chance to regain his throne. I imagine he'll do his very best to convince you to change your mind."

"I won't."

"He'll try to force you."

"He can't."

"If he kills me, there won't be anyone to stop him," Luke pointed out. "If you fight him, he'll have no reason to keep you alive."

"But you said a woman could have her own money in America."

"The ranch is yours. I don't know what will happen to the money in Belgravia."

"I don't want that money. I'll give it to Rudolf. Then he won't have to marry me."

"Will your uncle let him have it, or will he try to keep it by killing you?"

"Are you trying to scare me?"

"No."

"Well, you are."

"I'm just trying to show you what you're up against. You've got to have a plan."

"I do. I want to marry you. My uncle and Rudolf can fight over the money. I don't want it."

Valeria had mastered one aspect of becoming an American woman very quickly. She had taken to being stubborn like a duck to water. The woman had a one-track mind and obviously didn't intend to change it just because her idea wouldn't work.

"You've got to have a plan in case something happens to me."

"What could happen to you?"

"I could fall off this trail." They were following a game trail barely wide enough to to keep their legs from rubbing against the rocks. He doubted anyone at Rudolf's ranch knew of the trail. He was certain they'd never believe he could get a princess to go more than a hundred feet on it before turning around. But Valeria was too busy arguing to be frightened by the precipitous drop. "Rudolf could have me killed. I could die of pneumonia," he said.

"You're indestructible," Valeria said.

She didn't know a bullet in the back had brought many a gunslinger's career to an end.

"You still need a plan. What would you do without me?"

That kept her quiet long enough for Luke to try to answer the same question for himself.

Try as he might, he couldn't envision a future without Valeria. She had become an inseparable part of his life. It didn't matter where he went, how many miles separated them, she would still be with him, in his heart, his thoughts, his dreams. She was everything he wanted in a woman. She was perfection.

It was precisely because of her perfection that he couldn't allow himself to have her.

It wasn't just that he had no life to offer, no career that allowed for a wife. He wasn't the man she thought he was. He wasn't a man at all. He had been nothing more than a reputation. Now he didn't even have that.

He had no finer aspects of character, no deeply held convictions. He was for sale. He was no better than a woman who sold her body to any man with the price. He had always hoped there was something of value to him. He'd left Jake and Isabelle, hoping to find it. But the last sixteen years had only confirmed what he'd suspected from the start. His parents had been right.

He wasn't evil. He was simply empty. Hollow. A shell guarding nothing, shielding nothing, preserving nothing. Valeria deserved a chance to enjoy all that life in America could offer a beautiful and wealthy young woman. She deserved a husband who could expand her horizons, not bring them crashing down around her.

"I'd go to New York," Valeria announced.

Luke had nearly forgotten he'd asked her a question. "Why New York?"

"I have a friend there. Her husband's family immigrated to New York after the Prussians overran his country."

"Are you sure they'd want you? I mean, not everybody

welcomes visitors from home. It's dangerous sometimes."

"Not Lillie. She tried to get me to come to New York when Uncle Matthais lost his throne. She even tried to get me to escape from Hans and Otto."

Luke wanted to be cynical, to say he'd have been spared a lot of trouble if she'd followed Lillie's advice, but all he could feel was cold fear at what could have happened without someone to look after her. Lillie and her husband would never have guessed her uncle was trying to kill her.

"Where do they live?"

"Lillie said they have a house near a place called Central Park. Do you know where that is?"

"Yes." Only the wealthiest could afford to live there. "What does her husband do?"

"I don't know, but she says he makes a lot of money doing it."

That was exactly the kind of connection she needed, a wealthy, titled ex-nobleman who could introduce her into the highest levels of society. With her friends to watch out for her, she wouldn't be in danger of being cheated out of her money or marrying a fortune hunter. With her wealth and beauty, she'd be an instant success.

"I always wanted to visit New York," she said. "Will you take me there someday?"

"Yes." A lot sooner than she expected.

Unless she decided to marry Rudolf after all.

He couldn't get that possibility out of his mind. Once she finally understood he didn't intend to marry her—and he would convince her if it took every minute until they reached the ranch—she would feel lost. It would be only natural for her to turn to someone of her own background, culture, and language, someone she'd have been content to marry only a few weeks earlier. She'd have a home, a husband who probably wouldn't mistreat her as long as she didn't object to what he did with her money. She'd be safe from her uncle's plans to kill her.

He couldn't offer her as much.

"I think New York is a good idea," Luke said. "But right now I'd like you to concentrate on Rudolf. We've reached the top of the Rim. We will be at the ranch in about an hour."

They stopped for a moment to allow their horses a breather. Luke expected Valeria to be excited by the thick pine forest that covered the Rim. She ought to feel she was back in Belgravia. Instead, she turned to look at the panoramic view of the land they'd left more than two thousand feet below. Forests of oak, fir, and pine stretched across hills swallowed in a blue haze until they merged with the sparsely covered ridges of the distant Mazatzal Mountains.

"It's magnificent," Valeria said. "When I got off the train in Bonner, I thought everything was desert."

"You can find almost anything you want in Arizona," Luke said.

"Including happiness?"

He was afraid his own hopelessness showed before he could wipe all expression from his face. "You can find happiness anywhere, even in the desert."

"Have you ever found happiness?"

"Not everybody wants happiness."

"Why not?"

"Happiness isn't trustworthy. It can disappear in a moment or die a slow, painful death over years."

"But isn't the chance of happiness worth the risks?"

"Only when the chance exists."

"Does it exist for you?"

"No."

"Are you sure you can't change that?"

"Yes."

"Have you tried?"

No. He'd lived too long without love. Now, even if Valeria could love him, it was too late. Whatever value he'd brought away from Jake and Isabelle's ranch had been used up long ago. "I never had a reason to try. Now it's too late."

"Why?"

"Valeria, we've been over this time and time again. Talking about it isn't going to change anything. I'm not the right man for you."

"But I love you."

"That's not enough."

"Then what is?"

How could he explain to her what she wouldn't believe until bitter experience brought home the truth of his words?

"I've told you I have nothing to offer you, that I can only—"

"You haven't given me any reasons."

"Yes, I have. You just won't listen to them."

He turned and started into the pine forest. After being in the open with the sun blazing down on their heads, the contrast was dramatic. The temperature, twenty degrees cooler up here than in the Verde Valley below, dropped ten more degrees. After the desert heat, he wondered if Valeria might feel chilled.

"Okay, I'm listening," Valeria said, apparently impervious to the towering ponderosa pines that surrounded them.

Maybe it would be better to tell her. His own resolve had been slipping. Every time he looked at Valeria, made love to her, thought of leaving her, he felt himself reaching for excuses to believe a future as her husband might be possible. Maybe if he heard the reasons all over again, he would stop trying to convince himself he could be mistaken.

"You come from a hundred generations of royalty. I come from two parents who were barely better than vicious animals. They had no morals, no standards, no limits. There was nothing they wouldn't do for money, a drink, momentary gratification. I don't know if my brother and I even had the same father, though my mother swears we did. But she would swear to anything. She did nearly a hundred times a day. She died of pneumonia because she was too drunk to come in out of the rain, and the man she was with didn't care whether she lived or died.

"My father cheated at cards. He was fast with a card and fast with a gun. One day he cheated a man who wasn't as fast with cards or a gun, so he shot my father in the back. That's my heritage, Valeria. Is that the kind of man you want for your husband, for the father of your children?"

"You're not your parents. You're—"

"I'm a gunfighter!" Luke exploded. "I kill people for a living. Do you understand that?"

"I'm sure you haven't—"

"You don't know the people I've run off, shot, or killed. You haven't seen the faces of their families. I have, and I kept right on doing it. Do you know why? *Because I'm just like my parents!* There's nothing inside me to save, so get that missionary look off your face. I wish there were. I'd hoped there would be, but there isn't. I won't marry you, Valeria, not now, not ever."

He didn't know when their horses had stopped, but they sat their motionless mounts, staring at each other in silence. He'd expected her to argue, but she didn't say a word. Twice he saw her lips part to form words, but she changed her mind both times.

So he waited, wondering what she was thinking. He'd hoped she would argue with him. As long as she still wanted to marry him, he could tease himself with the possibility that he might figure out how to make it work. If she decided she didn't want to marry him, or that he wouldn't marry her no matter what she said, the door would close. He knew it was best, but he didn't want to lose that last glimmer of hope.

"If I ask you one question, will you answer it truthfully?"

His stomach did a flip, warning of danger, but he had to answer. He owed her that much.

"Yes." He held his breath.

"Do you love me?"

It was worse than he'd expected. He hadn't asked himself that question. There were some things too painful to know. Yet he'd known the answer for some time. He'd been telling himself it didn't matter what he felt, that he wasn't going to marry Valeria, so there was no point in thinking about it, but he'd promised Valeria an answer.

"Yes. But—"

"That's all I wanted to know," she said, cutting him off. She spurred her horse forward. "We'd better get started for the ranch. It's chilly under these trees."

She had surprised him again. He didn't think for a minute that was the end of it. Valeria was a very stubborn woman with a powerful liking for getting her own way. She had something up her sleeve.

But suppose she agreed with him!

Suppose she'd finally given up, accepted his conviction that he wouldn't make a good husband. Luke could stand knowing Valeria could never be his own—at least he thought he could—but he couldn't stand knowing she thought as badly of him as he did of himself.

* * *

Valeria was so angry it took her nearly half an hour before she could formulate a rational thought. It did no good to lose her temper. She wasn't a royal princess who could send Luke to the guillotine, but she would have exchanged her best emerald necklace for a rack and some thumb screws.

He was not a stupid man, but to go around saying he was unworthy of marriage because he had rotten parents was stupid. She didn't believe for one minute he'd killed innocent people just for money. He might have strayed close to the line—he might even have leaned rather far over it on occasions—but she was certain he'd never crossed it. She'd seen too many instances of the good in him. He'd truly grieved over Hans's death. He'd agreed to help Neely and Albie. Despite trying to appear indifferent, he had strong feelings for his adopted brothers. There was good in Luke Attmore, and she didn't understand why he couldn't see it.

Maybe his parents had convinced him he was rotten. Maybe something else had happened. It didn't really matter. He'd tell her someday, but right now she needed to figure out a way to convince him to marry her. If he thought she was going to be miserable for the rest of her life just because he'd gotten on a misguided high horse, he could think again. She wasn't the scion of a house of successful generals for nothing. When someone in her family wanted something, he or she got it.

And she meant to have Luke Attmore.

But it wouldn't do any good to keep badgering him. He'd dug in his heels. She had to think of a way to get them undug. In the meantime, she would deal with Rudolf and decide what to do about her ranch. She really liked the idea of using the ranch to breed her horses. Nearly everything in her life had been controlled by men. This was one of the few things she'd been allowed to do on her own. She was studying the terrain for good grazing when they came upon a small meadow.

"You'll see more and more of these as the trees thin out," Luke said. "The farther you get from the Rim, the closer you get to desert."

She should have known they weren't far from the desert. She hoped Rudolf had chosen a spot in the forest to build the ranch house. She loved the clean scent of pine.

"Have you decided what to do about Rudolf?" Luke asked.

"There's nothing to do. I'll tell him I don't want to marry him, and he'll leave."

"How are you going to make him leave if he doesn't want to?"

"That's your job."

"My job ends once you reach the ranch."

"But you won't leave me there," Valeria said, throwing him a knowing look. "You'll stay to make sure nothing happens."

"So you plan to let me take care of everything."

"Yes. Isn't that what men are for? I'm just a poor, helpless female." She nearly burst out laughing at his expression. Maybe he hadn't thought she could catch on to being an American so fast. Neither had she, but it just came naturally. The more angry she got at Luke, the more natural it became.

"I'm beginning to think you've been playing me for a fool all along," Luke said.

"Why should I when you're so determined to do it yourself?"

She didn't care if he got angry. It would do him good. Maybe it would melt some of that icy control, let some feelings out. She was certain he had them. He'd just buried them so deeply he'd forgotten about them.

"Is that the ranch?" she asked, pointing to some buildings visible through the trees.

"It looks that way. Get ready to meet your ex-fiancé."

Valeria hadn't noticed the riders approaching through the trees north of the ranch buildings. She saw at once how Luke knew it was Rudolf. He wore his army uniform. Even the men riding with him were in uniform. Obviously, being in America hadn't changed Rudolf.

His greeting contained none of the friendliness that had characterized their meetings in Belgravia.

"Where have you been? I had begun to think this man had run off with you."

He said *this man* as though Luke were some nameless servant beneath his notice. It shocked Valeria to realize that only a few weeks ago she wouldn't have noticed his attitude. She cringed inwardly at the memory of her own behavior.

"After the second attack, he decided to bring me by a different route," she explained.

"It was extremely rash of you to leave the wagons. Anything could have happened."

"I could have stayed with the train and been killed in the next attack. I nearly was, you know."

"Those *men* who brought the wagons told me what happened. Have you no more appreciation of what is due your rank than to be traveling with people like that? And what happened to your clothes? You look like a gutter wench."

Valeria had been feeling a little guilty about refusing to marry Rudolf after having promised to do so, but his attitude changed that. Even if they didn't go back to Belgravia, he would expect her to behave the way her mother had behaved, her mother before that, and countless mothers back into the mists of history. Their marriage would have been a disaster, even if they'd loved each other. She had changed, but he'd stayed the same.

"You can't ride horseback in court dress," Valeria said, impatient to be done with this greeting. "Did Zeke tell you Luke tore up the marriage contracts?"

"I don't talk to people like him. Or the other one. He was an Indian."

"You should have talked to him, Rudolf. He was supposed to tell you I've decided not to marry you."

"One of my men told me he said something like that. Naturally I didn't believe it."

"It's true. I've decided I don't want to go back to Europe, not even if you could regain your throne. I want to stay in this country. I want to choose my own husband."

"You're suffering from too much sun," Rudolf said. "Come up to the house. You'll feel better in a few days."

"Didn't you hear a word I said? I'm not going to marry you. This is my ranch. I'm thinking about living here and breeding horses. You'll have to leave."

Rudolf looked at her as though she'd suddenly gone stark raving mad. "Elvira said you hadn't been acting like yourself since you got off the train."

"Elvira is still here?"

"Yes. And a good thing, too. From the way you look, even she will have a difficult time making you presentable by dinner." He reached out and took hold of her horse's bridle. "I've had a priest waiting for nearly a month. We'll be married immediately after we dine."

Valeria tried unsuccessfully to break Rudolf's hold on her mount's bridle. "I've already told you I'm not going to marry you, Rudolf. Not tonight or any other night."

"As soon as I can arrange for the transfer of your money to my bank, we'll return to Europe. It'll take at least a year to make preparations for an invasion." He pulled on the horse's bridle, forcing it to follow him.

"Let go of her horse," Luke said.

Rudolf looked at Luke as though seeing him for the first time. "You may leave. Your services are no longer needed."

"Let go of her horse," Luke repeated.

Rudolf turned to the four men who'd accompanied him. "Take care of him," he said over his shoulder as he started toward the ranch, forcing Valeria's mount to follow.

At Rudolf's command, the four men drew their swords and started toward Luke.

Chapter Twenty-four

A volley of shots shattered the silence, sending birds squawking through the trees. Four swords flew through the air. The shots had been so close together, it was impossible to tell how many times Luke had fired his gun, but Valeria knew it was only four. Luke didn't miss.

"Now I will tell you once more to let go of that horse's bridle," Luke said to Rudolf. "If you don't, I'll put a bullet through your hand."

Rudolf looked stunned. When his hand fell to his side, Valeria turned her horse back toward Luke.

"Don't bother telling your men to draw their pistols," Luke advised Rudolf as he drew a second gun. "I can shoot them out of their saddles before the first one can get his pistol out of his holster." Luke turned to the soldiers. "Go back to your barracks, your bunkhouse, or your kennel, wherever you stay. Collect anything that's yours and clear out. If you're here an hour from now, I'll kill you." One man glanced at his sword. "Leave them where they are."

The men turned and started toward the ranch.

"Come back here," Rudolf shouted, but they kept going. "You can't come in here and order my men off my ranch," he said, turning his regal fury on Luke.

"This isn't your ranch," Luke told him. "It belongs to Valeria. She's already told you she's not going to marry you. I'm giving you until noon tomorrow to be gone."

"I'll have you court marshaled! I'll have you shot!" Rudolf raged.

Luke laughed. Valeria was embarrassed to think she'd ever considered marrying such a fool.

"This isn't one of your toy kingdoms," Luke said. "Now show some courtesy to Valeria, or I'll run you off with your men."

"You can't possibly mean to trust yourself to this man," Rudolf said to Valeria.

"Since you couldn't be bothered to send anyone to meet me, I had no other choice. If it hadn't been for him, I'd be dead now."

"But he's not a gentleman," Rudolf said. "He's not one of us."

"It's you who aren't the gentleman, Rudolf. You were going to force me to marry you against my will."

"But you signed a contract."

"Everything changed when I realized that contract could get me killed."

"But you'll be safe once you marry me."

"Even if I won't let you use my money to raise an army?"

"It will be my money when we marry," Rudolf said, the old arrogance coming through.

"I don't want you to recover your throne, Rudolf. You're a tyrant. You think people exist only to obey your wishes. When they're unwilling, you force them. I don't like that, and I won't have any part in it."

"What's come over you?"

"America's come over me."

"Why? It's nothing but a country of deserts and peasants!"

"I'm finding deserts aren't as bad as I thought, and I actually like the peasants."

"Now I know you're suffering from brain fever. Come back to the house. I won't mention marriage again until you've had time to recover your senses."

"You have to be out of here by noon tomorrow," Luke said.

Rudolf puffed up, preparing to act like he was still an absolute monarch. Then he noticed Luke hadn't put his gun away. He exhaled slowly.

"I'll leave the ranch, but I won't leave the area until I'm certain Valeria is in her right mind."

"You can live in a pine tree for all I care," Luke said, "as long as you're off the ranch tomorrow."

"What are you going to do?"

"That depends on Valeria."

Rudolf turned to Valeria.

"I told you I'm thinking about breeding horses."

"But you can't live here by yourself."

"That won't be your concern," Luke said.

"Of course it's my concern," Rudolf shouted. "I can't allow my wife to live in the woods by herself. It makes her sound like a witch in some fairy tale."

"Aren't his ears attached to his brain?" Luke asked.

Valeria couldn't help smiling. "Rudolf doesn't like to be told no. He thinks if he keeps talking, I'll change my mind. Now I'm very tired. Wandering through the desert can be fun, but I want to get out of these clothes and take a hot bath. You do have hot water at the ranch, don't you?" she asked Rudolf.

"Of course. Certain amenities are absolutely necessary if one is to support life."

Rudolf had no idea how little was actually necessary to support life, but she wasn't in the mood to tell him. She'd deal with that once she'd had her bath.

"I was hoping you'd still be here," Luke said when he saw Zeke.

"You didn't think I'd leave without knowing what happened to you, did you?" Zeke asked.

"I wasn't sure old Rudolf would let you stay."

"He tried to get rid of us, but there's nine of us. That's more than his boys were willing to tackle."

"How many does he have?"

"An even dozen that jabber away in something foreign. Nasty looking devils. I don't trust them not to be talking about cutting our throats with those swords they like to carry around. I was hoping you'd get here before they got tired of our faces."

"I came as fast as I could."

"The hell you say. I was beginning to think you'd decided to take your princess and ride off into the sunset. What the hell took you so long? I could have made love to that woman every night and still have gotten here before now."

Luke didn't know which part of his face gave him away, but comprehension suddenly changed Zeke's welcoming smile to a fierce scowl. "Dammit to hell! You did make love to her."

"Where's Hawk?"

"Don't try to change the subject."

"What I did is none of your business."

"It is when it keeps me sitting here with those foreign devils growling at me like a set of guard dogs. I thought your precious reputation was more important than any woman." Zeke's gaze narrowed. "You've fallen in love with her, haven't you?"

"What do you know about love? Or me or Hawk for that matter."

"Enough to know it's got you at last. You going to marry her?"

Luke could see no reason to pretend any longer. "You're not a fool, Zeke. What could I offer a woman like Valeria?"

"It depends on what she wants."

"Well, she sure as hell doesn't want a gunfighter with no home, no future, and no family."

"The no family part is your doing," Hawk said. He came out of a building Luke figured was the bunkhouse. He looked like he'd been taking a nap.

"Is she in love with you?" Zeke asked.

Luke felt hemmed in. "She doesn't know any more about love than the rest of us. Why else would she agree to marry a man like Rudolf?"

"That one's a back-stabber," Hawk said.

"He's an arrogant bastard who thinks he has the God-given right to step on anyone born below his station. He refuses to believe Valeria won't marry him."

"You marry her," Hawk said. "That convince him."

"I'm not marrying anybody!" Luke snapped.

"You love her," Zeke said. "Why not?"

"Because I do love her," Luke replied.

Zeke rolled his eyes. "You were stubborn before. Love has made you stupid."

"You love her. She love you. What's the problem?" Hawk asked.

"We come from two different worlds. We have nothing in common. We'd hate each other in a few months. I don't want to talk about it anymore," Luke said when

Zeke started to argue. "We've got something more important to do."

"What?"

"Come up with a battle plan. I figure Rudolf will try to kill me tonight. He may try to kill you and the drivers, too."

Valeria had expected to enjoy her return to a semi-civilized life. Rudolf had done everything he could to make the ranch support his former way of life. The house itself was made of wood, but some of the walls had been painted to resemble marble. The main room was about thirty feet wide and sixty feet long, its ceiling supported by huge pine beams that had been carved and painted with classical scenes. Carpets covered the wood floor. Louis XVI furnishings formed an elegant contrast to the forest setting. Valeria thought he would have been better advised to decorate the ranch in the style of a hunting lodge. It would have been more comfortable and more appropriate. The French furnishings looked miserably out of place. Even the dining room, paneled and painted in white and gold, made her uncomfortable.

Dinner was like a court affair, consisting of seven courses, each served with its own wine. Rudolf hadn't wanted Luke to join them at the table, but Valeria had insisted. Now she wished she'd eaten in the kitchen with Zeke and Hawk. The three of them sat around the huge table, a servant standing behind each chair, avoiding the issues that hung in the air around them.

Luke didn't appear to be uncomfortable, but then, he hadn't bothered to dress up. Rudolf had worn his best dress uniform. Valeria had put one of her prettiest gowns. Luke had washed his face, changed his shirt, and come to the table in dusty boots.

Rudolf was furious.

Rudolf watched Luke like a hawk during dinner. She didn't know whether he expected Luke to use the wrong fork, ask for beer instead of wine, or steal the silver. Luke had surprised them both by appearing perfectly at ease. He'd stunned her by saying he liked the red wine served with the beef well enough, but that he preferred a burgundy. Rudolf turned the conversation to life in Belgravia.

Valeria wasn't interested in talking about Belgravia. She was even less interested in talking of Rudolf's pitiful lost kingdom, Ergonia, a place so small it made Belgravia seem large. She wanted to know about the ranch.

For the most part, Luke ate in silence.

By the time the dessert plates had been removed and liqueurs set on the table, Valeria was ready to throttle Rudolf.

"You must be relieved to finally get a decent meal," Rudolf said, justifiably proud of the dinner.

"Everything was wonderful," Valeria said, "but I feel heavy, almost drugged. I can't believe I used to eat like this all the time."

"It has to be better than anything cooked over a campfire. How did you survive? You know nothing about cooking."

"Luke cooked after we left the wagons."

"An all-around nursemaid," Rudolf sneered. "And he can shoot."

Luke poured out a small amount of a dark amber liquid into a liqueur glass. He swirled it around before taking a sip.

"I hope it meets the approval of your discriminating palate," Rudolf snapped.

"It's very good," Luke said.

"It ought to be. It's Napoleon Brandy."

"I know," Luke said. "It's written on the bottle."

Valeria smothered a smile. "I think I'll go to bed."

"It's early," Rudolf said.

"I was in the saddle before dawn. Luke doesn't believe in lounging in bed."

"I don't see how you managed to sleep at all."

"After being in the saddle all day, even rocks don't keep you awake."

"You can sleep as long as you want tomorrow."

"She needs to be up early," Luke said after swallowing the last of his brandy. "We plan to ride over the ranch." He looked directly at Rudolf. "That way you'll be gone when we get back."

Valeria was surprised to see Rudolf contain his anger. It was very much unlike him. "You'll find plenty of room in the bunkhouse."

"I'm sleeping in the room next to Valeria," Luke said.

"You haven't been invited to sleep in the house."

"I invited myself."

The two men stared at each other across the table.

Rudolf was the first to look away. "The room hasn't been prepared."

"I can use my bedroll."

"I will give orders for the room to be prepared immediately," Rudolf said. "I will not allow anyone to say he had to sleep in a *bedroll* while a guest in my house."

Valeria started to point out that it was her house, then stopped. It must be hard for Rudolf to give up his plans to return to Ergonia. There was no point in making it more difficult. The two men rose when she stood.

"I'll go up with you," Luke said.

"Your room won't be ready for nearly an hour," Rudolf said.

"I have to check out Valeria's room."

"There's no need. She—"

"She's still unmarried. Her uncle still inherits her estate if she dies."

"You didn't have to remind him of that," Valeria said after they left the room.

"Seemed like I did."

"Why are you coming to my room?"

"To make sure you'll be safe."

"Surely you don't think my uncle would try to kill me here?"

"No."

"Then who?"

"Rudolf. I think he means to get rid of both of us, claim your uncle did it, and claim your estate as your husband."

"But I didn't marry him."

"If we're both dead, there won't be anybody to challenge anything he chooses to say."

Valeria started to protest that Rudolf wouldn't do such a thing. She stopped when she realized she would have said the same thing about her uncle only a short time ago. "What do you want me to do?"

It started with shots somewhere behind the house. Luke figured Rudolf's henchmen were attacking Zeke and the drivers. They were in for a rude surprise. The sound of the shots from outside the house had barely reached Luke's ears when he heard a short burst of gunfire from the bedroom down the hall. He hadn't heard the sound of splintering wood.

Whoever had entered that room had done so with a key.

Leaning against the wall next to the door in Valeria's room, Luke heard the key being inserted in the lock, the tumblers falling as it was turned. A man entered the room on silent feet, approached the bed, and fired into the shape outlined by the covers. He let the gun fall to his side.

"Nobody goes back on a promise to me," Rudolf said.

"Some men never know when it's time to stop reaching for the moon and settle for what they have," Luke said, his voice soft and menacing.

He saw Rudolf's body freeze, his hand tighten on the gun.

"You didn't think I was fool enough to let Valeria sleep in that bed, did you?" Luke asked. "I knew you were going to try to kill me and the boys. I really hoped you wouldn't try to hurt Valeria."

"You were supposed to be down the hall," Rudolf said.

"Hawk offered to take my place. He's the Indian you wouldn't talk to. Hawk doesn't like soldiers."

"Maybe your friend is dead."

"Hawk never misses. Neither does Zeke. He and the drivers were waiting for the rest of your men. I don't think there'll be too many of them left."

"Where is Valeria?"

"I'm over here, Rudolf."

Luke saw him jump, then slowly turn his head in the direction of Valeria's voice.

"I could hardly believe it when Luke told me what he thought you would do. Why would you want to kill me, Rudolf? I would have given you the money."

"You couldn't give it to me," Rudolf said. Suppressed fury made his speech hard to understand. "Your uncle would have had it all. He doesn't want me to go back to Ergonia."

"Why couldn't you stay here? You have enough money for a ranch, for—"

"I'd rather die than live in this uncivilized wilderness. The whole country is full of peasants, criminals, and people like your Hawk and Zeke. I wanted to go back to

Ergonia, to take my proper place as the ruler of my country."

"It's not a proper place," Valeria said, "any more than my uncle's was a proper place. Our ancestors invaded our countries and conquered the people. For hundreds of years we ruled them for our advantage, not theirs. They're in control of their own destiny now. We can't turn back the clock."

"*I could!* I could if I just had the money. I would have if you hadn't listened to that damned gunfighter."

"If it hadn't been Luke, it would have been someone else. I never wanted to go back, Rudolf. I told you that when I agreed to marry you."

"I would have gone back as a king!" Rudolf shouted. "Do you understand what that means? I would have been received with honor anywhere I went."

"It's an empty honor to rule over people who don't want you," Valeria said. "Much better to stay here and start a whole new life. You could be a rancher, a banker, anything you want, Rudolf. You could be an important man."

"Five minutes of being a king is worth a lifetime of being anything else. I would have had it if it hadn't been for you." Rudolf whirled as he spoke, brought his gun up. The deafening roar of a gunshot echoed through the room. The gun fell from Rudolf's hand. "I would have been a king," he said.

Then his lifeless body sank to the floor.

Luke started at his reflection in the mirror of his hotel room, something he did so seldom he felt he was looking at a stranger, one dressed like a tenderfoot. He thought of what Zeke would say and smiled. He had no business being in New York, certainly not dressed like this. He belonged on the back of a horse, at the bar in a saloon, camped in the desert. Facing a man with a gun. He hadn't wanted to come. He wouldn't have if Valeria hadn't needed him, but she was settled with her friends now. They would take care of her.

It was time for him to leave, but his feet wouldn't move. He might as well have been turned into a statue.

"You know you have to go," he said to the man in the mirror.

"No, I don't," the man said back to him. "She loves me."

"Nobody can love a man like you," Luke said, "at least not enough to make a difference."

"You'll never know until you try. Even black-hearted villains want love. Don't you deserve at least that much?"

Did he deserve love, or had his turning his back on everyone who loved him disqualified him forever? No, he'd never done anything worthy of love.

"Don't you want to be loved?" the man in the mirror asked.

All resistance to admitting the truth, to accepting his weakness, collapsed. Not even the fear of failure could keep him from admitting he wanted Valeria's love more than he wanted life. The last sixteen years had been an empty parade of jobs, women, people entering and leaving his life like so many cars on a passing train. A few passed his way more than once, but they usually kept going. When they didn't, he did.

Some had offered to make a place for him in their lives, but he always refused. Jake's support, Isabelle's devotion, his brother's loyalty—none of them had been powerful enough to reach the cold hard center that was his parents' loathing for the son they created. Additional layers of hardness had been applied by orphanages, foster parents, communities that drove out homeless children. To cut himself off even further from his feelings, he'd added layer after layer until he was certain the core was impregnable.

Then he found Valeria.

From the very first, he'd been helpless to control his feelings for her. Nothing he said or did had been able to drive her from his mind. Or heart. With Valeria came hope that she could love him enough, that he could trust her love to last, that he could believe there was something inside him worthy of love.

But even though his heart told him not to give up, his head counseled him to stop being a fool. Not even she could dissolve the layers of self-loathing that cut him off from his feelings, from connection to his family. Valeria had fallen in love with the first man she saw who wasn't after her money. As soon as she discovered the world was full of fine, honorable men who could love her just as much as he did, who could give her the kind of life she deserved, she would find she didn't love him after all. As soon as she got back among people of her own kind, she would see they didn't fit, that he didn't belong. She would be sorry, she would try to hide it, but they would both know it had ended.

"It's better not to begin something you know can only end in pain," Luke told the man in the mirror.

"You're a coward," the man said. "You face men with guns all the time, but you haven't the courage to trust your heart, to trust *her* heart to see in you things you can't see in yourself."

"I know myself."

"You could be wrong. Isn't the chance to be loved, to be *saved,* worth the gamble?"

"I still have to leave," he told the man in the mirror.

But he hoped he was wrong.

* * *

"Nothing exciting ever happens to me," Lillie Tegetthoff complained after Valeria finished telling Lillie about her trip through the Arizona Territory.

"You could have had most of it with my compliments," Valeria said. "You can have no idea how horrified I felt when Rudolf calmly fired into what he thought was me asleep in the bed."

"You poor darling."

They were sitting in the Tegetthoff's salon in New York City. The sumptuously decorated house was nearly as big as Valeria's palace in Belgravia. Obviously Americans liked to live in splendor just as much as Europeans. Luke would certainly disapprove of the number of servants it took to run the place.

"But that wasn't half as bad as having Otto try to kill me and learning my own uncle had paid him to do it," Valeria said.

"You must have been overjoyed to hear Matthais died of apoplexy when he heard your Mr. Attmore had put out a contract on him."

"What?"

"Didn't you know?"

"Of course not. I wouldn't have let him kill my uncle, regardless of what he'd tried to do."

Lillie smiled as if she knew a secret. "I guess that's why he didn't tell you."

"I'll have a lot to say to Luke when I see him."

"I hope it's to thank him for saving your life, several times over."

Despite Valeria's objections, Luke had insisted upon bringing her to New York immediately after Rudolf's death. She had worried he might try to get rid of her since he still flatly refused to consider marrying her. But when he settled into an expensive hotel next to the exclusive apartment building where Lillie and her husband lived, Valeria knew he loved her. She just had to figure out a way around his foolish objections to marriage.

One of the massive oak doors to the sitting room swung open, and Lillie's husband entered. "You're looking absolutely beautiful today. The New York air must be good for you."

They all laughed at that. Valeria had coughed the whole first day. "I never thought I'd long for desert air."

"Is it really the air, or are you looking for a way to escape from all those fortune hunters?" Marcus Tegetthoff asked. "With so many young men anxious to get to know you and your money better, you might be getting married before we know it."

"I think Valeria had a magnificent debut," Lillie said. "And not every handsome young man is a fortune hunter."

Valeria tried to smile. Lillie had thrown a lavish party to introduce her to New York society. As an ex-princess of wealth, beauty, and fame, she'd had dozens of men vying for her attention. The heat, the crush of bodies, the noise, the extravagant flattery, the brilliant flashes of white in too wide smiles—all of it reminded her of Belgravia. Form lacking substance. Despite the attention, her thoughts had remained on the only man who'd refused Lillie's invitation.

Luke.

"I don't think I'll be getting married just yet."

"Not even if a certain man should ask you?" Lillie asked.

Her husband's eyes widened with interest.

"That might change things," Valeria said, trying to hide a smile. "But I haven't been able to convince him he's good enough for a princess."

"Surely you jest?" Marcus asked.

"No," his wife said. "Valeria is blessed with beauty,

money and brains. Instead of being thankful, the idiot thinks he's not good enough."

"He's not an idiot," Valeria said.

"I'd say he was a sensible man," Marcus said. "You did say he is a gunfighter, didn't you? What could you two possibly have in common?"

Valeria knew it was impossible to explain why Luke was the only man she'd ever be able to love. Like Marcus, people generally saw what she had at first, what Luke lacked.

The appearance of the butler saved Valeria from having to answer.

"Mr. Luke Attmore," he announced.

Chapter Twenty-five

Luke entered the room, and Valeria's breath caught in her throat. She couldn't believe how handsome he looked. She'd thought he was beautiful in the desert. But here in New York, bathed, shaved, his hair perfectly cut, wearing fashionable clothes that fit him like a glove, he was every bit the image of the prince Rudolf would never have been. His blond hair gleamed like wheat in the late summer sun, his blue eyes glistened like the azure sky. His deeply tanned skin looked radiantly healthy in comparison to the pale skin of the New Yorkers. The fact that he was so tall and broad-shouldered only enhanced his appeal.

He would have made a perfect king. People would have worshiped him.

Lillie rose to greet her visitor. "I'm very angry with you for refusing to come to my party."

"I would have been a curiosity," he said, "not a role that appeals to me."

"I'm a little curious about you myself," Marcus said.

"I've asked around. It seems you've got some very good connections."

Luke searched his memory but couldn't think of anyone among his clients who would have admitted knowing him.

"Madison Randolph speaks very highly of you."

"We were sort of neighbors back in Texas."

"I understand Jake Maxwell is your father."

"He was kind enough to adopt me and my brother when the orphanage threw us out." He smiled. "We were too much for the good people to handle."

"Is that why you turned to being a gunfighter?"

Luke's expression turned wintery. "It's a way of making a living."

"From what Madison tells me, a very good one."

"He's made a few investments for me."

"It must have been more than that. He tells me you're a rich man."

"Rich!" The word exploded from Valeria. "Is it true?" she asked. "The whole time you were telling me we had nothing in common, you were rich?"

"I'm not really rich."

"He's a millionaire," Marcus said. "That qualifies as rich in my book."

Valeria could tell Luke hadn't wanted her to know this. It hurt. She didn't understand.

"I hate to change the subject," Luke said, "but I came to say good-bye. My train is leaving this evening."

Valeria felt her heart in her throat, but she refused to panic. Five hundred years of successful monarchs counseled her to remain calm, to rely on tactics, not to let emotion prod her into rash action. "Where are you going?" she asked.

"To Texas."

"Why Texas?" Marcus asked. "They can't need more gunfighters there."

"You can't leave tonight," Valeria said, ignoring Marcus.

"Why not?" Luke asked.

"Because I won't have time to pack. And don't ask why. You know I'm coming with you."

"You can't."

"You can't stop me. It's a free country, remember? I can buy a ticket to anywhere I want. It won't matter if you change your mind and go somewhere else. I'm rich, too. I can buy lots of tickets."

"You can't come with me," Luke said.

"I can, and I will."

"Marcus, I have to ask you about the new rug I mean to buy for the salon," Lillie said. "Now is a perfect time to check the colors. The sunlight is just right."

"It's overcast," Marcus pointed out.

"That's why it's perfect. I'll keep the curtains drawn so the sun won't fade the carpets." She stood, started to leave the room. Finally figuring out what she was doing, her husband followed.

"Did you put her up to that?" Luke asked.

"No, and don't change the subject."

"I'm not. The discussion is over. You can't follow me, and that's final."

"It will only be final when you agree to marry me."

"Valeria, we've been over this time and time again."

"And you've put forward the same stupid argument."

"You don't know me. You don't understand."

"*You* are the one who doesn't understand. You think you're rotten, corrupt, evil, but I think you're just about the finest man I've ever known."

"I'm not. I'm—"

"Shut up, and listen for a moment, dammit."

"Now I've ruined your language. You never used to cuss."

"Maybe I should have. You might have listened to me sooner. I love you, Luke Attmore. I always will. There's not a woman in New York who wouldn't understand that the instant she set eyes on you. You're gorgeous. Big, strong, handsome, and a wonderful lover. What woman could want more?"

"You didn't tell—"

"Of course not, but I would if it would make you believe I want to marry you more than anything else in the world."

"Why me? And don't mention my muscles or my blue eyes."

"I didn't fall in love with your looks. They're a nice bonus, but they're not the real you. You saw something in me no one else saw. You saw a person who was too ignorant, too locked into one way of thinking, to realize she was little more than a painted doll. And you cared enough to make me see that. I fought against it, but you wouldn't give up. You kept chipping away at the porcelain until you exposed the person inside.

"Then you told me what I could be if I just had the courage to try. You called them freedoms, but they were ways for me to become a real person. To be my real self. You made me feel important. Me, not Princess Valeria of Badenberg. I'd never realized until you showed me that there was a difference. When I held back, you bullied me. When I was frightened, you comforted me. All the time you protected me."

"I didn't have any other job at the time."

"Don't lie, Luke. You've never done that before."

"Okay, dammit, I won't lie. I love you so much it hurts. Do you think I want to walk out of here knowing I'm leaving my only chance for happiness?"

"Then why are you doing it?"

"Because I love you too much to hurt you."

"You can't hurt me. You're much better than I am. I really ought to be ashamed of asking you to marry me. I come from a long line of murderers, pillagers, generals who sacked towns and encouraged their men to rape women. I couldn't possibly count the number of men they've hanged or beheaded. Then there's robbery."

"Valeria, be serious."

"I am. Do you know my great-grandfather had his own son killed? It's true. Hans told me. My heritage is far worse than yours. If our children are vicious killers, white slavers, or cattle rustlers, it'll be my fault."

"So we should probably strangle them at birth to spare society the trouble."

She saw a twinkle in Luke's eyes, and her heart leapt with hope. "Couldn't we first give them a chance to prove they can become worthwhile citizens?"

"Be serious, Valeria. You can't really think your parentage is worse than mine."

"I know it is. And I can document it for five hundred years."

"And you'll follow me?"

"Zeke promised to tell me every place you go. He said he and Hawk would make certain you couldn't hide."

Luke didn't know whether he wanted to find his brothers and knock them down or thank them for making it easier to do what he had wanted to do almost from the moment he first saw Valeria.

"You're sure you love me enough to follow me no matter where I go?"

"Don't ask stupid questions. I followed you all over that desert. You can't go anyplace worse than that."

"And you won't stop thinking I'm wonderful?"

"How could I? Nobody is more wonderful than you are, not even Marcus, and Lillie thinks he's perfect."

"I'm not rich compared to you."

"I don't care."

"I have a terrible temper."

"So do I."

"I don't like New York."

She practically laughed. "Neither do I. I haven't stopped coughing since I got here."

"Do you truly want to marry me?"

"How many times do I have to tell you?"

"Millions. Maybe then I'll believe it."

She jumped up and threw herself into his arms. "I love you, Luke. I never thought it was possible to love anybody as much as I love you. I'll never stop. And now that you've lost the shield of honor you hid behind for so long, maybe you can see yourself for the man you are, for the man I've seen all along, the man so many people love."

Could what she said be true, that he'd been hiding behind his reputation so long, using it to judge himself, that he couldn't see himself anymore? Could Isabelle have been right when she said he'd avenged Chet because he couldn't turn his back on people who loved him even though he didn't love himself and didn't want others love him? Did his hiring Zeke and Hawk have more to do with the need for family than the need for dependable men?

He was shocked to realize Valeria had done for him exactly what he'd done for her. She'd seen behind the protective barriers, the image, the fear he was as bad as his parents believed. And she'd liked what she saw enough to want to marry him.

A hard, tight knot in Luke's chest started to unravel. He felt some of the tension, some of the self-loathing, some of the feeling of hopelessness begin to fade. Not much. Just a little bit. But if Valeria could keep loving him, maybe it would keep fading away until one day he could actually believe he was as wonderful as she thought.

He wasn't, but he would bust his butt to be the man she saw when she looked at him. He didn't know how, but he would learn. This was one lesson, by God, he meant to learn good and proper.

He knelt at Valeria's feet.

"I make this solemn promise—"

She put her fingers over his lips. "Sit on the sofa with me. We're going to start on the same level. No special favors for me or for you. I want only one promise, that you'll love me as long as you're able."

"Is forever long enough?"

"No, but it's a good place to start."

Epilogue

"I'm not going back to Arizona without you," Valeria said.

"But I may be gone for months at a time," Luke argued.

He'd decided to spend a year working for the Texas Rangers. It was his way of paying back a debt no one but he understood. Isabelle called it his attempt at atonement. Maybe she was right.

"You can't stay on our ranch," Luke said. "We haven't even started on the house."

"She can stay with us," Isabelle said.

"She could get to know your nephews," Melody said. "Being with Anne and me when we have our babies will help her learn what to do when she has her own."

Luke had been stunned upon returning to Jake's ranch to discover that everybody but Hawk and Zeke had bought ranches and settled within riding distance of each other. As far as he could tell, they'd spent all their time having babies. The valley and the surrounding hills resounded with the cries, yelps, and shouts of more than twenty boys and girls, all delighted to welcome home their famous uncle.

He found it hard to imagine Pete was about to become a father, that Drew had three girls. Most moving was seeing his brother Chet and his two young sons, perfect images of what their father must have looked like at that age.

His reunion with Chet had been the most difficult. Too many angry words had passed between them during the years they had both hired out their guns. Nearly everything that was really important had been left unsaid. Seeing Chet again was like finding the other half of himself, the part of him he'd struggled so hard to deny, the part without which he could only exist.

Luke felt like he'd missed half his life.

"I talked to Zeke and Hawk," Valeria said. "They agreed to take the horses to the ranch and run it until we decide what we're going to do."

"I'll see about making sure your new ranch gets started right," Jake volunteered.

"I don't want you to have that extra work shoved on you," Luke said.

"It won't be extra," Isabelle said. "He's bored with a ranch that doesn't need him to fight off rustlers or mountain lions."

"Chet has made everything too scientific," Jake complained. "It's not half as much fun anymore."

"Then you can help Zeke and Hawk run my ranch," Valeria volunteered. "You'll find more than enough fun in Arizona."

Everyone had enjoyed Valeria's description of her trip with Luke. He thought a few of his brothers actually felt nostalgic for some of the adventure of the old days.

"If you're not going to Arizona and you won't stay

here," Isabelle said to Valeria, "what are you going to do?"

"Go with Luke."

"No, you're not," Luke said.

"I hope they give him interesting jobs, something like chasing bank robbers or going into Mexico after rustlers."

"You're definitely not going into Mexico after rustlers," Luke said.

"You told me I had to buy some good stock to cross with my thoroughbreds. Jake says South Texas is the best place to look."

Isabelle started shooing people out of the room. "I suggest we leave them to fight this one on their own."

"I won't let you go looking for breeding stock all over South Texas," Luke said.

"And I won't stay cooped up here waiting until you're done playing cops and robbers."

"You could get hurt."

"*You* could get killed."

"You forget my fearsome reputation. Once the rustlers hear my name, they'll get religion and vow never to steal again."

A spurt of laughter escaped Valeria. "It didn't work on Soderman."

"I was so worried about you, I forgot to tell him who I was."

Her smile vanished. "I'm not leaving you. I couldn't forgive myself if anything happened to you and I wasn't there. Besides, I'm determined to have two little boys just like Melody."

"I was thinking about a couple of girls, dusky-haired gypsies like their mother."

"Maybe we can have one of each."

Luke put his arms around Valeria. "You'll have to promise to come back here the minute you're pregnant."

She made a face. Then unexpectedly she pulled away, gave him an arch look, and laughed. "I know. We can have separate beds."

"The hell we will," Luke said, grabbing her and pulling her close. "I plan on getting you pregnant as soon as possible."

"Is that a threat?"

He kissed her soundly. "It's a promise. And you know, I always keep my promises."

TEXAS TRIUMPH

ELAINE BARBIERI

Buck Star was a handsome cad with a love-'em-and-leave-'em attitude that had broken more than one heart. But when he lost his head over a conniving beauty young enough to be his own daughter, he jeopardized all he valued, even the lives of his own children.

Ever since leaving his father's Texas Star ranch, the daring Pinkerton agent and his lovely partner Vida Malone made it their business to ferret out the truth. But the twisted secrets he begins to uncover after a mysterious message calls him home might be more than anyone could untangle. Saving his father will require all his cunning and courage, as well as the aid of the most exasperating and enticing woman ever to go undercover or drive a man to distraction.

Dylan

NORAH HESS

Dylan Quade is a man's man. He has no use for any woman, least of all the bedraggled charity case his shiftless kin are trying to palm off on him. Rachel Sutter had been wedded and widowed on the same day and now his dirt-poor cousins refuse to take her in, claiming she'll make Dylan a fine wife. Not if he has anything to say about it!

But one good look at Rachel's long, long legs and white-blond hair has the avowed bachelor singing a different tune. All he wants is to prove he's different from the low-down snakes she knew before, to convince her that he is a changed man, one who will give anything to have the right to take her in his arms and love her for the rest of his life.